RUNELIGHT

JOANNE M. HARRIS

GOLLANCZ
LONDON

First published in Great Britain in 2017
by Gollancz
an imprint of the Orion Publishing Group Ltd
Carmelite House, 50 Victoria Embankment
London EC4Y 0DZ

An Hachette UK Company

1 3 5 7 9 10 8 6 4 2

A CIP catalogue record for this book
is available from the British Library.

ISBN (Hardback) 978 1 473 21708 9
ISBN (Export Trade Paperback) 978 1 473 21709 6

Typeset by Input Data Services Ltd, Somerset

Printed in Great Britain by Clays Ltd, St Ives plc

www.joanne-harris.co.uk
www.orionbooks.co.uk
www.gollancz.co.uk

PRELUDE

In the days of the old gods, the Worlds were very different. Magic was in everything. Demons and giants walked the land. And in the sky was a citadel, linked to our World by a rainbow bridge, in which the Æsir of Asgard dwelt, and shaped the Worlds to their purpose.

In those days, stories and fairy-tales were perfectly Lawful and nothing to fear, and even dreaming was considered to be safe and natural. Then came Tribulation: the war that some called Ragnarók; when the Sun grew dark, and the Moon filled with blood, and the old gods and their citadel fell into the darkness. For a long time, confusion and violence reigned. The Worlds went back to fire and ice. Brother slew brother, blood rain fell, and evil creatures preyed on mankind.

Then from the University of Immutable Truths in the great City of World's End, came the Order of Learned Historians, chroniclers of the Last Days. From Tribulation they brought the Worlds, and gave them a new religion, bringing Order from Chaos and new Laws out of anarchy. Their god was Nameless; supremely wise; and he gave them the mystic powers of Communion and of the Word. Thus armed, and on his orders, they began the Cleansing of the Worlds, to bring them back to the righteous ways and to rid the Folk of their evil past. All mention of the old gods was forbidden, their works erased, and even their names were forgotten, except in those parts of the Good Book to which only the Order had access. The Æsir became the Seer-Folk; the University became the Universal City. Magic and runes were declared a crime punishable by death. Reading and writing were limited to those whom the Order deemed worthy. Even stories were outlawed, for fear that through Dream, the old gods might return, and bring the Worlds into Chaos.

But in the North, a rebellion had already started to ferment. It began in a village called Malbry, by an ancient site called Red Horse Hill. Strange forces had been sleeping there, but they were awoken by Maddy Smith, a girl whose reputation for being too imaginative would already have been bad enough, without the runemark on her hand. With the help of her dubious friends, the Outlander One-Eye and Lucky the Trickster (both of uncertain origin, bearing broken runemarks and all the signs of depravity), and a goblin creature from World Below, Maddy retrieved an ancient glam, awakened the Seven Sleepers, and travelled into the Netherworld – with the help of her friends, Ethel Parson, Dorian Scattergood and Black Nell, a rather unusual pig – to rescue the old gods of Asgard, prisoners since Ragnarók. One-Eye and Lucky were revealed to be Odin, chief of the Æsir, and Loki, his erstwhile Captain, while Maddy was something even worse. For Maddy was Modi, child of Thor: one of the new gods whose birth was foretold years ago, by the Oracle. The Nameless, too, knew of her, and feared her, and sent the Order to challenge the gods, armed with the holy fire of the Word.

On the dusty plains of Hel, the gods met with ten thousand warriors. Odin fought with the Nameless; named at last as Mimir the Wise, Odin's former counsellor. Odin fell with his enemy; both of them swept away into Dream. The Order, too was completely wiped out in an event the Folk now call the Bliss. But victory was hard-won: Odin had fallen, Hel's gate had been breached, and the gods of the Æsir had been reborn into most unexpected Aspects.

Thor the Thunderer had taken the Aspect of pig farmer Dorian Scattergood; the cowardly goblin Sugar-and-Sack was serving as host for the war god Tyr; Ethelberta Parson had assumed the form of Frigg, the Seeress, and Sif, the goddess of grace and plenty, was currently incarnate as Fat Lizzy, a pot-bellied pig.

Since then, three more years have passed. The Folk have begun to recover from the fall of the Order. The Universal City is once more a place for trade and industry. But a breach in Hel's gate, however small, is not without serious consequences. During the few seconds of that breach, who knows what might have escaped into Dream, and thus into the world of the Folk? And where are the rest of the *new* gods, bearers of the new runes foretold long ago by the Oracle, of which Maddy Smith is only one?

MAP OF THE NINE WORDS

ORDER
The Firmament

ASGARD
(The Sky Citadel)

The Rainbow Bridge

YGGDRASIL
(The World Tree)

THE MIDDLE WORLDS

WORLD ABOVE

THE ONE SEA

OUTLANDS

INLAND

WORLD BELOW

THE FUNDAMENT

HEL
(The Underworld)

DREAM

NETHERWORLD
(The Black Fortress)

WORLD BEYOND
(CHAOS)

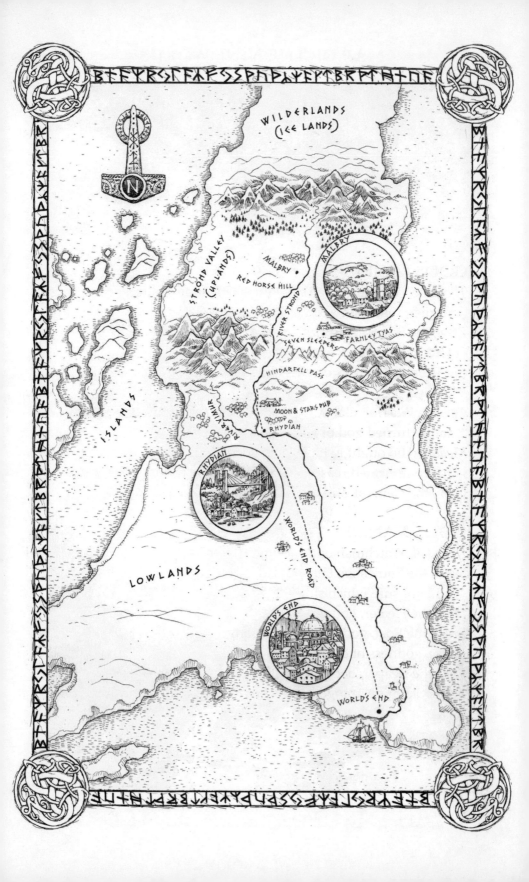

CHARACTERS

GODS (ÆSIR)

Thor, the Thunderer, son of Odin, aka Dorian Scattergood, ex-pig farmer, rebel and acting leader of the Æsir

Ethel, the Seeress, his mother, aka Frigg, Ethelberta Parson, Oracle and merry widow

Sif, Thor's wife, the goddess of plenty, aka Fat Lizzy, a pot-bellied pig

Tyr, the Warrior, aka Sugar-and-Sack, an erstwhile goblin reluctantly turned god of war

Maddy, who ought to have been born Modi, son of Thor, but who for complicated reasons turned out to be his daughter instead

Odin, the General, still dead, but working on a solution

GODS (VANIR)

Heimdall, Watchman of the Golden Teeth

Skadi, the Snowshoe Huntress, daughter of the Ice People and still not sure which side she's on

Idun, the Healer, goddess of youth

Bragi, the Poet, god of wine and song

Freyja, goddess of desire

Frey, the Reaper, her twin brother

Njörd, Skadi's estranged husband, the Old Man of the Sea

OTHERS

Loki, blood-brother of Odin, known as the Trickster, fitting into neither camp but grudgingly tolerated – at least for the present – on account of how he saved the Worlds

Jormungand, his monstrous son, aka the World Serpent

Sigyn, Loki's late ex-wife

Hel, his daughter, Ruler of the Dead

Fenris, his other son, Devourer and demon wolf

Skól and *Haiti*, aka Skull and Big H, friends of Fenris, Demon Wolves, Devourers of the Sun and Moon, and dedicated followers of World's End fashion

Jolly – just don't call him 'short'

Hughie and *Mandy*, aka Hugin and Munin, ravens with a sweet tooth

Angrboda, one of Loki's more dangerous liaisons, aka the Temptress; hag of Ironwood, mother of Hel, Fenris and Jormungand – and person of Chaotic origin

Maggie Rede, a daughter of the Order, and more

Adam Scattergood, a young man with a dream

Crazy Nan Fey, a crone of unruly ambition

Captain Chaos, an entertainer

Sleipnir, an eight-legged Horse and harbinger of the Apocalypse

Mimir the Wise, aka the Whisperer, a disembodied entity with revenge on its mind

The Old Man, see above

Perth, an entrepreneur and dealer in other people's property

Surt, a Lord of Chaos

RUNES OF THE ELDER SCRIPT

ᚠ   *Fé*: wealth; cattle; property; success

ᚢ   *Úr*: strength; the Mighty Ox

ᚦ   *Thúris*: Thor's rune; the Thorny One; victory

ᚩ   *Ós*: the Seer-folk; the Æsir

ᚱ   *Raedo*: the Journeyman; the Outlands

ᚲ   *Kaen*: wildfire; Chaos; World Beyond

ᚻ   *Hagall*: hail; the Destroyer; Netherworld

ᚾ   *Naudr*: the Binder; need; distress; the Underworld; Death

ᛁ   *Isa*: ice

ᛄ   *Ár*: plenty; fruitfulness

ᛇ   *Yr*: the Protector; the Fundament

ᛋ   *Sól*: summer; the sun

ᛏ   *Tyr*: the Warrior

ᛒ   *Bjarkán*: revelation; truth; vision; dream

ᛘ   *Madr*: mankind; the Middle Worlds; the Folk

ᛚ   *Logr*: water; the One Sea

RUNES OF THE NEW SCRIPT

Ethel: the Homeland; motherhood

Aesk: the Ash Tree; Creation

Ác: the Oak Tree; strength; determination

Daeg: day; the Thunderbolt

Iar: the Builder; industry

Perth: a game; hazard; chance

Wyn: gain; winnings; temptation; gambling

Eh: Wedlock; loyalty; a bond

Ea: the tides; Eternity; Death and beyond

Gabe: a gift; a sacrifice

BOOK ONE

World's End

The river Dream runs through Nine Worlds,
and Death is only one of them.

Old proverb

1

Five past midnight in world's end, three years after the End of the World, and, as usual, there was nothing to be seen or heard in the catacombs of the Universal City – except, of course, for the rats and (if you believed in them) the ghosts of the dead.

Maggie Rede had no fear of either. A tall, slim girl with straight dark brows and eyes of a curious amber-grey, wearing a white headscarf of the type World's Enders called the *bergha* and a scarlet tunic over leggings and boots, she was the only remaining custodian of those abandoned catacombs, and rats were her especial prey. With crossbow or sling she could hit a rat at three hundred paces without missing a step; the rats knew her very well by now, and kept their peace when Maggie Rede was on the prowl.

As for ghosts, Maggie had been walking the secret passageways every night for almost three years, and she had never yet seen a glimpse of one. There were still tales of a terrible battle here, with ten thousand of the Order wiped out in a single day. But there were no signs of them, nor of the enemy they had fought. Not even the ghosts were telling that tale.

Outside, of course, tales were rife, but Maggie Rede mistrusted such tales, and even more the folk who told them, and she ignored them just as she did the ghosts, concentrating instead on what she could see, and keeping the rats from the catacombs.

The Good Book, of course, had its own version of events. According to the Book of Apocalypse, the ten thousand had all been lost to the Bliss, a time predicted since the birth of the New Age, when the Nameless would call the faithful to arms, and they would shrug off their mortal flesh and be reborn into their perfect bodies upon the shores of the First World.

Maggie believed in the Good Book. Like her father and her brothers before her, she had been a true follower of the Order, and if she had been a boy she too would have known the Bliss by now, and would have been taken up into the Celestial City, instead of being left to deal with the mess at World's End.

Part of the problem, Maggie thought, was that although there had been much discussion on the subject of the Bliss and the precise nature of the delights in store for the faithful when the happy day arrived, no one had ever been entirely clear on what was to happen afterwards. She had imagined a kind of celestial spring cleaning, whereupon the bodies would be miraculously tidied away, but when it had finally come round, with ten thousand members of the Order suddenly vacating their earthly bodies (including Professors, Magisters, prentices and Examiners in the field), the results had been catastrophic.

It had taken six months to dispose of the corpses. Part of this was because no one in World's End wanted to take responsibility. The cleanup was the Order's business, or so the sanitary services maintained, and ought to be dealt with (and paid for) by official representatives of the Order.

The grim truth remained, however, that there *were* no representatives of the Order, either official or unofficial. And so the corpses festered and stank until, many meetings and committees later, they were declared a public health hazard and carted away and burned.

That had been three years ago. Maggie had been fourteen that year, and just before the plague broke out she had been sent to stay with her great-aunt Reenie in the Ridings, while her mother searched among the gruesome remains for the three Examiners who had been her sons.

Officially, of course, an Examiner of the Order has no family. The first thing a prentice has to do before taking his place as a son of the faith is to turn his back on his parents, to give up his name and to accept a number in its stead. Maggie's father respected this. The brother of an Examiner recently honoured with the gift of the Word, he knew better than to shame his sons with his interference. The younger son of a Ridings wool merchant, he had longed to enter the Order himself, but his father could only afford to lose one of his sons, and so his brother Elias had won the chance, while Donal had learned his father's trade.

Years later, himself a father, he had moved to the Universal City, swearing to give his own sons the opportunity he had been denied and, when the time came, to disown them entirely, as was right and proper according to the rules of the Order. But Maggie's mother had made no such vow. Many were the mothers like her, who defied the Law and sneaked into the University buildings at night, risking arrest – and sometimes worse – for the chance to offer a decent burial to their lost menfolk.

Susan Rede had paid dearly for that chance. A haemorrhagic fever, caught on one of her night trips among the remains, had put an end to her searching and to her life, though not before she had passed on the sickness to her husband, the nurse, the grocer, his cousin, all his customers and the fellow who came to collect the dead.

By the time Maggie came home, a hundred thousand people were dead of the plague; World's End was out of quarantine; the bodies had been cleared away; and the University of Immutable Truths was nothing but a hollow shell, its wealth looted, its libraries abandoned, its great halls and amphitheatres empty of everything but dust.

She could have stayed with her aunt, she supposed. Nothing remained of her previous life. But Reenie had children of her own, and a job milking cows at a neighbouring farm, and Maggie was unused to the ways of Ridings people, who seemed to her almost disorderly, with their country customs and casual attitude towards going to church and holy days; who laughed at the way she dressed and at her World's End accent and at what they called her 'city ways'.

And so, with no family, no home and no friends, Maggie went back to World's End. She found herself a job in a tavern close to the old University, which offered her board and lodging and a penny a day for expenses. She didn't like the customers, who were often rude and drank too much; but the tavern was called The Communion, which had led her at first to think that maybe it was somehow connected with the Order. The landlady was a Mrs Blackmore, a prude with a widow's *bergha* and a beady, sharp, acquisitive eye, who had made a fortune during the plague selling charms to the credulous. Her husband had died *helping the sick,* or so said Mrs Blackmore; in fact he had caught the fever himself while looting the bodies of the dead. Now his widow made her trade on her sainted husband's reputation – telling tales of his bravery; warning of the Seer-folk; keeping an eye out for ruinmarks and such; and solemnly preaching abstinence, while selling the worst and sourest watered-down beer in the whole of World's End.

And as Maggie became accustomed to new ways and to her new life in the Universal City, she understood that the great plague was not the worst thing that had happened there. In the absence of the Order, another plague had come to town – a plague of greed and lawlessness that swept the whole of Inland's South.

Odin One-Eye would have understood. Order and Chaos have their tides, and the rise of one leads inevitably to the decline of the other. Not that the Seer-folk had risen far; but the fact remained that ten thousand members of the Order had been eliminated in a single day, and Chaos had rushed in to fill the spaces they had left.

It was not, however, a victory that would have given Odin any great comfort. The Order was gone, certainly; but in the three short years that followed the war, World's End had become a wretched place. Without the Order to keep control, it had succumbed, as money often does, to excess, anarchy and greed. Gone were the solemn dark-robed figures; gone the chattering groups of prentices; gone the quiet coffee shops and the oratories and books.

Now, instead of Cleansings to entertain the masses, the streets were awash with traders from abroad, rushing in to ply their wares. In the days of the Order, the port of World's End had been kept under very strict control. Foreign traders had been heavily taxed, and illegal wares seized and destroyed. Only respectable merchants had been allowed, selling respectable and necessary goods. Hard drink had been banned, along with whores and dancing girls, and although a black market had existed (for luxury and exotic wares), such undesirables as gypsies, pedlars, rogues and Outlanders were more likely to have been put in the stocks, Examined, expelled or even hanged – than welcomed into Cathedral Square.

But now the gates had been opened up. Ships were no longer turned away, and once this knowledge had been passed around, a plague of traders from abroad had descended upon the port of World's End.

These traders sold anything and everything you could imagine. Silks and leathers and pasties and pies; monkeys and persimmons and purple dyes; sea shells and poisons and barbarian slaves from over the One Sea; gemstones real and fake; hard drink; odd gadgets; love spells; oranges and glassware and the dried organs of wild beasts. And gradually these traders had invaded the city, bringing hordes of buyers and gawkers and gamblers and thieves tumbling in their exotic wake. They also brought crime of every kind, diseases, drugs and violence. They made and lost fortunes in gambling, selling into slavery those who could not pay their debts. They lived like kings or warlords, draped themselves in jewellery, carried swords, kept slave girls, and seduced the young and credulous with promises of easy wealth.

For Maggie, who scarcely had enough money to survive, and who worked all hours in the grimy tavern, it looked as if the world she knew had turned to Pan-daemonium. Even the University had been taken over by the new arrivals – empty refectories converted to dancing halls and colleges, to brothels and taverns and gaming halls.

At first there had been some resistance to this – mostly from native World's Enders, who feared that one day the Order might return. But as time passed, their followers had grown fewer and less fervent. No one had come to take control. The Order had not returned, nor the plague. A few people claimed to have seen ghosts around the deserted buildings, but the eerie corridors of what had once been called the Universal City proved themselves to be a lot less eerie when filled with dancers and musicians; and slowly but steadily the rot spread inwards, claiming chapels, studies and halls; even the Great Quad itself, now converted to a forum where half of World's End – or so it seemed – came to cavort on Seventh-day nights.

Here were dancing bears on chains, and sumptuous banquets eaten off the backs of naked whores, and smokers of exotic weeds, and fake magicians and fortune-tellers, and mad prophets preaching the words of vanished demons and conquered gods. Where modesty had always prevailed, wild new fashions now appeared. Some women even went out in the streets with heads uncovered and shoulders bare. In three years, it seemed, the world Maggie knew had come to an end; and no one but Maggie seemed to care.

She had always kept the faith. She covered her head with the *bergha,* as the Good Book instructed. She ate no meat on holy days and always washed before saying her prayers. Even though the Order was gone, she kept its fast-days and followed its Laws, for in this new disorderly world, the old rites and rituals made her feel safe.

Of course, she had never known the plague, nor had she actually witnessed the Bliss. Coming home from the Ridings to find herself an orphan, penniless and alone in a city she barely recognized, she had found her romantic young soul turning inwards for comfort, and she had convinced herself (at least in part) that she was the hero of some tale of the Elder Days, a lone survivor of Tribulation.

The youngest child – and the only daughter – of a family of four, Maggie had always been the brightest. Though she had never been to school, she had secretly taught herself to read, and over the years, in tantalizing fragments between Jim Parson's Sunday sermons and passages snatched from her brothers' books, she had collected more knowledge than anyone could have suspected. Tales of the demon Seer-folk of old; of the Æsir and the Vanir, their wars, and finally how they had stolen the runes of the Elder Script and built themselves a citadel from which to rule the Nine Worlds. She knew how they had gloried; made weapons and magical artefacts; had gone on quests and adventures; waged war against the Ice Folk; and, finally, had been betrayed by one of their own, Loki, the Trickster, and defeated at last in their arrogance by the Nameless.

That had been Tribulation – or Ragnarók, as they called it then. But Tribulation had not finished the Seer-folk. Instead it had driven them into hiding, weakened but still dangerous, like wildfire creeping underground. And the Good Book had promised that one day soon, the final Cleansing would arrive, and Perfect Order would triumph for ever over Chaos . . .

In the days of the Order, of course, *all* tales had been seen as potentially dangerous – even the ones in the Good Book – and only the Order's initiates had been permitted to enter the great libraries of the Universal City. But now Maggie was free to do as she pleased. Though most of the Order's gold had been plundered – including the strange key-shaped tokens that Examiners wore around their necks – many of their books remained, and these she sought out with a growing hunger, knowing that it was dangerous, but filled with a mounting nostalgia for the half-forgotten worlds inside.

Some were books of science and alchemy, naming the various properties of metals and salts. Some were books of geography from before the New Age. Many were in languages she could not read, or in words she did not understand. Some were illustrated with tiny pen-and-ink drawings of animals and birds. Some were indecent, containing erotic poetry or pictures of naked women. Some were long lists of ancient kings. As the desecration of the University by the traders progressed, Maggie knew that it was only a matter of time before some enterprising person dismantled the libraries and sold the books to burn in their hearths, and so she removed as many as she could and took them to a place of safety, a newly discovered passageway that lay below the Communion Chapel.

At that time this tiny chapel at the heart of the University still remained almost intact. Some of its glass had been plundered, but at the great oak pulpit a lectern still stood, and on it was the largest Book Maggie had ever seen. Too big to have been looted as yet, it was almost the size of a child's cradle, tooled in leather and bound in gold and heavy with the mysterious weight of words. Maggie longed to see inside – but it was securely fastened with a golden hasp, and none of her efforts to force it prevailed.

But it was what she found *under* the lectern that day that made catch her breath in excitement; for behind a panel in the huge carved pulpit Maggie discovered a secret door, left half open during the Bliss – the first of many hidden entrances into the catacombs of the Universal City.

From that day forth Maggie spent most of her nights in the catacombs. The ransacking of the University was already underway, and she knew that before long, the once-abandoned buildings would no longer be so, and her solitary occupancy would be no more.

But the catacombs were a different matter. The passageways beneath the University stretched out for miles in every direction: cold stone lanes, labyrinthine tunnels, draughty caves, abandoned stores, depositories of bone and dust. Above her head the looters grew bold; but no one ventured underground, and no one came to disturb her forays as she moved ever deeper under the city.

It became more than a game to her. Over three years Maggie made several hundred maps showing the location of more than a thousand rooms, caverns, crypts, passages, wells, stairways, hidden doors, loose panels, avenues, entrances, exits, crawl-spaces and cul-de-sacs.

Some of these passageways were clean; others were almost knee-deep in dust. Most of them were bare and unused, but once she found a high vault constructed entirely of human bones, the skulls arranged in a decorative pattern along the architrave, the columns made of long dry bundles of femurs and ulnas mortared together with hair and gristle and dirt and fat. Another time she found a room filled with canned meats and vegetables; then some cases of wine. She also found rats in great number; but mostly she found only lifeless rock, echoing chambers, frozen arteries – the dead heart of the Universal City.

And then, on one of her nightly forays, Maggie tripped over a loose stone, under which was wedged a long golden key. She took it and kept it around her neck. It was a pretty thing, though surely too ornate to be of any practical use. Then, one day, it occurred to her to try it on the gold lock that sealed the colossal leather-tooled Book she had found on the lectern in the Communion Chapel—

And that's how a Ridings wool merchant's daughter found and read the Book of Words.

The pages were unwieldy and large, and the paper was both stiff and curiously brittle, so that Maggie had to take great pains to avoid breaking it. But the hand-lettered script was exquisitely beautiful, and the pictures – tiny enamelled scenes from the Closed Books; portraits of heroes, rampant snakes, dragons, demons and long-vanished Seer-folk – were often stories in themselves, mysterious and terrible and luminous with promise.

Fearing vandals or thieves, she had hauled her treasure (not without difficulty) into the space under the pulpit, and from thence to her secret library. Here she kept all her stolen books, and here she set up the Good Book respectfully against the wall. And although the text was very old and its meaning was often hard to make out, Maggie sensed the power in the ancient script, and she would creep back to the library at night and, by the light of a candle, run her fingers over the illuminated text, and whisper the strange and lovely words to herself, and dream.

As a child she had been taught to be wary of dreams. But as Maggie grew older, scraping a living down in the bilges of the Universal City, she found increasing pleasure in dreams. Her parents and relatives were gone. Such friends as she'd had were scattered. Dreams were all she had now and, primed with images from the Book, she dreamed of battles and of demons, Seer-folk and gods; of the Sky Citadel and the Black Fortress and the Chaos beyond; but most of all she dreamed of the Last Days, of Tribulation, of the ultimate Cleansing of all the Worlds, when plague and crime and famine and death would be outlawed for ever, and three great Riders with swords of flame would charge across the Middle Worlds, striking down the wicked and raising the faithful from the dust.

And there shall come a Horse of Fire –
And the name of his Rider is Carnage.
And there shall come a Horse of the Sea –
And the name of his Rider is Treachery.
And there shall come a Horse of Air –
And the name of his Rider is Lunacy . . .

It was Maggie's favourite dream by far. She knew what a dangerous game she played – for the Order had always taught that demons could enter the world through dreams – but still she could not let it go. And so in the darkness of the Universal City, surrounded by forgotten books, lulled by the murmur of wind in the tunnels and by the distant sounds of music from above, she dreamed of the Word, and of the Bliss, and of the Tribulation to come. Most of all she dreamed of the Riders of the Last Days, coming closer as time went by; and she found that if she closed her eyes, she could almost see them – one of them especially, his young face weathered by the sun, light hair pulled back with a hank of hide, and the blue of his eyes, so different to the blue of the Sea; a misty blue, like mountains seen from afar, and as cold as the peaks of the distant North.

It was a strange and beautiful dream. Strange, because somehow she *knew* he was real, and that *this* – this dead and all-but-forgotten place – was the place to which he was destined to come. Stranger, because she sometimes felt that the *dreams themselves* were calling him in a language of their own; a secret language like that of those books in which she had found a new purpose.

And so, where most people did all they could to stop themselves from dreaming, Maggie became a hunter of dreams. And

12

the more she dreamed, the more real they became to her, and the more she grew to understand that it was here, among the ruins of the Universal City, that the End of the World was destined to start, and that *she* would have a part to play.

It was this thought – and not the books or the rats – that brought Maggie Rede here every night, walking down deserted passageways, reading strange and forgotten texts, turning keys half gobbled with rust, and dreaming of that glorious day when everything she had longed for all her life would suddenly come true.

One day it would happen. One day her moment would come.

And so Maggie waited amongst her stolen books, and kept the faith, and studied, and dreamed; little knowing that six hundred miles away, in the far frozen North, in a village half hidden between mountains and snow, a pair of ever-watchful eyes had turned at last to the sound of her voice; and that, after three years of waiting, her dreams were finally marching home.

2

THOR WAS SPOILING FOR A FIGHT. That in itself wasn't unusual. The Thunderer wasn't best known for his patience, especially not before breakfast, and you had to admit he'd had a lot to deal with over the past three years.

First had been the arrival of Modi – one of a pair of twin sons predicted by the Oracle, but who, due to the unreliability of oracles in general, had actually turned out to be a daughter, Maddy. Then there had been her rescue of the surviving Æsir – with the help of Loki, the Trickster, of all people – from the Black Fortress of Chaos; which operation had led, if not to the *actual* End of the Worlds, then at least to something very like it, something that had wiped out the enemy, taken the life of the General, and culminated in the cataclysmic event between Order and Chaos that had caused Dream to burst its banks and to release its contents into the Middle Worlds.

She hadn't meant to do it, of course. In Thor's experience, women never *meant* to do anything, which was why – in the Elder Days, at least – they hadn't been involved in the dealings of the gods. Let a woman in your life, thought the Thunderer bitterly, and before you know it, you're sitting in an ice cave somewhere with your beard in knots and your glam reversed, and your wife nagging at you for a new body every ten minutes, as if you didn't have enough to do keeping the Worlds safe for mankind.

Bloody women, grumbled Thor. *A son would have done things properly. A son would have made a difference. A son would have made his father proud—*

Of course, it had ended in victory for the gods. Four of them had escaped the Black Fortress. Loki had gone even further, escaping the realm of Death itself. But though it was true that the Order had been defeated, never had victory tasted less sweet.

The Oracle, who had promised them new Worlds, had turned out to be the enemy. Odin was dead, the Æsir divided, the Vanir resentful and hostile; all of them weakened and irresolute. Without the General they were once more at odds – the Vanir, under Heimdall's command, keeping mainly to their stronghold under the chain of mountains called the Seven Sleepers (except for Skadi, who hadn't been seen since the End of the World and was generally assumed to have gone back home to the Ice People).

The Æsir too were divided. Elevation to godhood is not easy to come to terms with, even such beggarly godhood as theirs, with their broken runemarks and unfinished Aspects. On the shores of the river Dream, with magic flying around like snow and the disembodied Æsir fighting desperately for their lives, there had been no chance for discussions or explanations. Four largely unsuspecting hosts had found themselves suddenly embodying various Aspects of the divine with greater or lesser degrees of comfort.

Ethel and Dorian had accepted the change wholeheartedly, and had therefore come to terms with the situation rather better than Sugar, whose role as Brave-Hearted Tyr was still something of a trial to him; or Sif, whose complaints at her reincarnation into the body of a pot-bellied pig had been a trial to *everyone*.

As a result, the Æsir were split between Malbry Parsonage, which still belonged to Ethel; the pig farm at Farnley Tyas, which was the home of Thor and Sif; the smithy, which Tyr had claimed as his own (possibly because it was closest to the inn); and the smith's cottage, which had fallen to Maddy after her father's death.

Maddy's elder sister Mae, who might in other circumstances have been expected to take an interest, had married out of Malbry to a relative of Torval Bishop's, and now lived across the river

15

in the little village of Farnley Tyas, which was about as far from Maddy as could be managed, and where Mae could sometimes pretend to herself that they were not related.

The folk of Malbry had been reluctant at first to accept the strangers into their midst. But Maddy was still one of their own; and Dorian Scattergood, though something of a black sheep, was the son of a most respectable family. A pity his new wife was so muffin-faced, said the village gossips. Dor – or Thor, as he called himself now – was a fine-looking fellow, and some had expected him to pair up with the parson's wealthy widow – though, to be sure, even Ethel Parson had grown quite peculiar following her escapade under Red Horse Hill.

Still, to be peculiar was not against the law, they said, and the strangers were tolerated, if not liked, as long as they kept to themselves and caused no trouble.

There *had* been a scally with them at first – a red-haired young man with a Ridings accent and a disrespectful manner – but thankfully his visit had been a brief one, and had not been repeated. Loki, who could no more refrain from causing trouble than he could from breathing, had lasted all of three weeks in Malbry before going back to Red Horse Hill on pain of dismemberment (Thor wouldn't even have bothered to give him the warning, even though, as Maddy pointed out, he *had* just saved the Nine Worlds). Here he had remained, watching the valley from his subterranean stronghold and cataloguing the weird and uncanny things that sometimes emerged from the flanks of the Hill.

Still, reflected the Thunderer crossly, there were worse things to deal with than Loki right now. Bad as he was, and undoubtedly crazy to the last drop of his demon blood, at least things *happened* when Loki was around. And Thor was bored; so terribly bored that he would have welcomed even the Trickster's company.

The cause of his present annoyance was sitting at her dressing-table mirror, combing her famous golden hair and getting ready for an argument.

Thor watched her and wondered vaguely how a woman's back was able to convey such a wide range of negative expressions.

It wasn't as if *he* had been in any way responsible for what had happened three years ago. You'd think she'd be grateful for some of it – her escape from Netherworld, her release from torment, the embodiment of her Aspect into that a living host – but Bright-Haired Sif had been angry since the End of the World, and showed no sign of changing her mind.

'You all right?' said Thor at last.

'I'm fine,' said Sif in a voice that suggested she was anything but.

That's the problem with women, thought Thor. *They say one thing, and mean another.*

'What's wrong?' he said.

'I *said* I'm fine.' The comb tore at the fabled locks, releasing a fine dusting of dandruff onto the dressing table. All the gods had done what they could, but even in full Aspect – or what passed for it, with that broken runemark – Sif continued to share some of the imperfections of her host body.

It could have been a lot worse. Apart from a few excess pounds and a tendency to grunt when provoked, Sif could have passed for human almost anywhere. True, there was little in her present Aspect to suggest that she had once been an immortal beauty; but neither was there any indication that it owed much of its existence to a pot-bellied sow called Fat Lizzy.

Sif, however, was acutely aware, and took it out on everyone.

It didn't help that Thor had fared better. It's true that he still bore a striking resemblance to Dorian Scattergood, the man into whose body he had been reborn; but his colouring and stature were those of the Thunderer, and Dorian's mind was rarely in conflict with his. Sif had never ceased to begrudge him this, and, pulling out a rogue bristle from under her chin, she shot him a look of pure venom – wasted on Thor, as he happened to be looking the other way.

Behind him, an arrangement of flowers suddenly turned brown and died, but since neither Thor nor Dorian had ever cared for such things, that too went unnoticed.

Sif pulled in her stomach with her hands and looked at herself side-on in the mirror. For a moment her expression softened. 'Notice anything different?' she said.

'Different?' said the Thunderer. Such questions were always tricky, he knew – referring as they might to a new hat, or a different dress, or a fancy hairstyle, or any one of a thousand things that only a woman would care about.

'Something about . . . the dress?' prompted Sif.

'Yes. It's new,' said Thor with relief. 'Noticed something straight away.'

'This is my oldest dress,' said Sif, her eyes beginning to narrow again. 'I haven't worn it for ages. I haven't been able to fit in it.'

'Well, perhaps you should go on a diet, dear.'

Sif gave a snort. 'For gods' sakes, Thor. Are you blind? I've lost fourteen *pounds*!'

But Thor had apparently found something outside that demanded his full attention. The fact that it was six in the morning, pitch-black, and already snowing heavily did nothing to endear him to Sif, whose chins were trembling furiously by now, and whose blue eyes burned like magnesium flares.

'What are you gawping at out there?' snapped the goddess of grace and plenty.

'Something's wrong,' said the Thunderer.

Sif was about to make a scathing remark when she saw it too – a signature in the sky above Red Horse Hill, diffusing its light against the clouds in a pattern that both of them recognized.

'That's Loki,' said Thor. 'He's in trouble.'

'Ignore it,' said Sif.

Of course, she and the Trickster had never quite seen eye to eye; and though she accepted that Loki was not *directly* responsible for the transference of her Aspect into the body of a pot-bellied pig, it was true that he had taken a lot of unnecessary amusement from the situation. If he was in trouble, she thought, then he could get out of it on his own. Bright-Haired Sif had more pressing concerns.

But now another signature emerged, this one dark red, rather than violet. Both signatures were very bright, like fireworks in the turbulent sky.

Thor frowned at them for a moment, then made for the door, pausing only to collect the heavy fur cloak that hung there. 'I have to go, Sif. That's my son.'

Sif grunted. '*What* son?'

'That's, right, rub it in,' muttered Thor under his breath. 'I mean, isn't it bad enough that my wife's a pig, without my son being a girl as well?' He raised his voice. 'I have to go. Something's up. They're using glam.'

That meant a fight, as Thor well knew, and in a place like this, in the heart of the Uplands, there wasn't really much else for a thunder god to do but be terribly bored – or get into a fight.

In recent years the gods had done both, at first only fighting among themselves; but as time passed they had realized that there was a more serious foe to be reckoned with. Its name was Chaos, and it meant just that.

Three years ago, on the shores of Dream, the gates of Netherworld had been breached for a period of exactly thirteen seconds. During that time, while Chaos raged, an unknown number of its inhabitants had crossed over from Damnation into Dream. Most were assumed to have perished there – Dream is hostile territory so close to its source – but some, the strongest, had clearly survived, surfacing occasionally into the minds of the Folk, and thence into the Middle Worlds.

Fighting such creatures was Thor's only sport. Not a thinker by temperament, he rather enjoyed being at war, and given that the Order had been completely eliminated, these beings from Chaos were now the only foe worthy of the name. Even without a complete runemark, and lacking Mjølnir, the hammer that had once made him almost invincible, the Thunderer was still a force to be reckoned with.

He tried to hide his eagerness, but Sif was quick to notice the gleam in his eye and the way he didn't quite meet her gaze as she said, in a deceptively silky tone: 'So, you're going, are you, dear?'

He faked a sigh. 'Well, it's my job.'

'Leaving me here alone?' said Sif. 'With all kinds of . . . *creatures* loose out there?'

'Be reasonable,' said the Thunderer. 'Big, strapping lass like you, I'm sure you can look after yourself.'

Later, Thor had to admit that the choice of words had been unfortunate. Like the cry that starts off the avalanche, it set off a reaction in his beloved, characterized firstly by certain sounds, then by a furious change in her colours, and finally by a fretful explosion of glam that melted the snow around the house to a distance of almost a quarter of a mile and vaporized a family of mice living under the skirting board.

'*Strapping?*' echoed Bright-Haired Sif. 'Who in Hel's name are you calling *strapping?*'

There are times when even a thunder god knows when to beat a strategic retreat. Thor took one look over his shoulder, mumbled, 'Uh— sorry, love. Must dash,' and, hastily throwing on his cloak, escaped into the driving snow.

3

On the top of Red Horse Hill, Loki was having a difficult time. The Hill was a marvellous stronghold, of course, but it had one major disadvantage. It was a gateway to World Below, and the Faërie – goblins, demons, and sometimes worse – were drawn from a hundred miles around.

Loki could usually cope with that. Being a demon himself, he had a certain sympathy for the goblins, his little cousins under the Hill. And he could usually cope with trolls and other everyday nuisances, even in his present state, in human Aspect, with his runemark reversed (a consequence of having been dead, which still irked him considerably). But when it came to ephemeral beings squeezing their way through between Worlds and converging upon Red Horse Hill, Loki felt he'd had enough. He'd already saved the Nine Worlds once. It wasn't his job to save them again.

Of course, the gate itself was a source of power. But unless he felt like playing King of the Hill to every stray demon that came his way, he was going to have to give up his position sooner or later. At least, this was what went through his mind as he stood in the Eye on Red Horse Hill, flinging runes at the monstrosity that reared above him.

It had come out of nowhere, like the others. His mindbolts had barely slowed it down. Five feet over his head it hung, swaying sleepy-eyed above him with its fangs dripping venom into his face. He flung up an arm to protect himself and wondered what he'd ever done to deserve to be victimized in this way.

Naturally he'd encountered monsters before, but this was something that had no place in the Middle Worlds; an ephemera, a thing of dreams, born from Dream and obeying only dream logic. It shouldn't be there, Loki knew. And yet it *was* – and it wasn't the first.

It looked like a snake with a woman's head, although Loki knew that it might just as easily have come to him as a giant wolf, or a clockwork clown, or a swarm of wasps, or any other form given it by the dreamer from whose dream the creature had been fledged.

In this case a snake.

He hated snakes.

In his true Aspect, with his runemark intact, Loki could have dispatched the thing easily. Such things were still possible in Dream – and, of course, in Asgard. But this was no dream, Loki knew; and Asgard had fallen years ago, leaving the gods weakened and lost and stripped of most of their power.

He shrank back as far from the thing as he could and reached for the crossbow at his belt. Over the years he'd become accustomed to carrying ordinary weapons, and this one had come in handy on several occasions. Not against ephemera, of course. *Still, there's always a first time,* the Trickster thought, and levelled the weapon ready to fire.

'What's thisss?' said the snake, looking amused.

Loki tried for a confident grin. 'This is *Tyrfingr*,' he said. 'The greatest crossbow of the Elder Age. What? You don't think the gods would have left me here on my own with no protection, do you? *Tyrfingr* the Annihilator, they used to call it. Gift from the god of war himself. If I were you, I'd run for my life.'

The snake gave an undulating shrug.

'I'm warning you,' said Loki. 'One shot from this, and you'll be fried calamari.'

The ephemera spat a concentrated gobbet of venom that smashed the crossbow from Loki's hand and burned a smoking hole in the ground. Droplets of venom showered him, and although he was wearing winter furs, the venom burned through his wolfskin gloves and scorched the tough leather of his winter coat right through to the skin.

'Ouch! That was unnecessary!'

'I know you, Trickssster,' said the snake.

Loki cursed and flung a handful of small, quick runes at the ephemera, spinning them through the air like knucklebones. He had little hope they would do the trick, however. *Isa*, ice, and *Naudr*, the Binder, might stay its approach for a while, but as for driving it away—

With all his strength, Loki cast *Hagall* at the creature. It was a good hit, taking up much of Loki's glam. But the mindbolt went straight through the ephemeral body, lighting up its internal organs in a flare of colours as it passed.

'Iss it my turn now?' said the snake.

'Who sent you?' said Loki desperately. 'Who dreamed you, and why come after *me?*'

'I come when I am ss-summoned, Trickssster.'

'Summoned? By whom?'

The ephemera smiled and drew a little closer. Its face seemed vaguely familiar, though Loki couldn't quite place it just then – the eyes a troubling golden-grey, the shapely mouth lined with a double row of fangs.

'*You* did. You freed me. From the Black Fortresss.'

'Oh. That.' Loki sighed. Saving the gods had been the first genuinely selfless thing he'd done in over five hundred years, and it had brought him nothing but trouble. 'That was a mistake,' he said. 'You see, there was this Serpent—'

The ephemera flexed its jaws.

Loki took a final step back and cast *Yr* like a shield between himself and the creature. 'If *I* freed *you* from Netherworld,' he said, 'then doesn't that make me your master, or something?'

The snake gave him a pitying look and drew a little closer.

Loki avoided its hypnotic gaze. The runes that had held it at bay were already failing. Loki could feel *Naudr* and *Isa* flexing against his will, and when they failed, *Yr* would follow.

23

'Just tell me what you want from me.'

'Come clossser, Trickssster, and I will.'

'D'you know, I think I'd rather stay here.'

There was powerful glam in the Horse's Eye – a combination of ancient runes dating back to Ragnarók. Glam enough, even now, to keep *Yr* active for thirty seconds more – maybe even a minute or so. After that – there was nowhere to go. Retreat was wholly impossible. Loki was cornered. Even if he shifted to his wildfire Aspect, a creature that could move between Worlds would have no difficulty in tracking him into the Hill. His own glam was almost completely burned out; to leave the protection of the Horse's Eye at this stage would amount to virtual suicide.

He had no choice but to signal for help.

Ós, the rune of the Æsir, crossed with Loki's own rune, *Kaen,* and cast as hard as he could against the clouds, should leave the gods in no doubt that he was in peril. The question was: did anyone care? And if they did, would they make it in time?

He addressed the snake. 'Who dreamed you up? And for gods' sakes, why pick on *me*?'

'Don't take it perssssonally,' said the snake. 'Think of it as a compliment that you ss-still command the attention of Chaos-ss.'

Now *Isa* was slipping; *Naudr* had dissolved. Only *Yr* still held it fast, and through the circle of his finger and thumb Loki could see the mindshield fading from its original colours to the thin gleam of a soap-bubble in the sun.

He sent the signal again. Weaker this time, but he saw it flare, casting his signature colours against the snowbound sky.

Droplets of the snake's venom had penetrated the mindshield now, leaving little pockets in the snow where they had struck.

'Why me?' repeated Loki, summoning the dregs of his glam. 'Since when did Chaos have a grudge against me?'

The ephemera opened its jaws, releasing a powerful stench of venom and rotting flesh. Its fangs dripped like stalactites. It was smiling. 'Ss-suffice it to ss-say, your time is done. You have no place in As-ssgard.'

'Asgard? What about it? It fell. From rather a height, as I recall.'

'Asgard will be rebuilt,' said the snake.

'You seem very sure of that,' said Loki, glimpsing a spark of hope. A spark of runelight, to be precise, approaching fast in the swirling snow. The ephemera, like so many beings from the lands beyond Death, apparently had oracular powers, and Loki knew from experience that what an oracle craves above all things (even more than killing things) is the chance to listen to itself talk.

'So— you say Asgard's going to be rebuilt?' he said, keeping an eye on the failing mindshield.

'Why should you care? You will have no hall there.'

'Didn't have a hall in the old one, either.'

'Ss-serves you right for betraying Chaos-ss.'

'Hang on a minute,' said Loki, falling to one knee as Yr collapsed. 'Is Chaos behind this, or isn't it?'

The ephemera smiled. A gentle smile – or would have been, but for those fangs. 'Order built Asssgard. Chaosss will rebuild it. New runes, old ruins. Sssuch is the way of the Worldsss, Trickssster.'

Loki flinched at the droplets of venom that landed on his shoulders. 'Perhaps we can do a deal,' he said.

'What exactly are you offering?'

'Oh, I don't know. The goddess of desire, the sun and moon, the apples of youth – you know, the usual thing.'

'You're ss-scum, you know that. You'd ss-sell anyone to ss-save your ss-skin.'

'I happen to rather value my skin. Anything wrong with that?'

'Ssssss,' said the ephemera, and struck.

Loki had been expecting it and, with a sudden burst of energy, he launched himself out of the Horse's Eye. Rolling, he tumbled fifty feet down the frozen side of Red Horse Hill, and came to a sharp halt against a fallen rock, once part of the castle long ago.

The fall left him winded and gasping for breath; and now the ephemera, which had followed him down as smoothly and as quickly as a jet of spring water from the source, reared its half-familiar head and bared its glassy fangs for the kill.

'I take it that's a no . . .' Loki said.

But then, just as the creature struck, there came a blinding flash, followed by the double *crunch* of two missiles striking at serpent speed. A flare of runelight pinned the snake to the side of the hill, sending forks and runnels of fugitive glam writhing and scurrying across the snow.

Hissing, the ephemera twisted and thrashed in protest as its body began to revert to the dreamstuff from which it had been woven.

Loki, who had dodged the strike, now scrambled out of the creature's range, avoiding the whiplike tentacles of runelight that thrashed crazily this way and that; and, looking up at the top of the Hill, saw a tall, slim figure standing there, a mindbolt in each outstretched hand.

Below her, half a mile away, he could just make out a familiar trail – Thor's colours, like a cloud of angry red dust, along the winding road to the Hill.

'Maddy. You left that a little late.' He hid his relief with an impudent grin.

'Not half as late as *you* nearly were.' She began to move towards him down the side of the Hill, making sure not to slip on the snow and keeping a cautious eye on the stricken ephemera. 'Are you all right?'

'Damn, that hurts.' He rolled up his sleeves and, wincing, rubbed a handful of snow onto his venom-scorched skin.

'You should let Idun see to it.'

Loki said nothing, but looked at her, thinking, not for the first time, how much she had changed since first they'd met. In three years Maddy Smith had grown from a sullen, uncertain fourteen-year-old into a striking young woman with granite-gold eyes and dark hair hidden beneath her wolfskin hood. Three years ago she had been mostly untrained, unsure of her powers and cut off from her tribe. Now, with her youth and her unbroken glam – one of the new runes, *Aesk*, the Ash – she was stronger than any of the Vanir or the Æsir; a power in her own right, a true child of the New Age.

The stricken ephemera watched her too. Even as it faded and died, it stared back at Maddy without fear, its grey-gold eyes widening in what seemed like recognition.

26

Behind them, Loki's eyes widened too, going from Maddy to the snake as finally he understood why the creature had looked so familiar. He opened his mouth to speak, then thought better of it as Maddy approached the ephemera, mindbolt in hand, keeping a safe distance between herself and the woman-faced thing that twisted and writhed on the ground before her.

'Do I know you?' Maddy said.

The snake-bodied thing just stared at her, and Maddy couldn't rid herself of the thought that she'd seen something like it before, that she knew it somehow, or that it knew her . . .

She turned to Loki. 'Did it speak?'

'More than that. It prophesied.'

Maddy looked curious. 'What did it say?'

'It told me Asgard would be rebuilt. It spoke of runes and ruins, and—'

'Asgard?' said Maddy curiously. Of course, she was the only one of the Æsir who had no memory of the Sky Citadel. She knew it only from stories – the Cradle of the Gods, they'd called it – and there were many tales of how Asgard had shone above the clouds, linked to the Worlds by the Rainbow Bridge; of how it had been built for them, using the runes of the Elder Age; how each god had had his own hall there – except for Loki, which rankled with the Trickster even now, given that he'd been instrumental in the construction of the Sky Citadel in the first place, and that without him there would have been no Asgard and no halls, and probably no Gødfolk, either.

Loki shrugged. 'That's what it said. Don't ask me what that means.'

He wondered whether to mention to her what he'd seen in the snake-woman's features. He had no idea what it meant, of course – but Maddy clearly wasn't aware, so he filed the information away for use at some later time.

Maddy was talking to the snake. 'Do I know you?' she said again. 'Have I seen you somewhere before? Why did you come after Loki?'

The dying ephemera flexed its jaws. 'Ss-see you in Hel—' it

27

hissed. And vanished in a cloud of sparks, returning to the fabric from which it had been spun, leaving only a stench in its wake, and a broad bare strip of melted snow.

'Well, whatever it was, it's dead now.'

Behind her, Loki made no sound. She turned, half expecting to see him passed out, either from exhaustion or from the snake's venom. But Loki simply wasn't there – not by the rock where the creature had been, nor lying breathless in the snow, nor even at the top of the Hill.

By the time Thor arrived on the scene she had searched the Hill from foot to crown, but still there was no sign of the Trickster; nothing but his discarded glove, and the scuffle of snow where he'd tried to escape, and his footprints – only three of them – leading away into nowhere at all, as if something had plucked him from out of the sky, or dragged him into the side of the Hill, or maybe simply swallowed him whole, leaving not even the smallest gleam of runelight to mark out the place where he had stood.

4

'Out of the question,' said Heimdall at once. 'I'm not sending out a rescue party for someone who may not even be missing. I mean – who in the Worlds would take Loki, and why? Chances are he got scared and took off. You'll see. In a couple of days he'll come crawling back with some lame excuse about why he had to leave in a hurry while you dealt with the enemy.'

It wasn't often that Maddy called for a meeting of the gods. Apart from the time this usually took – an hour at least to fly to the Sleepers in bird form; another hour to fly back – she knew that Æsir and Vanir were allies by force of circumstance, nothing more. But Loki's disappearance, she felt, counted as an emergency. Surely they could agree, just this once, and face the crisis together?

'He *didn't* run,' she tried to explain. 'I told you, Heimdall. The thing was dead. I turned away for a second or two, and when I looked back, Loki was gone.' She gave the Vanir a sharp look. 'Now I know several of you have issues with Loki—'

'*Issues!*' exploded Bragi, the Poet.

'Bless you,' said Idun kindly. The Healer had an annoying tendency to see the good in everyone, including Loki – even though the majority held that, in his case, there was nothing to see. 'I think that's a little unfair, Maddy. I know Loki can be a bit – well, *wild* – but we all care about him really . . .'

'Can't stand the little bastard,' said Njörd. The Man of the Sea

29

had never quite forgiven Loki for bringing Skadi to Asgard – Skadi, Njörd's warlike ex-wife, who had proved to be a far cry from the shy, domesticated lady Loki had led him to expect.

Idun looked reproachful. 'Well, you wouldn't want to see him *hurt . . .'*

'I'd rather see him dead,' said Heimdall through his golden teeth. The Watchman also had issues with Loki; not least the fact that they'd been on opposite sides at Ragnarók.

'Well, if you're going to be *negative . . .'* Idun turned to the four Æsir. 'I'm sure the rest don't feel that way .

'Don't look at me,' said Bright-Haired Sif. 'I'm sick and tired of his stupid jokes. *Can I pour you a glass of swine, Sif? So nice to see you snout and about. Shall we go for a pork in the park?* Honestly. It's juvenile.'

There came a faint choking sound from behind the goddess of grace and plenty. Of all of them, Sugar-and-Sack had found it hardest to come to terms with his new identity as a god. Even in his Aspect – as Brave-Hearted Tyr, the god of war – he still retained far more of his goblin characteristics than was entirely appropriate. One was an appetite for beer, and the little paunch that went with it. Another was the kind of humour more suited to Loki's company than that of the gods of Asgard.

'Sorry. Bit of a cough,' he said.

Sif gave him a long, hard stare.

'I agree entirely,' said Freyja, buffing her fingernails. 'If anything could make life in this putrid little village even *close* to bearable, it would be knowing that Loki was somewhere else.'

'But you can't just abandon him,' Maddy said. 'You owe him something for saving the Worlds—'

'Gods alive,' exploded Thor. 'If I hear that whole *Loki-saved-the-Worlds* thing one more time I swear I'm going to wring someone's neck—'

'Stop it,' said Ethel. 'All of you. Shouting won't solve anything.'

The gods had assembled in the Parsonage – the only place that afforded both space and privacy for their purpose – and if Nat Parson had lived to witness the sight of the ten of them in their full

Aspects, sitting around his coffee table, drinking tea from his best china and discussing the workings of demons – and with his *wife*, of all people – he would probably have dropped dead on the spot. Not that the casual observer would have seen much to remind him of Ethelberta Parson in the calm and thoughtful woman who had spoken with such authority. And yet there was more than you might have expected. Ethel's patience, her loyalty, her kindness and her good sense served Frigg the Seeress well in her present Aspect, and the gods turned towards her instinctively as she put down her cup and addressed the group.

'Friends,' she told them quietly. 'A lot has changed since the End of the World. Three years ago was a time of disorder. Now we have a chance to rebuild. And just as Loki helped build the Sky Citadel, we may well need him to build it again.'

'Build it again?' said Heimdall. His keen blue eyes were two points of ice. 'Since when was *that* an option?'

The Seeress smiled at him. The runemark *Ethel* on her arm – one of the runes of the New Script, mystic and full of power – glowed a hazy blue-white. 'The cards are about to be re-dealt,' she said. 'I speak as I must, and cannot be silent.'

'Why is she talking like that?' said Sugar.

'Shhh,' said Maddy, who knew a prophecy when she heard one. Ethel went on in a distant voice:

'I see a mighty Ash that stands beside a mighty Oak tree.
I see a Rainbow riding high; of cheating Death the legacy.
But Treachery and Carnage ride with Lunacy across the sky.
And when the 'bow breaks, the Cradle will fall,
Then down comes Oak, and Ash, and all.'

She paused, as if waiting for inspiration. The gods waited expectantly – Heimdall with his eyes averted; Njörd with a look of hope; Thor with a growing scowl on his face; Frey, Freyja's twin, with a narrow smile; Idun with the wide-eyed look of a young child listening to a story.

'I hate it when she gets cryptic like this,' said Thor at last,

31

scratching his beard. 'Call that a prophecy? Sounds more like a forester's manual.'

But Ethel was already speaking again, reciting in clear and measured tones:

'*The Cradle fell an age ago, but Fire and Folk shall raise her*
In just twelve days, at End of Worlds; a gift within the sepulchre.
But the key to the gate is a child of hate, a child of both and
  neither.
And nothing dreamed is ever lost, and nothing lost for ever.'

Maddy thought it sounded like one of Crazy Nan Fey's nursery rhymes. Maddy's knowledge of these was not vast – in the days of the Order it had been rumoured that even the most seemingly harmless rhymes hid knowledge of the Elder Days – but everyone knew the old rock-a-bye about the baby in the treetop, and of course, as everyone knew, the Sky Citadel had once been known as the Cradle of the Firefolk.

'Is there any more?' she said.

But nothing more came from the Seeress. Instead, Ethel blinked at them, her Aspect fading once more to that of a simple parson's wife, a puzzled expression on her face.

'You're all very quiet,' she said, looking around the circle of gods. 'Was it something I said? Now, what was I doing?'

They looked at her.

'Ah, yes. Tea.' She smiled and reached for the china pot. 'Nothing like a nice cup of tea to put everything in perspective again. Shall I be Mother, everyone?'

5

LOKI AWOKE IN DARKNESS. All of him hurt: he was bound hand and foot, and as he tried vainly to summon light and found that his glam was as thoroughly wiped out as the rest of him, he was forced to conclude that he might be in trouble.

He seemed to be in a kind of cave. He knew that from the cold, the echoes, the nuggets of rock on the hard floor that seemed to know exactly where to dig into him most painfully, and the unmistakable cave-smell – the creeping scent of cellars and holes, like dust and earth and seeping moisture and blind things growing from cracks in the stone.

He wasn't under Red Horse Hill. Loki knew that Hill too well, and he would have sensed his territory. No, this place was unfamiliar, and whoever – whatever – had brought him here must have dragged him from World Above. He remembered standing on the Hill, rubbing snow on his hands, and then . . .

Just flashes. He remembered a light – not daylight, but brighter and shining with a red-white glow.

He remembered being hit on the back of the head so hard that he fell to his knees.

Then a voice saying, *Got him, dude.*

Then nothing but the dark.

So maybe I'm dead again, he thought. But Hel didn't generally tie up her guests. And Loki had been most efficiently bound, hands and feet roped together, the cord looped around the back of his neck.

At least he was alone, he thought. To have left him unguarded was careless – Loki had a knack of escaping from confinement – and he began to feel more optimistic. Those ropes would last for precisely as long as it took his weakened glam to recover – after which he would be out of here as fast as his wildfire Aspect could take him.

He tried to move to a more comfortable position, and all around him the echo awakened like a nest of shifting snakes, slithering all around him, projecting their voices to a thousand lost places, a thousand cavities in the rock.

Startled, he cursed, and once more the echoes picked up the sound, and soon the cave was percussive with it as it ricocheted against the stones, going deeper and deeper into the caves until nothing was left but a low vibration that tugged at his eardrums and made his hackles stand on end.

So much for escape, Loki thought.

No wonder they hadn't left a guard: he couldn't make a move in this underground echo chamber without sending out signals for miles around. Gods knew what any sound might attract from out of the labyrinth of World Below: rats, bears, trolls – snakes . . .

Terrific, thought Loki. *That's all I need.*

After that he tried to keep still, but his position was not a comfortable one. His back hurt; he was shivering; and now hunger was starting to worry at him, sharpening its claws on his belly.

Why me? he thought desperately. *What did I ever do?*

On further reflection, however, Loki had to admit he'd made a few enemies over the years, all of them more than capable of trying for a bit of revenge. There was Hel, whose hospitality he had just managed to escape during their last encounter, and who had promised to see him dead sooner rather than later. Then there were the Tunnel Folk, whom he'd conned out of some rather unique and very valuable merchandise several centuries ago, and whose long memories and ability to hold a grudge would have made an oliphant look fickle. Then Skadi, of course – the Snowshoe

34

Huntress – who would be more than happy to collect his hide, or cut it to ribbons with her runewhip. In fact, *none* of the Ice People were likely to show him any mercy if they chanced to get hold of him; nor were most of the Faërie; nor the Sea Folk; nor the Cloud Folk; not to mention selected members of the Æsir, the Vanir *and*, of course, Chaos – perhaps the least likely of all factions to forgive a traitor in their ranks.

Loki sighed, making the cavern walls exhale despondently. In Ridings parlance, he was toast.

Suddenly he heard a sound, something not caused by the shifting of his body against the pebble-strewn floor. The sound of bootheels against the stone. A single pair? No, more than one – pattering and scattering and chasing each other across the rock walls until soon they became a cavalcade that seemed to approach from every side, so that even if Loki had managed to break free, he would not have known which way to run.

His glam was still out, worse luck. All he could do was wait and see.

He did not have to wait long, however. He listened for five minutes or so to the sound of approaching boots before he saw a light somewhere to his left, and a hulking figure, made taller and more sinister by the leaping shadows, came into view. Behind this Loki could just glimpse two more dark figures, the first holding a lantern that spat out an oily, reddish light. He fought the urge to shrink back, and looked up calmly as they approached, trying not to betray his surprise.

For instead of being minions of Chaos (or the Tunnel Folk, or the Ice People), his captors were simply three youths of the Folk – all three dressed in uniform black and each of them, for some reason, wearing a bandage on his thumb.

The one with the lamp seemed to be in charge. He stepped up to Loki without any sign of hesitation – which made him either very secure, or incredibly stupid, or both – and scrutinized him for a moment in the reddish light of the lamp.

Loki squinted up at him. He thought he looked vaguely familiar. For some reason this was less than reassuring.

The new arrival looked to be in his late teens. His face was pale and angular behind a curtain of lank brown hair, and there was a keen intelligence in his grey-gold eyes that seemed absent in those of the other two. His comrades were very much alike; Loki guessed they were brothers. Both were shaggy and heavy-set, with oily skin prone to spots and thick-fingered hands carpeted with hair. Both were wearing heavy boots, and shirts of a design unfamiliar to the Trickster – some World's End fashion, he assumed – embroidered with a pattern of skulls.

One of them – the bigger one – peered suspiciously at Loki. 'Dude. You sure it's him?' he said.

'You think I'd mess up?' said the one with the lamp. 'Sure it is.' He stepped forward, took Loki's arm and, with a single sharp gesture, tore his shirt sleeve to the shoulder, exposing the runemark *Kaen*, reversed.

The hairy brothers took a step back.

'It's all right. He totally can't get away.' The stranger narrowed his eyes at the captive Trickster. 'You know, I thought you'd be taller in real life.'

'You're making a mistake,' said Loki. 'Whoever you think I am, I'm not.'

'Yeah, right,' sniggered the larger, hairier brother. 'Tell him, Big H,' said the shorter one.

The lamp-bearer silenced him with a growl and turned again to Loki. 'Don't lie to me,' he said softly, staring into Loki's eyes. 'I know *exactly* who you are. A named thing is a tamed thing. I hereby name you child of Chaos. I name you Keeper of the Fire.'

Loki sneered. 'That's rather vague . . .'

The pale young man showed his teeth. 'Oh, I haven't finished yet. I name you Sky Traveller, Farbauti's son, Begetter of Serpents, Father of Wolves—'

'Father of *Wolves?*' Loki frowned. The words were beginning to take effect – words or Word, he did not know – although what a trio of boys of the Folk would be doing with one of the secret texts from the Book of Invocations he could not at present begin to guess. But words – even Words – were only words without the power to use them. The Order had taken its power directly from the Nameless. But the Nameless was gone, and besides, these boys had never been part of the Order. And yet, the words were powerful. *A named thing is a tamed thing.* That cantrip dated back from a time when Frigg commanded the Nine Worlds to swear allegiance to her son Balder. How could a boy of the Folk know his names – names that only the gods had known?

Not that they stood a snowball's chance of actually taming Wildfire. Even Frigg had failed to do that. But in his present Aspect, subject to all the weaknesses and imperfections of his human form, they could perhaps come painfully close.

'Look here,' said Loki, playing for time. 'This really won't get you anywhere. But if you'll just tell me what you want, then maybe we can do a deal. I can get you anything – gold, weapons, runes – *women . . .*'

The hairier brother – the one called Big H – looked up at this with some interest. Loki guessed that the three of them hadn't had much luck with women – not entirely surprising, he thought. Their social skills were hardly impressive, and one – or maybe all – of them smelled.

'Women,' he went on silkily. 'Oh yes. I know ways to make you irresistible to the sweeter sex. I can teach you cantrips you wouldn't believe – runes to melt an ice maiden's heart. I swear, by the time I've finished with you, they'll be queuing up halfway to the Ridings to see you. Redheads, blondes, brunettes – or if you like exotics and you're not too worried about the progeny, then I know some demons who'll blow your mind and spoon up your brains like ice cream—'

'He can talk, can't he?' said Big H.

'He sure can,' grinned his friend.

The pallid youth ignored them both. He simply went on with the canticle as his two friends watched with eager eyes, nudging each other in suppressed excitement, and Loki felt what was left of his strength ebb slowly away into the dark.

'I name you Trickster, Father of Lies. I name you sire of Half-Born Hel. I name you Fire-Bringer, Architect and Destroyer of Worlds.

I name you Archangel, Fallen One, Opener of Forbidden Doors, builder of the Citadel. I name you Dogstar, Lighter-than-Air—'

The ritual words rolled over Loki like stones onto a burial mound, and once more he struggled against the ropes that held him, pointlessly chafing his sore wrists. He didn't know all these names himself; but there was no denying their power. 'Please,' he begged. 'Just tell me one thing. Tell me who you're working for—'

The force of the words pinned him again, making him writhe in anguish. Where in Hel was the power from? The Order was gone, its followers dead. The Nameless was a spent force. And these boys were not Examiners. They had no power, no training. So – who was the one supplying the glam? And how could he negotiate if he didn't know who he was dealing with?

'Tell them they're making a big mistake. Hurt me, and my people will— *Oww!*'

Now the force was unspeakable; a loathsome, crawling sensation, something far worse than mere pain. It seemed to reach right *into* him, and he screamed aloud – or thought he did – helplessly, without calculation, just because he had no choice.

'You haven't got any people,' said the youth. 'All you've got is some tired old gods and a handful of noobs. How pathetic is that? I name you Wildfire, son of Laufey—'

'All *right*! I'm sorry! Whatever it is you think I've done—'

'I name you Loki, wielder of *Kaen*—'

'Please,' gasped Loki. 'I'll do anything . . .'

The pale youth smiled. 'I know you will.'

6

IT TAKES A CERTAIN STRENGTH of mind to force a promise from a god. Even the Seeress had failed in the end – a weakness which had once led to the death of Balder the Beautiful and to the unfortunate chain of events that had ensued in the weeks that led up to Ragnarók. Even now, it wasn't easy; but out of Aspect and with no glam to speak of, Loki was at his most susceptible; and the force of the words, along with a powerful combination of the runes *Úr, Naudr, Isa* – and some others he couldn't quite make out – was enough to force him into sullen acquiescence.

But a god's sworn oath is binding, as Hel had found out four years ago at the End of the World, on the shore of Dream, and to break it would have disastrous effect. Basically, the nasty truth was this, the Trickster realized: whatever the pale young man told him to do, he was bound to do it now, or face the cosmic consequences.

'So what do you want?' he said at last, when it was clear that he was trapped. He felt uneasy, as well he might: the last time he'd been caught like this, it had been by Thiassi, Skadi's father, who, after three weeks of none-too-gentle persuasion, had finally wrung a promise from Loki to kidnap Idun, the Healer, and to deliver her into the custody of the Ice People. Such an oath, once made, cannot be broken without incurring the most serious cost, and it had taken all Loki's guile and glam to find a way to avoid both payment and retribution.

39

'Whatever you want, I'll give it to you. Just tell me what it is, OK?'

The pale youth shrugged. 'We're waiting,' he said.

'Waiting? For what?'

'You'll see.'

It occurred to Loki once again that perhaps Skadi was behind all this. Perhaps she *hadn't* gone home, after all. Perhaps she'd been planning this all along. His young captors might be her creatures; although they looked to be of the Folk, there was something feral about the three of them, an animal gleam in their golden eyes, their mouths crammed with too many teeth . . .

'So – won't you tell me who's in charge?'

'You'll find out soon enough,' came the reply.

The pale youth who seemed to be in charge now turned to his companions. 'Watch him for me, both of you. If he tries to move, hit him.'

Loki gave him a hurt look. 'Who, me? What did I do?'

Big H squinted down at Loki, looking, if possible, even bigger and more menacing than before. A faint rank scent of rotting meat seemed to emanate from him. Loki sensed that personal hygiene was not high on this young man's list of priorities.

'I'll give him a belt of my glam,' said Big H.

Glam? thought Loki. *What glam?*

More than ever, he wished for the truesight, which would show him what he needed to see. But his own glam was still burned out, and the brothers showed no colours at all, nor any sign of a rune-mark, though now that he looked more closely, he could see that they bore matching tattoos. A flaming sun on Big H's arm, a full moon on his friend's, each flanked by the symbol that Loki knew as the Wolf Cross. Not a runemark, exactly, but a sign of allegiance to Chaos in one of its darkest, most sinister forms.

Their leader had moved to the back of the cave, apparently waiting for someone. Loki, seizing his chance to gain information, turned to the smaller of his captors and gave him his most innocent smile.

'So, Big H—' he began.

'I'm Skull,' corrected the youth.

'Dude . . .' Big H gave him a nudge.

'Oops, sorry.'

Loki said nothing, but grinned inside. Now, at least, he knew their names. Nicknames, both of them, he guessed; but every piece of information was valuable. He put on his most guileless expression and turned to the brothers once again.

'So – what happened to your thumb?' he said, indicating the bandage that adorned Big H's hand. It seemed rather too much of a coincidence that all three of his captors should meet with identical accidents; and now that he came to think of it, wasn't there something strange about all this – something that rang a distant bell?

'We – uh – like, we swore an oath.'

'Blood-brothers, man,' said Big H.

'Really?' said Loki. 'So – you're not actual brothers, then? I mean, you both look – very alike. What does the H stand for? Handsome? Hairy? Hefty? Huge? I *said* handsome, right? I *meant* handsome. Oh, and I don't think I caught your friend's name?'

'Don't talk to him,' warned the voice of their leader from the far side of the big cave. 'Didn't she say not to talk to him?'

'She?' said Loki apprehensively. Once again, images of Skadi and her runewhip took unsettling shape in his thoughts.

'Dude,' said the hairy youth. 'You heard what Fenny said. Shut up.'

Loki hid a triumphant grin. *Fenny*, he thought. He squinted across the cavern once more, trying to see if there was anything at all in the young man's face that could give him any kind of clue as to the nature – as well as the scale – of the trouble in which he had landed himself.

Nothing. Just the light of the lamp and the shadows that leaped like flung spears against the rock walls of the cavern. Then . . .

Just for a moment he saw something. Maybe it was a trick of the light, but it brought the gleam back into his eyes and a flicker of

41

recognition into his mind. There was something about that profile. Something about those matching tattoos. And something behind that human form – a hint of colours imperfectly concealed, a distant thread of violet . . .

Ah. Hello. There it was. A trace of a signature in the air, so faint that Loki had missed it at first. Now, as his spent glam began to recover, the colours also slowly returned, filament by filament, bracketing his silhouette with their fleeting rainbow sheen.

Loki fingered the runeshape *Bjarkán* and, through it, tried to see Fenny more closely, but his hands were tied too tightly for that, and the momentary impression he thought he'd had was gone in a blur of light and shade.

'Stop that, you,' warned Big H.

'Stop what?'

'*You* know what.'

Frustrated, Loki shook his head. It was no good, he told himself. There was nothing he could do. Unless . . .

I'll give him a belt of my glam, he'd said.

Now Loki considered Big H's threat. If he could persuade him to use his glam – or whatever he counted as such – then the explosion of runelight that would inevitably follow might well be enough to identify his signature, or at least to find out how strong he was. Of course, Loki had no wish to be belted by anything – but sometimes you needed to take a risk.

He gritted his teeth. 'You stink,' he said.

Big H looked at him. 'You talking to me?'

'Well, duh,' said Loki. 'Who do you think? It's bad enough having to look at you both without having to smell you too. I mean, don't you people wash?'

'Dude, his ass is *so* dead,' said Skull, not without admiration. 'No one disses the Brotherhood. I don't care whose father he is—'

'Shut up,' said Fenny from the far end of the cave.

Loki ignored him. 'Brotherhood? What Brotherhood? Brotherhood of BO? And what kind of dialect is that, anyway? The North Ridings? Sheep country? You look to me like the kind of man who might be lucky with his sheep—'

'Lucky with his *sheep?*' Big H's face was dangerously congested. 'Well, you do *look* like a—'

The whack, when it came, was every bit as powerful as Loki had feared it would be. It caught him squarely across the side of the head, knocking him sideways into the rock wall. The only problem was that Big H didn't use glam, just one of his big, hairy hands, and the only colours Loki could see were the stars that danced in front of his eyes.

Not such a great plan, after all.

He lay on his side, breathing hard, trying to link the few facts he had. *Fenny. Skull. Big H.* The Brotherhood. Those matching tattoos. Those colours. He'd seen them before, he knew he had. If only he could remember *where . . .*

Loki's flame-green eyes opened wide in the darkness.

The Wolf Cross.

Father of Wolves.

I don't care whose father he is . . .

'Oh *no*,' he whispered.

And then there came a thrashing of wings as something large flew into the cave. *Some kind of bird,* thought Loki, and once more he thought of the Huntress – but Skadi, he knew, would have chosen a form that reflected that of the natural world. A hawk, perhaps, or a mountain cat, or her favourite Aspect, the snow wolf.

This creature was something like a bird, but no bird Loki had ever seen. Instead it looked like a child's drawing of something only glimpsed in dreams: its wings were a violent purple, its head a fiery scarlet. It settled on an outcrop of rock, sparks crackling from its fiery tail, and fixed Loki with a piercing stare.

Behind it came running a small, bandy-legged, aggressive figure, rather less than a goblin in height, but with a squarish, massive head that gave it a look of the Tunnel Folk.

It gave Loki a look of contempt. 'Oh, it's bloody *you*,' it said.

7

LOKI LIFTED HIS HEAD FROM THE FLOOR. 'Should I know you, or something?' he said.

The dwarfish creature shrugged. 'Who cares? The important thing is, you know my lady. And my lady needs to have a word with you.

Loki swallowed. 'A word?' That sounded ominous. In his experience, *a word* often turned out to be something that hurt. 'Who's your lady?'

'Can't you guess?' The female voice was deceptively pleasant, and it took Loki several seconds to identify it as that of the firebird, now perched on a rock above him. 'I thought you were smarter than that, Loki.' It opened its long, sharp beak and gave a very human yawn.

'Poor sweetheart,' it went on. 'Have my boys been rough with you? Untie him, Jolly. If he tries to run, break his legs.'

Jolly was the dwarf, it appeared. A somewhat inappropriate name – Loki had met jollier people in Hel – and he glared and grimaced at Loki as he cut through the ropes that secured him, leaving the Trickster even more certain that he and Jolly had met before.

But there was no time to think of that now. Fenny, Skull and Big H were closing around him menacingly, and Loki knew the firebird was right. Trying to run would be a mistake.

'Thank you.' Painfully, he stood up.

The firebird watched him unblinkingly.

'Looking good, Angrboda,' he said. 'Feathers always suited you.'

The bird lifted a careless wing. 'So you do recognize me,' she said.

'Oh, Angie. How could I not?' he said. 'You know you're the love of my life, right? And Fenris . . .' He smiled at the youth who called himself Fenny. 'One minute he's a cute little wolf cub, gambolling happily through Ironwood, chasing squirrels and disembowelling birds; the next thing you know, he's hit puberty and he's into the whole released-from-Netherworld, kidnapping-Dad, aligned-with-the-forces-of-Chaos thing. Doesn't it make you feel proud?'

Fenris growled. 'Shut up, *Dad*.'

'Articulate as ever,' said Loki. 'And your little friends, Skull and Big H – Skól and Haiti, by any chance? Demon wolves with an appetite for celestial bodies?'

The hairy brothers grinned. 'Yeah.'

'Dude. We're the Devourers.'

Loki sighed. 'OK,' he said. 'So— to what do I owe the pleasure? Not that I don't appreciate this little family reunion, but did you have to send a snake after me? Wouldn't a postcard have done just as well?'

The firebird spread its purple wings and fluttered down from its perch on the rock. The moment it touched the ground, it changed, appearing now as a slender young woman dressed in a close-fitting black tunic and sporting big boots and purple hair. She looked to be in her late teens. So much for appearances. Loki happened to know that Angie was as old as the hills – actually, rather older than that – and that behind her look of innocence there beat an ancient, savage heart. Her eyes were heavily circled with kohl, and there was a row of purple studs going through her left eyebrow. One arm was bare. The other was intricately sleeved with tattoos: stars, birds, concentric patterns, and something that looked like a runemark, amethyst against her skin—

Interesting, Loki thought. She'd never had a rune before. And this one was somehow different; not a rune of the Elder Script, but brighter than a bastard rune. A *new* rune, then? Was it possible?

He indicated the mark. 'Nice. Is this what they're wearing in Chaos these days?'

'Not quite,' Angie said. 'And I *didn't* send that ephemera. In fact, we were all set to rescue you when your funny little friend intervened.'

'Really? How touching,' Loki said. 'I should have known you were on my side when you ordered Shorty to break my legs.'

Jolly gave a little growl.

'Dude,' said Skull. 'Don't call him short.'

But Loki was thinking furiously. The fact that this was family didn't mean he was home and dry. Quite the opposite, in fact. This was Angrboda – otherwise known as Angie, the Witch of Ironwood; the Temptress; the Mother of Wolves; cruel as a mountain cat, wily as a snake, unpredictable as – well, Loki.

Now Loki, looking back, wondered how he could ever have been so rash as to get involved with the Temptress. She *was* very alluring, he thought. That, he supposed, was his only excuse. But you don't fool around with Chaos. Five hundred years, three demon children and two Apocalypses later, it still sounded like a bad idea, and his absence had clearly done nothing to make her heart grow fonder.

Still, he wasn't dead yet, which probably meant one of two things. One: she needed him alive. Two: her plans for his execution involved something more elaborate than three wolf brothers and a sulky dwarf.

Of the two possibilities, Loki much preferred number one.

He grinned at Angrboda. 'So – first of all, I'd like to say how happy I am you made it here. I'm guessing you left the Black Fortress during the little fracas I caused there, and managed to enter the world through Dream.'

Fenris gave a low growl.

Jolly looked disgusted.

'That *little fracas,* as you call it,' said Angie, 'damn near ended everything. Chaos was breached, Death was wide open and Dream was awash with ephemera fighting to get into World Above. Fortunately, Jormungand had already made his way out of Dream and back into the One Sea, from which he freed us – no thanks to you.' She shot Loki a scornful glance. 'Yes, we escaped. But only just. And as for *your* contribution to events – Loki, don't you ever grow up? I've never seen anything so irresponsible.'

Loki blinked. '*You're* lecturing *me* about responsibility?'

'That rift you opened,' the Temptress said. 'A rift from Death into Netherworld. For thirteen seconds that gate was open, letting Hel knows what into the Worlds. And you're here, with that *Who? Me?* expression on your face, pretending it's nothing to do with you?'

'Be fair,' said Loki. 'I *was* dead—'

'Being dead is no excuse. You were given a second chance, and it's up to you to put things right. The Order is gone. That means *you're* the Order now – you and the rest of the surviving gods. It means that it's up to *you* to redress the balance – to help rebuild Asgard, to hold back Chaos, to bring stability to the Middle Worlds – and what are you doing instead? Hiding out in Nowhere-land, getting drunk, picking fights with each other, hob-nobbing with the Folk, for gods' sakes, while all the time those ephemera are munching their way through the fabric of the Worlds—'

'Now wait a minute,' Loki said. 'Since when did you care about maintaining Order? I thought Chaos was your business.'

Angrboda looked away and played with a wisp of her purple hair. 'Let's just say that in this case . . . I have a personal interest.'

'An interest? In what?'

'In the new Asgard, of course,' said Angrboda impatiently. 'Listen, Loki. At this rate, with the Universal City overrun, with ephemera coming out of Chaos, with the Nine Worlds so full of holes that they might as well be Ridings cheese, things will probably come to an end in another twenty years or so. But rebuild

Asgard and you have a chance. A chance to regain your Aspect. To reestablish Order again. To be *gods*—'

'What's in it for you?' said Loki.

'The truth is,' she said, 'I *like* it here. I've built a niche in World Above. And if Chaos comes to the Middle Worlds—'

'You mean – Chaos might not be thrilled to find out that you've gone totally native?'

Angie shrugged. 'Something like that.'

'To say nothing of a new rune – and how did you get that, by the way?'

'Suits me, don't you think?' she said. 'That's *Wyn*, the rune of high stakes and big prizes. Play your cards right, and you may even find that some of those prizes come to *you*.'

'So— what do you want from me?' Loki said.

'Darling – I want to *help* you, of course. I'm willing to put all my resources at your disposal. You'll be needing all the help you can get if you're going to rebuild Asgard.'

'Rebuild Asgard?' Loki said. 'But I don't build things. That's not me. I cheat, steal, swindle, misappropriate, sabotage, disrupt, commandeer and demolish – but *build*? Angie, you've got the wrong man. You need Thor, or Heimdall.'

She shook her head. 'I need *you*. I've heard there's been a prophecy.'

'You've got to be joking,' Loki said.

'Not even a bit,' said the Temptress. 'I take these things very seriously. And so should you, when the enemy sends an ephemera after your hide—'

'You *knew* Chaos was after me?'

Angrboda shook her head. 'This didn't come from Chaos,' she said. 'Someone from the Middle Worlds pulled that creature out of Dream. Someone who clearly wants you dead . . .'

'Wonderful,' said Loki.

'Oh, we were keeping an eye on you,' said Angie reassuringly. 'The boys would have stopped you getting hurt.'

'Well – er – thanks,' said Loki. 'Forgive me if I'm not entirely overwhelmed with confidence at the thought of the Wolf Brothers and Fenny-boy standing between me and extinction. Not forgetting Shorty here . . .' He shot a look at Jolly, who responded at once by showing him a set of alarming yellow fangs.

'Don't call me Shorty,' said the dwarf.

Loki suppressed the urge to laugh. 'You spoke of *resources* earlier. I'm assuming you have more up your sleeve than this little band of comedians here . . . Because if you haven't, Thor and Heimdall are going to laugh themselves into a seizure, after which they're going to play ball with my head—'

'Now, Loki,' Angie warned. 'I hope you're not going to be difficult. You'll deal with us whether you like it or not – the only real choice you have is whether you want to do it the easy way or the hard way.' Her kohl-rimmed eyes narrowed menacingly, and at her side, Fenny gave a warning growl.

Loki shrugged. 'So what's the deal?'

'Well,' said Angie, 'it's simple enough. I have something the Æsir thought lost, which they'll need when it comes to a fight. I also have a new rune to put at their disposal. In exchange, I want guarantees . . .'

Uh-oh. Here it comes, Loki thought.

'First: amnesty for my people. When the Æsir get back into power, I want to be sure we'll be left in peace. Two: the return of our rightful territories. Ironwood for Fenris. The One Sea for Jormungand. And for myself? A place in Asgard. A hall of my own amongst the gods.' Angrboda took a step forward and playfully kissed Loki's nose. 'So those are my terms, sweetheart,' she said. 'Now it's your turn. What do you say?'

49

8

LOKI WAS SILENT FOR A LONG TIME. When at last he found his voice, all the humour had gone from it. 'You know they'll never agree to those terms. A deal with the Witch of Ironwood? They'd never believe it wasn't a trap. The moment I tell them I've spoken to you, they'll peel me like a grape. And if you think holding me hostage will help . . . Well, you'd have more chance if you brought them my head – which, incidentally, they'll probably relieve me of the minute I even mention your name—'

Angie raised an eyebrow, and the row of studs caught the light. 'Always so dramatic,' she said. 'Your folk can't afford to turn me down. I mean, without me, what have you got? Washed-up has-beens like Heimdall and Njörd. Flower children like Idun and Bragi. Recalcitrant recruits like Tyr. Narcissists like Freyja and Frey. Besides, you haven't heard the best part yet. If the Æsir meet my terms, then this is what I'm willing to offer them. First, an alliance with my people. Of course, I can't answer for all of Chaos, but as far as our little group is concerned, the Gødfolk make better allies than enemies, and we want them on our side. And to show our goodwill, as well as my rune, we're prepared to give you the Hammer of Thor the moment the treaty's agreed.'

Loki's eyes widened. 'The Hammer of Thor? Mjølnir?'

'None other,' said Angie, looking smug.

'How? It was lost at Ragnarók. Swallowed by— Ah.' He smiled. 'I see.'

'That's right. Jormungand.' Angie shrugged. 'Apparently his . . . digestive functions take a bit longer than we'd thought.'

'Ew,' said Loki.

The Wolf Brothers grinned.

'He can't help it,' Fenris said. 'Devouring things runs in the family.'

'And so we retrieved it,' Angie went on. 'And we're prepared to return it to its rightful owner – a gesture of good faith, if you like – as soon as the gods have given their word.'

And at that Angie turned away and began to inspect her finger-nails, which were painted purple, while Loki, who was thinking hard, tried to make sense of her plan in his mind.

On the whole, he thought he understood. Chaos was prone to rebellions. That was the nature of its folk. He himself had thrown in his lot with their enemies when it suited him, which had earned him no friends among his own people. Now, it seemed, Angie was doing the same. But she and her renegades would not risk an open confrontation. Much better to march under some other banner; then, when the Sky Citadel was rebuilt and Order restored, they would use their alliance with the gods to protect them from the retribution of Chaos – while doing precisely as they pleased, like delinquent children wanting their freedom, yet happy to be shel-tered and fed by parents too soft to turn them away.

Yes, thought Loki, it did make sense. And yet there were things that troubled him. The first was how organized they seemed. Chaos is – well – *chaotic.* There are no generals in Pan-daemonium. And Angie had been no exception, proving as volatile as Loki himself. But here she was, speaking of treaties and oaths and strategies and the rebuilding of Order and Asgard. It wasn't the Angie he knew at all. Which led the Trickster to conclude that perhaps there was someone else involved.

He knew better than to say so, however. If they had Thor's Hammer, he thought, they needed careful handling. The hammer, Mjølnir, Thor's Right Hand, had been one of the great treasures

of the Elder Age, lost forever, so they'd thought, in the great up-
heaval that the Folk liked to call Tribulation, and the Æsir knew
as Ragnarók.

Since then, the gods had barely survived. Even Maddy's rescue
attempt had resulted in only partial success. Their numbers now
stood at thirteen – including a goblin and a potbellied pig – which
was hardly the stuff of conquest, he thought. Angie's assessment,
though harsh, was not entirely unfair. The Æsir were a spent force;
the Vanir scarcely better. And with Skadi gone off on her own,
and Maddy the only one of them whose powers had not suffered
dramatic reversals, it had seemed unlikely that the gods would
ever make much of a comeback.

But with Mjølnir, they might have a chance. The mighty hammer,
carved with runes that made it indestructible, heavy enough to
gouge great chasms into the mountainside, and yet able to shrink
itself small enough to tuck into your shirt—

No such weapon had been forged since the start of the Elder
Age. Even the Tunnel Folk had lost the skill; and Loki was torn between suspicion of Angrboda and of her motives, and the simple
knowledge that with Mjølnir anything might be possible: the
defeat of Chaos, the rebuilding of Asgard and, with the new Sky
Citadel, the return of their primary Aspects; and, with them, the
power to rule the Worlds . . .

'All right,' he said, looking up to where Angie was now sitting
on a rocky ledge above him, swinging her legs. 'Angie, I'll try. I'll
put your suggestion to the gods. I can't make any promises.'

She narrowed her kohl-rimmed eyes at him. 'You'd better be
persuasive,' she said 'I want my hall in Asgard.' She turned to
smile at Fenris, who had been watching Loki with open mistrust
throughout the conversation. 'And there'd better not be any treachery, either, or Fenny and the boys will be paying you another call.'

Big H winked. 'Believe it, dude.'

'And just to ensure your *complete* support, I'm sending Jolly to
keep you on side.' Angie smiled at the dwarf, who was watching
Loki with a look of distaste. 'You'll like Jolly,' she said. 'In fact,
you'll be inseparable. He'll wait on you, he'll follow you home,

he'll be your constant companion. And if you try anything – a trick, a scam, a double-cross – then you'll be in big trouble.'

'*Big* trouble?' Loki scoffed. 'So what'll he do? Bite my knees?'

Jolly gave him an evil look. 'What're you sayin'? You sayin' I'm short?'

'Who, me?' Loki said.

Jolly pushed back his jacket sleeves, revealing meaty forearms on which were inscribed the symbol—

The dwarf's fists were also unusually large for such a small person, and Loki just had time to read the words *Fadir* and *Modir* tattooed across the knuckles before the dwarf lowered his head and butted him squarely in the solar plexus, knocking all the air out of his lungs and leaving him gasping on the floor.

Jolly brought his misshapen head very close to Loki's face. 'Don't call me short,' he said. 'I don't like it when folk call me short.'

'Right,' said Loki.

'Now stand up.'

Loki did so with difficulty. He'd spent rather too long on the floor that day, and was beginning to feel victimized. He eyed the dwarf with cautious respect. Short he might be, Loki thought, but there was a lot of glam in the little fellow. The twin runemarks on Jolly's arms shone out with a baleful red glow.

From her ledge, Angrboda smiled. 'We call it *Daeg*, the Thunderbolt. Packs a punch, doesn't it?'

Loki had to admit it did.

And the thought that Angie had access now to *two* of the runes of the New Script made an even greater impact. Where had she managed to find the glam that should have belonged to the new gods? It made him *very* uneasy to think of Angie equipped with such things. And what would the other gods make of it? Nothing good, that was for sure. In fact, they would probably assume that he himself was somehow to blame.

'I'm giving you twenty-four hours,' Angie said. 'That should be enough to convince the gods that they need my people on their side.'

'And if they decide against?' he said.

'I'm sure you can persuade them.'

'And if I can't?'

Angie laughed, swinging her legs against the rockface. Beside her the Wolf Brothers sniggered, and Fenris snarled his amusement.

'Loki,' she said. 'You crack me up.'

'Thanks,' said Loki mirthlessly.

'No, really,' said Angrboda. 'You're going to need that positive outlook for when you rebuild Asgard.'

'Yeah, I'm always at my most positive when I'm about to be disembowelled by my friends.'

She gave him an indulgent look. 'I'm sending you back to World Above. Skull and Big H will look after you. And if you need to contact me, just tell Jolly. He knows what to do.'

The little man bared his teeth again. He was definitely a carnivore, Loki thought. Maybe even a cannibal.

Loki sighed. 'OK. Let's go.'

'That's my boy,' said Angie.

9

BACK IN WHAT WAS LEFT OF the Universal City, Maggie Rede was dreaming again. It was a strangely powerful dream, lit with the colours of Chaos and peopled with shapes that twisted and writhed. The Folk of the Order do not dream; but Maggie was no longer entirely their child, and after reading the Good Book, the rules that had bound her for so many years had begun to unravel like windblown flax, and the dreams had come soon after . . .

Now she dreamed of a man with red hair and eyes of a searing fire-green. She'd seen him before in dreams, and knew that he was somehow her enemy. But this time he was in trouble, she thought, and she grinned and clenched her fists in her sleep. She could see that his colours were very strong – demonic colours such as she'd seen depicted in the Good Book; and there were *runes* among them – unholy fire-runes like those she had seen in the Book of Words. The same kind of symbol shone from his arm – the ruinmark of the Firefolk.

By his Mark shall ye know him . . .

Kaen. The name of the ruinmark was *Kaen.* Reversed. She did not ask herself how she knew. Perhaps she'd seen it in the Book that lay open against the wall at her side. The golden key that opened it now hung on a chain around Maggie's neck. It was her most treasured possession. She always closed the Book when she left, but when she was alone in her secret place, she liked to keep it open at the Chapter of Invocations, where the secret names of the Firefolk were written in letters of silver and gold.

She struck out at the red-haired man, slamming him against the ground. He threw up a shield to protect himself, but the shield was weak. It would not last. Her enemy cried out in pain; venom spattered the Northlands snow.

Good, thought Maggie in her dream. *Let's see you talk your way out of this.*

Now the man was on his knees. She could see the fear in his eyes. She couldn't hear what he said, but knew that he was pleading for his life.

Mercy? I don't think so, she thought.

Moving closer, she could see him lying helpless at her feet. Triumph bloomed in her like a rose. She could have killed him easily, but she wanted the pleasure to last a while. She wanted to see him suffer first; she wanted him to grovel and beg before she sent him to Netherworld.

But now there came a flare of colours, and Maggie saw a figure approaching; a small but somehow ominous shape, bracketed with runelight. And yet there seemed little to justify the surge of panic Maggie felt as the figure came closer. It was only a girl, after all – a girl of about her own age. A girl with curious grey-gold eyes, hair loose around her shoulders, and one of those ruinmarks on her extended palm . . .

Maggie thought: *She looks just like me!*

And then there was another bright flash, and the world flipped over like a leaf—

And Maggie awoke with a loud cry, sheathed in sweat and trembling, and found herself back in the catacombs, head resting close to the open Book, over which she must have fallen asleep, and the afterimage of the dream stamped against the shadows.

But now, as she struggled to banish her fears, Maggie saw that she was no longer alone. A young man was sitting opposite her, cross-legged upon the stony floor. A young man who might have been seventeen or eighteen, but whose face bore the marks of experience. His hair was like that of the northern folk; his eyes were blue as distant ice.

Maggie realized that as she slept, the *bergha* she was wearing had slipped, and, blushing, she tugged it back into place before addressing the stranger.

'Who are you?' she said sharply. 'Who are you, and what are you doing here?'

The young man smiled, and Maggie Rede felt a funny little shiver go down her back, as if a tiny feather of ice had brushed against her shoulder blades.

'My name is Adam,' the young man said. 'And I've come a long way to find you.'

10

THREE YEARS HAD PASSED SINCE Adam Scattergood had
found his way out of World Below. Little now remained of the
boy who had once been Maddy's tormentor. Little now remained
of the boy who had once pissed his pants on Red Horse Hill and
had come so close to losing his mind at a hint of things uncanny.
Little remained of the boy who had seen his mentor possessed by
the Nameless. Now it was he who stood his ground while other
people fled in fear; and he had seen so much that was uncanny,
unnatural and downright impossible that all trace of fear in him
had gone, leaving him with nothing but a hatred of Seer-folk. This
hatred was at its strongest when he was thinking of Maddy Smith
– which was often, and with rage, a rage that was nine-parts envy
and one-part that of his passenger – the whispering Presence in
his mind that had been with him for the past three years.

The Seer-folk had the power to build Worlds. Why should
Adam not have it too? But Adam had no ruinmark, and Adam
had no Book of Words, and even if he had, he knew that there was
no particle of glam in him, and the words would lie useless on the
page, however hard he tried to awaken them.

The Voice in his head had told him this – the whispering Voice
that had guided him out of Hel and back into the Middle Worlds;
the Voice that had taught him so many skills, but which sometimes still ranted and railed at him, calling him useless, stupid and

weak – a nonsense, as Adam had trained relentlessly these past three years, and his body was all muscle.

At first Adam had wondered *whose* Voice it was that guided him. He had seen, three years ago, how the Nameless had come in Aspect out of a stone head, and had fought with the Seer-folk, and killed their one-eyed General; after which it had tried to possess Maddy Smith, but had been lost in the river Dream. Adam also seemed to recall that the Nameless actually *had* a name: Mimir the Wise, or the Whisperer; an ancient being with a bitter grudge and the power to enter minds and control the actions and thoughts of the weak.

But here Adam's native caution had blunted the edge of his memory. The affairs of gods were no business of his, and all in all he was happy to stay in ignorance. He sensed that the less he remembered of the events of three years ago, the less likely he was to incur the rage of the passenger inside his mind.

Besides, there were compensations. His unseen passenger had skills. Now Adam shared them too: he had knowledge and instincts he'd previously lacked. Emerging from World Below, he'd astonished himself by hunting for food – killing a deer with his bare hands and dressing the skin for later use, though these were skills he'd never learned.

Later, he discovered that he could fight – as a group of hill bandits learned, to their cost. Sword, bow and throwing knife – all seemed strangely familiar. He could also ride a horse, trap fish, and find his way at night by the stars, all of which had ancient names – names he'd never known before.

He was not strong at first, of course; but walking and exercise hardened him, and by the time he reached the Universal City, he was a foot taller and a hundred pounds heavier than when he'd left Malbry at the age of fourteen. In fact, Aileen Scattergood's spoiled, lazy son had grown into a fine-looking young man, skilled in all manner of combat, speaking four dialects, and more learned in the Good Book than the most senior of the Order's Magisters.

His name was no longer Scattergood, although he had kept the Adam part. Scattergood was a provincial name, fit for a rustic from the North. Instead he had taken the name of Goodwin, a trusty, dependable Lowlands name, and invented a plausible history to account for his presence in World's End.

Not that he would need it now, Adam Goodwin told himself. No, after weeks of searching the city he had found the prize he sought. *Two* prizes, in fact – and the Voice in his head seemed to caper and howl in glee, reinforcing Adam's occasional (but always unspoken) fear that the thing in his mind was insane.

'Adam?' repeated Maggie. Her eyes were dark and expressive, and coloured grey-gold like mountain granite. Just like her sister's, in fact, he thought, and a new surge of hatred blossomed within him, seeing the face of his enemy . . .

Of course he hadn't *seen* her – except in his dreams – for the past three years. But those eyes were unmistakable; and that mouth, with its hint of sullenness; the hair pulled back in a thick braid . . .

Why don't we just kill her now? Send the Seer-folk her head in a bag—?

You fool, whispered the passenger. *Just leave the thinking to me, will you? And try to be charming, for once in your life. This girl is extremely valuable.*

And so Adam swallowed his hatred and gave the girl his most winning smile. It was a little cold, perhaps; but all Maggie saw was his blue eyes and the firm line of his jaw and the fair hair that fell almost boyishly across his forehead . . .

Good, said the passenger. *Now tell her what I told you. And for gods' sakes, be courteous. None of your village-boy ways in World's End.*

So Adam put out his hand and said: 'Adam Goodwin, at your service. Maggie Rede? I've been looking for you.'

11

'How did you know my name?' she said. 'Are you a dream, a demon – a ghost?'

There *were* ghosts in these catacombs, though until now Maggie had never encountered one. But the handsome young man with the piercing blue eyes had none of the look of the ghost about him.

In fact, Maggie Rede had never seen anyone so vital. He glowed with health; his hair shone; he moved with the easy, effortless grace of one who is completely at ease with every muscle and nerve in his body. He was a stranger, and yet there was something familiar about him. Had she seen him in one of the markets? The tavern?

'A dream?' said Adam. 'Far from it. In fact, if anything, *you're* the dream. The dream I've been following all my life.'

It was a good line, he thought. The Voice gave him lots of good lines, and he had become quite adept at delivering them. Besides, he knew girls, and he guessed that this girl was no different to the rest of them. A few good lines, a kiss or two, and she would be his for the asking.

But Maggie didn't seem impressed. In fact, he thought she looked furious. For a moment she seemed to struggle to speak; then she turned away from him, drawing her scarf protectively close.

'Whoever you are, you shouldn't be here. You woke me. I was sleeping.'

'I know. I'm sorry to intrude,' said Adam in a humble voice. 'But now that I'm here, aren't you even a little bit curious about what I've come to tell you?'

'No,' said Maggie. 'You shouldn't be here. It isn't – *right* for you to be here.'

Adam Scattergood clenched his fists. The girl was going to be troublesome. Of course, he should have expected as much – knowing who the girl *was*.

He swallowed his impatience. '*What* isn't right?' he asked her.

'You and me, alone like this. Here. Alone. Together.'

Adam turned his face away, not wanting his expression to show. Clearly the girl was some kind of prude. He should have guessed she would be. The *bergha* she wore told him as much; and, of course, no respectable daughter of the Order would want to be alone at night – with a man – in such a place as this.

'Trust me. I've no interest. All I want is to talk to you.'

He thought she bridled a little at that, and grinned to himself in secret. *There's nothing like a show of indifference to get a girl's attention.* From the corner of his eye he watched as she fought curiosity, fiddling with the little gold key that hung from the cord around her neck.

At last she seemed to relax a little.

'What did you want to talk about? And how did you know I'd be down here?'

Adam shrugged. 'I know lots of things. Those dreams you've been having, for instance.

She shook her head. 'I don't dream.'

'Of course you do,' Adam said.

Maggie narrowed her eyes. 'Do *you*?'

'Oh yes,' said Adam. 'I've dreamed of *you*. I've dreamed of you every night for years. And you've dreamed of me. You know you have. You really think you can lie to me?'

Maggie felt all the breath in her body suddenly leave it, as if she had been punched in the stomach. Then she looked into Adam's face directly for the first time, and knew why he'd seemed familiar.

This was the face she'd seen in her dreams – her dreams of

Tribulation. The blue of his eyes. The line of his jaw. She felt a surge of panic. How could this man have come from her dreams? How could she have known his face?

'You *are* a demon,' Maggie said.

Adam smiled. 'Quite the opposite. I'm a *demon-hunter*. I know all about you, Maggie Rede. Daughter of Donal, niece of Elias, known within the Order as Examiner Number 4421974.'

Maggie's eyes widened still further. 'No one knows the secret names,' she said in a voice that trembled a little.

'I know much more than that,' Adam said. 'I know what you've been doing here, Maggie, delving into forbidden books. I know what dreams they've given you.'

Guiltily, Maggie raised her hand to the golden key that hung round her neck.

'It's all right,' Adam said. 'I'm not going to try to take it from you. But I know how you lost your family – your brothers when the Order fell, your parents to the plague that came after. I even know how your uncle died.'

Maggie went pale. 'The Bliss—' she began.

'There was no Bliss. That tale was concocted to hide the truth.'

'The truth?'

Adam sighed. 'I know it's hard. But the Bliss was just a Faërie-tale invented by the enemy. Those people – the Order, your family – they weren't reborn to celestial Bliss. There was no Nameless waiting for them on the shores of the First World. The First World fell long ago, in the days of the Winter War. The Order was trying to build it again – when all this happened . . . this massacre – what your people call the Bliss.'

Maggie stared at him. 'No,' she said. 'I don't know why you're telling me this. The Order was fighting Chaos. Bringing perfection to the Worlds. And when their task was finally done, then the Nameless called them home—'

'Maggie,' said Adam. 'Open your eyes. Does this world look perfect to you?' He paused to let his words sink in. '*Look* at it,' he went on. 'Thousands of people dead with the plague. The Universal City reduced to a sink of corruption and vice. Foreign

63

traders in every square, stinking up the place with their food, their animals, their heathen ways. Slaves being traded where libraries stood. Opium-dens and liquor-traders on the steps of the cathedral itself – Chaos where Order used to be. Is *this* what the Order was fighting for? Is this what you call perfection?'

Slowly Maggie shook her head. Now that she came to think of it, the stories didn't really make sense. Souls swept up to celestial Bliss; bodies left to rot on earth. And the plague – surely *that* had not been part of the plan—

'But if you're right,' she said at last, 'then what happened to the Order? How could ten thousand people die, all at once, in a heartbeat?'

Now Adam smiled to himself. 'That's what I came here to tell you,' he said. 'That's why my mission led me here. Your parents, your brothers, your uncle Elias – all the other Magisters and Professors and Examiners of the Order, all those good folk who gave up their lives to keep the Worlds clear of corruption and Chaos . . .' Now the young man's blue eyes gleamed, and his face was alight with a fervent glow. He turned once more to Maggie and gave her his most earnest look.

And then he put his hand on hers, and Maggie felt a shiver of something pass through her body, a sudden surge of mysterious heat as he looked at her and whispered: 'They didn't die from the Bliss at all. Maggie, they were murdered.'

12

'MURDERED?' REPEATED MAGGIE REDE in what sounded
to her like a stranger's voice. She knew she ought to feel angry
– shaken, distressed, grieving, shocked – at the news Adam had
given her. But in truth, the overwhelming sensation she felt was
simple relief – relief that she had been right; that the feelings she'd
had over the past three years had turned out not to be simply a fig-
ment of her lonely imagination, but the shadow of a deeper truth;
that the forces of which she had read so avidly were not only real,
but more sinister than even she had been led to suspect – forces
that could wipe out ten thousand people at a single stroke, forces
that threatened the very Worlds.

Maggie already knew their names. They were names she had
seen again and again in the pages of the Good Book; names that
filled her with unease and with a kind of fevered excitement. *The
Æsir. The Vanir. The Seer-folk.*

'Have you seen them?' she said at last. 'The Seer-folk – have you
seen them?'

Adam nodded. 'Once,' he said.

'Tell me,' said Maggie, eyes gleaming.

'If I do,' he said, 'there'll be no going back. It'll eat up your life,
as it did mine. And the things you'll know – the things you'll *see*—'

Suddenly the young man's face changed: a shadow seemed
to pass over it – his eyes darkened, his mouth twisted – and if

Maggie had been of a whimsical nature, it might almost have seemed to her that another face had surfaced briefly beneath the young man's features: that of an older, harsher man, with a smile of infinite malice and guile . . .

But Maggie was too excited to be deterred by shadowplay.

'Tell me what you know,' she said.

'All right,' said Adam with a smile. 'But don't say I didn't warn you.'

And so Adam Goodwin told his tale. And as Maggie listened in silence, she began to be conscious of a most curious sensation. Not *pleasure* – though her face was flushed. Not *anger* – though her heart was beating faster than a hunting hawk's wing. Instead, she felt unexpectedly *alive*; like something that enters a cocoon to emerge, months later, as something else.

It didn't matter any more that she'd never been close to her family; that she'd almost forgotten her brothers, who had joined the Order when she was a child. As for her uncle Elias, Maggie had never met him at all. Still, those things didn't matter now. Grief; loneliness; sorrow; guilt – all that belonged to the past. Now there was only the certainty of what her enemies had done – and the equal conviction that they had to be stopped.

'These Seer-folk,' Maggie said. 'They won the war by a trick. A cheat.'

'That's right,' said Adam. 'They're devious. They have no Laws, no honour. They lured the Order into Hel and unleashed Pandaemonium onto them without a thought for the consequences. And that's why you see the Universal City as it is – overrun, in Chaos. But in the North it's far, far worse. There are gateways there through which things can pass – not just in dreams, but in the flesh. Things from before Tribulation, released into the waking Worlds like flotsam from the river Dream.'

Maggie's eyes grew wide with alarm. 'And is that what you do?' she said. 'Hunt down these things and send them back?'

'I used to,' said Adam. 'But not any more.'

'What happened?' said Maggie.

'Not here,' he said. 'Somewhere light. This place reminds me too much of—' Adam broke off. 'Too much of the Seventh World,' he finished in a low voice.

It took Maggie some time to take that in.

'You were there?' she said. 'You were actually *there*?'

Adam nodded.

'But how did you . . . ?'

'I wasn't in the Order,' he said. 'I'd never received Communion. So when the Seer-folk made their move, I alone was overlooked. I survived. I saw it all. Sometimes I wish I hadn't.' He paused. 'That's why you have to trust me now That's why I need you to understand. With the Order gone, there's no one left to continue the fight. No one but me – and *you*, Maggie.'

He looked at her appealingly, and Maggie thought she had never seen anyone with eyes so blue. World's Enders were most often dark – Maggie was like an Outlander – but Adam was like the sun on the Sea, and Maggie was bedazzled.

'*Me?*' she said.

Adam smiled.

'But how can I—?'

'Shh. You trust me, don't you?'

Maggie nodded. 'I think so,' she said.

'Then do as I tell you.' And Adam drew from his pocket a slim pearl-handled razor. 'I need you to keep very still . . .'

'Why? What are you going to do?'

'I'm going to show you a mystery.'

'You're going to cut me?' Maggie said.

'Power demands a sacrifice. Believe me, this is worth it.'

Maggie looked at the razor. The thought of being cut alarmed her a little; but blood, she knew, was a powerful thing. Perhaps this was some kind of initiation, she told herself; something like the prentice's rite when he first entered the Order.

'All right.' She held out her hand.

'No. Take off your headscarf.'

'Why?' said Maggie in surprise. Brought up in the ways of the Order, she had strict ideas of modesty. Even now that the Order was gone, to show her hair to a stranger – a *man*; a man who was not a relative – seemed almost indecently intimate.

'Do I have to explain *everything?*' said Adam, getting impatient. 'Come on, Maggie, it's only a scarf. You think I haven't seen a girl's hair before? Besides, where I come from, only married women cover their hair.'

For a moment Maggie was pulled two ways. She wanted to do what Adam asked, but still it felt obscurely *wrong*. It wasn't so much the *bergha* itself, but all that it had meant to her. To Maggie, wearing the *bergha* returned her to a more orderly time, a time when to be called *modest* was the greatest praise a girl could receive – that, and *unimaginative*, which was nearly as good as *obedient*. Maggie had tried to be all those things for as long as she could remember – and the urge to be obedient now, to do what Adam asked of her, was almost overwhelming. Adam had worked with the Order. That made him practically an Examiner. And the language he used – that of sacrifice, and power, and mysteries – was so close to that of the Order that to refuse him anything seemed so much worse than removing a scarf.

The *bergha* was pinned around her head and shoulders in a style that had once been popular, and that some of the older women still followed. It took Maggie a moment or two to remove the pins that held it in place; beneath it, her long hair was braided.

Adam nodded approvingly. 'Keep very still,' he told her,

'What are you going to do?' Maggie said.

'It won't hurt a bit. I promise.'

'But— this is going to help you, right? Help you fight the Seer-folk?'

'Trust me,' Adam said. 'This is going to hurt them *badly*.'

Maggie obeyed and closed her eyes as he reached to unfasten her hair. Clearly it had never been cut. The Good Book frowned on short hair in girls, just as it did on long hair in boys. *Each to his own, and each in their place,* the Book of Laws instructed them, and although this rule had never been particularly enforced in Malbry, World's End was closer to the Order, and therefore more likely to insist on such things.

'Remember, this is a sacrifice,' he said in his most persuasive voice. 'New times demand new Laws. New ways.'

For a moment Maggie still hesitated. It wasn't that she was vain, but her hair was all she had of her past life. She remembered her mother brushing it every night when she went to bed; her brothers tugging on her braids when they were playing together.

And then she opened her eyes again. She knew what she wanted. The past was gone. Her mother and brothers were all dead – and all because of the Seer-folk. And here was Adam, offering her a chance to hurt the enemy, and all she could think about was her *hair*?

'Give *me* the razor,' she told him fiercely.

'All right,' Adam said, and smiled.

Five minutes later, the job was done. Maggie's braids were gone, and the rest of her hair was shorn so close that in some places the scalp showed through. It didn't look too bad, Adam thought. Maggie's hair was curly and thick, and would grow back soon enough. And under a *bergha* or a veil, no one would guess at the silvery mark – the silvery mark at the nape of her neck, just where the Voice had said it would be.

He'd had to shave that part himself – Maggie couldn't see to do it properly – and when he uncovered the ruinmark, the Voice in his mind gave a cry of triumph, making Adam flinch. The razor gave a tiny jump, leaving a faint line of crimson.

'Ouch!' said Maggie.

'I've found it,' he said.

Adam folded the razor and put it back in his pocket. 'I can see how they missed it,' he went on. 'Even when you were a baby, I'm guessing your hair must have hidden it. But now that your powers have grown—'

'Hidden what?' Maggie said. 'Please, Adam – what do you see?' Now there was tension in her voice, and he could feel her trembling as he traced the rune with a fingertip. It seemed to brighten as he did so, like tarnished silver beneath the polishing cloth. A forked shape like a fallen twig, gleaming now with a ghostly light—

'What is it?' Maggie said.

'A sign,' said Adam, smiling.

Maggie raised her hand to her neck and gently explored the uncovered mark. It tingled slightly at her touch, but that might just have been the unaccustomed feel of stubble at the nape of her neck. 'How did you know it was there?' she said. 'And what does it mean?'

He smiled again. 'It confirms what I knew: that you're the one. The one we've all been looking for. *I see a mighty Ash that stands beside a mighty Oak tree . . .*'

'I don't understand,' Maggie said.

'Those are the words of a prophecy made by a famous oracle. And this . . .' He touched the runemark lightly with his finger-tips. 'This is *Ác*, the Thunder Oak, and with it, we're going to raise Asgard.'

BOOK TWO

Thor's Hammer

Beware of Gødfolk bearing gifts.

Northlands proverb

1

'You're saying i'm a *demon*?'

Adam took a deep breath. That the girl had taken it badly, he thought, was in some ways understandable. But he hadn't expected this outburst of rage; this furious denial.

'No, you're not a demon,' he said, for what seemed like the fortieth time. 'This mark is why I came here. That's why I came to find you. It's a powerful rune—'

'It's a *ruinmark*! A filthy, horrible ruinmark!'

Adam put his arm around her. 'I know,' he said. 'I know you're upset. But listen to me. This runemark makes you *special*—'

'There's nothing special about me!' Maggie said. 'I've always believed in Order. Am I possessed?' She clenched her fists. 'Is this something that came from my dreams?'

Adam shook his head. 'No. But it gives you power over Dream. Power to change the Worlds, Maggie. Power to challenge the Seer-folk . . .'

Maggie stared at him. 'How?' she said. In the horror of discovering the filthy ruinmark on her neck, she had almost forgotten the reason for cutting her hair in the first place.

'Remember your dream?' Adam said. 'About the red-haired man on the hill? That was *you*, Maggie. You did that. Without any knowledge or training, you were able to summon a creature from

73

Dream, and send it after the enemy. Do you know who that man *was?* Have you any idea how close you came to taking out one of the Æsir for good?'

'How could you know about that?' she said.

'I told you. I know lots of things. That's a remarkable power you've got—'

'I don't want it! Take it *away!*'

At that Adam's patience finally broke. The part of him that stood aloof, watching and measuring from afar, saw his anger and judged it good. Anger could sometimes be useful, he thought; especially when dealing with this girl, whose fury, he sensed, almost matched his own. Sympathy hadn't worked on her; neither had seduction. Now Adam turned on Maggie Rede, and slapped her face as hard as he could.

For a moment nothing happened. The girl simply stared at him, her eyes dark with rage and astonishment. The mark of Adam's fingers stood out in scarlet on her cheek; the other side of her face was white. Adam was suddenly reminded of Hel, the two-faced Guardian of the Underworld, and in spite of the closeness of the cave, he shivered.

Then he felt it: a prickling, something like static. It surged; it built; and Adam felt the hair at the back of his neck rise up as if there were lightning in the air. He felt a sudden urgency to get away before it struck, but the Voice in his mind was jubilant; and Adam was rooted to the spot while the power of Ác, the Thunder Oak, spat and crackled around him.

When it struck, it struck hard, and if Adam had not been expecting it, it might have done more damage. As it was, he managed to drop to the ground just as the static was discharged, but even so he felt it close, like a rush of dark air above his head – air that was filled with ephemeral particles, radiant and lethal.

Adam had seen mindbolts before. This was not a mindbolt. It felt more like a gust of wind – an icy draught from Chaos itself – and even the Presence inside him ceased its gloating and whispered in awe, *Gods! Gods!* as the draught passed right through the cave wall with a shrug that made the Worlds tremble, before losing itself at last in the foundations of the Universal City and the labyrinth of World Below.

Now Maggie looked down at Adam, and the expression in her granite-gold eyes reminded him so much of another girl that for a moment it might have been Maddy Smith, watching him from Red Horse Hill, the day she'd made him wet his pants. Adam had long since passed the pant-wetting stage, but even so, looking at her, his mouth was as dry as a shingle and his heart felt like a ruptured balloon.

Gods! repeated the passenger.

'What did you say?' said Maggie.

Adam Goodwin shook his head.

And now, for a moment, Maggie froze, almost certain she'd heard something – a whisper – in some half-familiar language, remembered as if from a dream—

She looked at Adam. 'What did you do?'

Once more he shook his head. 'Maggie, I didn't do anything. What you felt just now – that rush – was glam that, if harnessed, could strike a man dead just as I might swat a fly.'

Maggie sat down on the rocky floor. Suddenly her legs – and much of the rest of the Worlds, she thought, that had once seemed so dependable – simply could not be trusted.

'Felt pretty good, didn't it?'

Maggie looked at him, horrified. She too had felt the explosion of glam, and for all the darkness it brought with it, for all its reek of Chaos and death, Adam was right. It *did* feel good. Was this possession? She asked herself. Did this make her evil? And how could a filthy ruinmark have been there, on her neck, all the time, without her ever suspecting it?

'Power isn't good or evil,' said Adam, echoing the words that Odin One-Eye had once spoken to Maddy Smith, years ago, on Red Horse Hill. 'It's something like fire. Out of control it can burn up a city – or, if you keep it in its place, it can cook you a batch of cakes and light your bedtime candle.'

'But how do I *do* that?' Maggie wailed.

'It's all right. I can help you. I can help you tame the fire – or use it on our enemies.'

She looked at him wildly. 'Teach me *now*.'

Adam smiled. 'Not here,' he said. 'It isn't safe. But you've already chosen the right path. You're on the side of Order now. And I'm here to help you. Think of me as your personal guide.'

Maggie gave a long sigh. It felt as if something inside her – a pressure on some vital organ, some nerve – had finally, blissfully, been released. The discovery of the ruinmark and the horror of what had happened next seemed almost insignificant now, compared to the relief of knowing that *this* was what had set her apart for all these years of misery; that this was the source of her unquiet dreams; and that someone wanted to help her – someone who wanted to be her friend.

'So I'm not a demon,' she said in a voice that wavered a little.

'Of course you're not' He took her hand.

'Then what am I?'

'You're a *warrior*,' he said. 'Perhaps the only warrior who can bring down the Seer-folk. Remember the Book of Apocalypse? *And there shall come a Red Horse, and the name of his Rider is Carnage?*'

Maggie took a deep breath. The Worlds still seemed to be spinning around her. Only Adam Goodwin was still. 'Carnage?' she repeated.

For a moment Maggie considered that perhaps she hadn't woken up after all, and that this young man and his tale were nothing more than another dream, a cruel gift from the river whose waters sent good people mad . . .

But Adam was still holding her hand. It warmed her frozen fingers. Maggie was suddenly aware of the fact that she hadn't touched another human being since before the time of the plague.

'But— I thought the Rider was *you*,' she said. 'I even saw your face in my dreams . . .'

'No. I'm only a messenger. I'll be your squire, your teacher, your friend, but without your glam I'd be helpless. I wouldn't stand a chance in Hel against even the least of the Seer-folk.'

'And I would?' Maggie said, feeling rather doubtful. She wasn't a violent person; except in dreams she had never killed anything larger than a rat. But the thought of the Seer-folk set her teeth on edge like biting down on a piece of tinfoil. And Adam's hand in hers was strong – warm and strangely comforting.

'What do you need me to do?' she said.

Adam looked at her tenderly. 'I want you to come with me. Bring the Good Book. You'll need it soon.'

'Where?' said Maggie.

'Trust me,' he said. 'I'll tell you when we get there. First, you'll stop by the tavern and pack. You won't be going back again. That part of your life is over.'

Maggie nodded, feeling dazed. It wouldn't be a great loss. She felt as if the past three years had been nothing but a meaningless dream. If Adam had asked her to follow him in nothing but the clothes in which she stood, Maggie would have said yes without even a pang of regret.

She looked at him, eyes shining. 'And then?'

Adam smiled approvingly. 'After that it's easy,' he said. 'All you have to do is dream.'

2

Twenty-four hours had already passed since his encounter with Chaos below Red Horse Hill, and Loki was feeling miserable. Miserable, nervous and hunted; and if Jolly had not been at his side, watching him all the time, he would long since have made a run for it and taken his chances across the Hindarfell. Gods and demons notwithstanding, the North was becoming too dangerous, and to Loki the Universal City, with its taverns and souks, sounded a likelier prospect than Ethelberta's prophecy.

Of course, the words of the Seeress had already spread like wildfire. Both Æsir and Vanir had their theories on how to interpret the prophecy. Originally it had sounded not unlike common speech, but rearranged in nine lines of verse, the words now seemed heavy and ominous, like the sound of chariot wheels rolling towards a battlefield:

The Cradle fell an age ago, but Fire and Folk shall raise her.

So far, so good. That part seemed straightforward. Most of the gods had already agreed that this meant the rebuilding of Asgard – otherwise known as the First World, the Sky Citadel or the Cradle of the Firefolk. The following line, however, had caused some disagreement:

In just twelve days, at End of Worlds; a gift within the sepulcher.

What was that supposed to mean? That the raising of Asgard would bring about the destruction of the gods? No one knew for certain. Oracles, as everyone knew, were not always clear on the details. And in twelve days – how could anyone hope to rebuild in such a short amount of time?

'I don't see that it matters,' said Frey. 'We don't have the glam to rebuild it. Not in twelve days or even twelve years. Look at us – the twelve of us; thirteen, if you count Loki. Skadi's gone, Odin's dead, and most of us have our glam reversed. It took all sixteen runes of the Elder Script to build the original Asgard. Sixteen unbroken runes, plus all of us, Æsir and Vanir, in full Aspect. And even *then* we needed help—'

'Nice of you to remember that,' said Loki sourly, under his breath.

'The point is,' continued Frey, 'that even at the height of our powers, that was a monumental task. We had new, unbroken runes; we had all our warriors. How many new runes have we got now? *Aesk* and *Ethel*. That's all we have.'

'My brother's right,' Freyja said. 'Why assume that *we're* involved? All the prophecy really said was that Asgard was going to be rebuilt—'

'Yes, by Fire and Folk,' said Thor. 'Don't you want to see Asgard rebuilt? To have your Aspects back again? To give Chaos a damn good kicking?'

'That would be *wonderful*,' said Sif in her most sarcastic voice. 'Now all we need is your hammer back – the hammer *you* lost at Ragnarók.'

At this, Jolly looked up with interest, but the Trickster shook his head. Tempers were running *far* too hot for him to stick his neck out now.

'But, Sif, the prophecy . . .' said Thor. 'It practically promised there'd be war—'

'*I* don't see why there has to be war,' said Sugar, whose anxiety, always high, had now reached unprecedented levels.

'But you're the god of war,' said Thor.

'About that . . .' said Sugar-and-Sack. 'I was thinkin' that mebbe I'm not cut out for that kind of thing. You know. Violence. War and stuff.'

Jolly gave a snigger.

'What?' said Sugar.

But Jolly just smirked. As far as he was concerned, the fun was only just beginning, and Æsir and Vanir would soon find themselves in the middle of Ethel's prophecy whether they understood it or not.

Loki had his own thoughts, none of them optimistic. He'd had enough of oracles the last time the Worlds had ended. Besides, raising Asgard was one thing, he thought, but Treachery, Carnage and Lunacy were all things he felt he could do without. All in all, he told himself, he would much rather be in World's End, sitting in a tavern somewhere, maybe drinking a glass of wine and watching the dancing girls.

But he still had a task to fulfil, and Jolly was never far away, and besides, even if he managed to flee, he knew that Angrboda's wrath would never cease to pursue him – not to mention ephemera coming after him through Dream.

His return to World Above had met with something of a mixed reaction, ranging from scornful displeasure (Freyja and Sif) to thunderous rage (Heimdall and Thor). Bragi, the most amiable of the Vanir, had treated the whole thing as a joke, but Heimdall had voiced the suspicion at once that Loki had betrayed them, had sold himself to the enemy and was secretly working with Chaos. (The fact that this was true, of course, made Loki all the more nervous.)

However, his tale of kidnap by the Tunnel Folk and of his subsequent release by Jolly – who looked enough like a dwarf, he thought, to make his story plausible – had convinced most of the others, with the possible exception of Ethel, who said nothing, but whose eyes betrayed more understanding than Loki found entirely comfortable.

But allaying the gods' suspicions was not the only task that Loki was to carry out. The second – and much more difficult – task was to talk them into listening to a scheme so wildly implausible that even the Trickster wasn't convinced that it wouldn't lead to disaster.

A pact with the Witch of Ironwood. Loki himself wasn't

convinced that such a thing was possible. And Angie – who was she working for? Her plan was far too well thought out to be simply the work of her crew; Loki knew from experience that Angie was as volatile as he was himself.

So who was behind it? Chaos? Old gods? Dark Surt himself? None of the options were promising. Whichever way you looked at it, Loki was sure it would all end in tears – or blood . . . probably his own. He needed an ally – and badly – before it all blew up in his face.

Maddy seemed the obvious choice, except that she was a new-comer and the others might not follow her. Heimdall? Forget it. Frey? Njörd? Likewise. Idun bore him no ill will, but her trusting nature meant that she believed no harm of anyone else either. Tyr would have been useful, but in his present Aspect he didn't have the willpower to stand up to the rest of them, and as for Ethel, the Seeress – *Never trust an oracle.* That watchword had served Loki well in the past, and he wasn't about to risk his life looking for exceptions.

Which left only one possibility. And at last, after a great deal of planning and thought, Loki finally knew what to do. It would be tricky, but it might work. He went to see the one member of the Æsir he knew – well, he *hoped* – wouldn't ask awkward questions and, once convinced of Loki's good faith, would offer him protection.

Thor.

The strongest of the Æsir, in spite of his reversed runemark, the Thunderer had always held a grudging respect for Loki's superior intellect; and this time, with the Hammer as bait, and in the light of the prophecy, the prospect of war on the horizon, he might be tempted to take up the fight. And with Thor on side, the others would follow, even to the End of the Worlds . . .

The Trickster arrived in the village at dawn, with Jolly trotting at his heels. No one saw him but Crazy Nan Fey, who was doing her laundry down by the Strond, and who recognized him instantly. Nan, of course, was famously mad, but she was no fool, either, and she knew Loki for a Fiery at once from the trail he left behind him. The little man at his heels, now, might have been a goblin, she thought, but for his colours, which crazed and spun . . .

'I see you, Dogstar,' cackled Nan Fey. 'Who's your little friend, eh?'

Loki gave her a sharp look. 'He's no friend of mine,' he said.

'Oh, so that's it?' said Nan with a grin. 'Gods keeping ye on a short leash? Is that because of the prophecy?'

Loki glared at her. 'Just because there's a prophecy doesn't mean Yours Truly's involved. Nothing's going to happen, all right?'

Nan gave another toothless grin. She didn't need any prophecy to know that something was on its way. The Auld Man had already told her that. Since the End of the World, the Auld Man had come to her many times in dreams, whispering and coaxing; telling her stories and songs from her youth that Nan had thought forgotten. The words often sounded like nonsense to her, but there was wisdom in nonsense, she knew, if one could only fathom it; and as she watched the Fiery trail, she hummed a little rock-a-bye that had been on her mind since she awoke – a little rhyme that went all the way back to the Elder Age:

See the Cradle rocking
High above the town.
Down come the Firefolk
To bring the baby down.
All the way to Hel's gate
Firefolk are bound.
Pucker-lips, a-pucker-lips,
All fall down.

She wondered if Loki knew that rhyme. Probably he didn't, she thought; which was no doubt for the best. Nan Fey liked the Trickster, and was genuinely sorry for what was to happen to him. But sentiment could play no part in the coming chain of events. The Auld Man's plans must always come first, and if he demanded a sacrifice.

And so she watched the Trickster go by, and gave her little toothless smile. *Pucker-lips, a-pucker-lips.* That wasn't *quite* the right word, of course. But something was coming. Something big. The Auld Man had told her so.

3

LOKI AND JOLLY'S FIRST PORT of call was Dorian Scattergood's farmhouse, from the open window of which came a thunderous snoring. Loki was quick to pick the lock, and to follow the sound to the four-post bed that Dorian had once occupied – but further investigation revealed the sleeper to be female, stout, with blonde hair of unusual wiriness.

Damn it!

Loki took a hasty step back onto Jolly's foot, which raised a growl from the little man. The goddess of grace and plenty gave a sigh and rolled over, eyes half open in the shadows.

Wincing, the Trickster held his breath. To be in the village at all was bad enough. But to be *here,* of all places . . .

'Shh,' he whispered. 'It's all right. You're only dreaming. Go back to sleep.'

Sif gave a sigh and rolled over again with a noise like a sousaphone in distress. Most of the bedclothes rolled with her, and Loki was treated to rather more than he wanted to see of the goddess's plump hindquarters, which still bore the mark of Dorian's livestock tattoo.

'Please, no,' whispered Loki. The last time he'd sneaked into Sif's bedroom had ended with his lips being sewn together – painful, but nothing at all compared to what had originally been planned;

or, indeed, to what Thor would do to him this time if he ever found out.

Sweating, he began to move back, inch by inch, towards the door. Jolly matched him step for step – he moved soundlessly, in spite of his gait. And as Loki breathed a sigh of relief and the bedroom door swung shut in his wake, there came a voice in his left ear as low and as dangerous as that of a distant avalanche, and at the same time a large hand clamped around his neck.

'So tell me,' growled Thor, ''cos I want to know. Exactly how do you want to die?'

'Ah, Thor,' Loki said, in a casual voice that lost much of its effect for being half an octave higher than usual. 'Believe it or not, I was looking for you.' He tried to extricate himself from the Thunderer's grasp, without success. 'In fact, I have some information that I know you're going to—' A thumb on his windpipe cut him off.

'No, I don't think you do,' said Thor. And he began to apply pressure against Loki's throat.

'Just listen,' said the Trickster.

Thor showed his teeth.

'Three little words—' gasped Loki, beginning to turn blue.

So it really happened, reflected Thor. He hadn't noticed it before. People really *did* turn blue . . .

'*Please,*' whispered Loki.

Thor eased the pressure from his thumb.

Loki coughed.

'That counts as one.'

'*Thor*—'

'That counts as two,' said Thor.

Loki gave him a vicious look. He put a hand to his bruised throat and took a deep breath, trying not to cough again.

Then he said: '*Mjølnir*—'

A heavy object moving at speed takes a certain time to come to a halt. For a moment Thor's fist continued its trajectory, and might even have reached its target if Loki hadn't managed to duck; then it stopped in midair and Thor's face took on an expression of doubt mingled with a dawning hope.

'The Hammer?' he said.

'No, dummy, the other Mjølnir. The one that flies through the air, catching birds.'

The Thunderer looked slightly confused.

'Of *course* the Hammer,' Loki said. 'Thor, listen – I know where it is. In any case, I know who it's with. And the good news is: they're willing to trade.'

Loki was used to death threats. A death threat or two before breakfast, he thought, was just the way to begin the day. Some people preferred cereal, but Loki ran on energy, and there was nothing better, to his mind, than a daily helping of menace and intimidation to sharpen his intellect and keep him on his toes.

Which was why, over the course of that morning, Loki had already received no fewer than twelve promises of immediate torture, beating, dismemberment, disembowling, and other acts of unpleasantness – none of which had been carried out, thanks to Thor, whose reluctant belief in Loki's tale had swayed the four Æsir and most of the Vanir, with the obvious exception of Heimdall (who would no more have believed the Trickster than he could have given birth to ocelots) and Skadi, of course, who wasn't there.

Which wasn't to say that they were pleased. In fact, during that morning's emergency council of war (convened in haste by Ethel and Thor, and held in the drawing room of the ex-Parsonage) Loki had to answer a great number of awkward questions and swear a good many binding oaths before anyone else would believe him; and even then, it was only the presence of Maddy and Thor that dissuaded the Vanir (who didn't enjoy being summoned like this) from trying out on Loki's person a variety of methods of interrogation designed to ensure he was telling the truth.

'But why would I lie?' said the Trickster.

'Because you're the Father and Mother of Lies,' said Heimdall, gnashing his teeth so hard that they sparked.

'Ah, come on, Goldie. Give me a break.'

'With pleasure. Legs or spine?'

'I swear there's nothing in this for me.' Now Loki directed a heartfelt plea towards his circle of judges. 'But you all heard the prophecy. Asgard's going to be rebuilt, with us or without us. A deal with Chaos gives us a chance to be part of it. And if Thor gets his hammer back, with the new runes Angie can share with us—'

'New runes? Are you sure?' said Frey.

'Absolutely,' Loki said. 'I only saw two, but there must be more. And—'

'And if there are,' Frey went on, 'then maybe Asgard *can* be raised, and we can recover our Aspects. And if Thor gets his hammer back . . .'

It was a powerful argument. To the gods, exiled for five hundred years, its power was irresistible, and finally even Heimdall was moved to grudging acceptance.

'They've got the Hammer? Are you sure?'

Loki nodded. 'On my life.'

'If you've lied to us, Dogstar, you're dead,' said Heimdall, bringing the total of threats to thirteen. 'Just as long as we're clear on that.' And he put his hand out to join the rest, completing the circle.

Loki gave a sigh of relief. 'All right. Now for the oath.'

Freyja sniffed. 'But there's no one else here!'

'Please. Just this once. Do as I say.'

And now Loki began to recite the terms Angrboda had laid out: 'Amnesty for our allies in Chaos. The return of disputed territories: Ironwood for Fenris; the One Sea for Jormungand; and a hall to be readied in Asgard for Angrboda, known as the Temptress, in payment for her loyalty—'

There came a low, impatient growl. The Thunderer was getting restless.

'Such pact to be sealed,' went on Loki in haste, 'by a gesture of goodwill from our new allies – to whit, the return of Mjølnir, the Hammer of Thor, such return to be effectuated as soon as the settlement is agreed—'

'For gods' sakes, get on with it,' said Thor.

'Are we agreed?' said the Trickster.

Æsir and Vanir nodded in turn.

There was a rather lengthy pause.

'So— now what?' said Freyja at last.

Loki shrugged. 'I suppose we wait.'

They waited, hands clasped, in a circle. They waited so long, in fact, that Thor regained his dangerous look, Heimdall showed his golden teeth, and even Loki, who had assumed an air of insouciance throughout the proceedings, seemed to lose some of his confidence.

'What's holding us up?' said Njörd at last.

'I suppose these things take time,' Maddy said.

Loki shot her a grateful look

'If this is one of your games . . .' Thor began.

'Leave it out,' said Loki. 'Fourteen death threats and counting, and I haven't even had breakfast yet. You're going to hurt my feelings.'

'I'm going to hurt much more than that,' said Thor, breaking the circle and taking two steps towards Loki, who took refuge behind one of Ethel's chairs. 'In fact, if something doesn't happen right now, I'm going to—'

But precisely what Thor planned to do was suddenly interrupted by a sound from behind him. The sound of laughter, to be precise, and if Loki didn't recognize it, that was simply because his diminutive comrade had previously shown so little sign of the explosive mirth to which he now gave noisy vent.

Lounging on the ottoman, teacup in one hand, biscuit in the other, Jolly the dwarf was laughing.

His presence had barely registered with any of the gods before. Only Tyr had noticed him, and that was because the god of war was still primarily Sugar-and-Sack, a renegade goblin from Red Horse Hill, who knew a dwarf when he saw one, and who, on seeing Jolly, had been quick to dismiss the comparison.

Now he turned to the little man. 'Have we met before?' he said.

Jolly gave an insolent smirk. Sprawled on the ottoman he looked even more misshapen than before, his massive head thrown back onto the cushions, the china cup held with exaggerated delicacy between his pudgy fingers. He seemed quite unafraid of Tyr, or, indeed, of any of the gods.

'I'm talkin' to you,' said Brave-Hearted Tyr, lapsing into goblin-speak. He levelled his gaze on the little man and, taking a step, addressed him thus:

'*Short-arse —*'

Jolly's laughter stopped at once. 'What?' he said in a dangerous tone. 'Who're you callin' short?' In a second he was out of his seat, his iron-grey eyes level with those of the reluctant god of war. Sugar had time to wonder how such little legs could ever support such a massive head before something butted him in the pit of the stomach and sent him flying across the room.

'My china!' said Ethel.

'*Don't* call me short!'

From behind the overturned china cabinet, Sugar gave a feeble thumbs-up.

Jolly resumed his place on the couch – as well as his good temper. 'As long as that's understood,' he said. 'Now p'raps we can talk.'

He poured himself a cup of tea, added nine lumps of sugar and rolled up his shirt-sleeves, revealing the double rune on his arms.

'Folks, the name is Mjølnir. But you can call me Jolly.'

4

THE LITTLE SQUARE-HEADED MAN'S revelation caused uproar amongst the gods. Only Loki seemed at all inclined to laughter, although he wisely kept out of the way as Æsir and Vanir faced each other with expressions of outrage and disbelief, and Jolly simply drank his tea and grinned all over his puglike face.

'Thor, what in Hel's name is going on?' said Heimdall, finding his voice at last. 'How can this – *this* – be a hammer?'

Jolly smirked evilly. 'Learned mesself some new skills while I've bin in World Above,' he said, looking pleased with himself. 'Couldn't just lie around waitin' for you lot to wake up, could I?'

Heimdall glared at Loki. 'And you're trying to tell us you didn't know?'

'Don't look at me,' said the Trickster. 'I didn't make Mjølnir. We all knew it had powers . . .'

'Powers, yes. But – arms? *Legs?*'

Jolly scratched his armpit and yawned. 'I'da thought youdda bin more pleased to see me,' he said. 'Seein' as you're goin' to be needin' me soon.'

Loki narrowed his eyes at him. 'You're not an oracle as well, are you?'

Jolly shook his head.

'Thank gods.'

'Still,' said Jolly cheerfully, helping himself to more tea. 'From what I heard, there's trouble ahead, and you're goin' to need every bit of help you've got. 'Cos if they come at you through Dream—'

'Bloody prophecies,' said Thor. 'Why don't they ever make proper sense? All this stuff about gates and dreams. All this stuff about new runes. Why can't we have war in the *real* world?' He bared his teeth at Jolly, who bared his own teeth in return. 'With Mjølnir and Brave-Hearted Tyr on our side, we'll give them a bloody good hammering.'

Brave-Hearted Tyr gave a sickly smile. 'Is war *really* the answer?' he said.

Jolly gave him a knowing grin. 'I' cold feet, are yer?' he said.

'Course not,' Sugar said. 'But god of war – shouldn't that job go to someone . . . more *warlike*?' He looked appealingly at Thor, who growled, and Frey, who gave him an apologetic shrug.

'Bit late for that now, innit?' Jolly said. He stretched out his feet on the ottoman. 'Nice tea, by the way. Got any more of them biscuits?'

'So – er – Jolly,' said Thor, whose baffled expression had gradually darkened to one of growing impatience. 'I mean, I'm glad you've kept busy and everything, but— when do I get my hammer back?'

Jolly gave him a look. 'What?'

'Well – of course I'm happy to meet you, but . . . when do I get my hammer back?'

Jolly's face took on an expression not unlike Thor's own. 'And that's all I get, is it?' he said. 'No *Hey, Jolly, I'm so glad you're here,* or *What was it like, bein' swallowed by the World Serpent?* Or even *How did you manage among the Folk?* No. It's just *Where's me bloody 'ammer* without so much as an if-you-please—'

'Well, you do belong to me,' said Thor.

'Belong to you?' Jolly snapped. 'I'll 'ave you know that things've changed a bit since I were anybody's property. I'm not just here for hittin' things. And if you're expectin' me to fold up and sit in your pocket like I used to do in the old days, then you've got another think comin', because I've got business of me own—'

'But— you're a *hammer*,' protested Thor.

'Not any more,' Jolly said, calmly proceeding to finish his tea.

Thor's face darkened even further. 'Loki . . .' he said in a dangerous voice.

But as the Trickster had wisely chosen that moment to find urgent business elsewhere, it was left to Thor himself to point out that perhaps there *was* someone, after all, who annoyed him more than Loki did.

This knowledge did nothing to improve his temper, and there were thunderclouds on Red Horse Hill throughout the whole of that afternoon, while, from another mountaintop, a penetrating eye was levelled on the valley of the Strond, and two black birds flew into the storm, skirted the lightning that stalked the skies, wheeled around the Sleepers twice and then were swiftly lost from sight.

5

Maggie's return to the Communion Inn had not been as easy as she'd hoped. Perhaps if she had managed to evade Mrs Blackmore's vigilant eye, then she might have been able to collect her few belongings and leave before difficult questions were asked. Unfortunately for Maggie Rede, this happened to be delivery day, and by the time she and Adam reached the alley behind the Communion Inn, her absence had already been noted.

'So here you are, madam – at *last!*' said Mrs Blackmore as she came in. 'And where do you think *you've* been all night?' Her gaze took in Maggie's furtive look, her crumpled clothes and the scarf knotted hastily around her head. 'You look a proper vagabond and no mistake. And who's *this?*' The beady eyes narrowed on Adam, standing quietly outside the door, holding the Good Book under his arm.

Mrs Blackmore at once dismissed the likelihood of his being a potential customer. If he had been, her scruples might have taken a back seat. As it was, she took in his travel-stained clothes, his long hair and impoverished look, and launched into a shrill tirade, in which she denounced all northerners, riff-raff and vagabonds, bemoaned the loose morals of young folk today and almost passed out at the sight of the Book.

'Oy!' shrieked Mrs Blackmore in alarm. 'I'm not 'avin' that

thing in 'ere! That's stolen, that is, stolen from the Order! You got no business takin' it!'

Maggie tried to explain. But Mrs Blackmore (whose plague charms had once included pages torn from books such as this) was already working herself into a state of high moral outrage. 'There's powerful words in there!' she said in a voice that could have shattered glass. 'Ye've not been trying to *read* them? Laws preserve us, what next, girl? Out all night gallivanting, and now what? Looting – *witchcraft*?'

Maggie tried to edge past her, acutely aware of the fact that her ex-employer was starting to attract attention. There were still lawmen at work in the Universal City, and while not *all* the Laws were strictly enforced, rumours of witchcraft were never ignored, and looting was a grave offence.

'All I want is to collect my things,' she told her. 'Then I swear I'll go.'

Mrs Blackmore gave her a piercing look. 'Ye're not in trouble, are ye?' she said. Her eyes went back to Adam. 'Because if ye are, there's easier ways than messing with the Order's books . . .'

'I'm not in trouble,' Maggie said.

'Ye wouldn't be the only one,' said Mrs Blackmore virtuously. 'Many's the girl as hides her shame under a maiden's *bergha*.' And with that she reached out suddenly and snatched at the scarf around Maggie's head. It pulled free, and Mrs Blackmore's feigned outrage turned to genuine alarm as Maggie's newly shorn head was bared and, with it, the ruinmark that gleamed on her neck.

'Oh my *gods*!' said the landlady, forgetting herself enough to sweat. 'Gods, ye have a ruinmark, an honest-to-godless ruinmark. Where did ye even get such a thing? Unnatural! *Unnatural!*' And she backed away as fast as she could, forking the sign against evil (a fingering of the runeshape *Yr*) and knocking over a coal-scuttle in her haste to get away. 'If my husband were still alive,' she declared in a tremulous voice, 'he'd have something to say, miss! Traipsing around the city at night, cavorting with Northern-ers, corrupting the Word, *flaunting* that ruinmark like a badge o' pride—'

Adam looked impatient. 'We don't have a lot of time,' he said. '*Deal* with her, Maggie, for Laws' sakes.'

'*Deal* with her?'

Adam put a finger meaningfully to his throat.

'Oh no,' said Maggie. 'I couldn't—'

'Why not? Use your glam. You used it on me, didn't you?'

Maggie looked at him helplessly. 'I can't. It would be murder,' she said.

'Oh, *please,*' said Adam impatiently. 'Do I have to do *everything?*' And he pulled the sword from the sheath at his side – a pretty blade from Jed Smith's forge, and sharp as a World's End fish-wife's tongue – and levelled it at the landlady, thereby reducing Mrs Blackmore to a quivering pudding, chin and lip both striving in vain to carry as much as a squeak of fear.

'I believe my friend said something about collecting her effects,' said Adam, punctuating his words with a slight increase of pressure from the sword-point.

Mrs Blackmore's chins shook.

'I didn't hear that,' Adam said. 'Is there some kind of a problem?'

'No problem,' said Mrs Blackmore.

'I thought not,' Adam said. 'In fact, we will be so discreet that you won't even know we were here.' And Adam reached into his pocket and drew out a handful of coins.

Mrs Blackmore, recognizing the gleam of gold, gave a shudder and forked the sign against evil again – which pious gesture would not prevent her from spending the money later, when the demons had fled. For demons they undoubtedly were, as she would say in a low voice to her friend Mrs Claymore, who ran the taphouse down the road; only a demon had such eyes.

'Go then,' she said. 'Give ye joy.'

Adam smirked. 'I think it will.'

In fact, he didn't care at all about collecting Maggie's things – she had little enough in the world, and Adam had plenty of money – but the Voice in his head had insisted, and now Adam thought he knew why. He had already cut off Maggie's hair. Now he had cut off Maggie's life – her job, her home, her acquaintances

95

– making himself her only friend, her ally and protector.

Of course, this never crossed Maggie's mind. In fact, in spite of everything, Maggie was happier than she'd ever been before. She was jobless and destitute – homeless, an outcast – and yet she felt lighter than air; and it was with a strange new sense of recklessness that she ran to join her new friend on the streets of the Universal City, to conjure up an army of dreams to ride against the Firefolk.

6

DREAM IS A RIVER THAT FLOWS BOTH WAYS – a fact often overlooked by the Folk, for whom dreaming had always been considered territory best left unexplored. Malbry's own Crazy Nan Fey was rumoured to be a victim of turbulent spirits, channelled into the world through Dream, though Maddy Smith had always suspected the *other* kind of spirit to be at fault – the kind that came in bottles. But Dream is far more than a river, as One-Eye could have told her. Dream is the stuff of Worlds – *all* Worlds – and all things come and go from it, as water comes and goes from the Sea, becoming clouds, rain, snowflakes, tears – all so ephemeral, all so unique, always changing but never lost, a universe of possibility where any thought can take form.

In Malbry, Maddy was dreaming. It was a quiet, comforting dream that took her back to her childhood years, when everything was new, and her old friend, whom she knew only as One-Eye, would tell her tales of the Elder Age and teach her how to fling cantrips to bamboozle Nat Parson and torment Adam Scattergood and his cronies.

Today she was only ten years old, and she and One-Eye were lying side by side in the sage-grass of Red Horse Hill, watching the fat fairweather clouds pass rapidly in the morning sky. It was just past Midsummer's Fair Day; the Sleepers were crowned with blue haze, and from the fields below Red Horse Hill came the distant sounds of grazing cattle, and birds, and the sleepy sound of the river Strond snaking across the valley.

For a moment, Maddy felt a great and overwhelming relief. The past seven years had been a dream. None of those things had happened. One-Eye was simply her old friend, not Odin of the Æsir. Her father was Jed Smith, not Thor; and though she was no dearer to Jed than she was to Thor himself, that didn't matter. One-Eye was there; and he would be there forever.

'That cloud looks like a serpent,' said Maddy (who of course had never encountered such a thing, except perhaps in One-Eye's books). 'A big one, with a shaggy head.'

'Aye, perhaps,' said One-Eye lazily, taking a puff of his stubby pipe. The smoke made two distinct little clouds of its own, like two tufts of rabbit-tail grass, which chased each other into the swift summer air and were lost on the crest of the Hill.

Maddy said: 'Did you see it too?'

One-Eye smiled. 'There's substance even in clouds,' he said. 'And dreams are no less potent or less perilous if the dreamer happens to be awake. Do you see those birds over there?' He pointed them out: two black birds, too large to be jackdaws, too dark to be gulls. Crows – or ravens, perhaps, thought Maddy.

'I see them,' she said.

'Good. You keep your eye on them. Birds are messengers, they say. Did you know that the General had the power to send out his thoughts in the form of a pair of birds?'

Maddy nodded. 'I've heard the tale.'

'Hugin and Munin were their names. Spirit and Mind, in the old tongue. Rascals both, but with their help he could scrutinize every one of the Nine Worlds. The Middle World. Dream. The Underworld. Even into Chaos itself – Odin's eye saw everything, for Mind can travel to every World. Now look for me, Maddy. What else do you see?'

Maddy squinted at the sky. 'That pink cloud looks like a horse,' she said. 'But with more legs than usual.'

'Really,' said One-Eye.

'Over there. Can't you see it?' Maddy said.

'No,' he said. 'But I'm sure you can. What else do you see?'
Maddy smiled. 'That one looks like a basket. A basket full of washing. And *that* one . . .'

'Yes? Is there anything else?'

Maddy narrowed her eyes at the sky. She thought the birds looked closer now, circling the brow of the Hill. And for a moment, in their wake . . .

She looked away. 'I don't think so. Can we play another game?'

'Of course we can, Maddy. You've done very well.' One-Eye tapped out his pipe onto a piece of rock at his side. 'But now I must ask you to do something else. Something that may prove difficult.'

'Of course,' said Maddy, her eyes lighting up. 'What is it you want me to do?'

One-Eye moved closer, and now she could see how *old* he suddenly looked, how sad, with his dusty cloak and his eye-patch and his battered hat on the ground at his side. And she wanted above all things to put her arms around him, but there was something in his manner that made her afraid to lay hands on him, as if at a touch he might disappear.

'You're not ill, are you?' she said. 'You look so . . . tired.'

'Aye. Maybe I am. But there's work to do before we can rest. Hard work. And I need your help.'

'You mean like digging for treasure?' asked Maddy, looking up eagerly. There *was* treasure under Red Horse Hill, everyone in the valley knew that. Relics from the Elder Age: gold and diamonds and rubies.

'Not that kind of treasure,' he said.

Maddy was disappointed. 'But I thought . . .'

'Never mind. Listen. I need you to trust me. I know you have little reason to. I lied to you once, and paid the price. Fair enough, that's what I do. But now I need you to trust me again. The fate of the Worlds depends on it.'

Maddy was puzzled. 'I don't understand. When did you ever lie to me?'

One-Eye looked grim. 'Trust me,' he said. 'I know you don't

99

understand – not yet. Nevertheless, I need your word. Trust me, Maddy. Do as I say. Remember this conversation. One day you're going to understand exactly what I'm talking about. That's when I'll need your trust, Maddy. That's when you'll know what you have to do.'

Maddy nodded.

One-Eye went on. 'I need you to search for something,' he said. 'An artefact of the Elder Age. A very special thing indeed. You can call it the Old Man. The Old Man of the Wilderlands.'

'The Old Man of the Wilderlands?'

Odin nodded. 'That's one of its names. Though it won't look like a man to you, but something else entirely. It may look like a piece of rock; but it's what's inside that matters.'

Maddy nodded solemnly. 'How will I find it? Where will you be? Won't you be coming with me?'

One-Eye smiled. 'Patience,' he said. 'By the time this message reaches you, you'll understand what I'm trying to say. For the moment, remember this. Someone's going to come here soon. For the Horse, and for the Old Man. And you're going to have to be ready.'

Maddy frowned at him. 'Who?' she said.

'You'll soon find out. Don't tell anyone we spoke. Not if the gods themselves were to ask—'

'The *gods*?'

'Please, Maddy. I don't have much time.'

'All right,' said Maddy. 'I promise.'

'Good.' One-Eye tucked his pipe carefully back into his tobacco pouch. The birds were very close now, spinning and circling the brow of the Hill. One-Eye turned to look at Maddy again. 'Now I have to go,' he said. 'Don't worry, you'll hear from me again. Keep dreaming, Maddy. Remember me. And keep an eye out for those birds.'

And with that he stood up and put on his hat and vanished into the sweet air of Red Horse Hill without even a flicker, and Maddy awoke with tears on her face to the sound of beating wings in the dawn.

7

AT FIRST MADDY THOUGHT SHE was still dreaming. Two black birds – two ravens, in fact – were perching on the window-ledge. Maddy could hear the whispering *squeak* of their feathers moving against the glass, and their cries – a loud, unmusical *craw* – were enough to wake the Sleepers.

She rubbed her eyes and got out of bed and walked towards the window.

To her surprise, the two big birds did not fly away at her approach, but simply watched her from guinea-gold eyes, occasionally shifting from one foot to the other in the half-comic, ponderous way that had always made Maddy think of Nat Parson, back in the days of the Order.

She thought of her dream.

Birds are messengers.

Maddy frowned at the two birds. They looked just like ordinary birds to her. Both looked glossy and well-fed. One – the smaller of the two – had a single white feather on its head. The other, a ring around its foot.

Birds are messengers. Why not? There was plenty of truth in dreams, she knew. Could Odin have somehow sent these two? And if he had, where was he now? Death, Damnation, or maybe Dream?

Maddy opened the window. Feeling slightly foolish, she spoke to the birds. 'Do you have a message for me?'

The larger bird pecked at its wing.

The smaller cocked its head. *Craw.*

'Sorry. I don't speak raven.'

Crawk.

'What do you want?'

Craw. Craw.

Maybe they wanted a bribe, she thought. Ravens and crows were greedy, she knew; she had often watched as One-Eye fed them with crumbs from his pocket. Maddy had never quite understood why – the birds were thieves and scavengers, ready to peck the eyes from your head if they could get away with it – but for some reason One-Eye had always liked them, calling them *my tattered ones* and laughing at their antics.

'Do you want something to eat?' she said.

Two pairs of eyes swivelled up at her.

'All right. Wait here.'

There was a half-eaten biscuit on a saucer by the bed. Maddy turned to pick it up, meaning to scatter the crumbs on the ledge—

But the ravens were there before her. Without waiting for an invitation, both had flown into the room, one now perching on the bedpost, the other on the mantelpiece. Maddy hadn't quite realized how very large a raven could be. The sound of their wings was disquieting in the little room; their beaks looked sharp and dangerous.

'Who asked you in?' Maddy said.

The smaller of the two birds hopped from the bed onto Maddy's arm and pecked at the biscuit in her hand. Maddy dropped the biscuit, and the bird caught it in midair, bearing it off to the corner of the room. The larger raven gave pursuit, and there followed a vicious scuffle as the two of them uarreled over the food. A china candlestick – one of two – fell into the fender and smashed.

'Stop it!' said Maddy, just managing to rescue the second candlestick.

The ravens paid no attention at all.

Maddy stared at them helplessly. What an idiot she was, she thought – so eager to believe her dream was real that she'd thought a pair of scruffy ravens might be messengers from another world. She looked around for some kind of weapon – a broom, a carpet-beater, perhaps – with which to shoo the birds away.

A voice – the smallest of voices – came to her as if from a dream.

Rascals, both, it whispered, and laughed.

'Odin?' said Maddy.

Craw, Crawk.

The birds stopped squabbling at once. They seemed to be waiting for something; two pairs of golden eyes stared fixedly at Maddy.

'I don't know what you want,' she said.

Crawk. Crawk.

'Why don't you tell me, you stupid birds?' Maddy was starting to lose her temper.

And then she suddenly knew what to do – it was so simple that she'd missed it; but if the birds were what she hoped, then there was a way to know for sure.

She made the sign of Os with her hand. '*A named thing is a tamed thing,*' she said in a voice that trembled a little.

Two pairs of eyes blinked.

Maddy made the sign again. 'I name you *Hugin* and *Munin,*' she said. 'Spirit and Mind, in the old tongue. Now – will you tell me what you're doing here?'

The two birds disappeared at once, to be replaced by two tattered figures, one lounging on the ottoman, one perching on the bed. To Maddy they looked almost identical, but for the difference in gender and size, and the broad streak of white in the girl's long hair. Both were dressed in shiny black, in a fabric that might have been feathers or silk, but which somehow resembled neither. Their hair was wild and tangled, and they both wore a great deal of silver jewellery – rings on every finger; bracelets stacked halfway up each arm – earrings that jangled with feathers and bells; strings and strings of gleaming jet beads.

They looked like Chaos folk to Maddy, and each bore a black

design on their arm that she did not recognize – the woman's on the right arm, the man's on the left—

'Shiny,' said the taller one.

The other grinned and flashed its teeth.

'Hugin and Munin?' Maddy said.

'We dinnae go by them names any more,' said the taller of the creatures. 'Call me Hughie. It's close enough. And this is my sister Mandy. Get us both a drink, will ye, and maybe a quick bite of something tae eat? We've come a long way to see ye, and you're going tae want tae hear what we say.'

8

MIND AND SPIRIT, MY FOOT, Maddy thought with bitterness as, some time later, over what seemed like half the contents of Ethel Parson's pantry, her two visitors unburdened their tale. *Wines and spirits, more like. Gods, who are these people?*

But Maddy had soon learned that when dealing with Hughie and Mandy, certain things took time. Time and sustenance, it seemed – and as far as their joint appetites went, the two were more like locusts than birds. A raised mutton pie; a cold roast ham; several loaves of bread; some cakes, including a plum pudding set aside for Yule; a cheese; a whole barrel of biscuits; various jars of jams, preserves, cherries in brandy, dried apricots; plus wine, ale, a bottle of mead and, lastly, tea – with six sugars.

'What, no cream?' Maddy said.

Mandy grinned and made a sound very like a raven's *craw*.

'She disn'ae talk much in this Aspect,' said Hughie apologetically. 'But she's a fearsome thinker.'

'So, what do you want from me?' Maddy said. The clock on the wall now said nine o'clock, and it was only a matter of time, she thought, before one of the gods came looking for her and found her entertaining guests.

'Well, if ye had a dozen eggs, I'd no say no tae an omelette—'

'*Apart* from food,' said Maddy. '*And* drink.'

105

Hughie looked disappointed. 'Well, ye already know that, a-course. We've a message from the General.'

For a moment Maddy could hardly breathe. 'One-Eye?' she said in a choked voice.

'Aye, that's him. He called us from Dream.'

Maddy cast her mind back to the last time she'd spoken with the General. That had been three years ago, on the ravaged shores of Hel. *Look for me in dreams*, he had said. And Maddy had done precisely that, waiting and hoping for a sign that somehow her old friend might have survived – in spirit, if not in Aspect. But Maddy had taken his words as little more than cold comfort. One-Eye in dreams was not the same as One-Eye in the living flesh, and as time had passed, she had finally come to believe that dreams were all that remained of him.

'Odin's still *alive*?' she said.

'Well – yes and no,' Hughie said. 'That's why he sent us, see?'

Craw.

'You leave the talking tae me,' said Hughie, addressing Mandy. 'Now what was that message again, eh?'

Crawk.

'No, I havenae forgotten.'

Craw.

'Mandy, I resent that. I am not inebriated.' He drew out the word to its full five syllables, spreading his arms for emphasis and knocking over a vase. Maddy winced inwardly. Ethel was partial to her trinkets and, even in her newfound Aspect as Frigg, wouldn't take kindly to these intruders in her home.

'I don't understand,' Maddy said. '*Is* Odin alive, or isn't he?'

Hughie shrugged. 'That's a little hard tae say. Dream runs through all Nine Worlds, Death and Damnation included.'

'But you said he gave you a message for me—'

Mandy crawed impatiently.

'Aye, aye. Give me time.' Hughie seemed to gather his thoughts. 'So we heard there'd been a prophecy. Regardin' the rise of the First World.'

106

Maddy nodded. 'That's right.' She struggled to recall the words of the Seeress.

'The Cradle fell an age ago, but Fire and Folk shall raise her
In just twelve days, at End of Worlds; a gift within the sepulchre.'

'Crawk.' That was Mandy, attempting to speak. *'Crawk. Craw.'*
'Shhh,' said Hughie.
'But what does it mean?' Maddy said. 'The Cradle – that's Asgard, isn't it? How can anyone build it again, let alone in twelve days? And all that stuff about Fire and Folk . . .'
'What it means is trouble,' said Hughie. 'And you're right at the heart of it. You think those things coming out of Dream are coming at you by accident? The snakes, and the gribblies, and the what-d'ye-may-call-'em, ephemerae . . .' He paused to scratch at a feathery armpit.
'The rift between Worlds—' Maddy began.
Hughie interrupted her. 'Dreams need to be summoned, hen. And for that they need a dreamer.'
Mandy nodded approval at this, and flapped her arms in encouragement. *'Drea-mer. Dreamer, Crawk.'*
'I don't understand,' Maddy said. 'You're saying this is something more? That someone's attacking us through Dream?'
'Pull something out of Dream, hen, and it isn'ae a dream any more.'
Maddy knew, of course, that Dream, by its very nature, was *complicated*, to say the least. A World awash with contradictory truths; a state with no rules or natural laws; a river that runs through all Nine Worlds from a source that can never run dry.
But could it be diverted like this? And who would want to do such a thing?
'Who?' said Maddy. 'There's no one left. The Order's finished. The Whisperer—' Now her eyes widened. *'The Whisperer.'*
It *could* have survived, she told herself. In those thirteen seconds of Chaos, when Death, Dream and Damnation were one, Mimir

the Wise could have escaped. Into Damnation, into Dream – and from there, to find another host . . .

A dreamer?

For a moment Maddy considered her own dream. In it, Odin had mentioned an artefact – had told her to seek out the Old Man of the Wilderlands. Could he have meant the Whisperer? It seemed more than likely, she thought, in the light of what she had just heard. The Whisperer in collusion with a dreamer of extraordinary ability – and they'd *have* to be something special, she thought, to do what Hughie had described.

'Look, what *exactly* did Odin say?'

'That's what I'm tryin' tae tell ye,' Hughie said, looking pained. 'He said, first of all, tae trust us. We speak for the General. We're his eye and his ear in the Worlds. That makes us practically family.'

Maddy looked at him doubtfully. 'Is that a runemark you've got?' she said.

'Aye, hen. That it is.' Hughie preened a little. 'It's *Ea*, the rune of eternity. One of the runes of the New Script that's going tae build the new Asgard. That's how important we are, hen. That's why ye've got tae do what we tell ye.'

'Mm,' said Maddy. 'What else did he say?'

'He said we should say to remember your dream. The one on the Hill, with the cloud game. Then ye must find the dreamer. She'll lead ye tae the Auld Man. But not a word tae anyone, mind? Especially not the other gods.'

Maddy was puzzled. 'But why?' she said. 'If the Whisperer's still around, then—'

'Ye cannae tell them,' Hughie said. 'The General was very clear about that. *Just find the dreamer*, that's what he said. After that, everything's shiny.'

Find the dreamer. Yeah, right.

Like all Odin's plans, of course, it sounded absurdly simple. As simple as finding the Whisperer in the tunnels under the Hill, a task that had ended in Hel and Damnation and the near-destruction of all the Worlds.

So much for simple, Maddy thought. With Odin, nothing ever was.

'This dreamer could be anywhere. I wouldn't know where to start looking!' she said.

'But *we* do,' said Hughie impatiently. 'What do you think we've been doing all this time, flying about from World to World, spying for the General? Her name among the Folk is Rede. Maggie Rede – d'ye kennet? Maggie Rede of World's End.'

'Rede?' It sounded familiar.

'Aye. Follow her tae the Auld Man. That's what the General says.'

'But how does he know her?' Maddy said.

'He's had his eye on her for a long time,' said Hughie. 'Been watchin' her since before the war.'

'But if Odin *knew* she was there all the time, then . . .'

Hughie shrugged. 'Ye're askin' me? But he had other concerns back then: the war with the Folk and the Order; his own people sorely divided. If the Vanir had known of a rogue in World's End – and one of the General's own kin, at that—'

'What d'you mean, his own kin?'

Mandy gave a sharp *craw*.

'No, I *hadn'ae* forgotten,' said Hughie. He turned once more to Maddy and flashed her his crazed and brilliant smile. 'So there ye are,' he said. 'Oh yes – and there's just one more thing ye ought to know about Maggie Rede of World's End. The General said tae tell ye first, in case it came as too much of a shock . . .'

'Tell me *what*?' Maddy said.

'Why, hen. She's your sister.'

9

In a room in distant world's end, Maggie Rede was trying to dream. Over the past twenty-four hours she had learned a great many things from Adam Goodwin, including a number of truths and half-truths and outright lies about his life, the Seer-folk, their plans and how to combat them; and Maggie listened wide-eyed to his tale; her runemark burning the back of her neck as if something hot had been placed there.

Adam had found them a place to stay in one of the more fashionable quarters of the Universal City. A penthouse suite near Examiners' Walk, not ten minutes from St Sepulchre's Square – with a sitting room, a balcony, a chandelier, a claw-footed bath, an ottoman couch and an enormous canopy bed with curtains of crimson velvet.

Maggie Rede had never seen such a luxurious dwelling. It made her slightly uncomfortable – how much money did Adam have? – besides which, she told herself, surely a man of the Order, used to prayer and abstinence, would prefer to be in less opulent surroundings, a place more fitting to their task.

'Don't worry, I'll sleep on the couch.' Adam had noticed her unease.

Maggie blushed. 'That's not what I meant— I . . .'

Adam made a dismissive gesture. In fact, he too was wondering why the Voice in his mind had been so insistent on spending their gold. He gave the most obvious reason.

'I chose this place,' he told her, 'because if your Mrs Blackmore talks – and she *will* – then news of both of us will be all over the city in days. They'll look for us in cheap inns, in taverns and in chop-houses. They'll be looking for two vagabonds. They'll never expect to find us here.'

All of which was true, of course, but the *real* reason, Adam suspected, was something very different. Between them, he and his passenger were preparing Maggie to play a part in something of great importance. Adam had already gleaned as much from what the Voice had allowed to let slip and, because he was no fool, had guessed what role *he* might have been chosen to play. It didn't trouble him at all that the Voice was using him. Revenge was the glue that bound them together – revenge against the Gødfolk, and most especially against Maddy Smith, whose interference had cost them dear, both Adam *and* his passenger, three years ago on the shore of Dream.

Over the past twenty-four hours Adam and his passenger had watched as Maggie explored her glam. It was hard, and sometimes frustrating work; Adam had warned her not to expect immediate results. Examiners of the Order, he said, might wait thirty years for the power of the Word; some, for all their labours, had never managed to earn it at all. But Maggie, with her runemark, with her untrained instincts, was already far more powerful than any mere Examiner.

With Adam at her side, she learned to flex her glam like a muscle; to tease it into simple shapes; to strike it into flame like a match. With Adam's help she learned to cast *Bjarkán* for perception; *Thúris* for strength; *Hagall* to strike at an enemy.

In just one day Maggie had changed beyond all recognition, her fear and uncertainty shorn away as easily as her cropped hair. This was largely Adam's doing, of course; in twenty-four hours Maggie had come to trust the young man implicitly. Not just because he stood up for her when Mrs Blackmore saw her runemark, but because he seemed to accept Maggie as she really *was* – to accept, and even to like her.

Now, in their penthouse, just before dawn, Maggie closed her eyes at last and tried to banish the world around her.

'I don't know if I can do this,' she said, opening one eye again.

'Concentrate,' Adam said. 'Focus on the words in the Book.'

Maggie tried again. Closed her eyes. The Book at her side was open at a page that Adam had indicated. A section of script – all in runes – stood out against the parchment. Above it there was a picture of a horse. An odd kind of horse, Maggie thought. It looked as if it had eight legs.

'But I don't even know what the words *mean* . . .'

'Trust me. It doesn't matter,' Adam said.

Maggie sighed and tried again. Focused on the words in the Book. Closed her eyes and tried to dream . . .

At the nape of her neck, the runemark *Ác* lit up with a sudden silvery flare.

'Are you sure it's safe?' she said.

'You trust me, don't you?'

Maggie nodded.

'Then trust me now. Open your mind. Open your mind and let it float. Don't worry, I'm standing guard. Nothing's going to happen to you.'

Maggie gave another sigh. 'I'll do my best.'

'You must be exhausted,' Adam said. 'Close your eyes. Let yourself go.'

She lay down on the bed. She *was* very tired. More than twenty-four hours had passed since she had last slept. She closed her eyes. The bed was soft – softer than any she'd ever known. The pillow was stuffed with duck down; the coverlet was tasselled silk.

Gently Adam drew the bedspread over her shoulders.

Good, a soft Voice whispered.

'Good,' repeated Adam.

Now Maggie found herself floating, rising gently into the air; rising out of herself, the room, floating above the alley. For a moment she saw herself, her cropped curls ablaze with runelight. She saw Adam at her side, watching her with a curious – and not entirely pleasant – expression, and for a split-second she saw him unmasked, saw the meanness, the arrogance beneath the handsome exterior.

She tried to call him, but she was already half asleep, rising above the silent streets, the little shops and drinking dens deserted now in the cold pre-dawn. She saw St Sepulchre's Square, lit up like a crown of lanterns; she saw Mrs Blackmore's inn; she saw the maze and network of the streets; and, far away in the distance, the harbour with its tall ships, and the Outlanders' camp with its tents and bazaars and pens filled with horses and sleeping slaves.

'This is amazing!' Maggie said.

Higher, said the whispering Voice. It was something like her father's voice – quiet, clever, a little dry. *It's all right. I'm a friend*, it said.

'A friend of Adam's?'

Yes. That's right. I'm here to see that you come to no harm.

Now Maggie was rising higher still, far above the Universal City. And now she could see the avenues, set out like the spokes of a giant wheel around the University of Immutable Truths, with all its colleges, libraries, chapels, quads embedded into the pattern like escutcheons on a battle-shield, and the sweep of blue cliff to one side and the roll of green hills to the other, and at the centre of it all, the great glass-domed cathedral of St Sepulchre—

'It's so beautiful,' Maggie said.

Even in defeat, said the Voice, *Asgard was always beautiful.*

'Asgard?' she said. 'But wasn't that—?'

Yes. Fallen more than an age ago. But the seed never falls very far from the tree. Don't you agree, Maggie Rede?

'You know my name,' Maggie said.

There came a whisper of laughter. *Oh, I know much more than that. I used to be an oracle.*

'Used to be? What happened?' she said.

Again, that distant laughter. It made Maggie feel uneasy somehow. What kind of a dream was this, anyway? What kind of a dream gave the power to fly, to speak with spirits and oracles? Was this the place she'd been warned about, where demons and Gødfolk and Faërie awaited their chance to steal her soul? And if Adam had known about the Voice, then why hadn't he told her?

Don't be afraid, Maggie, it said. *No harm will come to you with Me.*

Who are you? she said. *A demon? A god?*

Neither, said the dry Voice. *But if you still feel the need for names, then you may call Me . . . Magister.*

If ever there had been a name to instil trust into Maggie Rede, then surely this was it. A title of the Order, with all its associations of culture, learning and purity. She responded as she'd been taught, with instant respect and relief, and the thing that had named itself Magister smiled inwardly and addressed her again.

We're going to travel through Dream, it said. *You may see things that disturb you.*

'What kind of things?'

You'll see.

And now she was flying higher still: higher than the rooftops; higher than the cathedral spire. Clouds like muslin drapery parted to allow her to pass; a couple of black birds – ravens, perhaps – shrieked their warnings across the sky.

Dream is a river, said the Voice. *It carries all kinds of flotsam. Nothing here is ever lost. Everything returns here in the end. Whatever you want, you'll find it here, somewhere, among the islets of Dream. As long as you know what to look for . . .*

'And what are we looking for?'

A Horse.

Later, when Maggie tried to recall her trip through Dream, she found that only fragments remained – pieces of a larger picture of which only details had survived. She remembered a river, all in mist, with islands that rose and sank like drowning men on the surface; and as she watched, Maggie understood that every island was a dreamer, each in his own little fleeting world.

There were dreams of chance meetings and dreams of the past; of food; of being buried alive; of cats; of duties undone; of battles fought; of being naked in public places; of flying; of sailing ships and abandoned buildings; of oceans and battlements and the dead. A maelstrom of shrieking shadowy things took monstrous shape around her – a creature with an eye for a head glared at her from the vortex.

Ignore them, said the Magister's Voice. *They're nothing. Just ephemera. Look for the Horse.*

But which horse? Dream was alive with horses. Riding, leaping, grazing, running; carousel horses with gilded manes; wild horses galloping free; cart-horses pulling ploughs; hobbyhorses with skirts of straw; horses with hooves like sledgehammers; ponies with ribbons in their manes; race-track horses – *and they're off!*

For what seemed like a very long time Maggie searched through the islets of Dream. The Voice had assured her that she would know when she saw what they were looking for, but so far she had no idea what that was.

And then, at last, she saw something. Something in one of those passing dreams that spoke to her like a memory. At first sight it seemed like nothing much: just two figures on a hill, a long, long way below her. But something about them caught her eye; casting *Bjarkán*, Maggie saw a skein of bright light that crisscrossed the hill and rose into the morning sky . . .

What's that? she said. *St Sepulchre's Fire?*

Not that she'd ever seen such a thing – except, of course, in books. But the northlights – or St Sepulchre's Fire, as they were better known in World's End – was something she had always wanted to see in spite of the tales that surrounded it; tales of sky-demons in the clouds who carried away the unwary to a place once known as Asgard.

No, it's a signature, said the Voice. *The banner of the Firefolk. Move closer now. Do you see the Horse?*

Maggie narrowed her vision once more. Her eyes had become an eagle's eyes; the scene below her was stark and clear. And now she was right above the Hill – a hill that was half covered in snow – looking down at the shape of a horse cut into the red clay.

'A horse,' she said in surprise. 'A red horse . . .'

That's right, said the Magister. *There's an old Northlands saying* that goes like this: *'If wishes were horses, then beggars would ride.'* Do *you know that saying?*

'No.'

The Voice in her mind gave a harsh laugh. *Well, that's what these beggars are going to do. All the way to Asgard.*

10

BACK IN MALBRY, Maddy Smith was struggling to take in the news.

'You're saying this girl's my *sister?*'

Hughie nodded. 'Aye, your twin. Magni, child of the Thunder Oak, twin of Modi, the Lightning Ash. The General spent years looking for her, but never managed tae reach her. And all the time she was in World's End, right in the lap of the Order. Hard tae believe, isnae, hen?'

Maddy narrowed her eyes at him. In fact she found it quite easy to believe. That Odin could have neglected to tell her of such an important matter as this, and that having deceived her thus far, he should still have the audacity to expect her now to obey him without question, even though he was technically dead.

'My sister . . .' she said slowly. How she had longed to hear those words. To have a sister of her own age with whom to share her thoughts, her dreams. Mae, Jed's other daughter, had been as different to Maddy as cowslips to crabs; but when Maddy had learned her *true* parentage, she had hoped that one day her dream might come true. Of course, she had known that the Thunderer was meant to have *two* children; but oracles often fail to reveal the things that are most important. After the war with the Order, three years ago on the plains of Hel, Maddy had finally assumed that her longed-for sibling was lost in Dream, unborn among its islets, never to wake in the Middle Worlds. But now, here were Odin's messengers telling her that the girl was alive – and working with the enemy.

'You're *sure* that this is the same girl?'

'Oh aye. The General was verra particular.'

Yes, that sounded like One-Eye, all right, Maddy thought bitterly. He'd known all about her twin sister – perhaps even from their earliest childhood – and, for reasons of his own, had decided not to tell her. Why? Could it have been that he was afraid, even then, of dividing Maddy's loyalties?

Once more she thought of the prophecy. *I see a mighty Ash that stands beside a mighty Oak tree . . .* Did that mean that she and her twin were supposed to work *together?* And what about the rest of it? Where did the Old Man come into this? Why would her sister want to send out ephemera against Loki?

Maddy frowned. She understood now why she couldn't tell her friends. Announce to the Gødfolk that one of their kind had turned renegade in World's End, and the uneasy alliance between Æsir and Vanir would turn to conflict in an instant. The Vanir would want to kill the traitor; the Æsir, to try to win her back. As for her father – Thor's reaction on learning that he had a daughter, and not a son, would have been funny if it had not been bitterly disappointing. The news of *another* daughter – and a disloyal one, at that – would be no cause for rejoicing.

And the enemy – whoever that was – would have little more to do than watch while the gods tore each other apart.

But if Maggie *was* the enemy . . .

Maddy dismissed the half-uttered thought. Her sister, according to Hughie, had lived in the lap of the Order ever since she was a child. She'd had no One-Eye, no Æsir to teach her the meaning of family. How lonely – how different – she must have felt. How easy it must have been for someone – someone a little like One-Eye, perhaps – to mould her to his purposes and make her believe he was her friend.

'What about the Old Man? Does my sister have it?' she said.

Hughie shook his head. 'Not yet.'

'And *is* it the Whisperer?'

Hughie shrugged. 'I cannae say. Just find it, sez the General. Bring it home, whatever it takes. She mustn'ae get a hold of it.'

But Maddy, uncomfortable from the very start of this troubling conversation, was feeling increasingly ill at ease. Communication through dreams was, at best, a most imperfect medium, and Odin – if it was Odin at all – had managed to convey only fragments of the whole. Maddy's *heart* wanted to believe that Odin's spirit survived in Dream, but she had changed over three years. She was no longer the innocent little girl who had opened the Horse's Eye that day. Since then, her world had been overturned. The life she'd thought was hers had turned out to be a lie from the start: no-one was as they seemed to be, not even those she'd counted as friends. If she had learnt anything during that time, it was the value of mistrust. And as for Hugin and Munin – they might once have been loyal, but who was to say they hadn't switched sides and were working with the enemy?

'So how do I know this isn't a trick?'

Hughie looked offended. 'A trick? Now who in the Worlds would do that?'

'Oh, let me see now—' Maddy said. 'Order, Chaos, old gods, new gods, demons, Ice People, Tunnel Folk, ephemera, flying snakes, goblins, escapees from Netherworld, magical artefacts with a will of their own – or anyone else with an axe to grind. The Worlds are full of our enemies. Did you want the full list?'

There was a rather lengthy pause. The ravens exchanged glances. Mandy, whose transition from bird to human Aspect still looked somewhat incomplete, *crawk*-ed in what seemed like frustration and pecked the bed-post savagely.

Hughie said reproachfully, 'You have some serious trust issues, hen.'

Maddy shrugged. 'So persuade me.'

But Hughie was getting agitated; he put down the empty sugar bowl and took a few paces around the room. The feathers on his garment – which seemed to be part tunic, part cloak – unfolded like dark wings in the air.

'We'll have tae do it now,' he said.

Mandy gave a sharp *craw*.

'The General said she'd be like this. He said we'd have tae persuade her.'

Mandy gave a whole-body shrug that reminded Maddy of Sugar. Then, reaching into her tattered sleeve, she pulled out a piece of faded blue cloth. Hughie took it from her and handed it to Maddy.

'What is it?' she said.

'Open it.'

Maddy did. Folded into the piece of cloth was a strip of leather the size of her thumb, onto which was fastened a piece of steel. A buckle, or maybe a brooch, she thought, the metal darkened and pitted with age. And there were runes cast into it: *Tyr*, *Raedo* and *Úr*, the Ox – bound together to form a sigil that Maddy knew to be Odin's—

'Where did you get this?' she said.

Hughie grinned at her. 'Shiny, eh?'

With a hand that was not quite steady, Maddy cast the rune *Bjarkán* and looked through it at the runeshape. Its glam was almost burned out; only a faint gleam of butterfly-blue animated the sigil. Even so, it awakened in her a powerful sense of nostalgia. This had belonged to her oldest friend; his signature was on it. A sudden wave of grief and loss threatened to overwhelm her.

'Where did you get this?' she said again.

'Pulled it out of Dream, hen, lookin' for the General.'

Maddy narrowed her eyes at Mandy, whose attention had wandered again and who was now investigating the contents of a tea caddy on Ethel's mantelpiece.

'We're talking about Dream,' she said. 'You don't just pull things out of Dream like driftwood from the river.'

'We do,' Hughie said. 'We overlook the Nine Worlds. We've been doing it for five hundred years – looking for pieces of salvage like this . . .' He gestured towards the leather strap. 'Do ye know what this is, hen?'

Slowly Maddy shook her head.

'It's from a horse's bridle. Where there's a bridle, there's a horse. And where there's a horse, there's a rider.'

A rider, she thought. *A general.*

Was Odin *really* behind all this, orchestrating his own release?

Such thoughts had crossed her mind before. But she had always pushed them away. That Odin might have escaped Hel's sphere during those seconds of Chaos, when Dream burst its banks and Netherworld released its ephemera into the Worlds – such a thing had happened before, but the odds were so desperately against it that Maddy was afraid even to hope.

Dream was a perilous state in which, if he *had* escaped, her old friend might have been driven insane – assuming, that is, that he had managed to avoid his fellow-travellers from Hel: demons, ephemera, fire-fiends, shadow-folk and Aspects of doom, as well as a whole world of living dreams, lethal as a river of snakes. And yet Loki had managed it. And where one could lead, others might follow. What was Odin's plan, she thought? How was her twin sister involved? And who – or what – was the Old Man?

'It's hardly proof,' she said at last. 'Now, if you'd brought the Horse itself . . .'

Mandy flapped her arms and *craw*-ed.

Hughie looked puzzled. 'But hen—'

'*Stop* calling me *hen*!' she said.

'Maddy, then. But I thought you knew.'

'Knew what?' Maddy said.

'The General's Horse. Sleipnir, born of Loki and Svadilfari, who built the walls of the Sky Citadel. Sleipnir, Odin's eight-legged mount, who, according tae legend, has a foot in each World except in Pan-daemonium . . .'

'Yes?' said Maddy impatiently. 'Please, Hughie, just get on with it, for gods' sakes!'

'Aye, well, it's right here.'

'What do'you mean, *right here*?' she said.

'I mean it's been here all the time. Five hundred years, since the Winter War, practically under your noses. Hiding in plain sight, ye might say. Aye, he's a sly one, the General. And he *always* has a plan.'

Maddy uttered a silent curse at the General, his plans *and* his ravens. But now, at last, she knew where to go. Where else would Odin have hidden the Horse that could carry him between the Worlds? Where else could he hide it in plain sight without arousing suspicion? Where else could he be sure that neither Folk nor Faërie would interfere in his plans?

Where else, thought Maddy, *but Red Horse Hill?*

11

WINTER IN THE NORTHLANDS meant that for nearly three months in the year, the sun barely grazed the horizon. Today it had risen just high enough to brighten the Seven Sleepers, but Red Horse Hill was still in shadow.

Well, thought Maddy, perhaps the business in hand was best conducted away from the light. Even to Maddy, who had seen many strange things over the past three years, the idea that Sleipnir, the General's Horse, might actually be under Red Horse Hill was difficult to swallow.

Wouldn't she have seen him, she thought? Wouldn't she have sensed him there, as she had sensed the Whisperer? And if One-Eye had known that he was there, then why in the Worlds had he not tried to awaken him himself?

Hughie looked slightly uncomfortable. 'Some things don't like being wakened,' he said. 'I mean, one moment there you are, nice and snug under the ground, sleeping off the End of the World, and the next you're bein' wakened up again. It stands tae reason ye'd be a little – ah – *ratty*.'

Mandy, who had resumed her raven Aspect for their little trip up to the Hill, gave a harsh, impatient *craw*.

'Something's coming,' Hughie said. 'I can feel it in the air.'

He was right, Maddy thought. Something was building in the air like static before a thunderstorm; something that came, not from under the Hill, but from all around them. And with the static came a sound – a distant, wrenching, *ripping* sound, as if something were actually tearing its way through the fabric of Worlds towards them, making the land raise its hackles and the winter trees bend and sway.

The sound was getting closer. A tremor ran through the snow-covered ground. Above them, the clouds seemed to ripple and warp . . .

'What in Hel's name is it?' she said.

Hughie shot her a hunted look. 'Something's coming out o' Dream. Hurry, before it gets here! Ye have to wake the General's Horse!'

'And how do we do *that?*' Maddy said, raising her voice against the sound. 'A cup of tea and some toast soldiers?'

But now the raven's voice was lost in a final rending crash as whatever it was came through from Dream. An overwhelming flare of light; another tremor that shook the Hill and tumbled Maddy to the ground, and then . . .

Silence. A dead calm.

Maddy, scrambling to her feet, had time to hear the birds resume their singing; to hear the sound of sheep in the valley; to catch the distant scent of smoke from chimneys in the village. Hughie, back in his bird form, was cawing raucously above her head. Everything seemed so *normal,* she thought – as if what had happened a moment ago had been just a fragment of one of her dreams.

What had come through the rift? she thought. What demon, what ephemera, had birthed itself into the Worlds? She looked around. There was nothing there. No snakes, no skeletal warriors, no wolves, no swarms of killer bees. Nothing but a young girl standing no more than twelve feet away, studying Maddy through granite-gold eyes as direct and luminous as her own.

For a moment Maddy stared at herself.

At herself? No, not quite. A scarlet tunic, faded and worn, in the place of Maddy's wolfskin cloak. That, and the newcomer's close-cropped hair, marked the difference between them. But for those details, the girl on the Hill might well have been Maddy's reflection; the figure was slightly transparent, as if glimpsed through a darkened mirror.

Then the girl stepped forward, and suddenly Maddy could see her more clearly: the plume of her breath in the cold air; the gleam of sweat on her forehead. This girl was no ephemera; she looked as solid as Maddy herself. *Well, almost,* Maddy corrected. The tiniest shimmer in the air, like a summer heat-haze, like the most transparent of veils, stood between her and the girl in red.

Maddy said: 'Do you know who I am?'

The other girl's lips moved silently.

'Can you hear what I'm saying?'

Once more the girl's lips made no sound.

'Are you my sister? What do you want?'

'Never ye mind talkin' tae her,' said Hughie, resuming his human Aspect. 'She'll be after the General's Horse. Without it, she can't cross over completely from Dream into this part o' the World. But if she gets the General's Horse she'll have entry to all Worlds but Pan-daemonium. She'll be able tae speak to ye then. She'll be able to use the Word—'

Again the girl appeared to speak.

At the same time a tremor went through the Hill. It was a tiny movement, but it lifted every blade of grass like the hackles on a dog's neck and made the fallen snow shift like a sheet on a restless sleeper.

'Did you say . . . the *Word*?' Maddy said.

Hughie flapped his arms at her. 'Please, hen, there isn't much time! She's still half in Dream, she's not prepared, she wasn't expecting to find us here. But with her glam and that runemark, she's so much stronger than we thought. And—'

Ack! Ack! From above their heads, Mandy's cries became increasingly urgent.

'Please, Maddy! We're wasting time!' Hughie's voice was almost a scream, and Mandy, still in raven form, swooped and chopped around their heads with increasing agitation. 'Do it now. Pick up the reins. Without the Horse she can't come through—'

'What reins?' Maddy said.

'The bridle! Get the bridle!'

The piece of strap was in Maddy's pocket. Quickly she took it out. Old and worn out as it was, it had glam; Maddy could feel it. And Odin's sigil had started to glow with a bold blue light that she recognized.

'That's it,' Hughie said. 'Now *use it*, for gods' sakes!'

But under their feet the Hill was moving. Only very gently at first, but with definite signs of wakefulness. To Maddy it looked like a giant shoulder under a mountain of blankets as the sleeper turns over, opens one eye and says he'll be up in five minutes.

She tried a command. 'Sleipnir, to me!'

Nothing else happened. The sigil glowed. The passageway into World Below, breached by digging machines and by the Word, stood, all bare rock and blasted earth, in a ring of melting snow. From the air it must have looked like the eye of a horse about to bolt – wide and white and terrified.

She tried again. 'Sleipnir, to me!'

This time she *pulled* at the bridle. Not with her hand, but with her *mind*, and with all the force of the rune *Úr*, the Mighty Ox . . .

As if in response, the nine other runes that surrounded the Red Horse began to light up, one by one – *Madr*, brown; *Raedo*, red; *Yr*, green; *Bjarkán*, white; *Logr*, blue; *Hagall*, grey; *Kaen*, violet; *Naudr*, indigo; *Ós*, gold – each ribbon of runelight connecting with the others until they had formed a bindwork of runes that enclosed the Red Horse completely.

The reins, thought Maddy. *Of course. The runes—*

'But where's the Horse? I've got the runes. Now where in Hel's the General's Horse?'

It suddenly occurred to Maddy that she had never ridden a horse before, let alone an ephemeral one. *What if he throws me off?* she wondered. *What if he won't let me ride him?*

Maddy's eyes flicked back to her twin. As she'd struggled to take the reins, the girl from World's End had not been idle. Filaments of runelight now shuttled from her fingertips. Her mouth uttered soundless phrases; her fingers formed shadowy runeshapes. What was she doing? Around the Horse, the girl in red was weaving *another* cradle of light, another set of reins from the glam that poured out of the Horse's Eye—

Gods, but she's fast, Maddy thought – not as fast as Loki, perhaps, whose reckless style of rune-casting, was almost too quick for the eye to follow, but fast enough for Maddy to know that in matters of glam, the girl was at least her equal. She raised her right hand – the runemark *Aesk* gleamed in her palm like a firebolt.

At the same time her twin raised her left hand. In it, a mindbolt of equal force burned like a nugget of molten glass.

For a moment the twins faced each other, perfect mirror-images but for their clothes and the length of their hair. Runelight shuttled around them; each held a set of reins in one hand and a deadly bolt in the other.

'Ye have to stop her!' Hughie said. 'Hit her with everything you've got!'

Of course, he was right, Maddy told herself. But this was her sister, her long-lost twin. Misled by the Order, corrupted, confused, unable to hear her – but all the same, a child of Thor and Jarnsaxa. And whatever the General's orders, she could not strike at her twin – at least, not like this, without knowing why they found themselves on opposite sides.

'Remember what the General said,' croaked Hughie, hoarse with anguish.

'But One-Eye isn't *here*,' Maddy said, and, turning away from her target, she discharged her glam – *Aesk,* the Ash – as hard as she could at the Horse's Eye.

At precisely the same moment her twin did likewise; though the mindrune she used was new to Maddy. In fact, it was *Ác,* the Thunder Oak, flung with all Maggie's untrained glam, and as it collided in mid-air with *Aesk,* there was a thunderous double crash and a sudden, massive release of glam that flung Maddy forward onto the ground and ripped through the Hill like an earthquake, and all these things happened at once:

Hughie and Mandy took wing and fled.

Maddy dropped the broken strap.

The Horse's Eye split open, and a shudder went through the hillside.

A whinnying sound cut through the air. It sounded like no kind of horse that Maddy Smith had ever heard; but it raised the hackles on her neck and brought a coppery taste to her mouth.

The girl from World's End, still standing, smiled and raised a fistful of runes.

And *something* came slowly out of the Hill – something that slouched and strained and dragged, all heavy with clay and glamours – and birthed itself laboriously, inch by inch, out of the ground, so that to Maddy it seemed as if the entire Hill were trying to reassemble itself, acquiring ribs, legs, nostrils, mane, hooves the size of boulders, and an eye that fixed on the girl who sat quite fearless atop its spine, holding in her left hand a glam that Maddy recognized, glowing a radiant butterfly-blue against the darkening winter sky.

And as Maddy fought for balance, or for something steady to hold onto, she realized that Sleipnir was not just *coming out* of the Hill. Sleipnir was the Hill *itself*, and if she wanted to survive, then she would have to reach solid ground, or be swallowed as the whole of Red Horse Hill slowly but surely began to collapse.

Loki, she thought, would have wasted no time in taking bird Aspect and flying away. But Aspect-shifting needs practice, and Maddy, whose Chaos blood ran only on her mother's side, had never been very good at it. To be fair, she hadn't really tried since her last attempt, eighteen months ago, to assume the form of a seagull. The wingless result of her morning's work had been more like a half-plucked chicken than anything else, and Maddy had spent the rest of the day picking feathers out of her hair, while Loki cracked bird-jokes, Freyja looked smug, and even Sugar found it hard to keep a straight face when she was around. Since that day Maddy had tried to concentrate on her strengths rather than her weaknesses, which meant that any attempt to Aspect-shift would certainly end in disaster.

No, she would have to try something else. Desperately, she looked around. There had to be a way out of this. The Hill was pulling itself apart: a crown of red clay lurched out of the ground; boulders tumbled away from its flanks. The snow was mostly melted here; though along the more sheltered flank of the Hill, where the runoff snow had re-frozen and set into crevices between the rocks, Maddy could see a long stretch of ice, almost like a toboggan run, that reached from the highest slopes of the Hill right down towards the Malbry road.

In simpler days Maddy Smith, riding a battered tea tray, had sped down just such ice-runs as this, screaming like a savage. There *had* been some collisions, of course. But most of the time it had worked rather well.

She glanced down the slope. It seemed mostly clear, except for a single cluster of rocks that, with luck, she hoped she could dodge. It was steeper than her childhood runs, and of course she was lacking the tea tray, but even so Maddy thought that the principle must be the same. *Well – here goes,* she said to herself, and, casting *Yr* for protection, she flung herself down the glassy slope.

The run was even steeper than she'd thought, and for a moment Maddy was sure that she would lose control of her descent. But she quickly remembered her old technique, using her hands and feet to steer, and, missing the cluster of rocks by an inch, she rapidly gained momentum, and shot as fast as a mindbolt down the side of Red Horse Hill, her hair streaming out like a pirate's flag and her old defiant war-cry ringing through the air as, with a ponderous flick of his mane, the General's Horse unfolded his legs and arose at last from his long, long sleep.

A bank of snow broke her fall, but even so Maddy was half stunned by the impact. For a minute or two she lay on her back, looking up at the dull yellow sky and trying to work out where she was. Overhead, two ravens flew.

Two ravens . . . Maddy thought dreamily.

She sat up, shaking the snow from her hair. She turned her face towards the Hill – at least, at what was left of it. Because, as Maddy now realized, the thing that had once been Red Horse Hill, the thing that straddled eight Worlds and galloped at the speed of Dream, now stood before her in Aspect – and it wasn't really a horse at all, but something defying description; something born of nightmare.

It looked like some madman's dream of a horse. The body's proportions were almost right; but the legs – all eight of them, no less – were grotesquely long and thin, like the legs on a midsummer crane fly, digging so far into the ground that they might have been the roots of trees and reaching so far above her that Maddy had to tilt her head back to see the creature standing over her, its colours like St Sepulchre's Fire, obliterating half the sky.

Its mane was every colour of red, from rose-pink to vermilion to almost-black. And among those savage colours Maddy could see the net of runes – with Odin's glam to hold it in place, just like the reins on an ordinary horse, saddled and harnessed and ready to ride.

And as Maddy stared, half stunned at the sight, the girl from World's End looked down at her, and said in a calm and even voice:

'A named thing is a tamed thing.'

12

IT HAD BEEN A LONG, strange dream. Maggie had never had such a dream, not in all her seventeen years, and at several points in this one she had been on the verge of retreat, of telling Adam she couldn't do this, that some things were never meant to be dreamed and that she was not a warrior.

But her courage, combined with the Voice in her head, drove her on; though most of all, it was the thought of Adam's disappointment that kept her from just opening her eyes and leaving Malbry to its monsters.

The thing that had dragged itself out of the Hill was bad enough, Maggie thought. But now she could see what followed it; what seethed into the gap it had left; what gurgled darkly in its wake, awaiting its chance to enter the world.

It looked like a smear of black smoke, or a cloud of ink, or a swarm of bees, and Maggie could hear it under the ground – ten thousand voices clamouring; ten thousand footsteps; ten thousand tortured prisoners all clawing and scrabbling to be born.

But most disturbing of all was the girl who was lying in the snow at her feet. Such an ordinary-looking girl, with her leather tunic and wolfskin cloak and braided hair like an Outlander's.

Was this really the enemy? The Voice in her head had told her it was. And yet she looked so normal, so very un-demonic. Maggie knew that demons could take whatever form they chose, but this girl – this very *familiar* girl – seemed such an unexpected choice. Did she know her? A part of her thought maybe she did. Those eyes, that stubborn mouth . . .

Why, that girl looks just like me!

Quick! The Word! said the Voice in her head. *Quick, while you still have the chance!*

Maggie cast aside her doubts and searched for the relevant canticle. She knew the Book of Invocations verse by verse, list by list. And she knew that ruinmark, *Aesk*, the Ash, that gave her Maddy's true name . . .

She held the bridle of light in one hand and recited the Words of the Good Book:

'I name thee Modi, Thunderchild. I name thee *Aesk*, Lightning Ash. I name thee Destroyer and Builder of Worlds. I name thee . . .'

The canticle was working. The girl – the *demon* – was weakening. The Word seemed to have this effect on her kind; every syllable a blow. Now she lay helpless at Maggie's feet, a line of red across her cheek where something – a bramble – had scratched her. The Word had robbed her of speech, but her breath still clouded the cold air – and that was when Maggie realized that none of this was a dream any more; that somehow all of this was *real*—

Finish her! While there's still time!

The Magister's Voice was commanding. But Maggie Rede had never been used to blind, unthinking obedience. The Order would never have taken her on, not even if she'd been a boy. To kill in a dream was one thing, she thought. But to kill like this, using the Word, in a manner opposed to all the Order's teachings, and without even knowing the first thing about this girl who looked so much like her—

Never mind that, snapped the Voice in her mind, the being that called itself Magister. *Do as I say, girl! Finish her! Remember the Book of Apocalypse! Maggie, this is your destiny!*

Destiny? Maggie thought. Like all the Order's children, she believed very strongly in such things. She remembered the Book of Apocalypse, the verse that dealt with the End of the Worlds:

And there shall come a Horse of Fire,
And the name of his Rider is Carnage.
And there shall come a Horse of the Sea,
And the name of his Rider is Treachery.
And there shall come a Horse of Air,
And the name of his Rider is Lunacy . . .

Could this be her destiny? Was Maggie Rede from World's End fated to ride the Horse of Fire? She'd dreamed of this for so many years, alone in her underground labyrinth. She'd read so many stories of the Universal City and the great Apocalypse; of Tribulations and Cleansings; of warriors and demons and gods. And in her darkest, wildest dreams Maggie had always fought alongside them, riding across the Nine Worlds, wading through rivers of unholy blood, an angel with a crossbow.

Nevertheless, in three years she had never killed anything bigger than a rat; and now, with the face of her enemy – so very like her own face – staring up at her from the snow, Maggie found that she simply could not obey the Voice without question.

'Who are you?' she said to the girl at her feet. 'Who are you, and how do you wear my face?'

The girl climbed painfully to her knees. The canticle had silenced her momentarily, but now her glam – and her voice – had returned. Her ruinmark flared in the palm of her hand, a brilliant coppery colour, but she made no visible move to attack.

Do it, Maggie! Finish her! The Voice had lost its calm authority; its tone was one of anguish now. *Maggie Rede, I COMMAND YOU—*

But Maggie's attention was on the girl. Her voice was almost lost in the sound of Maggie's ghostly passenger, but even so, she could hear it – a pleasant voice, much like her own, but with a trace of a Northlands accent:

'Maggie. Listen. That voice in your head. The one that tells you what to do.'

Maggie felt her throat contract. 'How did you know my name?' she said. 'How did you know about the Voice?'

The presence in her mind had become a savage, snarling animal. *YOU WILL OBEY MY COMMAND!* it said.

Maggie shook the Magister aside like a terrier shaking a rat. It hurt, but she was stronger; she felt its rage and frustration clawing for control of her mind . . .

'How did you know?'

'I guessed,' said the girl. 'It's the Whisperer. An enemy of my people and yours. I've seen people under its spell before. And I know you're not really a murderer.'

Maggie frowned. 'You're lying,' she said. 'You're one of *them*. The enemy. The filthy, treacherous Seer-folk.'

'That's right,' said the girl. 'I *am* one of them. But we are not the enemy. The Whisperer is the enemy. It lies. It wants to use you. It knows who you are, and it's using you to wreak revenge on your family.'

'I don't believe you,' Maggie said. 'The Seer-folk killed my family.'

'That isn't true,' said the girl from the North. 'Maggie, I'm yours—'

It was then that the ground began to explode. A geyser of earth and rocks and grass erupted twelve feet to Maggie's left, followed by another one just in front of her spectral mount. The Red Horse reared; he bared his teeth; cold fire shot from his nostrils. At the same instant something began to flood uncontrollably out of the Hill: a squealing, snickering tide of life that swarmed out of the holes in the broken ground and fanned out onto the seamless snow.

At the same moment Maggie felt something *snag* at her thoughts, like a fishhook caught inside her mind. It was her passenger again, battling its will against hers. For a moment her vision blurred. A spike of pain went through her head. Her dream-hands clutched the cat's cradle of reins even more tightly than before.

Below her, the girl from the Northlands was struggling to get to her feet. Earth and rubble showered them both, bouncing off the crust of snow. Maggie's head was pounding now; her vision doubled, trebled. She was vaguely aware of the girl from the North turning once to look at her, then beginning to run across the snow.

Above her, two ravens circled mystically.

The fishhook in Maggie's mind pulled again, urging her to give in, to obey.

YOU CANNOT RESIST ME, MAGGIE REDE. I ORDER YOU TO OBEY ME! STRIKE HER DOWN! USE THE WORD! DO IT NOW, BEFORE IT'S TOO LATE!

But Maggie was no Adam Scattergood, to be reeled in like a caught fish. *STOP IT!* she said, and *shoved* at the unseen presence with all the considerable force of her will. The Red Horse beneath her reared up, almost as if to encourage her.

She felt the Magister's astonishment.

GET OUT! she ordered, and lunged again. Once more the Horse responded.

The Voice grew plaintive, pitiful. *Please, Maggie. Let Me explain—*

GET THE HEL OUT OF MY MIND, Maggie said, and gave a final violent push. Beneath her, the Horse gave a giant leap; there came a sudden flare of light . . .

And Maggie opened her eyes again and found herself back in the Universal City, sitting up in bed with the Good Book open at her side, and Adam watching her wide-eyed, and the old familiar city sounds like music in her waking ears.

For a moment she was so relieved to find herself back home again that she almost didn't notice the fact that she and Adam were not alone. A sound brought her back to reality; a gentle, familiar whickering – the kind you might hear on any street corner or in any place where livestock is kept.

Maggie turned and saw a horse standing by the bedside. It looked just like a regular horse – a strawberry roan with a long black mane. It had the usual number of legs. Why then was she so sure that this was no ordinary animal? And what was it doing in their room?

She turned to look at the Good Book, still open at the picture of the strange, eight-legged Horse. Had the picture caused her dream? Or had dreaming driven her mad?

The picture in the Good Book showed the Horse with a rider.

Had that rider been there before? Maggie couldn't remember. But it was so dark in the room that she'd probably missed it. A tiny figure with cropped dark hair, wearing a scarlet tunic . . .

Maggie closed the Good Book and locked it with the golden key. Then she turned to look back at the Horse through the circle of finger and thumb. Through the rune *Bjarkán* she caught a brief, unspeakable glimpse of red. And on its bridle, a flash of blue signalled the presence of some kind of glam.

She'd thought it was a dream. But no. Here it was, in the real world. The Red Horse of the Last Days . . .

Which now, it seemed, belonged to *her*.

BOOK THREE

Odin's Horse

I saw an eight-legg'd horse trot by.
(Fie, oh fie, ye drunken fool!)
Nine Worlds were in his gleaming eye.
(Fie, ye drunken scally!)

World's End drinking song

1

THE GODS (EXCEPT FOR MADDY, OF COURSE) knew nothing but the aftermath. For five hundred years the Red Horse had slept, awaiting the time of the Last Days. Now he was gone, the Hill was no more, and Dream – raw Dream, undiluted, uncontrollable – was unleashed upon the valley.

It was the greatest wave of ephemera the gods had seen since Ragnarók. It started under Red Horse Hill, where all the dregs of World Below – Faërie, goblins and other undesirables, including Loki, who was still in disgrace – had made their quarters out of reach of Æsir, Vanir and the Folk.

It had come quite early that morning, when the sun was barely grazing the Hill. The villagers of Malbry had mostly still been in their beds, except for a few early risers and Crazy Nan, who got up at dawn to feed her cats and had seen the chaotic signatures in the sky above the Hill. For most, however, the first sign had been a kind of rumbling sound, as of an impending storm, followed by an explosion, as if all the geysers of World Below had chosen to erupt at once.

The rats had felt it first, and fled upwards in their thousands, swarming from the darkest depths, streaming through holes in the porous rock, squealing and biting and tearing each other – and at anything else that stood in their way – in an increasingly frenzied struggle to escape.

Sugar, with Thor in the blacksmith's house, found the courtyard full of them: brown rats, black rats, grey rats and red-eyed albino rats, pouring out of sewers and drains as World Below prepared itself for a massive evacuation. Some even popped right out of the ground like corks from bottles of ginger beer, and Sugar saw that a cloud of birds had begun to assemble over the village; eagles, carrion birds, hawks and crows and jackdaws and gulls, excited by the swarming prey, were circling over Malbry in numbers hitherto unseen.

Maddy, running as fast as she could away from the scene at Red Horse Hill, had time to remember the occasion when, three years ago, while trying to capture a goblin, she had accidentally summoned *all* Malbry's vermin into Mrs Scattergood's cellar. The present disruption was something like that, but magnified ten thousand times. *Something* was coming – something big – released by her twin and by the Horse they had awakened between them. As she ran for cover, Maddy couldn't help wondering why Maggie had not made a move to attack as she lay helpless and dazed at the foot of the Hill.

Had she lost control of the Horse? Had she simply run out of glam? Had she decided to leave the job of finishing off the enemy to whatever was corning from World Below? Was it some vestige of loyalty, a sense of kinship that had stayed her hand? Or was it because she knew somehow that Maddy too had disobeyed orders, preferring to lose the Red Horse rather than strike at her sister? Was she being used by the Whisperer, an innocent caught up in its plans? And if so, could she be saved from herself and brought back to her family?

There was no one to answer these questions, of course. Hughie and Mandy were long gone, lost in the growing maelstrom of birds. Odin's bridle was also gone. The plan to harness Sleipnir had backfired in a most spectacular way, and as for going to the Universal City – that was surely out of the question, now that this new threat had raised its head.

No, this attack must be dealt with first, Maddy said to herself as she ran. And yet for the moment, she realized, what had happened on the Hill would have to remain a secret – at least, until she knew the truth about the Whisperer and her mysterious twin. To betray her to the gods at this point would be nothing less than disastrous – and if Maggie, in spite of the assault, had sensed any kind of bond with her, then Maddy owed it to her to find out.

She made ready her glam for the inevitable, while around her the air turned black with birds and the ground came alive with vermin, swarming from holes and rents in the earth towards the village of Malbry.

Meanwhile Loki, to whom no movement under the Hill was lost, had sensed the disruption immediately and taken to his bird form, as the network of tripwires and runes he had laid in place these five hundred years was torn apart like a spider's web, and first the rats, and then a tidal wave of ephemera surged upwards from the Eighth World, driving all things before it.

His escape came not a moment too soon. As he soared in hawk Aspect above the chaos on the ground, there came a wave of turbulence that almost knocked him out of the sky, though he had time to see Maddy's signature vanishing into the maelstrom, and to wonder what she was doing there. And what was that *other* signature, submerged in the general confusion? Had he imagined it? Was he simply seeing stars?

Then the third wave came out of the Hill, and Loki lost interest in everything but getting as far from the epicentre as possible. A sudden release of water – ice-cold water from the Seventh World – erupted from fissures in the earth, so that the river Strond increased to ten times its normal size in as many minutes, and the flood barriers at Malbry Riverside were broken, and the first great wave of flood water charged like a herd of buffalo down Malbry High Street, past the church, knocking down the wooden houses closest to the river before spilling out across farmlands and pastures all the way to Nether's Edge.

This was no ordinary flood, Loki knew. It was the river Dream, unleashed, awash with the flotsam of Chaos. Faced with such a powerful threat, Loki didn't stand a chance, and, abandoning all loyalties, he fled in bird Aspect as fast as he could towards the

Seven Sleepers, where the Hindarfell Pass, just newly cleared, would provide him with the best means of escape from whatever was after him.

In the village, the Folk were in chaos. Some ran out to see what was happening and were swiftly borne away by the flood. Some fled to the church for safety; some hauled bags of sand and earth to their doorsteps to form a breakwater against the tide. But water was not the end of it: now came fire out of the ground; and boiling mud, which, meeting the floodwater, caused great gouts of steam to erupt from the already swollen Strond, rolling like thunder across the land, so that some of the oldsters remembered the tales of demon wolves that swallowed the Sun, bringing darkness even in summertime.

Maddy saw it coming, and found the nearest tree to climb. A stunted oak, but large enough, she hoped, to withstand the tide of water and mud. Settling into a fork in the trunk, she looked up into the roiling sky, trying in vain to distinguish the forms of Odin's ravens among the thousands of circling birds.

'Hughie! Mandy! Are you there?'

From the cloud she thought she heard the faintest of replies.

Craw. Crawk.

'Stay close!' she cried.

Again, that harsh note of reply.

From her refuge in the tree, Maddy drew her mindsword, for now, after fire and flood, came the rest: Pan-daemonium unleashed.

After the billows of steam and the plagues of rats and the subterranean waters came creatures that only Dream could have spawned: clawed things and flying things and things with the features of the dead. The deadliest kind of ephemera, fashioned from the raw stuff of Dream and spawned from the wells of Chaos, tearing their way through the rent in the Worlds towards the lair of the Seer-folk.

The Æsir were quick to react to the threat. Assuming as much of their true Aspects as they were able to summon, with mindswords and runeweapons they took their stand against the advancing enemy. No one was at their best, of course; runemarks

142

broken or reversed; muscles weakened; instincts dulled; subject to all the imperfections of their host bodies. Still they stood. Still they fought.

Outside the Parsonage Brave-Hearted Tyr, in spite of his inferior size, was making a fair job of dispatching every rat that came his way. They lay in drifts around the square, their bodies creating a barrier against the rising water.

Ethel's priority was the Folk. As panic seized the villagers in their struggle to escape, she spun runes into the air to shield the innocents from harm; directed them into the church, which was large enough to take them all; reunited families and promised them that all would be well. And in spite of her Aspect as Frigg the Seeress there was still enough of Ethelberta Parson in her to reassure the village folk – who otherwise might well have assumed that the strangers were to blame for all this, and turned their rage against their protectors.

Meanwhile the Vanir had not been idle. From under the Sleepers, they too had seen the plague of rats that poured from the Hill, flooding the many passageways that ran from beneath the Horse's Eye; the noxious tide that followed them – the waves of ephemera from Dream, the verminous geyser from World Below that rushed to fill every hole, every crack, every crevasse in the ice.

Now, from their ice-cave underground, Njörd worked to hold back the flood while Bragi struck power chords on his guitar. Frey had unsheathed his mindsword and was scything methodically through the enemy's ranks, while Freyja, in her Carrion Aspect (which she despised most of the time as unglamorous, but whose skeletal features were enough to strike fear even into the heart of Dream), flew around the battle scene, shrieking and striking out with her claws, dislodging clusters of stalactites that fell like spears from the ceiling and onto the heads of the enemy.

Back in the village, however, Thor was having staffing problems. Faced with a cloud of ephemera, the soul-eating parasites of Netherworld, he quite understandably assumed that his mighty hammer would be at his side during the mêlée. But Jolly seemed less than willing to take part, and the Thunderer spent several

143

minutes wheedling before he could persuade him to put aside his breakfast and to assume his Aspect as Mjølnir.

'Me toast'll go cold,' he protested. 'Can't you manage on yer own?'

Thor attempted to explain that this was a bit of a crisis.

Jolly pulled a face. 'Well, I don't think much of yer timin',' he said. 'I can't bloody stand cold toast. And what about me sausages?'

Thor took a deep breath, smiled and promised Jolly all the sausages he could eat – but later, when they'd saved the Worlds.

'Say *please*,' Jolly said.

At which time Thor's patience expired at last, and he erupted into full Aspect in Ethel Parson's breakfast room – all seven feet of Thunderer, red beard spitting fiery sparks, eyes like torches, fists like anvils, thick blue veins running up his arms – and there was Mjølnir at his side, still looking strangely like Jolly, with its huge misshapen head, its double runemark gleaming, illuminated with glamours and light.

Thor gave a growl of satisfaction and, seizing the weapon in his fist, strode out into the courtyard again and proceeded to do what he did best, which was to hammer things.

And there were so many things to hammer. Not quite as many ephemera as the gods had encountered in Netherworld three years ago, but far more than they had seen in World Above since Ragnarók, five centuries ago, when Surt had marched out of Chaos and Asgard had fallen from the sky.

There were feathered snakes and birds with teeth; fire-cats and mud monkeys; there were spiders, and swarms of flying eyes, and eagles with human faces, and bats, and things that were nothing but tentacles, like creatures of the One Sea.

Ephemera can take any shape; and even when smashed into pieces, they can often reassemble, but Thor and Mjølnir made a powerful team, and with Brave-Hearted Tyr at their side, killing rats, as well as Sif – who had dropped her current Aspect and now faced the enemy as a ferocious battle-sow, with golden tusks and eyes like coals – they laid into the hordes of Netherworld with the vigour of a small army.

'What are they *after?*' yelled Brave-Hearted Tyr, hurling a mind-bolt at a platoon of marching umbrellas. On contact, the umbrellas broke up into a shower of spinning crescents, each one as sharp as a razor-blade, that sliced screaming through the air before embedding themselves in the frozen ground.

Thor shrugged. 'How in Hel would I know?' He levelled his hammer at an oncoming ice bear and sent it howling back to Netherworld. 'I'm not the one who opened the rift . . .'

'No, that was Loki,' said Brave-Hearted Tyr. 'It must have given way at last!'

'Well, if that's who they're after,' said Thor with a growl, 'they're welcome to him. Anytime.' And, lifting his hammer, the Thunderer returned once more to the business in hand.

2

LOKI HAD NEVER DOUBTED FOR A moment that he *was* the one they were after. He'd automatically assumed from the start that his deal with Angrboda and her folk must have come to the attention of Chaos, and that this offensive was the result.

Certainly, it made sense. An alliance between demons and gods might threaten even Surt's domain, especially if the Sky Citadel were indeed to be rebuilt, and the First World reinstated as theirs. Of course, that didn't explain what he had seen in the sky before the eruption. Maddy's signature was hard to miss, and he was more than familiar with the colours of the General's Horse, which he had glimpsed in the moments before the Hill had started to erupt, emitting so many signatures that all trace of Sleipnir and Maddy had quickly been obliterated.

Loki, of course, had known all about the creature sleeping under the Hill. Technically, in Horse Aspect, he was Sleipnir's parent – a relationship he would rather forget – and as such he could have awoken the Horse quite easily; but he had no interest at all in doing so. Quite apart from the fact that Odin would have torn him limb from limb if he'd tried anything of that sort, the Trickster didn't much like horses, preferring his bird Aspect to anything four-or eight-legged. Maddy, it seemed, had no such qualms. The presence of her signature so close to the source of the eruption suggested that she had taken the Horse. Perhaps she'd assumed that the aftermath would provide her with adequate camouflage to make her escape before anyone made the connection. Perhaps, now that Odin was dead, he thought, its power had been too much for her to resist.

All the more reason, Loki thought, for him to take his flight while he still could. Maddy couldn't help him now, even if she'd wanted to. If he could reach the Hindarfell, he might have a chance of finding shelter outside the valley, and thereafter make his way southwards into the Universal City and beyond, where, he thought, he could probably find better, safer, more comfortable – and certainly more lucrative – opportunities to develop his skills.

But Hawk-eyed Heimdall, at his post in the Sleepers, had been waiting years for just such a move, and his sharp eyes were quick to notice the small brown bird flying towards the Hindarfell. Ignoring the chaos below him, he took to his own winged Aspect – that of a white sea-eagle – and set off in pursuit of the bird, whose gaudy violet signature-trail marked it conclusively as the fugitive Trickster.

For a time it seemed that the smaller bird might almost evade its pursuer. But Loki was tired, Heimdall was stronger, and the many eruptions from World Below had conspired to create a turbulence in the thin mountain air that battered and shook the Trickster until, at last, he was forced to the ground just as he reached the Sleepers.

With the white sea-eagle still on his tail, Loki headed for a space between two peaks, where, halfway down the mountainside, a pool of white mist spilled out from beneath a glacier, partially obscuring the scene below. If only he could reach it, he thought, then maybe he could find somewhere to hide . . .

The mist was thick and creamy, like the head on a glass of ale. He plunged into it, feeling the drop in temperature as soon as he passed through the cloud layer. As he came to land on an outcrop of rock, Loki had a moment to appreciate the unusual *thickness* of the fog – its ghastly pallor; its sickening cold; the stench that enveloped everything within its reach – before something happened that made him forget his pursuer, his flight; that startled him right out of his bird form and back into his human Aspect, sprawling him clumsily into the snow in his hurry to escape.

The white sea-eagle swooped into view, but Loki barely even glanced his way. He simply lay shivering where he had fallen, his eyes widening in disbelief as *something* came slithering out of the mist in the glacier's shadow. Something large. Something dark. Something monstrously familiar . . .

Loki swallowed painfully. 'Jorgi? Is that you?' he said.

3

LOKI'S DREAD WAS NOT MISPLACED. The last time he had encountered the World Serpent – otherwise known as Jormungand – the circumstances had been less than amicable. But at least he'd been in full Aspect then, with Maddy by his side, and with the (somewhat reluctant) support of Hel, the Guardian of the Underworld.

This time he was alone, freezing cold and, worse still – one of the disadvantages of shifting to bird Aspect being that he'd had to leave his clothes behind – clad in nothing but his skin. *Not* the way he had envisaged their reunion – in fact, Loki thought, the only way he would have willingly submitted to such an encounter was with a large army standing between himself and the Serpent (which would be safely bound with runes – Loki saw no virtue at all in settling scores in person).

He looked at the open jaws of the beast, bared his teeth in a feeble smile and said: 'Jorgi. Uh. Long time no see.'

Heimdall, meanwhile, recognizing his prey's attempt to escape, had taken a fast, steep dive into the pool of white mist. The first thing he saw on arrival was Loki, stark naked, backed up as far as he could go against an outcrop of white rock, and such was the Watchman's eagerness to dispatch his enemy at last that it took him several seconds to notice the massive, dark, undeniable head of the World Serpent leering from under the skirt of the glacier, his interminable coils lost in mist, his jaws half open and drizzling venom onto the snow.

'Heimdall!' said Loki gratefully.

The Watchman resumed his Aspect.

Jormungand gave a beastly yawn and slithered forward another twelve feet. Heimdall shot Loki an evil look and summoned a handful of fire-runes – though whether these were intended as weapons or merely to combat the bitter cold could not easily be determined.

'Running out on us, Loki?' he said. 'I always knew you would, some day. And now I find you here – with *that*, and all Hel following after you . . .'

'Give me a break,' said the Trickster. 'Do I look like I have a death wish? If you recall, Jorgi and I didn't part on what you'd call friendly terms.'

'Really?' said Heimdall with sarcasm. 'And after you freed him from Netherworld too. You'd think he might show some gratitude.' He levelled the full force of his ice-blue gaze at the cowering Trickster. 'So – am I to take it you're telling me you *didn't* have anything to do with what's happening right now under the Hill? That you *didn't* open a gateway to unleash the hordes of Netherworld, and that you're *not* now planning to make your escape with the help of your monstrous son, the World Serpent?'

'Well, *actually*—' began Loki.

But what he'd been about to say was lost in a sudden flurry of wings as another bird – an outlandish bird, with purple and scarlet plumage – fluttered through the veil of mist and alighted on the outcrop of rock. Loki had barely a moment to react before the bird became Angrboda – fully clothed in a long hooded coat of scarlet fur and purple snow-boots with outrageous heels – sitting on the high rock and watching him disapprovingly.

'I'm *very* disappointed,' she said.

'Angie, please. I can explain—'

'You're telling me you *weren't* running away?'

'Damn right I wasn't,' Loki said. 'In case you hadn't noticed, there's a bit of a crisis going on. I was covering the rear – making

150

sure the pass was secure – while Goldie and the gang held the Sleepers, and Thor and the others dealt with the Hill. Thanks for the Hammer, by the way. Great little guy. I miss him already.'

Angie grinned. 'I thought you would.'

'Excuse me?' Heimdall bared his teeth. 'Can I ask what in Hel is going on?'

'Cool it, Goldie. She's on our side. We had an arrangement, remember?'

'Not with *that*, we didn't,' Heimdall said, with a sideways glance at the World Serpent.

'Well, that's where you're wrong,' Angie said, hopping down from her icy perch. 'Jormungand's going to help us. You gods think you're so clever, with your glamours and your mindbolts, but Jormungand here can snap up ephemera the way an ice bear snaps up fish. You'll need him – *and* the rest of us – if you're to have any chance against what's coming.'

'And what *is* coming, according to you?' Heimdall's eyes were very bright.

'War, of course,' said Angrboda. 'The battle for the Sky Citadel.'

'We lost that battle long ago. How can we hope to win it now? This is a trick—' He turned once more on Loki, the rune *Hagall* trembling in his palm.

Loki forked *Yr*, the Protector, with fingers that were numb with cold.

'Play nice,' said Angrboda, 'or I'll take your toys away.' She made a gesture with her hand, and something shot from her fingertips – a spray of purple sparks that struck *Hagall* from Heimdall's hand and showered Loki with shrapnel.

Loki remembered the runemark he'd seen earlier on her arm, and wondered silently to himself how Angie could have obtained such a powerful glam. The runes had been gifts to the gods long ago, from Odin Allfather himself – broken or reversed in defeat at Ragnarók. New runes had been promised to Odin's heirs, but now, with the General gone, he thought, there could surely be no more.

And yet she had hit him with *something*, he thought; something

151

very different from the unruly, gaudy glamours of her kind. Loki felt very uneasy.

'Come on, Angie. I'm cold,' he said. 'If you're here to help, then get on with it.'

Angie gave him a quelling look. 'We're here to prove to your stuck-up friends that they're going to need us on their side. And to make sure you don't get any ideas – like weaselling out of doing your bit and flying south to sunnier climes . . .'

Heimdall clenched his golden teeth. 'There'll be no weaselling,' he said.

'Good,' said Angrboda. 'We can discuss this further when Jormungand has cleaned up the mess.'

'Cleaned up the mess?' said Heimdall. 'You're saying he's *not* responsible?'

'Of course not. Weren't you listening? Something happened on the Hill. Something that fractured the rift in Dream and let out all this vermin. But there's nothing to suggest for now that we were ever its target. In fact, it's entirely possible that this wasn't meant for *us* at all.'

'What was it, then?' said Heimdall.

'That remains to be seen,' said the Temptress, with a sideways glance at Loki. 'But whatever – whoever's responsible, they've left us with plenty of evidence.'

'How so?' said the Watchman, narrow-eyed.

Angrboda arched an eyebrow. 'They came to us through Dream,' she said. 'How better to know them than from their dreams?' And with that, she stepped towards Jormungand and climbed onto his scaly neck, holding herself in place with the aid of a strap placed around his jaw.

'I'll see you back in the village,' she said. 'There's someone there who needs our help.' Then, turning back with a grin: 'Oh, and for gods' sakes, boys – put some bloody clothes on.'

4

No ONE BUT MADDY HAD seen the Horse as he birthed himself from the Hill. But the signs of his passing were clear enough. Something large had broken free; and given the signature he had left, it was only a matter of time before they came to the obvious conclusion.

The initial surge of ephemera from the Hill had dwindled to a verminous ooze, and the Æsir had now been joined by the Vanir, who in their animal Aspects had raced down from the Sleepers towards the source of the attack. Now, regrouping by Red Horse Hill – at least, by what was left of it – they surveyed the damage with anxious eyes as the horrible truth became clear to them.

'So all this time that wretched Horse has been right here under our noses?' said Frey. 'But who could have known where to find him? And why?'

'Loki,' said Thor. 'He *made* the damn thing.'

Sif, still in battle-sow Aspect, grunted her approval.

'But why all this mess?' squeaked Idun, who, of all the Vanir, had no animal Aspect and had taken the shape of a hazelnut, which Njörd carried in his talons. 'Couldn't he just have stolen the Horse without waking half of Netherworld?'

'This is Loki we're talking about,' said Bragi. 'Who knows why he does these things?'

No one knew the answer to that. But what was clear to all of them was that what had once seemed little more than a nick between the boundaries of the Worlds had now become a gaping wound. There was no way of knowing when another wave of ephemera might strike; but on one thing the gods were all agreed. Such damage to the boundary between the Worlds had not been seen since Ragnarök, and as far as most of them were concerned, Loki was the obvious culprit.

There *was* some justification for this. After all, it was he who had caused the original rift in Dream. Afterwards, from Red Horse Hill, it had been Loki's job to guard the Eye. But now the Eye had been pulverized, and Loki was missing, his trail leading south, with an ice-blue signature that could only belong to Heimdall shooting after him in pursuit.

'When I get my hands on the weasel,' said Thor, flinging his hammer into a cluster of *afreets*, 'I'll use him as a toothpick.'

'I'll chop him into fish-bait,' said Njörd.

Freyja, in Carrion Aspect, rasped: 'I'll make a necklace from his teeth.'

Sif grunted through her tusks. 'I'll spread him from here to Fettlefields.'

Jolly resumed his Aspect for long enough to remark, with a smirk: 'Well, I don't see him comin' back here in a rush, not with this little lot to clear up – Oops, watch out, here they come again . . .'

The lull in the battle had proved to be only a temporary respite. Now once more the Hill disgorged a new glut of ephemera, taking shape as they approached, coming towards them on nightmare hooves and wings that stole the sun from the sky.

Once more the gods prepared to face another offensive.

Bragi took out his guitar and struck a mighty power chord. A battery of sharp little notes scattered across the hillside, dropping ephemera in their tracks, although they still kept coming.

Bragi frowned and tightened a string. 'Am I in tune?' he said.

Thor shrugged. Dorian Scattergood had been tone-deaf, and he himself had never been particularly interested in music. As far as

154

the Thunderer was concerned, guitars, pipes – or, still worse, *lutes* – were usually best avoided.

Instead, he unleashed his hammer again, striking rifts in the valley floor that led right down into World Below. Tyr wielded his mindsword, Frey his double-edged scythe. But for every stray demon they managed to halt, for every mindbolt that struck the mark, for every piece of ephemera that was blown back into oblivion, ten more escaped into the air, becoming insubstantial, acquiring the shapes of vapours and clouds, or sank back into the marshy ground, following rootlets, rivers, streams, finding their way to the One Sea, fishing for dreams as they drifted.

From Malbry all the way to World's End, people sensed their presence. Babies woke up screaming; good dogs turned bad overnight; old folk died in their sleep; rabbits ate their litters. Dream had turned another page. Tribulation was closer.

Meanwhile, back at Red Horse Hill, the situation looked hopeless. The gods were outnumbered ten thousand to one. Poisoned by the toxic air, feathers singed, glam burned out, cut and bruised and aching, step by step and blow by blow, they were forced back, away from the Hill.

Tyr had a number of rat bites. Frey's right arm hung useless. Bragi's guitar had a broken string. Even Thor was limping, though Jolly still seemed to be enjoying himself. And the flow of ephemera out of the Hill was as steady as ever.

Maddy, less than a mile away, had fared even worse than the Æsir. Clinging to a stunted oak, a river of mud and fire at her feet, she had managed, with runes and her mindsword, to combat the worst of the attack. The beings that surged out of the Hill had for the most part avoided her, but a clash with a column of razor-ants, some giant leeches and something that looked like a pterodactyl (though she had never seen one, of course) had left her with cuts and grazes and a gash across her forehead that was still bleeding steadily. That, combined with the fumes from World Below and the continuous onslaught on her glam, now found her much weakened, her mindsword pared down to little more than a sliver, her grasp on the tree trunk – now slick with her blood – finally beginning to fail.

Her friends, though close, were out of reach. The air was charged with ephemera. Their presence formed a kind of mist – a mist that was filled with invisible shrapnel – that clung to Maddy's hair and clothes, freezing her limbs, dragging her down, eating away her resistance.

Odin's ravens were nowhere to be seen – in fact, it was hard to see anything under that creeping cloud of mist.

She wondered vaguely where Loki was. Somewhere safer, probably. The Trickster had always had the knack of not being there when trouble arose – a fact that had done little to earn him the trust of the Æsir during the current conflict. Besides, what now came out of the Hill would have tested the faith of even the most devoted of Loki's few remaining friends.

As before, it began as a rumbling from the channels of World Below; the surge of ephemera stuttered and stopped, like a water pipe blocked by some kind of obstruction. And there came a sound like a thousand steam-kettles all about to blow at once; a screaming, hissing, ratcheting sound . . .

As Jormungand made his entrance.

5

IT WAS AN IMPRESSIVE ENTRANCE, as Maddy conceded later, after she'd shaken the dust from her hair and marvelled over the fragments of rock – some of them gems that the Tunnel Folk would have sold their grandmothers to obtain – projected so high into the air that five minutes later they were still falling like shooting stars over Malbry.

Of course, she had seen the World Serpent before. But Jormungand in Aspect was a sight to challenge anyone's nerve. His head was as big as a team of oxen, his mane like a haystack of runelight. And his jaws – jaws that were open wide to engulf the fleeing shoals of ephemera – were like a pair of barn doors edged with teeth the shape and size of scimitars.

Maddy reached for her mindsword, knowing that it was hopeless. Jormungand reared his massive head; Maddy gathered the last of her strength and prepared to go out fighting. She could feel the Serpent's venomous breath, feel the heat of his approach. But he did not attack. He simply lolled and gaped at her, no more than twenty feet away. Perhaps he recognized her, she thought. Perhaps he would listen to reason.

Maddy lowered her mindsword. 'Remember me?' she said.

She was still far from confident. The last time she and the Serpent had met had been three years ago, in one of the dungeons of the Black Fortress, and although he *had* helped the gods to escape, that had mostly been due to Loki, who had used himself as human bait to induce the beast to wreak havoc.

'I'm a . . . friend of Loki's,' she said.

Jormungand gave a long hiss.

'Well, not so much a *friend*,' Maddy amended hastily. 'More what you'd call an associate.'

The World Serpent made an unspeakable sound and rolled over in his sheath of slime. His stench was almost palpable. She wondered what was to stop him from simply opening his jaws and gulping her down like a grape. Once more she reached for her mindsword. Worn down to no more than a toothpick now, it would scarcely have deterred a rat. The World Serpent gave an enormous yawn—

And then there was girlish laughter, and a ringing voice from above that said: 'Oh, *darling*. Put it *away*.'

Maddy looked up – just in time to see the Witch of Ironwood jump down from her position on the Serpent's flank, in scarlet furs from head to foot and looking very pleased with herself. At her side, the Wolf Brothers gambolled like unruly puppies in the wake of the devastation.

'Thought you could use a lift,' she said. 'Climb aboard, and I'll take you home.' She sternly addressed Jormungand, who had turned his attention to a shoal of ephemera that was drifting past. Opening his enormous jaws, he inhaled – and drew the ephemera into his mouth with the ease of a whale ingesting plankton.

Angie stroked his slimy mane. 'Hungry, darling? *That's* my boy.' She smiled at Maddy. 'My boys have always had a healthy appetite,' she said. 'Now come on, sweetheart, and take Maddy home. You can catch a bite on the way.'

Meanwhile, not far from the village, the gods were watching with apprehension. A fistful of glamours was all they had left; they were limping, exhausted, close to defeat. Regrouping on the higher ground, they had watched the river rise, while the Folk gathered in clusters in and around the soundest buildings – mainly the church and the Parsonage, where Ethel had remained to help – some carrying possessions, others silently glaring at those who had brought this disaster upon them.

Crazy Nan Fey was among the crowd, although she knew perfectly well that the gods were in no way responsible for what was happening. It was all written down in the Good Book, and in the nursery rhymes of her youth – which all went to show, said Crazy Nan, that the old wives' tales the Order despised were not as foolish as they'd claimed, and that if anyone could somehow avert that long-awaited Apocalypse, then it would most likely be an old wife—

And then came an almighty crash, and out of what little was left of the Hill burst Jormungand in full Aspect, throwing up a shower of stones as he erupted from the ground. Flaming pieces of half-melted rock showered the valley like shooting stars, and Nan and the villagers were forced to take cover wherever they could as the gods turned to face the new attack.

It was some five minutes before the dust and debris had cleared enough for the gods to realize that the World Serpent was not alone. A trio of wolves accompanied him, plus a fire-bird, two ravens and, approaching from the direction of the Sleepers, a sea-eagle, and a small brown hawk whose signature scrawled across the sky marked it unmistakably as—

'*Loki.* I should have known,' growled Thor, grabbing Jolly by the feet.

But Jolly had taken one look at Jormungand and resumed his goblin Aspect. 'That slimy bastard swallered me once,' he said. 'I'm damned if I'm goin' in there again.'

The Thunderer, finding himself disarmed, gave a howl of fury. 'You come back here right *now*,' he roared.

'Or what?' said Jolly, picking his teeth.

'But that's the World *Serpent*,' said Thor plaintively.

'So what if he is? He's on our side.'

As the gods looked on in silence, it became clear that Jolly was right. If being on the side of the gods meant swallowing ephemera, slurping shadows, gobbling dreams, snapping up demons by the shoal with what seemed like insatiable appetite, then the Serpent *was* on their side.

What was more, he had a rider. Almost obscured by runelight, she seemed to be clinging onto his mane, her russet-red signature shining through the miasma. The three wolves they had seen were still at her flanks; and although beside the Serpent these looked no larger than kittens, the gods could see from their signatures that they were no ordinary wolves, but creatures of terrible power and strength. And above them all flew the firebird – a bird unlike any in the Nine Worlds, its trail coloured that eerie rainbow's-end purple that the gods associated with Chaos.

'What in Hel's name is going on?' Thor growled in frustration. 'Isn't that Maddy riding the snake?'

The others squinted at the scene, and finally agreed that it was.

'She's coming this way,' said Freyja. 'I can see her colours now.'

'Thank the gods she's safe,' said Njörd.

Bragi picked up his guitar and strummed a chord of victory.

'*And there shall come a Horse of Fire,*' said Ethel in her quiet voice. '*And the name of his Rider is Carnage. And there shall come a Horse of the Sea – and the name of his Rider is Treachery.*'

'What is this?' said Njörd. 'A prophecy?'

'It's from the Book of Apocalypse.' Ethel, whose role as a parson's wife had sometimes included helping him – in a very unofficial capacity – to prepare his weekly sermons, had more than just a passing knowledge of the contents of the Good Book. 'The Horse of Fire – Red Horse Hill – and now, perhaps, the Horse of the Sea—'

'What? The Serpent?' Freyja said.

'But a serpent isn't a horse—' said Njörd.

'And the Good Book is often inaccurate,' said Ethel in her calm voice. 'But if I'm right, then the End of the Worlds is closer than we imagined. Two of the Riders are already here. We have to face the enemy.'

'I thought that's what we *were* doing,' said Thor.

Ethel shook her head. 'No. This is just a diversion. The final battle takes place in World's End. *In just twelve days, at End of Worlds—*'

'What?' said Thor.

'Where else?' she said. 'That's where Asgard fell, after all. They even built a memorial.'

'The cathedral of Saint Sepulchre.'

For a moment there was silence as the gods considered the End of the Worlds. Sugar in particular felt very apprehensive. In his newly acquired capacity as god of war, he was aware that the prospect of another Ragnarók ought to fill him with enthusiasm. But Sugar-and-Sack had not yet outgrown his previous – and somewhat unimposing – role, and had found the Aspect of Brave-Hearted Tyr unexpectedly hard to assume.

Perhaps, thought Sugar, when Asgard was rebuilt, he would take to Aspect more readily. For now, though, he still found killing rats a challenge, and the thought of a final battle gave him goosebumps all over.

'A Rider whose name is Treachery,' said Thor. 'That has to be Loki, hasn't it?'

'Let's not jump to conclusions, shall we?' said Ethel, still watching the Serpent's approach. He was moving very quickly now, blurring along the Malbry road, and now the gods could *smell* him too, like a stretch of mud-flats in the sun; a salty stink that caught at their throats and made their eyes water. At last he stopped, and Maddy climbed down from where she had been clinging; Maddy with a gash on her head and three enormous wolves at her heels.

'It's all right. Jorgi's on our side,' she said, seeing Thor almost ready to strike.

'What happened?' said Idun, in goddess Aspect. 'Are you all right? Have some apple.'

Idun's apples were legendary – a cure for age and sickness as well as for wounds in battle. She carried supplies wherever she went: the fruit was dried, but still good, and Maddy accepted a small piece, not so much for its healing properties as for the excuse it gave her to be silent a few minutes longer. The thought of lying to her friends was almost too dreadful to contemplate; and even the presence of Jorgi and the wolves now came as a welcome diversion.

Freyja, also in goddess Aspect, pulled out a scented handkerchief (one belonging to Ethel, whose wardrobe was rapidly diminishing) and applied it to her pretty nose. 'He may be an ally,' she remarked, 'but why does he have to smell so *bad?*'

'And what in Hel's name are *they* doing here?' growled Sugar, whose hackles had risen instinctively at the sight of the wolves – who now revealed themselves as Skull, Big H and Fenris, still clad in their customary black, but with the further addition of a large and flashy collection of studded belts, wristbands and silver jewellery (mostly designed around the skull motif), which clearly counted as battle gear.

Fenny looked down at Sugar with contempt. 'Is this what the Æsir have come to?' he said. 'Recruiting noobs to fight their war?'

Sugar-and-Sack growled again. 'Who you callin' a noob?' he said.

Fenny shrugged. 'Bit short, aren't you? I'm surprised you can even hold a sword. Now the *last* god of war . . .'

Skull and Big H exchanged grins.

'*He* was kind of a big guy,' said Skull.

'Yeah. Lots of meat on him, man,' said Big H.

Sugar growled and clenched his fists. Fenny gave his uneven smile and displayed the Wolf Cross on his arm. They might even have come to blows if, at that moment, the firebird had not alighted in front of the gods, resolving itself into the Aspect of Angrboda, the Temptress of Ironwood.

'*You!*' said Freyja with loathing.

'I have to say,' Angie said, 'I expected a *little* more gratitude.'

'Gratitude?' growled Thor.

Angie blew him a kiss. 'I told you you needed me,' she said. 'And my lovely Wolf Boys, of course. Imagine what a mess you'd be in if Jorgi hadn't been here to clean up.'

Thor frowned and narrowed his eyes. The World Serpent, who had retreated after dropping Maddy off, was now coiled companionably around what was left of Red Horse Hill, looking like someone at the end of a very long, very satisfying Yuletide dinner;

full of meat and potatoes, but still able to pick happily at a mince pie, a chocolate, a handful of raisins, some hazelnuts . . .

'You're saying you *weren't* behind all this?' said Thor, with some suspicion.

'Of course not,' said Angie. 'Why should I be? I want my hall in Asgard.'

'Which brings us back to Loki again,' said Thor, glancing up into the sky, where the hawk and the eagle were beginning their descent. 'Well, when I get my hands on him . . .'

'Why blame Loki?' Maddy said.

'Because it's *always* Loki,' said Thor.

Maddy shifted uncomfortably. The Thunderer did have a point. Time after time, when trouble arose, the Trickster was behind it. This time he was innocent, and only she could prove it. After all, this was *her* fault: *she* had woken the Red Horse; *she* had let Maggie take it from her. Of course, if she told the gods the truth, she would have to betray her sister – her twin – and any chance of redeeming Maggie would be lost. Her connection with the Whisperer would damn her for ever in their eyes. Even it if were finally proven that Maggie had been an innocent dupe, the gods would demand vengeance. Maddy imagined her sister chained underground, as Loki had been, or banished into Netherworld. She couldn't let that happen, no. But if she lied to protect her twin, then Loki was sure to take the blame . . .

Before she could fully make up her mind, the white sea-eagle and the small brown hawk had landed on a nearby fence, becoming Heimdall and Loki again.

Sif, catching sight of them, gave a grunt of outrage. 'Oy! Look what the cat dragged in!'

Thor's face took on the expression of one who, long since overtaken by events, finally sees his purpose in life. He lunged forward, and in less than a second Loki was dangling from his fist as all the gods gathered round to watch.

'Nice one,' said the Trickster, thoroughly tired of this by now. 'Nice way to treat the guy who just helped save all your lives.'

His fire-green eyes lit on Maddy, and a look of relief came onto his face. If Maddy was there, he told himself, then she would be able to vouch for him. Whatever her reasons for taking the Horse, she'd never leave a friend in the lurch.

'So— how *did* you save our lives?' said Frey.

'Well, if you'd give me chance to explain – and, by the way, I don't want to sound prudish here, but there *are* ladies present,' said Loki, indicating his state of undress, and adding with a malicious smirk, 'Oh, and Sif and Freyja, of course.'

'Shut up and take this,' said Heimdall, who had already found himself something to wear, and now thrust a bundle of clothes at Loki. With his usual economy of words, the Watchman explained the situation as he saw it to the little group of bewildered gods, while Loki struggled into a borrowed shirt (very much too big for him). Angie looked on with a sweet smile, while Fenny and the demon wolves stood around, grinning and showing their teeth and displaying their muscles and Wolf Cross tattoos.

Big H addressed the Trickster. 'Dude,' he said. 'You look terrible.'

'Friends of yours?' said Heimdall.

Once more Loki began to explain. It wasn't a straightforward explanation. He was just getting to the part where, fearlessly, he had taken bird form to reconnoiter the mountains, when two more birds – two ravens, in fact – alighted on the fence of the Parsonage.

Hughie and Mandy, Maddy thought; but before she could say anything, a sudden and violent commotion broke out.

The Wolf Brothers, all three acting as one, swiftly resumed their Aspects and, with a single giant bound, made for the Parsonage fence. At the same time, the new arrivals took wing, swooping low over the heads of the wolves and *crawk*-ing loudly and impudently. The three wolves howled in frustration as the birds kept safely just out of reach. Fenny snapped at the larger raven, which responded by pecking him on the nose.

'Oh, where did *they* come from?' said Angie crossly.

'Always causing trouble . . .'

Maddy couldn't help smiling at that. From what she'd seen of the Temptress so far, trouble seemed to follow *her*.

'Stop that,' said Angie sharply, addressing the ravens and the wolves. 'We have a truce, remember?'

'A truce?' said Hughie, resuming his human Aspect. 'What, with the mutt?'

Fenris gave Hughie a filthy look while holding his nose with both hands.

Sugar, who had loathed the wolves on sight, fingered his mind-sword and scowled back.

Maddy noticed that Mandy, who had also returned to her human form, was now wearing Fenny's dragon-claw earring. Her bright gold eyes were alive with mischief. She opened her mouth and *crawk*-ed.

Loki blinked at them for a moment, then looked down at himself again. 'You know,' he said, 'I think this may be a lady's shirt.'

'Don't worry,' said Heimdall grimly. 'You won't be needing it for long.' He turned to Maddy. 'Tell me,' he said. 'What exactly happened here?'

Later, Maddy realized that this had been her final chance to confess her role in the day's events. A window of opportunity, and foolishly she had missed it. But hindsight is a false friend, the kind that gets you into trouble, then follows you around looking smug and saying: *See? I told you so.*

If someone else had asked her, then maybe she could have come clean. Kindly Njörd, or Ethel, or Frey, or even Bragi, whose idea of a stern rebuke was to sing at the culprit as loudly as he could. But Heimdall, whose eyes were as hard as tempered steel and just about as forgiving; Heimdall, who saw everything, heard everything, trusted no one, and never slept . . .

'Tell them, Maddy,' Loki said, sensing her hesitation. 'Tell them this was none of my fault. You were there. You saw.'

Maddy looked away.

'*Please . . .*'

Loki addressed the circle of gods. 'Folks, I know how it looks,' he said. 'But this time it's nothing to do with me. I was under the Hill, hanging out, minding my own business, and suddenly

165

– *boom!* – surprise. Ask Maddy. She was there. She must have seen everything.'

Maddy shook her head. 'I'm sorry, Loki, I can't,' she said.

'What do you mean?' said Heimdall.

'I mean I didn't see anything. Nothing but ephemera. But surely you can't think Loki could have had anything to do with *that?'*

'Can't I?' the Watchman said. 'Given that I caught him trying to make a run for it just as things started to get nasty here – a situation for which he stands largely responsible – not to mention the appearance of the World Serpent, the Fenris Wolf – and now Sleipnir. That's *three* of Loki's children so far – at least three that we know about . . .' He turned to Loki. 'So— where's Hel?'

Loki looked bewildered. 'Hel? You know she doesn't leave her domain . . .'

'Not until now,' said Heimdall. 'But with things as they are, why shouldn't she? Maybe she knows how helpless we are. Maybe she's just waiting for someone – someone like *you* – to give the word.'

'That's right,' agreed Freyja spitefully. 'He sets us up with the Temptress. He talks us into a deal with Chaos, he gives Thor a hammer that only works when it feels like it, starts a battle that no one can win, and then, when the two sides are otherwise engaged, he strolls away to collect the loot, leaving the snake in control of the Hill, and the rest of us virtually powerless. Isn't that about right?'

Loki shot Maddy an anguished look. 'Tell them, Maddy. *Please,*' he said.

Once more Maddy looked away.

Heimdall bared his golden teeth and turned to Angrboda. 'Well, Temptress? What do you say?' His voice was low and dangerous.

'Let me remind you,' Angie said, 'that we had an agreement, the gods and I. You swore an oath. To break it now—' She smiled. 'There might be . . . *consequences.*'

Heimdall glared. 'The gods keep their word.'

'Well, that's good,' said Angie, smiling at him. 'The last time a god reneged on a deal was down in Hel, three years ago. And we all know what happened *then*, don't we?'

The gods exchanged glances, their faces grim.

Finally the Watchman spoke. 'You'll get what was promised, Temptress,' he said. 'You'll have your hall in Asgard. But we made no promise regarding Loki, and if he *has* betrayed us—'

'Betrayed you? How?' Angie said.

'Something happened here,' said Thor. 'Something that blew the Hill apart and set free the General's Horse. Loki was there. Loki ran. Loki knows more than he's telling.'

'Besides, there's the Good Book,' Freyja said. 'The Rider's name is *Treachery . . .*'

'Be fair,' said Loki desperately. 'You're quoting a prophecy of the Folk. You know how these things get twisted. For a start, my name is *Trickery*. Not *Treachery*. There's a difference, you know.'

'Not a very big one,' grunted Sif.

'Hardly a difference at all,' said Frey.

'Let me hammer the truth out of him,' said Thor, looking almost cheerful at the thought.

'At last, a practical solution,' said Frey. He turned for support to the god of war, who affected to be looking at something else. Sugar was still mostly goblin, and the prospect of laying violent hands on the Captain was practically unthinkable.

'I don't think we need to go *that* far,' said Njörd, 'but I would welcome some answers.'

'I agree,' said Bragi. 'I vote we keep an eye on him until we know what's happening.'

Loki gave his twisted smile. 'By *keep an eye on him*,' he said, 'I'm assuming that what you really mean is *clap him in irons and lock him away until we can prove he's guilty?*'

'Precisely,' said Thor, moving forward again.

'I thought so,' said Loki.

And with that, he assumed his Wildfire Aspect and shot across the courtyard in a lightning trail of flames. Of course, the gods were expecting it; but in the wake of the recent battle, glam was low and reflexes dulled. A dozen mindbolts shot across the yard, but none of them hit Loki, who, zigzagging round the Parsonage, had leaped through the half-open window, ricocheted off the kitchen stove, ended up in the fireplace and vanished in a cloud of sparks before anyone could catch him.

As far as the gods were concerned, this proved his guilt conclusively. Maddy Smith knew better, of course, but couldn't afford to take his side. Not against Maggie, her longed-for twin; Maggie, whose motives were still unclear, but who, she was certain, needed her help.

Loki could look after himself – after all, he had a long history of getting himself out of trouble. And if it came to a choice, well—

A Horse of the Sea, she thought ruefully. And a Rider whose name is Treachery . . .

Treachery it is, then, she told herself with an inward sigh, and, without waiting for further developments, she left the gods to their debate and set off again towards the Hill, where the Black Horse of the Last Days was waiting to take her to World's End.

6

ADAM SCATTERGOOD STARED AT THE Horse that Maggie
had brought with her out of Dream. Her communion with his
passenger had left him, for the first time in three years, without
its presence in his mind, and although the interval of separation
had lasted only minutes, it had made him feel terribly vulnerable,
as if all the knowledge he had acquired had been suddenly and
brutally stripped away, leaving him directionless, defenceless,
ignorant and . . .

Free?

The thought was a revelation. That he could be free, really free,
had never before crossed his mind. It began as a tremor in his
spine, spread to the pit of his stomach and leaped like wildfire into
his brain, filling him with equal parts of terror and excitement.

His head spun, his throat was dry; for a moment he felt as if he
might be having a seizure. In three long years of slavery, of serving his passenger's every whim, of living in fear of what it might
do if Adam dared to displease it, the thought of simply walking
away had never before occurred to him.

I could be free, thought Adam; and all at once he saw himself
laying aside his pack and his sword; forgetting his dreams of
destiny – which were not quite *his* dreams, he understood, but
those of the presence that had inhabited him for so long that, until
now, he had been unable to tell where he ended and his passenger

began. *I could walk away*, Adam thought, and the terrible tremor intensified. *I could do it right now!*

Whether or not he would have dared remains a matter for speculation. Could he really just have gone home, put aside his destiny and gone back to being Adam Scattergood: running the Seven Sleepers Inn; keeping in with the neighbours; marrying young, like his father; growing fat, like his mother; going to church every Sunday and trying his hardest to forget that he could have been magnificent? Or would there have been a part of him that rebelled against the ordinary? And Maddy, who had been in his thoughts almost constantly for so long – could he really have let her go?

In any case, there was no time to think. The tremor had barely a moment to plant its beguiling fishhooks in his mind when his passenger came hurtling back with such force that it knocked Adam to the floor and pinned him there, bruised and shaking and terrified, as the thing that had once been Mimir the Wise flung itself back into place in his mind like a petulant house-guest into a much-used armchair.

Thinking of his treachery, Adam began to whimper. The Nameless could be cruel, and it knew how to punish rebellion. But today it was preoccupied. Adam sensed at the same time a wild and frenzied excitement, and an ecstasy of rage that surpassed anything he had encountered since that day on the shores of Dream, when the two of them had first become one.

How dare she? How DARE she refuse Me? it screamed.

Adam glanced at Maggie, who was watching him with some concern.

'Adam? Are you all right?' she said. He didn't look it, Maggie thought. She could see him shivering. 'Adam? Please? What happened?'

'It's nothing,' said Adam. 'It's over now.' He sat up. 'Tell me what happened.'

Sitting beside him on the bed, Maggie recounted her journey through Dream, from Red Horse Hill to her flight through the clouds, to the whispering, guiding Voice, which she had driven from her mind when it had tried to control her.

Adam's blue eyes widened. 'You did?'

Maggie nodded. 'In my dream. But it wasn't really a dream, was it?' she said, with a glance at the roan Horse.

'Dream is a river that runs through Nine Worlds,' said Adam, who needed no prompting on this. 'It's a dangerous place, and just as real as anywhere else. More so, perhaps, because in Dream you can see things as they really are, stripped of all their disguises.'

'Disguises?' said Maggie.

He looked at the Horse. 'Well, I'm guessing it looks different to the way it did when you were in Dream.'

'But why is it here?' Maggie said. 'And whose was the Voice? And who was that girl? And why does she look exactly like me?'

The passenger spoke in Adam's mind. *Tell her you can't discuss it now. Tell her there's something you need her to do. Tell her it's very important. And for gods' sakes, tell her to stop asking questions!*

But Maggie was looking at Adam through the circle of finger and thumb. Her friend looked feverish, she thought, sick and anxious and afraid; and every time she spoke to him, he put his head briefly to one side, as if awaiting instructions before answering her, or as if he were listening to a voice that only he could hear.

She remembered what the girl from the North had told her about the Voice in her head. What had she called it? The Whisperer? And could it be that Adam heard it too?

She focused on the rune *Bjarkán*, searching Adam's colours. And then she saw it – an alien strand of runelight in his signature. Adam flinched; his colours flared – and that was when Maggie was certain. Someone else was watching her, a silent, ghostly onlooker . . .

She banished the rune. 'Magister?' she said. 'No need to hide. I know you're there.'

In Adam's mind, his passenger writhed and spat like a pit of snakes.

Adam, with a tremendous effort, forced himself to stay calm. 'I have no idea what you're talking about—'

'Don't lie to me, Magister. You tried to take control of my mind. You tried to make me obey you. That girl on the Hill – she said you would. She said you were the enemy.'

'No,' said Adam. 'That isn't true.'

'Then what *are* you?' Maggie said. 'And why won't you tell me what's going on?'

'*I will,*' it replied in Adam's voice. '*But first I need your obedience.*'

Adam, mouthing his passenger's words, could feel the intensity of its rage. He sensed that it was on the verge of some colossal eruption:

How dare she question ME!

He flinched. Maggie found herself strangely touched. When Adam had first come to her in the labyrinth under the Universal City, she had thought him rather arrogant. After that she had been slightly in awe of this young man who knew so much. But now that she saw his true colours at last, she felt a peculiar tenderness. He was only human, she thought; and the thing that called itself Magister had him in its power.

'I want you to let my friend go,' she said.

'Maggie, don't,' said Adam.

'Let him go,' she repeated. '*Then* we can talk.'

Adam was sweating now. 'Please,' he said. 'You don't know what you're dealing with. It saved my life in the Underworld. Now it tells me what to do. It knows what I'm thinking. Mercy, *please* . . .' He whimpered and fell to his knees.

'What's wrong?' Maggie said.

In Adam's voice, the Magister said: '*This is your doing, Maggie Rede. I don't enjoy inflicting pain.*'

Adam began to flail and scream, clawing at the floor with his hands. 'Please! Maggie! Make it stop!'

'Leave my friend alone,' she said.

'*Not before you agree to My terms.*'

'What terms?'

'*All of them.*'

Maggie put her hand to her mouth. She realized that she was trembling. 'Don't,' she said. 'I'll do what you want. I swear I will.'

'Swear on your true name?'

'Yes! Yes!'

At once, the presence in Adam's mind released its hold on him. The young man crawled to his knees and retched. Maggie's throat was pinprick-tight. She'd never felt such terror before. She never wanted to feel it again.

What's happening to me? she thought. *What is this treacherous weakness?*

'I didn't want to do that,' said the Magister in Adam's voice. *'But both of you needed a lesson, and our time is growing short.'*

Adam looked at Maggie. 'Thank you,' he whispered, and took her hand.

For a moment Maggie held it, not quite knowing what to feel. Alone and loveless for so many years, that simple human contact felt strange and exotic – and thrilling. She wondered what it would be like to kiss Adam, and found herself flushing wildly.

'Has it gone?' she said at last.

'It never really goes away,' said Adam. 'But I think we're all right to talk.'

This wasn't quite a lie – he knew that if he deceived her, she would see it in his colours – but it wasn't quite the whole truth. In fact, he could still hear his passenger, its small, sly Voice inside his mind, and he knew that if he made a mistake, retribution would follow.

'You wanted answers, Maggie,' he said. 'Are you sure you're ready?'

She nodded.

'All right. I'll tell you everything. Then, if you still don't trust me—'

'I trust *you*,' Maggie said. 'It's your Magister I don't trust.'

Adam looked uncomfortable. 'I hope I can change your mind about that. I need you, Maggie . . .'

Maggie smiled. It felt very strange to wear such a smile, like trying on some unaccustomed item of clothing. She remembered her feeling of disgust when Adam had found the glam on her neck; her reluctance to take off her *bergha* in front of a man who was not one of her family. Now those feelings seemed childish, absurd. What was there to be afraid of?

As a child she had seen her parents die and her world dissolve into Chaos. If she'd known then what she knew now, she might have been able to save them – to help them – or at least fight back. But now things would be different. Now she had *glam* – that mysterious fire that made common people into gods. Better still, she had a friend. Someone who listened. Someone who *cared*.

Maggie had dreamed of healing World's End, of Cleansing a city in anarchy. Now her dream had grown smaller, somehow; smaller, yet more significant. Lost libraries, scally traders, the breakdown of Law and Order – even her desire for vengeance against the agents of Chaos – all had suddenly given way to a deeper, more powerful kind of desire.

Maggie had no name for it. She barely even knew it was there. All she knew was that something had changed; some lever had been pulled or pushed, setting in motion a mechanism that had never been used before. And as another small piece of an intricate trap tumbled slowly into place, Adam Goodwin grinned to himself, while the Red Horse of the Last Days started to munch on the silk tassels of the bedspread and, for the first time in five hundred years, Mimir the Wise was satisfied.

7

As MADDY APPROACHED THE REMAINS of the Hill, she found that, to her surprise, all was calm. The aftermath of the battle had left little in the way of debris, as most of the casualties had been of the ephemeral kind, and had fled back into World Below, or vanished into nothingness. The few, mostly harmless, remaining creatures that had escaped the World Serpent's appetite were scattered across the wintry fields: a unicorn; a goblin or two; a cluster of baby dragons borne like dandelion seeds on the air.

And all around the toppled Hill lay a blanket of pale, bright mist; no ordinary cloudbank, but something that welled up from World Below and flooded the flatlands around the Hill in a way that Maddy recognized . . .

The river Dream, she thought; much of its power spent now; the force of its eruption quelled, dispersing its vapours at leisure. All the same, she approached it with care, knowing the potency of Dream, unsure of what might still be hidden away beneath the shroud of white mist.

'Jormungand?' she called at last.

The World Serpent, gorged on Dream, seemed reluctant to respond.

Raising her voice, she tried again, not wanting to enter the bank of mist. But the vapour dampened everything; and the dream-shapes that she'd seen at the start – that menagerie of Outlandish creatures – had dwindled to almost nothing. Only the ghostly mist remained, a residue of the battle, perhaps, and on the ground a kind of ash, interspersed with nuggets of slag, like cinders from a blacksmith's forge.

The cloud was right in front of her now. Maddy could see a wavering line, like the tide-line on a beach, which marked the boundary of Dream.

'Jormungand?' she repeated.

There came a rumbling from the dreamcloud. Maddy cast the rune *Yr* and took a step forward into Dream. Nothing happened. She took another step. The mist was cold, and disturbing in a way that Maddy could not quite explain. She – who had witnessed Netherworld in all its bewildering multiplicity, who had looked Half-Born Hel in the eye and had walked the road to the Underworld all hedged around by the souls of the dead – found herself shivering with fear at nothing more than a bank of cloud.

But as she moved further into Dream, she began to see what was happening. What she had assumed was just cloud was something far more sinister: it seemed to Maddy almost as if the air, the trees, the rocks, the ground – the whole fabric of reality was slowly dissolving around her, unravelling into the dreamcloud like a piece of knitting, reducing to its component parts.

As she watched, a brown rat crawling over a piece of rock slowed down, grew dim and then *popped* out of existence before her eyes, leaving just a smear in the air to indicate where it had been. The rock itself soon followed suit, and she realized that the ash at her feet was the residue of this process, a gradual dissolution of everything within the cloud. How long would it take for a human being? And what did this mean for the valley itself?

Once more she called for Jormungand. This time the Serpent heard her. There came a fearsome rumbling from the blasted remains of the Hill, and the glutinous head of the World Serpent emerged from the broken ground like a mighty earthworm scenting the rain, and levelled his gaze on Maddy.

'Listen,' she said. 'I was wondering if you could help me.'

Jormungand simply gaped at her in a way that redefined apathy.

Maddy tried a more forceful approach. 'I need to get to the Universal City,' she said. 'I mean – I need *you* to take me.'

The Serpent gave a colossal yawn. His breath was foul enough, Maddy thought, to stop any number of ephemera. For a moment she thought of giving up and actually *walking* to the Universal City. But if she was to find Maggie Rede before Heimdall and the other gods learned of her existence, she had to get there straight away – which meant travelling through Dream, of course – and, failing Sleipnir, Maddy thought, Jormungand would have to do.

'So – will you take me?'

A long pause, in which the Serpent looked just as bovine as ever.

Maddy gave an impatient sigh. 'I wish I could tell if you understood. Don't you have a human form?'

'He does,' said a voice from behind her, 'but this is by far his most appealing Aspect.'

'Loki,' said Maddy, without turning round.

'Oh, so you *do* remember me,' said Loki in a casual voice. 'Call me paranoid if you like, but after your *spectacularly* loyal defence of me back there, I wondered if I'd done something wrong.'

'Have you?' said Maddy.

'No. Have *you*?'

Maddy turned to look at him. He'd assumed his original Aspect – easy to do in Dream, of course – and was watching her from a cautious distance, his green eyes bright with malice. In Dream, she saw, as in Netherworld, his runemark was no longer reversed, and his colours shone more violently than they ever had in World Above.

'Listen – I'm sorry about that,' she said.

'That's all right, then.' Loki's scarred lips twisted in a dangerous smile. 'Because here I was thinking, for some reason, that *you* were the one who'd opened the Hill, taken Odin's Red Horse and let half the Underworld escape in the process, and were even now preparing to take off in secret with Jorgi, leaving Yours Truly to take the rap – and we're not talking a rap on the knuckles here, but something *much* more permanent – without so much as an explanation.'

Maddy cast the rune *Bjarkán* and shot a quick glance at Loki. That casual approach, she knew, was simply a ploy to take her off-guard, and as soon as he saw a chance to attack, he would try to tackle her. She could see it in his colours now – an acid-green thread of malevolence combined with the red of his anger – in this case, perfectly justified.

'If that's what you thought,' she said, 'then why didn't you tell the others?'

He shrugged. 'You think they would have believed me? I'm hardly the most popular guy in the Middle Worlds right now.' He narrowed his eyes at Maddy and smiled. 'Anyway, I was curious. Whatever reason you might have had for freeing the Red Horse from under the Hill, it must have been something important.'

Maddy gave him a sharp look. 'You think I knew the Horse was there?'

'Oh, *please,*' said Loki impatiently. 'Don't play the innocent with me. Remember, I know Red Horse Hill. I know every crack and crevice. You think I never suspected that something big was buried here?'

'The Whisperer . . .' Maddy began.

'That's what everyone assumed,' said Loki, with his disarming smile. 'But Mimir was never the main prize. Odin was planning to use him to get the gods back on his side before revealing his master plan.'

'What plan?' said Maddy.

'War with Chaos,' Loki said. 'The End of the World. Asgard reclaimed. It's all there, in the Good Book; with the Horse whose Rider is Carnage. Carnage. *Grim,* in the language of the Elder Age. And did you know – by some freak coincidence – that happens to be one of Odin's names?'

Silently Maddy shook her head.

'But the Whisperer betrayed him,' Loki went on implacably. 'You went off to Netherworld; he was blinded; the gods turned against him. He had to reassess his plan. Even so, it nearly worked; but without the Horse it was futile. He fell. We all thought he was gone. Then, suddenly, I wasn't so sure. Strange things began to happen. Like Angie cutting a deal with the gods, and giving Thor back his hammer. And then this business with the Hill. And if those weren't Odin's ravens back there, then I may just have to resign my position as Asgard's most brilliant exile.'

'What are you getting at?' Maddy said.

'The General survived, didn't he?' Loki's eyes blazed fire-green. 'He managed to escape somehow, and he doesn't want the others to know. That's fine. I'm cool with that. I mean, he must have his reasons. And if he's working with Chaos now – well, I totally understand. It wouldn't be the first time.'

'Odin would never do that!' Maddy said.

'Sorry,' said Loki. 'My mistake.'

'I mean it,' said Maddy angrily. 'Odin would *never* do that. I can't explain his plan right now, but betraying the gods isn't part of it.'

'OK. I'm sorry. Forget I spoke. So – he *does* have a plan, then?'

Maddy eyed him suspiciously. 'What do you want, Loki?' she said.

Loki shrugged. 'Same as always. Let me go with you to World's End. That's where it's going to begin, right? The war between Order and Chaos? I don't know why you're keeping so dark, or what you think you can do alone, but if the General *did* survive, then I know he'd want me to help you.'

Help me? *Help yourself, more like.* Maddy thought she understood. Loki, as always, was hedging his bets. Out of favour with the gods, he thought to gain Odin's protection, or at least to put some distance between himself and the carnage at Red Horse Hill. She might even have succumbed to his charm – alone and uncertain as she was – but for the thought of Maggie Rede. Loki, she knew, had no scruples at all, and if he found out about Maggie, he would not hesitate to use the information to restore his status amongst the gods – or, worse, to bargain with Chaos.

Maddy hated to leave him this way, but she simply couldn't take the risk of exposing her sister to further threat. And so she turned to Loki and smiled, and hoped that he would understand.

'Look, I'm really sorry,' she said. 'I promise I'll tell you everything. But first I have to do *this*—'

And with these words she summoned all her considerable glam and flung it at him as hard as she could. Just to slow him down as she fled – Loki in Aspect was no pushover, even for her – but the glam she chose instinctively from all those at her command happened to be the new rune she'd snagged that morning from her ghostly visitor.

For a second the rune *Ác* burned silvery white at her fingertips, then, without any further encouragement, swiftly merged with her own rune, *Aesk*. She felt rather than heard the *click* as the two runes locked together, then a mindbolt shot from her open hand, knocking Loki off his feet; then slammed him hard against the ground some fifty yards away from her.

At first she was afraid he was dead. But, narrowing her eyes, Maddy saw that his signature was there, although its potency was dimmed.

She considered the glam she had flung at him. It looked like an ordinary combination rune – *Ác*, the Thunder Oak—

—crossed with *Aesk*, the Lightning Ash—

—but in this case, dearly, *Ác* and *Aesk* had come together to make up something far more powerful—

— a glam that had knocked the Trickster out cold (and in his most powerful Aspect, no less) as effortlessly as swatting a fly.

Once Maddy had determined that Loki wasn't faking it – that he really *was* unconscious – she found herself faced with the awkward choice between leaving him there at the mercy of Dream, or dragging him into the open, where his signature would instantly betray his location to Heimdall and his people.

She opted for the second choice, hoping that Loki would understand. The gods would be furious at his escapade, and would probably give him a hard time, but he'd talked his way out of worse things before, and Maddy was certain that he would cope.

As for his suggestion that Odin might have turned his coat and struck a deal with the enemy, she dismissed it with a shake of her head. Odin might be devious – sometimes even dishonest – but he would never betray the gods. She had no choice but to follow her heart and go off in search of her sister, and hope that her search for Maggie would lead her to the Old Man.

She left the unconscious Trickster just outside the dreamcloud and ran back to the Horse's Eye, where Jormungand, stirred by his father's defeat, was showing signs of excitement – shaking his mane and hissing and generally giving the impression of a Serpent ready for anything.

Maddy gave him a wary look. 'We're on the same side, right?' she said.

Jormungand made a horribly puppyish sound.

'And you know where I have to go? Right?'

Jormungand almost frolicked.

'And when we get there, you'll behave yourself? You promise you won't eat anyone? I mean it. That would be *bad,*' she said.

Jormungand gave a half-shrug and slowly began to uncoil himself. Maddy took a double handful of the World Serpent's mane and hauled herself into position. *I hope you know what you're doing,* she thought.

And they lurched off into the heart of Dream.

8

LOKI WOKE UP WITH A HEADACHE. Not so much a headache, in fact, as a pain that began at the top of his head and extended as far as his body could reach. Even his hair hurt – which, on second thoughts, he decided wasn't all that surprising, given that someone was using it to yank him briskly to his feet.

Thor seemed the likeliest guess – though to be fair, the Trickster thought, it might just as easily be Heimdall. Or Frey. Or Njörd. Or even Angie. If she had been anywhere nearby, his best guess would have been Skadi of the Ice Folk, otherwise known as the Snowshoe Queen, the Huntress, and the Snow Wolf.

Fortunately, he told himself, Skadi was out of the picture for good. In the weeks preceding Ragnarók it had been she who'd had him chained to a rock with a snake spitting poison into his face, and the last time they'd met she'd come very close to bringing him down with her runewhip.

He blinked against the harsh light – the sun had finally risen above the mist that spilled from World Below, and its dazzle on the fallen snow was enough to blind him briefly.

He tried to recall what had happened.

For a moment he couldn't remember anything. Then it began to come back: Maddy, the dreamcloud, Jormungand – and the image burned onto his retinas of a glam he'd never seen before—

He would have liked to give all this more thought. But the present situation, he knew, demanded his full attention. Once more, cautious, he opened his eyes. At first there was too much light for him to see anything; and then things started to swim into place: the mist, the snow, the brilliant sky, a pair of luminous golden eyes peering at him from under a tangle of raven-black hair.

Loki blinked at the golden eyes, trying to read their expression.

Crawk, said Mandy.

'Ach, you're awake,' said Hughie, stepping into view.

'What happened?' said Loki, trying in vain to get free of the hand that was fastened in his hair.

'We thought maybe ye'd like tae tell us that,' said Hughie with a cheery grin. 'We found ye, passed out, by Red Horse Hill, surrounded by broken bits of glam.'

'Maddy,' said Loki. 'She caught me off-guard. And she has the World Serpent with her.'

Crawk, said Mandy.

Hughie grinned. 'Did she mention where she was heading at all?'

'She mentioned World's End.'

'World's End? Are you sure?' This new voice came from behind him. The hand seemed to clench more painfully. 'If you're lying, Dogstar . . .'

The Trickster stiffened. He knew that voice. He finally managed to free himself and turned to face its owner, and felt all the strength go out of his legs as he found himself looking at a familiar pair of ice-blue eyes and a smile like a cut-throat razor.

'Oh, *crap* . . .' Loki said.

'Hello again,' said Skadi.

9

MEANWHILE, ON DREAM'S THOROUGHFARE, Maddy had
decided that *any* other form of travel had to be preferable to this.
Certainly it was the *fastest* way; but moving down through Dream
at a speed she had once thought unimaginable, clutching at the
Serpent's mane with hands that had lost all sensation, trying not
to look at the *things* that lurched and clawed and snatched at her as
she and Jorgi hurtled down the sickening series of whirlpools and
falls that made up the boundaries between the Worlds, Maddy
began to realize that her jaunt through the Black Fortress of Netherworld had been nothing compared to this.

There were pockets of ephemera like deadly bursts of fireworks;
there were clouds of flesh-eating parasites and rains of knives and
geysers of flame. And then there were the dead, of course: a slew
of cold and hungry jetsam, bodiless fingers clutching at her, whispering voices pleading to her.

Help us, Maddy. Help us live . . .

It lasted only minutes, although when she emerged from
Dream, Maddy felt as if she had been travelling for half her life.
She opened her eyes into darkness; and for a moment almost believed that this had all been a *real* dream, and that she was still in
her bed at home, and that none of this had happened.

But there were no bedclothes around her, and the place had a
resonant sound – and a serpent-stench that Maddy knew only too

well. No. This was no dream. This, she thought, must be World's End.

She cast the rune *Sól*, and found herself in some kind of underground storeroom, the roof of which had partially collapsed under the weight of Jormungand, who had come to rest on the floor above with his head lolling happily in World's End and the rest of him hidden in World Below.

'I told you to look *inconspicuous*,' Maddy hissed reproachfully, and was surprised to see the Serpent's head begin to change its Aspect, becoming a large and shaggy black horse with a tail so long that it brushed the floor. It wasn't an especially handsome beast, and its breath did smell suspiciously carnivorous, but it would do, Maddy thought – at least until she had found Maggie.

She patted the black horse cautiously. 'That's much better, thank you,' she said. 'Now. Let's see where you've brought me.'

10

'You look surprised,' the Huntress said.

'Well, I'm not exactly at my best,' said Loki, rubbing his sore head. 'Besides, I was under the impression that you'd gone back to your people.'

'I did, at first,' said Skadi, fingering her runewhip. 'That is, until the rumours began. Rumours of mischief under the Hill. And a Rider whose name is Treachery.'

'And so you assumed I was to blame. Well, have *I* got news for you, folks—'

'Shut up, Dogstar,' Skadi said. 'You're not here to argue your innocence. If I had my way right now, you'd be chained to a rock in Netherworld with poisonous snakes for company. That could still happen if you mess me around.'

Loki gave her a cautious look. 'I'll try not to mess you around,' he said. 'So – where am I, and what do you want?'

Skadi gave him a cold look. 'You're near the Seven Sleepers,' she said. 'There's a cave about a hundred yards back that leads into the mountainside. It's dry enough, and there's water nearby. I think you'll be fairly comfortable. Of course, you'll have to stay hidden,' she went on. 'Otherwise they'll track you down. And given the feeling towards you right now, I wouldn't rate your chances. A Rider whose name is Treachery – who else could it be but the Trickster?'

Loki nodded. 'OK,' he said. His mind was working furiously. Could the Huntress be trying to help? It seemed improbable, somehow. And why were Odin's ravens with her? Had the General really survived? Or was this the prelude to something else – some form of interrogation?

Almost imperceptibly, Loki started to reach for his glam.

Crawk, said Mandy accusingly.

Skadi raised her runewhip. Its coils slithered across the snow like cables of electricity. 'I'm warning you,' she said through clenched teeth. 'It's bad enough having to save your life, but try that again and it's going to hurt.'

'OK.' Loki spread his hands.

'Verra wise,' Hughie said. 'Mandy doesn't talk a lot, but she can see across Nine Worlds.'

'See *this* . . .?' Loki made an obscene hand gesture. Then he turned back to the Huntress. 'So – forgive my mistrustful nature, but . . . why would you want to save my life? It's not like we're the best of friends.'

'You got *that* right,' said Skadi. 'But Balder wanted you to live, and I guess he had his reasons. As for the General, wherever he is—'

Mandy *crawk*-ed.

Skadi paused. Beside her, Odin's Spirit and Mind levelled twin pairs of golden eyes at the renegade Trickster.

'*Oh,*' said Loki. 'It's like that, is it?' His scarred lips twitched appreciatively. 'Listen, if Odin's alive somewhere, if *that's* why you're protecting me, then why not bring me in on it? I can totally see why you might not want the Vanir to know – but I'm his *brother*, for gods' sakes, and if he's planning to make a deal—'

'What kind of a deal?'

Loki shrugged. 'Damned if I know. But someone's pulling strings all right. The Red Horse is loose, the Black Horse is free – now all we need is the Horse of Air, and it's all aboard the Faërie bus for Ragnarók!'

Skadi gave him a scornful look. 'Got it all worked out, haven't you?'

'Well, it wasn't difficult.' Loki grinned. 'Maybe the General survived. Maybe he wants to take charge. But the balance of power has changed in three years: Heimdall's made an alliance with Chaos, and suddenly Odin isn't sure how many real friends he has left. So he does a bit of recruiting by stealth. It doesn't take much to get Maddy on side. But as for Yours Truly – I understand. We've had our differences in the past. But you can tell him, Skadi – I've changed. I'm on the side of Order now.'

Skadi's eyes gleamed ice-blue. 'Well, maybe that's the problem,' she said. 'Changing sides is your speciality. So what we're going to do is this. We're putting someone in charge of you. Someone to keep you on the right track. Someone to make sure you *don't* change sides.'

That sounded ominous, Loki thought. 'You don't think I'd rat on the General?'

'You did before, at Ragnarók.'

Loki shrugged. He could have explained the reasons for his defection. He'd spent the months before Ragnarók chained to a boulder in World Below, friendless and abandoned, with a snake dripping venom into his face (courtesy of Skadi, of course). Only his faithful wife, Sigyn, had stayed, collecting the poison droplets – and to be honest, Loki thought, the snake had been better company. There was something about total loyalty, uncritical devotion, endless patience, perpetual forgiveness and the general inability to believe that a loved one could ever do *anything* wrong that, frankly, just gave him the creeps.

A horrible thought occurred to him. 'Please. You don't have to lock me up. I'm *not* the second Rider. I swear. I mean – would *I* ride a giant snake?'

Skadi gave him a chilly smile. 'Begetter of Serpents? Father of Lies?'

'*That* hurt my feelings,' Loki said.

'Well, count yourself lucky that's all that got hurt. And she won't be your gaoler or anything. Think of her more as a guardian. Someone to watch over you.'

'She?' said Loki.

'Can't you guess?'

Loki went pale. 'Oh no. She *died* . . .'

Skadi smiled. 'You opened Hel. You let a whole bunch of dead people loose.'

'But the odds of getting anyone out . . .'

'I guess you must just be lucky,' she said.

And now the Huntress stepped aside to make way for a new-comer, and all the remaining colour fled from Loki's signature and from his face.

To a casual observer it might have been hard to determine why; for the short, round-faced woman who approached looked as inoffensive as one of the Folk. Her hair was brown and sensibly tied back; her dress was plain and practical. Her eyes were her best feature, being large and blue and soulful, and were at present fixed adoringly on the Trickster.

'Well, aren't you going to say anything?'

Loki stared at his ex-wife. His *late* ex-wife, he amended. His late, *unlamented* ex-wife – tenacious as a bloodhound; stubborn as a sunstruck mule; jealous as a housecat; crazy as a box of frogs.

He'd thought that seeing Angie again had been a stroke of ill-luck. But to be reunited with *two* ex-partners in the same week – not to mention Fenny and Jormungand – felt like persecution.

He closed his eyes. 'Gods, this is Hel.'

'*What* did you, say?'

'I said – I *said* . . . hello, Sig.'

Sigyn responded with a squeal and flung herself at Loki. 'I *knew* you'd be happy to see me!' she said. 'I've missed you so much – oh, *sweetheart*. Have you missed me? I *know* you have – and now we can be *together* again!'

Loki was trying as best he could to fend off the barrage of kisses. 'Great. Yeah. Thanks, Sig.'

She hadn't changed at all, he thought, half smothered in her scented embrace. Still as needy; still as sweet; still mad as a fish beneath that smile – and what was that mark on the back of her

hand? It *looked* like a runemark, Loki thought, though Sigyn had
never had one before—

'Where did you get *that*?' he said. 'And what in Hel's name is it?'

'Hel's name is right,' Skadi said. 'We've called it *Eh*, the Wedlock. Another rune of the New Script.'

But now Sigyn released her embrace and peered at Loki crit-
ically. 'You look *awful*,' she remarked. 'Hasn't that nasty Angie
person been looking after you at *all*? Hasn't she been *feeding*
you?'

'Sigyn, I'm fine,' Loki said.

Sigyn eyed him narrowly. 'So. She's still around, then? You've
seen her?'

'Well . . .' said Loki.

'It doesn't matter. Really. I know. I bet you've been seeing her all
this time. You *have* been seeing her, haven't you? After everything
I've done for you. You lying, cheating little *rat*!' And she dealt the
Trickster a ringing slap.

'But you were dead—' he protested.

Sigyn slapped him again. 'I see. That's your *excuse*, is it?' she
said. 'Just because I was *dead*, you thought you'd hook up with
that *floozy* again!'

Skadi hid a little smile. 'Men are so easily seduced. You have to
watch them all the time.'

'Oh, I plan to,' Sigyn said, and, raising her hand, she fingered a
sign that gilded the air with runelight. At the same time something
appeared around Loki's left wrist; something that looked like a
fine gold chain.

'What's that?' said the Trickster.

Sigyn spoke a cantrip – *Eh byth for eorlum* – and a similar glam
appeared around her own right wrist, linking them together.

Loki said: 'Please, don't do this.'

Skadi shrugged. 'It's for your own good. Or would you prefer
that rock in Netherworld?'

Sigyn's blue eyes lit up at that. 'Do you know, that might be *safer* . . .' she said. 'I'd be only too happy to stay with him there. I'd bring him his meals, and sing to him, and hold a basin over his face so the horrid snake couldn't hurt him—'

'What snake?' said Loki.

'Well, there'd *have* to be a snake, dear,' said Sigyn in a reasonable voice. 'You know, just like the old days. Just you and me – and the snake, of course.'

'I don't think that will be necessary,' said Skadi, interrupting her. Between them, *Eh*, the Wedlock, gleamed and crackled with runelight. 'Loki, don't try to escape,' she said. 'Sigyn – just take care of him.'

Sigyn gave a radiant smile. 'Oh, I will. I *promise*,' she said. 'I'll take *such* good care of him.' She turned to Loki. 'Are you hungry, sweetheart? I've got tea and cake in the cave.'

'*Tea? Cake?*' Loki said.

Kindly, Sigyn patted his hand. 'What? Did you think I was going to starve you to death? And then we can have a lovely talk. Now that I have you all to myself—'

'No – wait!' Loki said, seeing the Huntress turn away.

But Skadi just ignored him, resuming her favourite Aspect. In the form of a white snow wolf she padded away across the snow, while above her, Odin's Spirit and Mind took off into the sparkling air.

Tight-lipped, Loki watched them go. He'd been a prisoner many times – in dungeons, in Netherworld, under the Hill, in the lair of the Tunnel Folk, in the caves of the Ice People – but never before had he felt his imprisonment so keenly. The golden chain around his wrist was gossamer-thin but unbreakable, restricting his movements, though otherwise deceptively easy to overlook – except for the presence of Sigyn, the embodiment of constancy, never more than a few feet away, her eyes fixed adoringly on him.

Loki shivered. This was bad – worse even than Netherworld. At least in the Black Fortress he'd been able to scream. Here, he couldn't even do that. Instead he had to be *nice*, drink tea, make small-talk with his late ex-wife. Around his wrist, the Wedlock gleamed and glimmered pitilessly, binding the Trickster to his fate once more until the End of the Worlds; shackled with the bonds of love.

11

'In the beginning there was the Word. And the Word created Nine Worlds, from Firmament to World Beyond. And the Nameless ruled over everything, keeping Order and Chaos in place, enforcing the Laws of the Universe.

'Now in those days the Firefolk were always at war with the Ice Folk, and they wanted to possess the Word, to defeat their enemies for good. So they sent one of their people to bargain with the Nameless. This was Odin, son of Bór, and he spoke of building a citadel to protect the Worlds from Chaos. But the Nameless did not trust him, and wanted proof of his good faith. So Odin offered a sacrifice – one of his eyes in exchange for the Word, and a promise to keep Order. The Nameless agreed, and the Seer-folk were born, and they built the Bridge that spanned the Worlds and started to build their citadel.'

Now that Sleipnir had been relocated (not without some difficulty) to the stables, Adam felt much more comfortable. A bribe to the domestic staff meant that Maggie's occasional eruptions of glam could easily be overlooked; but the sudden appearance of a horse in a luxury penthouse suite above Examiners' Walk would certainly have attracted the wrong sort of attention.

Now, at last, Adam told his tale, while Maggie listened keenly. It was a story that she knew well, having read many different versions of it. Still she listened eagerly.

'How could they build such a thing?' she said, when Adam paused to take a breath. 'I mean, it was up in the sky, wasn't it? How did they get it to stay up there?'

'It's complicated,' Adam said. (In fact, he had no idea himself.)

Maggie looked expectant. 'Well?'

Inside Adam's mind, his passenger sighed. *Nothing comes out of nothing*, it said, and Adam echoed obediently: 'What do you do when you're building a house? The first thing is to cut down trees. Creation works through destruction. Well – the Word behaves in the same way. It breaks down the blocks of creation and shapes them to its purpose. Dream becomes reality. Reality helps fashion Dream. That's why the Word is so dangerous. That's where the Nameless made its mistake.'

Maggie stared at Adam, wide-eyed. Nowhere in the Good Book had she ever seen a reference to the Nameless making a *mistake* – or even a suggestion that such a thing was possible. It sounded almost like blasphemy. But by now she trusted Adam rather more than she did the Good Book, and her eyes simply opened wider.

'A mistake?' she said.

'Oh yes.' Adam smiled. 'Even the Nameless makes mistakes. And Odin was a plausible rogue, and he seemed to be on the side of Order. It was only much later that it became clear that Odin had allies on *both* sides – including a traitor from Chaos itself, brought in for his gift of trickery – and the Nameless began to regret its trust, and to be wary of the Seer-folk. And so it laid a trap for them, hoping thereby to clip their wings and reclaim some of its power.

'So it summoned a demon from World Beyond, a being by the name of Svadilfari, and enslaved it with the force of the Word, and gave it the shape of a great Horse. And the Nameless offered to help them complete the Citadel in less than a week – single-handed, except for the Horse – for a price as yet undetermined.

'It seemed too good to be true at first. A task that would have taken the Seer-folk years completed in less than seven days – but Odin One-Eye was wary. He'd already paid a high price for his bargain with the Nameless. To enter into a contract without even knowing what it would cost would be the act of a madman. But

194

Loki, his brother in Chaos, persuaded him to make the deal. The job would never be finished in time, he said; the risk was therefore minimal. And so they agreed, and the work began. But Svadilfari was by his very nature an architect of castles in the air, and rune by rune, glamour by glamour, the Sky Citadel began to take shape.

'Five days into the contract, the Seer-folk were getting anxious. Odin in particular was uneasy, not least because his people were beginning to whisper that it had been his intention from the first to throw in his lot with the Nameless. Typically, he blamed Loki, who, seeing where the land lay, set out in haste to redeem himself before they threw him from the sky.'

Maggie hadn't heard this part of the tale. Even in the Good Book's Closed Chapters, mention of the Seer-folk had been kept to a minimum, and all she knew was that somehow they had taken the First World through trickery, and in so doing had made themselves gods.

She thought of the Horse they had left in the stables, feeding placidly from a bale of hay. He looked so like any other horse that even she could hardly believe his true Aspect – that thing, half Horse, half spider, that had birthed itself from the side of a Hill with half of Dream in its terrible wake . . .

'The Red Horse . . .' she ventured shyly. 'Is he – Svadilfari?'

Adam shook his head. 'Not quite. Loki knew how to change his shape – an easy task in the First World – and he took the form of a little white mare – a very *pretty* little white mare – and lured away the demon Horse back into the realm of Dream. The Nameless tried to call him back; but Svadilfari was infatuated, and he and the white mare disappeared for two whole days and two whole nights. And so the seven-day deadline passed, and the Citadel was left unfinished. And the Nameless had to admit defeat, and forfeit Asgard to the gods.'

'And the Horse?' said Maggie,

Adam shrugged. 'No one saw him again,' he said. 'But when Loki came back in his natural form, he brought back with him an eight-legged foal, child of the demon and the white mare. He called him Sleipnir, and he gave him to Odin as a bribe, in exchange for being allowed to stay when all the others wanted him out.'

Maggie stared at Adam, enthralled. 'So . . . Loki was his *mother*?' she said. 'How did he manage to do that?'

'You wouldn't *believe* all the disgusting things that Loki's managed to do in his time,' said Adam, taking Maggie's hand and looking at her earnestly. 'But now we have him. Odin's Horse. The greatest steed in the Nine Worlds.'

'But why?' said Maggie. 'Why bring him here? Isn't he still dangerous? Besides, I thought our job was to wipe out demons, not release them into the Worlds . . .'

'Patience,' said Adam with a smile. In fact, by now he was feeling thoroughly impatient with Maggie, but three years of living with the thing in his mind had taught him a measure of self-control. 'Believe me, I understand how you feel. I was like that myself once. Of course I hate working with demons just as much as you do, but sometimes the end justifies the means, and this time the lesser evil is to bring these creatures into the Worlds, so that a far greater menace can be defeated for ever.'

'The Seer-folk,' said Maggie.

'That's right,' Adam said.

'But the Good Book says that the Riders will—'

'Herald Tribulation?' Adam smiled. 'That's right,' he said again. 'The End of the Worlds. Ragnarók. Apocalypse. The Winter War. But this time *we'll* be calling the shots. We'll be in charge. We'll name the date.' He put his hands on Maggie's shoulders and looked into her grey-gold eyes. 'Don't you see what this means?' he said. 'It gives us a chance to do things right. To bring Order out of Chaos. To save the Worlds from the Seer-folk.'

'You mean we can stop Tribulation?'

Adam nodded. 'Of course we can. You have what it takes to defeat them. You already have the Red Horse. Now all we need is one more thing: an artefact of the Elder Age that will help us destroy them once and for all.'

'An artefact?' She looked at him.

'People call it the Old Man.'

'What is it?'

Adam shrugged. 'All I know is we need it.'

'But what about . . .' Maggie lowered her voice. 'What about the Magister, Adam? Who – *what* – is he? And can't we get you free, somehow?'

Adam went pale and shook his head. 'You don't know what you're talking about,' he said in a low and urgent voice. 'My master's here to help us. I know back there it looked different, but you have to believe me. He's on our side. It's . . . complicated. All right?'

'All right,' said Maggie doubtfully. 'But tell me – who was that girl on the Hill? The one with the ruinmark, who looks just like me?'

In Adam's mind, his passenger uttered a distant warning.

Leave this to me, Adam said. *I know how to handle her.*

You'd better, said his passenger. *Or I'll take you both apart.*

Briefly Adam considered whether a quick prayer to Loki would count as blasphemy at this stage. He knew from the Voice in his mind that the Trickster had once been in similar shoes, had suffered this same communion and had somehow broken free at last . . .

'Trust me, Maggie,' he said, and smiled. 'You asked me once if I were a dream. Well, that's where everything begins. That's where you'll find your answers. Dream. Will you trust me?'

'Yes, I will.'

So Adam began his story.

12

MAGGIE REDE MISTRUSTED DREAMS, as she mistrusted dreamers. But Adam explained it all so well; and now she began to understand how Dream had been breached by the Seer-folk to unleash Chaos into the Worlds, and how from that Chaos they planned to rebuild the Rainbow Bridge and, from there, take possession of the Firmament itself, the First World of Creation.

'And so you see,' Adam said, 'the answer to everything lies in dreams. *Your* dreams, Maggie – yours and mine. That's how we freed the Horse of Fire. That's how we'll track down the Old Man. And that's how we'll vanquish the Seer-folk and bring Order back to the Nine Worlds.'

'But why does it have to be me?' Maggie said.

'Because of who you are,' Adam said. 'Because you carry their blood in your veins.'

'But *I don't,*' protested Maggie. 'My uncle was an Examiner. My parents were Orderly folk. My brothers were both in the Order.'

Adam touched the nape of her neck, where the runemark *Ác,* the Thunder Oak, still gleamed beneath her shorn hair. 'You didn't get *that* from Donal Rede. Or from his goodwife Susan.'

'Then who *did* I get it from?' Maggie said.

Adam sighed and took her hand. 'You asked me about the girl,' he said.

Maggie looked at him eagerly. Ever since her return to World's End she had longed to know more about the girl on the Hill, who looked so like her, and called her by name, and knew about her family.

'This may come as a shock,' Adam said. In fact, he was enjoying himself. For the first time since his passenger had taken residence in his mind, he was experiencing the joy of wielding power.

'Who is she?' Maggie said. 'She told me she wasn't an enemy.'

'Maybe not to you,' he said. 'But to me, to my master, to all the Worlds, to everything we hold most dear—'

'What do you mean? Who is she?'

He smiled. 'Her name is Maddy Smith,' he said. 'I knew her – *fought* her – long ago, before I met my master. She looks ordinary enough, but in fact she is one of the most dangerous and powerful of the Seer-folk. She hates me. She's always hated me. And . . .'

Adam paused for effect.

'Yes?'

'Maggie – *she's your sister.*'

He'd expected tears – hysterics, perhaps; to Adam, that would have been normal. But Maggie Rede was no ordinary girl, and although her lips tightened momentarily, her expression remained eerily calm. Her shock and disgust at finding the runemark at the nape of her neck now seemed like an eternity away; in fact, Adam thought resentfully, she was just like Maddy herself – pert, stubborn and too clever for her own good.

'How can we be sisters?' she said. 'I've never even met her before.'

Adam gave a narrow smile. 'Of course you haven't met,' he said. 'But you *are* sisters, nevertheless. You're the twin children of Thor and Jarnsaxa, of Chaos and the Firefolk. That's why my master wanted you to kill her while you had the chance. The link that binds you is dangerous, and until it can be severed, your soul will *always* remain in the balance, and the Seer-folk will never leave you alone.'

For a long time Maggie said nothing. Could it be that in one world, a person could seem so harmless – even apparently likeable

– while in another, they were as devious and destructive as Adam Goodwin seemed to suggest?

She thought of the Red Horse down in the stables. He seemed such an ordinary beast. And yet, in another world, he was the Red Horse of the Last Days. *Could* what Adam said be true? Could it be that the enemy was Maggie's own twin sister?

Adam put his hand on her arm. 'I know you don't want this, Maggie,' he said. 'Just as I never wanted it. But all that changed when I met you. Together, we can face anything. Together, with my master's help, we can change the Nine Worlds, take what was broken and build it anew.'

'Can we?' said Maggie.

'Of course we can.'

And at this he looked into her eyes, and all Maggie's common sense dissolved into a rosy haze. Here was someone who knew her heart; someone who accepted her; someone with whom she could share any secret, however dark.

Her hand crept to the nape of her neck, where the runemark *Ác* was glowing like a firebrand.

'You don't think I'm tainted? By *this*?' she said.

'Of course not.' Adam smiled. 'In fact – I think you're beautiful.'

Maggie looked at him in surprise. She had never been a beauty, of course; not even before she had cut her hair. Too poor to afford the expensive clothes that were the fashion in World's End, she had always been considered plain – too tall; too boyish; too clever; too pert; unwilling to play the seduction games played by other girls of her age. Her luminous eyes were too direct; her hair, which *had* been beautiful, was always hidden under a scarf. Now even that was gone, and just at the moment when Maggie, for the first time in her life, had started to care what she looked like.

Of course, Adam knew this perfectly well. Maggie Rede and Maddy Smith were alike in more than features; they shared a similar temperament, and even their different backgrounds had done little to alter the resemblance. Both had been solitary children – Maddy spending hours alone in Little Bear Wood, Maggie in her underground haunts beneath the old University. Maggie had her sister's pride; her courage and her confidence. But underneath all that he could see that Maggie longed for someone to trust; for a friend in whom she could confide – or even, perhaps, fall in love . . .

Love? Maggie Rede would have laughed at the thought only a few days ago. Now there was something in her eyes; a warmth that touched her plain face with something approaching beauty. Adam Scattergood had changed from the spoiled and sullen young man he'd once been. At seventeen, he was handsome; he had an air of mystery; he knew many things; he was different to all the other young men she had ever encountered. Most importantly of all, he was telling Maggie what she wanted to hear – that he *needed* her – that he wanted her – and to Maggie, to be needed was the greatest attraction of all.

He gently pulled at the *bergha* that covered Maggie's shorn hair. 'Must you really wear this? Now that I've seen you without it—'

Once more, and for the last time, Maggie hesitated. 'But Adam, my hair . . .'

'I like it this way. It makes you different,' he said.

It was the first time Maggie had heard that word used as anything but a negative.

'Different?' she said, allowing him to undo the headscarf and draw it away.

Tenderly Adam touched her hair. 'Beautiful,' he repeated.

He drew Maggie towards him; she rested her head on his shoulder. Her forehead seemed made for that cradle; she closed her eyes and settled there.

'I still don't trust your master,' she said.

Adam smiled. 'Do you trust *me*?'

Slowly Maggie nodded.

'Then come with me,' said Adam. 'And dream.'

13

MADDY KNEW IT ONLY FROM STORIES. Nat Parson had been full of tales of the Universal City, with its green parks and its gracious halls, its domes of glass and its spires of gold, its harbour with its tall ships, and the One Sea that stretched out for ever. But Nat Parson had always been prone to exaggeration, and, given that no one else in Malbry was in a position to contradict him (a pilgrimage was a costly thing, and no one had come back from the Universal City in something approaching forty years), Maddy had always assumed that his accounts of the place were much embellished, and that the reality would turn out to be something very different.

Even so, she found herself unprepared. The dark and eerie catacombs, the tunnels so like those of World Below, the hidden libraries infested with rats, seemed more like the ruins of an empire than any kind of a city. Exploring the labyrinth underneath the ancient buildings, she found herself marvelling at the amazement of riches, seemingly abandoned here: fragments of blackened silverware, cut up and hidden by looters who had lost their way in the darkness and whose bones still littered the catacombs; blocks of marble; toppled archways; uncut gemstones like nuggets of fire; papers and ledgers centuries old; and books – hundreds, *thousands* of books, some swarming with bookworms, some still intact, some locked, some coded, some lavishly illuminated, some written in foreign languages – some containing maps and charts of the World Beyond the One Sea.

Maddy would have liked to take time to investigate. Surely among these forgotten things she might be expected to find the Old Man. But she also needed to find Maggie Rede; because if all she suspected was true, then it was only a matter of time before the Seer-folk found their way to World's End. And Maddy needed the Old Man – not just because Odin had told her so, but because if, as she believed, the Old Man *was* the Whisperer, she could use it to prove to the other gods that Maggie was an innocent, a pawn in the hands of their enemy.

But first she had to find her twin; to try and explain the truth to her. *That* might not be easy, she knew. Maggie was a World's Ender, brought up under the Order's regime. For all Maddy knew, her sister might be a believer, devout in the ways of the Good Book, a willing convert to Mimir's deceptions, a soldier of the Nameless. It had taken One-Eye six years to teach Maddy what she needed to know. Maddy had only days, at best, to ensure that Maggie was prepared.

The Cradle fell an age ago, but Fire and Folk shall raise her
In just twelve days, at End of Worlds; a gift within the sepulchre.

The Æsir had assumed (too fast) that the twelve days of the prophecy referred to the building of Asgard. Now it seemed likely to Maddy that the twelve days were a countdown leading up to the End of the Worlds, whether the gods were ready or not.

Two whole days had already passed since Ethel had made the prophecy. Which left nine days to find the Old Man, which could be buried anywhere. Nine days to find her sister, and to persuade her she wasn't an enemy.

And so Maddy left the catacombs, and, using *Sól* to light her way and with one hand fastened in Jorgi's mane, managed to find a way aboveground into the University.

They emerged just south of the Great Cloister, once a place of mediation, recently converted into a teeming marketplace packed with stalls and businesses. It was lucky for Maddy that she did; for among the crowds of Outlanders, the slaves and the dancers and the entertainers, the veiled women and the painted ones, the thieves and the pickpockets, the cut-throats and the mercenaries, not even a rustic from the North and her strangely unconvincing horse was likely to attract much attention.

She tried to pass by unnoticed, but found it difficult to ignore a dog with two heads; a dancing snake; a tattooed prophet speaking in tongues; a man selling severed fingers.

'What kind of place is this?' she said to herself as she wandered from one plundered hall to another, among the cobwebs and chandeliers, avoiding the cracks in marble pavements, hearing the clamour of unknown voices against the ghosts of long ago. She'd expected to find it a shrine to the Order; a monument to her vanquished foes. That would have been appropriate. Ten thousand men had died, after all, in the name of what they believed. Maddy found, to her surprise, that she felt more sympathy for her dead adversaries than she did for these World's Enders, who seemed to have given themselves up entirely to the pursuit of pleasure and profit now that Law and Order were gone.

'Wanna buy a charm, lady?'

Maddy turned, and saw a journeyman addressing her, his face almost entirely concealed behind a grubby yellow scarf, his tall figure hidden beneath the coloured robes of the Outlands.

'Charm?' said Maddy.

The journeyman grinned, and Maddy thought she saw a glimpse of bright blue eyes above the yellow scarf. 'Love spell, miss? You look the type.'

She shook her head. 'Really. I'm not.'

'Then what about a good-luck charm? Genuine piece of the Elder Age. For you, only two bits.'

Still grinning, the journeyman held out a tray. It was piled with nuggets of black rock. They looked like the cinders from Jed Smith's forge – light and sharp-edged and pitted with holes. Some bore tiny crystals embedded in the surface; others, the ghost of a rainbow.

'I don't have two bits,' Maddy said.

'Ah, come on,' said the journeyman. 'Genuine piece of Asgard, this. Blasted to cinders by Screaming Lord Surt himself. Fell on the fields like black rain. Go on. Make me an offer.'

Discreetly, Maddy fingered *Bjarkán*. In the circle between her finger and thumb – a gleam of rainbow runelight.

'So you can see the colours, eh?' The journeyman peered at Maddy, and once again she caught a glimpse of his eyes above the grubby yellow scarf. She'd taken him for an older man at first, but those blue eyes were clear and bright. She guessed him to be forty at most; maybe even younger.

'If I were you,' he told her, 'I wouldn't do too much of that. Too many people watching. Ready to take an interest.'

Maddy banished the rune *Bjarkán*. The smallest gleam of kingfisher-blue flickered between her fingers. Had she imagined it? Probably. She'd done it so many times before. Her old friend was three years dead, and still she saw him everywhere – through a carriage window; sitting by a fountain; in a crowd on market day; walking by the side of a road. It hurt – perhaps it always would. And yet she almost dreaded the time when she would no longer see One-Eye in the face of journeymen from World's End to the distant North . . .

She looked more closely at the man. 'Don't I know you from somewhere?' she said.

The journeyman shrugged. 'You might,' he said. 'I've been a lot of places.'

That voice too was familiar. Maddy's heart gave a hopeful lurch. She reached out her hand and tugged at the scarf wrapped round the journeyman's head, exposing his features completely. The wry and slightly irregular mouth; the hair pulled back with a strip of hide; the mobile, humorous eyebrows – all were more than familiar, but the face was that of a stranger.

The journeyman raised an eyebrow. 'Excuse me?'

She looked away. 'I thought you were someone else,' she said.

'Aye, well, that's life,' said the journeyman, indicating his tray of wares. 'Take these little bits of rock. You wouldn't think that once they'd been part of something that spanned the sky. Look at 'em now – all burned out. And yet there's glamours inside of 'em, like seeds just waiting to up and grow . . .'

Maddy looked at him. 'Glamours,' she said. She picked up one of the black stones. 'Where did you find these, anyway?'

'They're all around the city,' he said. 'That is, if you know where to look. Most of the big ones were gathered up, but you can still find fragments lying around, and of course, there are the stories.'

Maddy thought of Red Horse Hill. 'What kind of stories?'

'The usual. That this is what's left of the Sky Citadel that fell during Tribulation. Fragments of Dream that the Firefolk brought to build the Bridge between the Worlds . . .'

'What's your name?' Maddy said.

The journeyman shrugged. 'What's in a name? Call me Lord Perth, if you feel like it. And you can be Lady Madonna. And then we can both pretend to ourselves that we're not just a pair of scallies, raking the footprints of the gods.'

A shiver went down Maddy's back. She cast the rune *Bjarkán* once more, and looked at him through her fingers. And this time she saw his signature, red as the heart of a midsummer rose, which shone out like a beacon, and on his arm, a patch of light . . .

A runemark?

'Show me your arm,' she said.

Perth gave her a quizzical look. 'What? *Here*?'

'Your *arm*,' she said, and, grabbing his wrist, pushed up the sleeve of his blue robe.

And there it was: a new rune, rose-red and burning with glam—

'What are you *playing* at?' hissed Perth, and pulled down his sleeve to cover the mark. 'This isn't show and tell, girl. Play that kind of trick again and I'm apt to end up in the stocks. Or even at the end of a rope.'

'I'm sorry,' said Maddy. 'I didn't know.'

'Of course, it's just a tattoo,' he said. 'Had it done on Saint Sepulchre's Day after a few too many pints. Could have kicked myself afterwards – I dunno what got into me. After all, the last thing I need is another set of distinguishing marks.'

Maddy nodded. She was thinking hard. She knew that rune was no tattoo. Did Perth really believe it was?

'So— what does it mean?' she said at last.

He shook his head. 'It's just my name. *Perth,* it says, in some Outlandish tongue. Supposed to bring me good luck, but it's brought me nothing but bad so far.'

'Really?' said Maddy. 'How so?'

Perth just shook his head again. 'I'd rather not discuss it here. And if you've got any sense at all, you'll hide yours. Yes, of *course* I see it,' he said. 'Right there in the palm of your hand. Wear gloves, for gods' sakes. The Order may be gone, but there are slavers in this city who'd pay good money for a girl like you – that is, if you don't get lynched first.'

Maddy put her hand in her pocket and frowned. There was so much she didn't know about the ways of World's End. Slavers, mercenaries, thieves – how in the Worlds would she find her sister? Perth – whoever, *whatever* he was, with his runemark and his pile of rocks – was hardly a trustworthy ally. But could he help her find Maggie? Or was she better off alone?

She peered at him once again, through *Bjarkán.* Yes, there was deceit in his colours, a green-gold thread that ran through his glam. The man was more than capable of lying to her, or selling her out, or stealing from her, or swindling her. He'd done those things before, she sensed. And yet in spite of all that, Maddy read no malevolence there; no real signs of wickedness. She concluded that he was harmless enough, as long as she didn't trust him with her purse. Besides, she badly needed a guide through this maze of a city.

'Listen, Perth,' she said at last. 'I'm a stranger here. I may need help. Perhaps we could help each other.'

Perth looked doubtful. 'That so?' he said. 'I thought you didn't have two bits.'

Maddy clicked her fingers, summoning the money-rune *Fé*. It gleamed provocatively in her palm, guinea-gold and glamorous.

Perth's blue eyes lit up at once. 'Nice trick.'

'I'll teach it to you.'

'Done!' Perth grinned. They shook hands. 'So – what have you come to find in World's End? And exactly what kind of horse *is* that?' He narrowed his eyes at Jormungand, who was apparently investigating a display of fresh fish on a nearby market stall. As Perth and Maddy watched, the Horse idly snapped up a live king crab as if it were a mouthful of straw.

Maddy grabbed Jorgi's bridle. '*No!*'

The Horse of the Sea rolled his eyes. For a moment the king crab's spidery legs twisted and clawed in his open mouth. Then there was a crunching sound, and a whinny of satisfaction.

The vendor in charge of the fish stall, who had barely had time to take it all in, now rubbed his eyes in disbelief. 'Did you see that?' he asked Perth.

'See what?' said Perth innocently.

'That *horse*,' said the fishmonger, looking shaken.

Perth looked sympathetic. 'I know how you feel,' he said kindly, putting his arm round the man's shoulders. 'The hooch they were selling here last night was enough to make anyone start seeing things. If I were you, I'd just sit down, take the weight off your feet for a while.'

The fishmonger, a burly man, sat down heavily on the ground. As he did so, Maddy saw Perth relieve him deftly of the fat purse at his belt. She glared at Perth in warning; the journeyman gave her a sunny smile.

'Come on, you,' Maddy hissed, dragging Jorgi away through the crowd.

Perth grinned and followed them, still carrying his tray of rocks. 'This is going to be *fun*,' he said.

Jorgi gave a fishy belch.

Maddy closed her eyes in despair.

They moved on into the Universal City.

14

MEANWHILE, BACK IN MALBRY, the gods and their allies in Chaos were engaged in strenuous argument. Maddy's disappearance, as well as that of the World Serpent, had already caused enough concern; but the signatures that she had left – the spent cantrips, her struggle with Loki, the unmistakable colour-trail of her escape into Dream – had triggered further division between Æsir and Vanir.

One faction (mostly Thor) was sure that she had been abducted, although the tracks were confusing. On the one hand, the presence of Loki's trail pointed to some kind of ambush. On the other, it was clear that she had *defeated* Loki – which seemed to suggest that whatever the reason, Maddy had entered Dream willingly. *How* she had entered it, whether or not Loki was still with her, and whether the presence of the World Serpent could positively identify either of them as the Rider whose name was Treachery, remained a matter for debate.

Heimdall's side was strongly in favour of finding Loki and making him talk. But to the Æsir, the rift in Dream – now growing at a visible rate – remained the more immediate concern.

'It has to be sealed,' argued Frey, whose runesign, *Madr*, marked him as a friend of the Folk. 'If we don't, then the valley Folk won't stand a chance.'

Bright-Haired Sif gave a grunt of contempt. '*Seal* it? You and

whose tribe?' she said. In fact, Thor had spent most of the afternoon working around the rift in Dream, tapping the ground
and blasting it with runes, and finally using Mjølnir, his mighty
hammer, to pound at the site of the Horse's escape – the only visible result being the line of enormous hammer-shaped holes that
now surrounded Red Horse Hill.

Since then, Jolly had refused to leave his dwarf Aspect, complaining of a headache, and Sif had had a great deal to say on the
subject of Thor's incompetence.

The Thunderer looked resentful. 'This isn't like fixing a leak,
dear,' he said, with the scowl that had once levelled giants. 'We're
talking about a fundamental breakdown between the fabric of
Worlds, not a faulty U-bend.'

Sif gave a very pig-like snort.

'More cake, dear?' suggested Thor.

By this time the Huntress had joined the gods in the front room
of the Parsonage, and, with her furs and her runewhip, was looking very out of place on Ethel's blue silk ottoman. Odin's ravens
– in human form – perched silently at her side.

'I know we've had our differences,' Skadi said, looking at Njörd.
'But this rift in Dream threatens us all. It has to be closed. Whatever it takes.'

'You think we haven't tried?' said Thor.

'I know you've tried,' said Skadi. 'But the rift is growing all the
time. It's like something's melting a hole in the ice, and we're all
about to take a dive.'

The image, though crude, was potent enough. The gods exchanged fearful glances. Only Jolly seemed unconcerned; apparently oblivious to the imminent arrival of the second Ragnarók, he
was picking the icing from a pile of cupcakes that Ethel had made
for afternoon tea.

It wasn't that she'd *wanted* tea. But in her days as a parson's
wife, Ethel had come to rely on certain routines, which was why
the table was set as usual, with its array of little sandwiches, scones
and cakes. Skól gave the cupcakes a hopeful sniff, but Jolly wasn't
about to share. He bared his teeth at the demon wolf and gave a

long, low growl. For a moment Skól was tempted to take up the challenge, but, seeing Jolly's ferocious expression, wisely decided against it. Besides – a wolf in a fight with a hammer? Dude, that was just *too* freaky.

'I don't understand,' said Heimdall at last. 'At first the prophecy seemed clear. Asgard rebuilt by the power of Dream. But so far, this rift in Dream has brought us nothing but Chaos.'

He looked out of the Parsonage window, where the rift was clearly visible in the late-afternoon sun – a column of cloud that towered above what was left of Red Horse Hill. He reckoned its diameter at about a quarter of a mile – not large, but growing steadily, expanding, consuming bushes, rocks, grass, trees at a rate of about three feet an hour. All the gods could hear it now – a sound like the *chirr* of crickets; a sound into which all other sounds were vanquished by a wall of noise.

Bragi fingered his guitar. Still out of tune after the battle, it gave a mournful jangling sound.

'Oh, please,' said Freyja. 'If I hear another one of Bragi's dirges, I'm going to kill myself.'

Bragi looked hurt. 'It's the strings,' he said. 'You know what it's like when you're out of Aspect. Nothing works the way it should. If only we could get Asgard back . . .'

Freyja sniffed. 'Yes, I know. In Asgard, everything's peachy. In Asgard, Sif gets her figure back, Tyr gets to play with the big boys, Thor gets to hammer whoever he wants, I get a change of clothes and a bath, and you get to play your lute again without making everyone's *ears* bleed.' She flicked back a strand of her red-gold hair. 'The only problem being, of course, that Asgard fell an age ago, taking our Aspects with it, and the only chance of getting it back is to decipher some lame prophecy that doesn't even *rhyme.*'

Fenny gave a smirk. *'Noobs.* You don't have a clue, do you, babe?'

'Who are you calling babe?' said Freyja, her Carrion Aspect beginning to show.

Heimdall had to intervene before it got any uglier. *'The key to the gate is a child of hate, a child of both and of neither.* Do you think that line could refer to Maddy? After all, she is the child of Thor and the demon Jarnsaxa. Though why she should be a child of hate—'

'Loki,' said Frey with conviction. 'He's the child of demons; and everybody hates *him*. Plus, he was the one who opened the gate to Netherworld in the first place. Who else could it possibly be?'

'I'm not sure I like the term *demons*,' said Angie, interrupting. 'Some people might find it offensive.'

'So what would you rather?' Heimdall said.

'Persons of Chaotic origin?'

'*Gods!*' exploded Heimdall. 'Maddy's lost, Loki's escaped, the End of the bloody *Worlds* is at hand, and you're lecturing me about political correctness?' But Ethel had suddenly gone very still. '*Now* what?' he said.

'Maddy isn't lost,' she said. 'How could I have missed it? It's obvious.'

'What is?' Heimdall said.

'*I see a mighty Ash that stands beside a mighty Oak tree.* We all thought the Ash was Yggdrasil, but—'

'Maddy's sign is the Ash,' said Frey. 'You mean, Maddy's involved in this? If that's true, then who's the Oak? And what about *Treachery, Carnage and Lunacy?*'

'The Three Horses of the Last Days.' Ethel dropped her knitting (a hat) and, for the first time, looked agitated. 'The Horse of Fire is Sleipnir, of course. The Horse of the Sea is Jormungand. And the Horse of Air is probably already on its way. And if Maddy is the key to it all, then World's End is where she'll be heading. That's where Asgard fell, after all. And that's where we should be right now.'

'Why? What's the rush?' said Sugar-and-Sack.

Ethel gave him a quelling look. '*In just twelve days, at End of Worlds; a gift within the sepulcher.* You all remember the prophecy I made the day before yesterday. That means that in nine days' time, in World's End, where Asgard fell at the end of the war, the final conflict will occur.'

There was silence as the gods took this in.

'What about the Folk?' said Frey. 'Leave now, and they're done for.'

'Leave too late, and *we* are done for!'

Frey sighed. 'Ethel's right,' he said.

'What about Loki?' Angie said, with a curious look at Ethel. 'Being the Trickster, and all that – don't you think we might need him?'

'Need him?' said Thor. 'I'll break his neck.'

'Not if I do it first,' said Frey.

'Leave him alone,' said Skadi. 'We don't have time to hunt him now. When we're finished in World's End, we can deal with him at leisure.' She looked around at the other gods. 'Agreed?'

Thor shrugged. 'World's End it is.'

'Agreed,' said Ethel with a smile.

And that was how, by sunset, anyone watching the Hindarfell road (through the circle of finger and thumb) might have seen the ill-assorted band – some on horseback, some trotting on foot, some running, some soaring overhead – approaching the narrow cleft in the rocks and passing out of the valley.

Such an observer, armed with the truesight, might have seen their signatures, ominous as the edge of a storm, spanning the dusk like a rainbow as they passed into the shadow of the mountains.

Such an observer, had they but seen her on her porch by the Malbry road, might have sighed and shaken her head, and muttered, *Kids, what will they do next?* before hitching her skirts above her knees and kicking her heels in a gleeful dance – not a pretty sight, to be sure, with her swollen old legs in their long stripy socks, but Crazy Nan Fey could dance a jig as merry as the next man when the occasion demanded it, and she had been waiting a long time for just this opportunity. The Auld Man had promised her a glammy of her very own, and a place at his side in Faërie, if only she did what he told her to do when next she came to him in Dream.

Crazy Nan Fey believed in dreams. She always had, even when they had tried to say that dreams would steal away her soul. They never had – maybe Nàn's soul was too old and dry for dream-demons to care about – but over the past three years it seemed that every time she closed her eyes she saw more when she opened them. Goblins and little folk; signatures and glammies. And now she had seen the Auld Man in Dream – aye, and his black birdies too – and they had taught her a skipping song like those she'd danced to as a child:

The Cradle fell an age ago,
But Fire and Folk shall raise her . . .

Which, to Nan Fey's mind, at least, meant that everything must come around-round, like the Serpent with its tail in its mouth circling the Nine Worlds, and she had smiled and nodded, because she knew the Good Book, including the Book of Apocalypse, in which the end of one World is announced, and the beginning of another.

To Nan, the signs were very clear. The End of the World was coming. The first sign had been the emergence of the new runes of the Younger Age; then the release of the old gods from the Black Fortress of Netherworld. Then had come the Nameless, and his defeat at the cost of the General's life. Then had come the rift from Dream, spilling into the Middle World. Then the return of Odin's Horse, and the escape of the World Serpent.

After that, as everyone knew, there was nobbut one step to Last Days. As the gods converged on World's End, it was told that Three Riders would come into the Worlds, three Riders on three Horses – red for the fires of World Below, black for the depths of the One Sea, and white for the clouds of the Firmament – and they would conquer the Nine Worlds, and Asgard would belong to them:

And there shall come a Horse of Fire,
And the name of his Rider is Carnage.
And there shall come a Horse of the Sea,
And the name of his Rider is Treachery.

And there shall come a Horse of Air,
And the name of his Rider is Lunacy . . .

And now Nan Fey laughed aloud. For years folk had mocked her visions, calling her crazy and lunatic and saying she had her head in the clouds. Well, very soon she would show them all. They would see who was crazy. Nan Fey would ride the Horse of Air to the Bridge across the Firmament, and the mark with which Nan had been born – a broken, reversed form of the rune *Fé* – would become a glam of the New Script, complete and full of power.

Meanwhile, so the Auld Man said, all Nan had to do was dream. And so she went back into her cottage and sat down on her narrow bed – the same box cot she had used as a girl, when she was Nancy Wickerman, the basket-maker's daughter – and folded her hands like faded petals across the bosom of her dress, and waited for Dream to take her into the clouds and over the moon and across the Sea to Asgard.

BOOK FOUR

The Old Man of the Wilderlands

There was an old lady so mad, they say,
That she flew through the air in a basket.
She flew to the Land of Roast Beef
With brandy in a flaskit.
Into the clouds and over the Moon and into
the Land of the Seer-oh
Where the Faëries play all the livelong day
and the oceans are made of beer-oh!

Ancient Ridings nursery rhyme

1

'OH, *PLEASE*,' SAID LOKI IMPATIENTLY. 'If I hear another nursery rhyme, or folk song, or Faërie story, or amusing anecdote from the everyday lives of the newly reborn, I swear I'm going to kill myself.'

Sigyn put down her lute and shrugged. 'Well, I think you're *very* ungrateful,' she said. 'Anyone would think you didn't *want* me here.'

Loki looked down at his left wrist, where *Eh*, in the form of a fine gold chain, sparkled and glimmered harmlessly. At first he'd tried to break it, but in vain; his wrist was scored with angry marks. Changing to bird form hadn't helped; even in his Fiery Aspect the Wedlock rune still held him fast, and hours later he'd had to accept the fact that escape was impossible.

Worse still was the fact that Sigyn was *happy*. Nothing Loki could say or do seemed to have any lasting effect on her. She remained implacably cheerful in the face of his initial rage, then his persistent rudeness and finally his silent resentment, plying him with food and drink and trying to keep him entertained with stories and songs of her homeland.

Sigyn had rather a pretty voice, and, as well as the lute, could play both the harp and the mandolin. With glamours she had managed to transform the cave into an airy boudoir, with silken drapes and vases of flowers and dishes of sweetmeats on every surface, but so far her efforts had borne no fruit, and Loki seemed as bored and uncooperative as ever.

'I *don't* want you here,' he told her now. 'Go away and leave me alone.'

Sigyn smiled uncertainly. 'Now you know that isn't true. It's just that you're tired and cranky. Let me fix you something to eat, and then I'll sing you a lullaby—'

'I don't want a lullaby,' he snapped. 'And I – am – *not* – getting – *cranky!*'

Sigyn shrugged and turned away. 'I don't see why you have to be so mean,' she said, with a tremor in her voice. 'I was going to make you a feather bed, with down pillows and satin sheets. I was going to bring you hot spiced wine, and rose-petal candies, and honey cake. I would have sung you my sweetest songs, even slept on the floor if you'd wanted me to . . .' Now her eyes were swimming with tears and her mouth had thinned to a stubborn line. 'And for all the affection you show in return, I might as well be a poisonous snake. Well, if that's the way you want it . . .'

She forked a little sign with her hand, and suddenly the Wedlock became a set of manacles linked to a chain so heavy that Loki fell to his knees. At the same moment, the shimmering outline of something long and sinuous appeared in the air above him, like something behind a silk screen. A distant tearing sound accompanied it.

Loki had heard that sound before, at the gates of Netherworld, and once again on Red Horse Hill. The fabric of Worlds seemed to stretch and yawn, and Loki suddenly realized that the powers of *Eh*, the Wedlock, extended to far more than glamours.

'Er . . . hang on a minute,' said Loki, pinned to the ground by the weight of the chain.

Sigyn pretended not to hear. She forked another sign with her hand, and now Loki saw something like a snake's head pressed against the troubled air like a child's hand pressing against a balloon. It gleamed with a sickly soap-bubble sheen, acquiring substance as he watched.

'Sigyn, *sweetheart* . . .'

She looked at him. 'Well?'

'You've got this all wrong,' Loki said. 'Of *course* I appreciate all you've done. And – yeah, maybe . . .' He gritted his teeth. 'Maybe I *was* kinda cranky.'

Sigyn's expression softened again. The manacles dropped from Loki's wrists, once more becoming a fine gold chain. The bubble (with the snake inside, like a worm in a dead man's eye) winked out of existence.

Loki took a deep breath. 'Where did you learn to do that?' he said.

'Do what?' said Sigyn.

'You know – the – ah . . .'

Sigyn ignored him. 'Rose-petal candy?' She held out the dish. It was made of pink porcelain, and had popped into existence just as quickly and effortlessly as the snake had popped out of it.

'Ah – yes. That would be nice.' Loki took a sugared rose and put it cautiously into his mouth, trying not to think of the fact that Sigyn, in her present mood, could probably turn it into a cockroach, or a stone, or a razor-blade . . .

'Delicious,' he said, forcing a smile.

'I know they're your favourites,' Sigyn said. 'And now . . .' she went on, and began to sing:

'There was an old lady so mad, they say,
That she flew through the air in a basket.
She flew to the Land of Roast Beef
With brandy in a flaskit . . .'

2

NAN FEY ALSO KNEW THE OLD RHYMES. There were stories hidden in all of them – tales of the Seer-folk and their time masquerading as nonsense as the years rewrote the language, subtly twisting and turning it so that solemn invocations, rumours of plague, and prophecies and heroes and lovers and generals and gods were turned at last into skipping songs and rock-a-byes; even when their histories had been outlawed by the Order, the words of the Seer-folk had remained in the mouths and hearts of children.

Young Nancy Wickerman had been a collector of skipping songs and nursery rhymes since she was nobbut a bairn, and now, grown old and mad (so they said), she realized that even at their most nonsensical, those words had a curious power.

The Land of Roast Beef, for instance. Absurd as it undoubtedly was, Nan had heard it mentioned in many a tale – a place where natural laws did not apply; where ordinary folk might fly through the air, and clouds were the manes of horses that galloped across the summer sky. According to legend, the Land of Roast Beef was a place where food never ran short and ale was always plentiful, where Death was banished forever, and from which the fortress of the Seer-folk, the legendary Sky Citadel of old, appeared as a castle in the sky, every brick and roof-tile all agleam with enchantment.

Folk of Malbry now identified this mythical land as a romanticized version of World's End, but Nan believed there was more to the old tales than a rustic's dream of the Universal City. The Auld Man had already told her as much; the Auld Man who came to her in dreams. According to all the old tales, the Sky Citadel had been linked to World's End by a fabulous Bridge, a construction of glamours and ephemera, born of Chaos, but serving the gods, and visible to the human eye only when sunshine and rain combined. It was this bridge, the Auld Man said, that still existed in children's rhymes, its true name – Bif-rost – reversed and corrupted, like Nan's own rune, and hidden away for five hundred years, forgotten until the End of the World.

But now the End of the World was nigh. The time had come for Crazy Nan Fey. Already two of the three Riders of the prophecy were on their way to World's End. The third still lacked a steed, of course – but Crazy Nan was not perturbed by trivial details such as this. She owned a number of baskets, one of them a wicker washbasket of more than comfortable size – certainly generous enough to take one old lady and any amount of brandy.

Nan liked brandy, especially when the weather was cold. She made it from apples in summertime, and when the dark months came around, she fancied she could taste the sun in every single mouthful. And dreaming, of course, came easier when Nan had taken a sip or two – which made it all the more crucial as serious dreaming was required. And now she opened her bright old eyes and reached for the bottle beside her bed, and tasted the sunny days of old, and felt the magic of summers past lighten her feet and fingertips.

Into the clouds and over the Moon and into the Land of the Seer-oh, thought Nan and, refreshed, stood up and went to find the big old wicker washbasket. According to the song, she knew, that was the way to reach the clouds, and crazy or not, Nan Fey meant to reach them, and ride her Horse of Air through the sky all the way to Bif-rost.

The basket was rather dusty, she found, having been kept in the cellar. Still, the wind would take care of that. Nan pulled it into the kitchen and very carefully stepped inside. The bottle of brandy in her apron pocket made a comforting sloshing sound.

She was wearing her warmest goat-hair shawl (it might be cold in the mountains), and the bonnet she got out for funerals. She closed her eyes and settled herself; the dry wicker creaked and complained at her weight. Her heart was beating fit to burst; excitement made her feverish. She took another sip of brandy – to calm her nerves, Nan told herself – and waited for the basket to rise.

Nothing happened. She took another sip.

Still the basket did not rise.

Crazy Nan began to feel a little foolish, sitting in the washing basket in her shawl and bonnet, waiting to be swept off to the Land of Roast Beef – a little foolish, and a little mad. Perhaps the Folk were right, after all – perhaps she really *was* crazy. She was tempted to open her eyes, just once, to see if anyone was watching. But the Auld Man had told her what to do, and Nan was not about to disobey. She screwed her eyes shut and thought of Dream, and this time she thought she felt something shift and grate on the floor beneath her. Her head swam from the brandy, but she kept her eyes resolutely closed. Meanwhile the sensation of movement increased, so that now it felt like the rocking horse that Nancy had had as a small child, a wooden horse she'd named Epona, which her father had thrown onto the fire when Nancy began to talk to it, telling it stories, pretending to fly . . .

It had been over seventy years since Nan had thought of Epona. Now the image of her returned, and Nan rejoiced at the memory. That had been a good time, she thought; a time when even a broken ruinmark could catch the eye of a General. Nan had been young in those days, strong as a mountain pony and keen; longing to serve the General, to learn from him, to help his plan. He could have asked her anything. *She* would have ventured below the Hill. *She* would have brought him the Whisperer. She would have tackled the Order itself, if only he had said the word. But that broken ruinmark of hers was too scanty for his purpose, and time had passed, her youth had flown, and Odin had never made use of her.

Then Maddy Smith had come along; Maddy, with her ruinmark. Special from the first day – a brighter star than the General himself. At first Nan had tried to be friends with the girl, teaching her songs and stories. But Odin One-Eye had taken her. Worse still, he had given her what Nancy had longed for all her life, leaving Nan to fend for herself while the Æsir reclaimed their birthright.

But then the Auld Man had come to her, promising salvation. Youth, her health, a glam of her own; the return of everything she had lost in the course of a wasted lifetime. What more could she hope for? The Æsir had lost their General; the Vanir were weak and dispersed. The Order had been annihilated. Runes – be they old or new – had proved themselves inadequate in the face of the threat from Netherworld, the rift between Worlds that reduced all things to a blanket of ash and cinders.

But the Auld Man could fix all that. He was, after all, an oracle. And when the Bridge had been rebuilt and the rift in Netherworld mended, all accounts would be cleared at last and balance would return to the Worlds.

Nan opened one eye. She was dreaming, she knew; it explained that sensation of flying. And as she looked around now, she saw that the snowy ground was far below, and that the wicker wash-basket was riding on top of a broad-backed cloud, with a mane all silvered with moonlight that stretched out across half the sky, and an underbelly that was swollen with rain—

Epona, thought Nan. *The Horse of Air* . . .

From the shadow of the Seven Sleepers, Loki looked up into a sky that was crazed with cold midwinter stars, and for a moment he saw her, riding high, shining in the moonlight, with a trail of glam streaming after her like the tail end of a comet, and said to himself: *What the Hel was that?* and fingered the chain around his wrist.

And in World's End the final piece of an intricate plan now fell into place and the Rider whose name was Lunacy (still tucked into her washing basket) rode Epona to the Land of Roast Beef, where the Auld Man was waiting.

3

In world's end, Maggie too was about to enter the realm of Dream. But this time, on Sleipnir, she had no need to sleep, but could reach the source of Dream directly, consciously, in her own Aspect. This time she was not afraid. Dream was no longer a threat to her, but a shining path that led to the Old Man; to victory over her enemies; and to Adam's release from servitude.

There was only one small problem. Outside of dreams, Maggie Rede had never actually ridden a horse. And the strawberry roan in the stall by her side, feeding placidly from a bale of hay, looked alarmingly big to her now that she came to mount him.

'Do I have to do this now?' Maggie appealed to Adam. Adam nodded. 'Our time is short. The sooner we find it, the better.'

Once more Maggie eyed the Horse. He looked just like any other horse – that is, until she peered at him through the circle of her finger and thumb, and saw the blaze of his signature and the runes that shone from his harness. In Dream, would he take on his true Aspect again – that flaming half-horse, half-spider that had dragged itself out of the Hill? And, assuming she found the Old Man, what then? What was the Magister's plan?

The Book of Apocalypse spoke of war; but although Maggie trusted Adam implicitly, she still did not quite trust his passenger. There were too many unanswered questions that it still refused to answer. What exactly did it want? What power did it hold over

Adam? What – or *who* – was the Old Man? And what about the girl from her dream, who Adam had said was her sister?

Her sister. The thought still came as a shock. For three whole years Maggie Rede had thought herself alone in the world, and the news that she still had a family filled her with confusion. She had never been close to her brothers; had never had sisters to talk to. Donal Rede had been proud of his sons, indifferent to his daughter; Susan, who had longed for a girl who liked pretty clothes and needlework, had found Maggie something of a disappointment. Now Maggie knew why. She had never been a Rede. She had been a cuckoo in their homely little nest, while somewhere else, her *real* tribe had been fighting the Order, bringing the plague, releasing demons from Netherworld and generally seeking to undermine everything she stood for.

Unless, of course, she stopped them. That was her destiny, Adam had said. To build a better world, he said. To claim it for the powers of good. The Order was gone. World's End was in disarray. Maggie alone stood between the Æsir and their citadel. But with Sleipnir, the Word and the Old Man, she could still hope to challenge them; to thwart their plans; to rid the Worlds of Chaos for good, to put an end to Tribulation once and for all.

But the Chaos that was in her blood spoke of possibilities. What if war *wasn't* the only way to end the conflict and heal the Worlds? If Dream could be used for good *and* evil, why couldn't Chaos do the same? And if so, couldn't she find a way to make peace with the Seer-folk?

These were the thoughts in Maggie's mind as she hoisted herself onto Sleipnir's back. Troubled, uneasy, heady thoughts, filled with contradictions.

She looked at Adam.

'Well done,' he said. 'Now tell him where you want to go. My master will guide you the rest of the way.'

Maggie glanced nervously down at the Horse. He seemed calm enough for the moment; in fact, he might almost be sleeping. There was no saddle on his back, but she kept one hand on the reins and fastened the other into his mane. In her mind, the Magister was a light and tentative presence.

'No more tricks,' she told it. 'Try anything like you did last time—'

No tricks, Maggie, it said. *Trust Me. We're on the same side.*

She turned her attention back to the Horse, who had made no move since she mounted him. 'I want you to find the Old Man,' she said, as boldly as she could.

Sleipnir opened one eye.

Good, said the Voice in her mind.

And with that, the air trembled in front of them, there came a blaze of runelight, the Horse took a single step forward, and the three of them slipped away into Dream.

Sleipnir never really slept, but then it would have been true to say that he was never completely awake. A creature with one foot permanently balanced in each of eight Worlds, a part of him was always in Dream, and he moved along the path of Worlds with the ease of a ray of sunlight. Death, Dream, the Worlds Above – all were the same to the Horse of Fire, and he led the travellers speedily along the shores of the river, where black birds flew and the thing they sought – which happened also to be his quarry – shone out among the skerries of Dream, a lone blue light in the wilderness.

Adam was *not* asleep, of course. Instead he stood guard in the stables, watching in astonishment as Maggie clambered onto the Horse, then vanished with Sleipnir into midair, leaving nothing but the empty stall and the sunny scent of hay in their wake. Once more the Whisperer's absence left him feeling strangely light, and for a moment he harboured a dangerous thought – *What if they never come back at all?* – and felt a little stab of hope. Then he dismissed the thought as absurd, and settled down in the hay to wait.

Meanwhile Maggie was riding across a vast, deserted, level plain, the terrain obscured by ground-mist, the sky a tarnished steel lid.

On the horizon, a river ran – or perhaps a part of the One Sea. Certainly Maggie had never seen any river as broad as this, not even in her stolen books.

Otherwise she was conscious of a feeling of disappointment. This was a far cry from the excitement of Red Horse Hill. Even Sleipnir looked normal here – a placid old strawberry roan plodding through the wilderness.

'What is this place?' she said aloud.

We're very close to the source of Dream. The Voice in her mind sounded almost smug. *Can you see the river? The islands? That means we're getting close.*

Maggie looked across the plain. The river in the distance was only faintly discernible; a movement against that layer of mist. Occasional marsh-lights flared at their feet, but otherwise there was nothing to be seen, and no sound at all but the muted baffle of Sleipnir's hooves against the ground, and the sound of her own heart, like the beat of a moth's wing in an empty cathedral.

'Close? But we've been here hours,' she said.

Time works differently in Dream. Believe Me, we are getting close.

Well, Maggie thought, the river at least looked no nearer than it had when they had entered this world. And she couldn't see any islands – just a formless clutter of clouds against the far horizon. Except that if she narrowed her eyes, she could see strange shapes in that jumble of clouds; shapes that sometimes resolved themselves into faces of people she'd once known. Her father. Her mother. Her brothers. Her childhood friend, Molly Carr, who had died when she was only eight. At that, Maggie gave a start of surprise – she hadn't thought of Molly for years – and made as if to dismount.

No! exclaimed the Voice in her mind. *You don't set foot on the ground here. Not even for a moment!*

'Why?' said Maggie. 'The Horse doesn't seem to be having any trouble.'

Must you question everything? The Voice sounded almost plaintive. *Can't you just do as you're told for once? Find Me the Old Man and leave?*

'Well, I don't see how you can find anything in this mist,' Maggie said. 'I thought that if I walked a bit – I mean, how do you know the Old Man's here? It might be right at our feet, for all you know.'

I don't have to know, snapped the Voice. *And you don't have to think, thank gods. All we have to do is ride. Can you do that, Maggie?*

Maggie gave a sullen sniff. 'All right. There's no need to be rude,' she said. 'I just wanted to—'

Yes, I know, said the Voice in her mind. *You just wanted to walk a while. Shall I show you what happens then? Will that make you happy?*

She shrugged.

There's a knife in your pocket. Take it out.

'How did you—?'

I just know, said the Voice. *Now take it out of your pocket, girl. Hold it out at arm's length. Then drop it at the Horse's feet. Well, what are you waiting for?*

'Will I be able to find it again?' Maggie said, still holding out the pocket-knife.

I very much doubt it, said the Voice dryly. *But perhaps then your interminable curiosity will be satisfied.*

Maggie let the knife fall. For a moment she thought it had vanished in midair; and then she was struck by a realization so huge that she almost fell off Sleipnir's back. She gave a cry, looked upwards, and tightened her hands on Sleipnir's mane until the knuckles showed bone-white. Above her, the sliver of metal that had been her pocket-knife streaked up into the iron-grey sky . . .

Except that it wasn't the sky at all, as Maggie now suddenly understood. They were travelling upside-down. The mist at their feet was cloud, she saw; the marsh-lights were far-off lightning; while the grey lid above them was the ground, some great, incomprehensible distance away.

I told you things were different here, said the Voice with a trace of smugness. *And especially here, in the heart of Dream, travel is rarely straightforward.*

'Is that why we needed the Horse?' said Maggie, trying not to be sick. How far above their heads was the ground? Half a mile? Ten miles? 'And how come *he* doesn't fall?'

Sleipnir isn't just a horse. He's a creature of ephemera, given the outward shape of a horse. In Dream, he could look like anything. Like this . . .

And, just for a moment, Maggie found herself at the helm of a long, tall ship with bright red sails, all fluttering with pennants and flags along the rigging.

Or this . . .

Now Sleipnir became an oliphant, his bridle studded with rubies, bearing a tower on his back and daubed all over with red clay.

Or maybe this . . .

The Horse's final transformation was something Maggie had never seen. It felt like some kind of a carriage, upholstered in red velvet, which moved so much faster than any vehicle she had ever encountered; blurring through worlds at the speed of Dream and making a sound like thunder—

Maggie clenched her fists. 'Stop that!'

Instantly the Horse was back, as placid and plodding as ever.

'How do you *do* that?' Maggie said.

I don't, said the Voice. *I simply redirected your glam – which, by the way, is impressive. As I'm sure you're aware, Maggie, I don't have a physical presence yet. But that will soon change. As soon as we have the Old Man.*

'So,' said Maggie. 'This Old Man – where exactly is it meant to be?'

In Dream, of course, replied the Voice.

'Yes, but—'

Dream is a place in perpetual flux, made up of countless islands. Some are very small, while others may contain whole worlds. Some last for only fragments of time, others may last longer. I have reason to believe that the object we seek has attached itself to one of these dreamlets.

'So – you don't actually *know* which one.'

If I knew that, why would I need you, or the Horse? The smugness had gone, to be replaced once again by the Voice's habitual petulance. *A thing can only be pulled out of Dream as a physical entity. Even a chunk of rock might do, if –* It stopped abruptly. *What was that?*

231

It looked like a streak of bright light shooting between the Horse's hooves. For the first time in their strange journey, Sleipnir showed signs of excitement. He pricked up his ears and shook his mane, and blew sparks out of his nostrils. The sparks were red and orange, and circled around them like fireflies.

'Is that it?' Maggie said.

No, it's not. The Voice was curt. *But we may not be the only ones looking for the Old Man.*

Maggie squinted into the cloud, trying not to think of the infinite space beneath it. She found that it was far more comfortable to recall the illusion of a mist-covered plain, beneath which occasional marsh-lights flared. The light she had seen was nothing like these: for a start, it was much brighter; and secondly it seemed to move below them with a definite intent. It was also getting closer. Maggie saw it shining out, brighter than the heart of a forge.

'Is it – one of the Seer-folk? Is it my sister?' Maggie said.

I hope not, said the Voice dryly. *After what happened on Red Horse Hill, I'm not exactly confident.*

'That's not fair!' Maggie said. 'I didn't know she was one of them.'

The Whisperer gave a mental shrug. *The fact is, you're unreliable. Your loyalties are divided. I can see it in your mind. You think you can win her over.*

Maggie looked defiant. 'Well, maybe I can win her over,' she said. 'If only I could *talk* to her—'

Listen, Maggie, said the Voice, sounding very cold now. *I know you don't trust Me. I understand. I hope the time may come when you do. But you care about Adam, don't you?*

'Yes.'

Then for Adam's sake, do as I say. I will tell you what to do. And when we have the Old Man, I will let the boy go.

Maggie nodded. 'All right.'

Beneath them, the light was dazzling now; a shield of brilliance under the mist. It was hard to see details in the cloud, but for a moment Maggie thought she could see the shape of something behind the brilliance. She narrowed her eyes, then, remembering that this was Dream and that here her inner vision was strongest, made a circle between her left forefinger and thumb and squinted through that at the moving light.

The result was dramatic. She suddenly saw, in the burning heart of that radiance, the image of an old woman – eighty, ninety, a hundred years old – her white hair flying out behind her, her legs tucked under her body, her hands clenched tightly onto the side of—

Was that really a *washing basket*?

For a moment Maggie could only stare. It certainly looked like a washing basket; its spectral form danced in the air, and beneath it, bearing it along, was something almost like a horse . . .

Of course, it bore no resemblance to horses Maggie had already seen. It did remind her of Sleipnir, though – Sleipnir in the Aspect he had assumed on Red Horse Hill. But whereas Sleipnir was fiery in Aspect, this creature – if it was alive at all – was very clearly a spirit of the air. It seemed to be made up of filaments of light, strung like luminous spiderweb across the darkness. Its tail stretched out interminably; its mane was a burning nebula. And, astride it, the old woman in her washing basket grinned and cackled and waved at her.

Gods! She sees me, Maggie thought.

But the Whisperer was showing signs of agitation.

Lose them! ordered the Voice in her mind. *Don't let them follow us any further.*

'Is she one of the Seer-folk?'

No, it's worse than that, said the Voice. *Wake the Red Horse of Tribulation, and soon the others will wake up too. If you'd done your job on Red Horse Hill* – Maggie heard it snap off the thought like someone cutting the head off a rose. *Never mind that now,* it said. *But we need to outrun it. It means to follow Sleipnir.*

As if he had heard his name spoken aloud, Sleipnir gave a nervous whinny. Maggie noticed that he was beginning to revert to his fiery Aspect – sparks shot from his mane and tail; his legs began to lengthen; the net of glam that bridled him began to shine a brilliant blue – and Maggie knew that in a few moments the

233

strawberry roan would once more become the creature she'd birthed from the Horse's Eye.

Hang on! warned the Whisperer. *We may have to travel on rough terrain —*

But before it had even finished the sentence, the fabric of Dream was already changing around them. Gone were the illusions of earth and sky; gone was the distant river, the clouds at the horizon. Now there was no horizon at all, but a cluster of lights in the distance towards which Sleipnir began to accelerate at some incomprehensible speed.

Keep firm hold of the reins!

But Maggie had no intention of letting go. Her only previous ride through Dream had been tame in comparison with this, and she did not have Maddy's experience of travelling through Netherworld. This was altogether different, and if it had not been for Adam, still waiting for her in the Universal City, she would have banished the Whisperer from her mind and escaped the horrors through which she now fled . . .

Islands, the Voice had called them.

To Maggie, they were nothing like any island she had ever heard of. But they *did* float; like Fair Day balloons they drifted around the travellers, moving in every direction, some circling, some rising, some clothed in glam, some almost dark. Some seemed to be travelling upside-down – whole cities floating in midair with their spires scraping the river bed; though for all Maggie knew, *she* was the one who had lost her sense of perspective.

There were places that looked almost like home, with its narrow streets and its harbour. There were valleys and peaks, forests and glades. There were stolen moments; lost loves; secret kisses; guilty thoughts. There were diamonds buried a million miles deep, and hidden fears and long-lost friends. There was standing in the marketplace, clothed in nothing but your skin, while a crowd of village Elders watched in disapproval. There were creatures shaped like musical instruments; hens with heads like trumpets and tuba-bodied pot-bellied pigs. There was swimming in the One Sea by night, watching the shooting stars overhead. There was running barefoot down an endless corridor, with terrible creatures in pursuit. There was the memory of birth and the certainty of death. There was nothing; there was everything – and through it all rode Maggie Rede and the Horse of Fire, while Crazy Nan and the Horse of Air followed in their turbulent wake.

And then, just as suddenly, they stopped, and Maggie found herself floating in a small red rowing boat down a swift-moving river. There were no oars on the rowing boat, and yet it moved freely enough, rocking violently to and fro. Maggie, mindful of Sleipnir's earlier transformations, kept a firm hand on the rudder and tried to avoid the debris that seemed to rise and fall in the murky water. She soon became aware that the Horse of Air had joined her – once more becoming the washbasket in which Crazy Nan had begun her journey – but, urged to greater speed by the Voice inside her mind, she concentrated all her efforts on following the current towards a third vessel, seemingly adrift, just visible through the thick mist coming off the water. The third vessel was unoccupied, but there was something there all the same; something that Maggie could *almost* make out in the runeshape made by finger and thumb . . .

'Is that the Old Man?' she said.

Whatever it was, she thought, it was bright. Its brightness baffled her truesight. It was like looking at something against the sun; and she found that even through *Bjarkán* she could not determine the size of the thing, or whether or not it was alive.

Don't waste time! said the Whisperer. *Just reach for it as you go past!*

'*Reach* for it? With what?' Maggie said. 'I don't even have a piece of rope.'

But already the time for discussion was past. The river Dream, here at its source, flows with incredible swiftness, and Maggie's little rowing boat was being carried along at such a speed that within the four or five seconds of their conversation they had almost reached their target. Crazy Nan was not far behind – perhaps a couple of boat lengths – and Maggie could hear her laughing and singing to herself above the roar of the river.

'Let it go!' cackled Crazy Nan. 'You can't outrun Epona!'

From which Maggie quite wrongly concluded that Epona was this mad old demon-woman's name, and wasted unnecessary seconds trying to remember if she'd heard it before, or indeed why the bizarre spectacle of an old woman riding in a washing basket should awaken in her memory the sound of her dead mother singing, and a sudden craving for roast beef—

Stop her! the Whisperer almost moaned. *Let her get in front of you, and all My work will be in vain . . .*

Maggie kept her hand on the boat while trying to see over her shoulder. The crazy old woman was six feet away. For a moment Maggie's granite-gold eyes met Nan's faded blue ones, and she raised her hand, where the rune Ác flared, ready to strike

'Maddy Smith!' cackled Nan. 'Fancy seeing you here! We're going to the land, girlie!' she cried, shaking her head in glee. 'The Land of Roast Beef, where the Faëries play, and no one ever goes hungry!'

Perhaps it was hearing that name, Maggie thought, when she later recalled what had happened. Or perhaps it was the sudden idea that the old woman had pulled a thought from her mind. Either way, it spoiled her aim, and Ác flew harmlessly past Nan's head and vanished into the slipstream.

At the same time, a wave propelled Nan's washing basket a fraction *ahead* of Maggie. Nan's skinny arm shot out and grabbed something out of the third boat, and then the Horse of Air was off, careening through the waters of Dream and right up into the rapturous air, with Nan's voice shrieking with glee in its wake and the Whisperer's rage, immense and all-consuming, crushing Maggie like a vice and roaring in her head:

NO! NO! IT WAS IN OUR HANDS!

And then the impossible happened. Crazy Nan dropped her prize. Perhaps it was the excitement, or the fatigue of that ride to the gates of Hel, or the fact that her old arms were not as strong as they used to be. In any case, she dropped it, and for a moment the object that both of them sought fell like a star across the face of Dream.

Maggie, who had gone cold at the thought of what her failure might mean for Adam, found herself acting on some instinct she never knew she had. With uncanny speed she flung out Sleipnir's reins like a fishing line and *dragged* at the falling object. For a second she thought it hadn't caught . . . and then it was somehow in her hands – a thing that *might* have been a rock, but which gleamed a curious kingfisher-blue.

And then, in a moment, she was back: Dream closed like a curtain behind her. She almost fell as the Red Horse gave an eager lurch towards the hay net above his stall. The ride must have given him quite an appetite, thought Maggie, clinging to the object she had brought out of Dream; then she slid off the Horse's back and into Adam's waiting arms.

'Adam, I got it! The Old Man!'

Let me see it, the Whisperer said, resuming its place in Adam's mind. The boy was not an ideal host – it would have been far better to possess the girl, with her marvellous, untrained, unbroken glam, but it already knew from experience that Maggie was too strong to break. Unless she gave herself willingly, beggars could not be choosers.

Take it! it commanded, and Adam obeyed, at the same time wondering what was so wonderful about a piece of rock. It looked like the volcanic glass that, long ago, he and his friends used to dig out of the sides of Red Horse Hill, although this was by far the largest piece that Adam had ever seen. It was heavier than he'd expected, and when he turned it in his hands, he thought he could almost see features there, bluntly fashioned into the stone.

'It doesn't look much,' Maggie said. 'Are you sure this is it?'

Adam nodded. 'Quite sure.' He ran his hands across the glassy surface. It was warm; much warmer than ordinary stone, as if it might almost be alive. And now he even remembered it, although his acquaintance with the Whisperer's previous incarnation had lasted only minutes – most of them spent in abject terror as gods and demons did battle in Hel . . .

Now he remembered the goblin, who had seized hold of the stone Head and flung it into the river Dream – where the being who had once been Mimir the Wise had tried and failed to possess Maddy Smith; and how at that moment a Voice in his mind—

That's right, interrupted the Whisperer. *That's why I needed you for so long. A vehicle for My consciousness. Of course, you were only a temporary solution. You had no further potential. Not even a broken runemark with which to enter Asgard. I did what I could with what I had, but I knew that one day I would have to move on.*

'You want to go back in there?' Adam said.

Go back to my old cell? Oh no. I have something rather better in mind. Besides, it's already occupied.

Maggie was feeling restless. Unable to follow the conversation between Adam and his passenger, she had turned her attention to the rock that she had fought so hard to retrieve.

What was so special about it, then? Maggie formed the rune *Bjarkán*, and peered at the object through its lens. What she saw was something that looked rather like a big cabbage inside a shopping net; but the net was made of runelight – dozens and dozens of woven strands – and the cabbage—

She gasped and banished the rune. 'It's alive!' she exclaimed. 'It looked at me!'

The being that had once been Mimir the Wise felt a rare pang of amusement. It used Adam's voice to say: *'Did it now? Shall I introduce you?'*

Maggie stared at the stone Head. Now that she knew how to look, she could see the features quite clearly: the outline of a lean jaw; a jutting nose; a clever mouth now bracketed with double lines of anguish; and across one empty eye-socket a ruinmark that she recognized as a broken form of *Raedo*, the Journeyman, in reverse.

In its stall, the Horse of Fire made a shrill, uneasy sound.

'For pity's sake, who's *in* there?'

Adam looked at her and smiled. 'Maggie, meet the General. Otherwise known as the Old Man.'

4

MAGGIE STARED AT THE CHUNK OF ROCK. So this was the
Old Man she'd heard so much about; the thing that Adam valued
so much. Looking at it closer now through the circle of finger and
thumb, she could clearly see its features, dimly illuminated inside
the volcanic glass, and if she concentrated very hard, she thought
she could even hear its voice—

They had moved it to the penthouse where Adam and Maggie
had their rooms. Now, with the curtains prudently drawn, the two
young people examined their prize.

'Is it alive?' Maggie said.

The Whisperer laughed with Adam's voice. *Alive, and at My
mercy. Yes.*

'What is it? Who is it?'

*'Never mind. What matters is its value to us. With your power and
My knowledge, there's nothing that we cannot achieve.'*

Once more Maggie stared at the rock. The being that seemed
to be trapped inside mouthed frantic, silent phrases. Inside the
cradle of runes, it shone with a faint luminescence, and a brighter
glow lay at its heart, like a piece from a fallen star.

'A fallen star?' said the Whisperer. *'Yes, I suppose you could call it
that. Fallen from the Firmament into the depths of the Underworld; rescued from the realm of Dream; and now at last, at long last, My prisoner,
bound by his own glamours into the Aspect in which I was trapped for so*

239

long . . .' Once more Adam gave the Whisperer's laugh. *'What does it feel like, General, to be as helpless as I was?'*

'You mean it's one of the Seer-folk?' Maggie said in disbelief. 'Is that a demon trapped in there?'

'A demon, or a god. Who cares? There's hardly any difference. Make it talk,' it told her. *'You can do it. You have the glam. You can make it prophesy. You can make it give to you the runes of the Younger Script – the ones that will rebuild Asgard and make us lords of the Nine Worlds.'*

'I can?' said Maggie doubtfully. She put her hands on the piece of rock. The light at its heart shone fretfully. She followed the contours of its face, tracing its features in the stone. 'How do I *make* it do anything? It's a *rock,* for gods' sakes . . .'

With an effort, the Whisperer tried to contain its impatience. *'You have the Good Book. Use it!'*

Maggie gave Adam a doubtful look. That rasping note in his voice was not his, she knew, but that of his passenger. She hated the fact that her friend could be manipulated in this way, like a puppet in a sideshow; and she didn't much care for the offhand way in which the Magister spoke to her.

'You promised you'd let Adam go,' she said. 'I've kept my part of the bargain—'

'Bargain?' said the Whisperer. The rasping note was harsher than ever. *'Must we talk of bargains when the End of the Worlds is upon us? We have the Old Man in our grasp, and you're haggling over it like a loaf of bread in a village bakery?'*

Maggie opened her mouth to reply, but Adam interrupted.

'It's all right, Maggie,' he said, now speaking in his own voice. 'My master's manner can be abrupt. But if we want to save the Worlds, these new runes are all we need.'

Maggie looked doubtful. 'How many new runes?'

'No one knows for sure,' Adam said. 'We know the Firefolk have at least two.' He glanced at the Old Man, now glowing even more brightly. 'Maggie, this is our chance,' he said. 'This thing's a kind of oracle. It can tell us about the Seer-folk. Their plans. Their powers. Their numbers. With the runes, we can stop them. We can win this war before it even starts.'

Maggie looked at the Good Book lying open at her side. A text, all in runes, seemed to shine from the page where *Raedo* glowed a kingfisher-blue.

'Is this the text?'

Adam nodded.

Maggie fingered the journeyman rune. Even to her untrained hands, it felt uncommonly powerful. She aimed it at the stone Head, making its cradle of runes flare, and started to read from the Good Book:

'I name thee Odin, son of Bór.'

And was that a tiny glint of response, deep inside the heart of the stone? Was it just a reflection from the sunlight through the curtains? Or could it be a wink, she wondered, from a single gleaming eye?

'Be careful,' said Adam. 'It's dangerous.'

Maggie nodded and went on: *'I name thee Grim and Ganglari, Herian, Hialmberi—'*

The Head was glowing fiercely now, as if the being inside the rock knew that it was under attack. Maggie's own head began to ache, and she realized that this was part of the thing's defence; this demon, with its broken glam, was stronger by far than the Whisperer. She was already halfway through the verse when a voice spoke up inside her mind – a voice that was, for a demon, both surprisingly cultured and vaguely amused. She faltered and stopped mid-sentence.

Maggie Rede. At last, it said. *Can I just say how proud I am?*

'What?' said Maggie.

Don't be modest. For a torturer's first attempt, I think you're doing very well. Though you may have to work on your intonation.

'Who said I was going to torture you?'

Given the company you're in, it seemed a reasonable guess.

'You don't know the first thing about me,' said Maggie, turning back to the Book.

You're wrong. I know all about you. I've known all about you all your life. Did you think you were alone, under the old University? What did you think you were doing down there? Didn't it ever occur to you that every time you read from those books you were calling out at the top of your voice to anyone who could hear you?

Maggie looked back at the Good Book. 'You're trying to distract me,' she said.

Not at all, said the Old Man. *By all means, feel free to continue. You're very powerful, by the way. You certainly scared the sunshine out of my brother Loki. The snake was a clever detail, I thought. I wonder what you'll dream up for me.*

Maggie shot the Old Man a look and went back to the canticle. '*I name thee Bolverk,*' she went on. '*Grimnir, Blindi, Har-Harbárd—*'

Hárbard, corrected the Old Man. *The accent on the first syllable, please. And try not to stutter. A sensitive person might mistake it for mockery.*

'I don't need your help,' said Maggie.

No? I rather thought you did.

'Just let me read the canticle. *Then* you can help me all you want.' She went on with the ancient text, reading from the Good Book, and as she read, the runes on the page lit up, one by one, with a hectic light.

'*I name thee Omi, Just-as-High.*

I name you Sann and Sanngetal . . .'

The canticle was working. As she spoke, the net of runes flared, each rune lighting up in turn. As it did so, Maggie felt the Old Man's power recede and fail; its broken glam no match for hers.

Maggie, please. It hurts.

She flinched. The disembodied thing could feel. Its anguish set her teeth on edge, like walking over broken glass. She tried to steel herself to go on, but suddenly her mouth was dry. The Old Man was right, she told herself. She really was a torturer.

Maggie, you have to listen to me. The Seer-folk are on their way. You can't stop them, whatever you do. Even if you kill me now—

Maggie clenched her teeth. '*I name thee Vili, and Wotan, and Ve—*'

Maggie! Please! Just listen to me! Is this the Order you dreamed about?

Maggie faltered, then stopped.

She thought of Adam, a prisoner of the being that called itself Magister. She thought of her parents, dead of the plague, and of her brothers, dead of the Bliss. She thought of the Universal City, overrun with cut-throats and thieves. And then she thought of herself, dreaming of death and destruction, taking joy in the prospect of seeing her enemies suffer and bleed . . .

The Old Man was right, Maggie thought. There was no Order in all this. For three years her life had been nothing but Chaos, grief and loneliness. Could it be that the Old Man might give her something different?

Adam was looking impatient. 'What are you *doing*, Maggie?' he hissed.

Good question, Maggie thought. The Old Man was at her mercy now. One more couplet would break its will. But something inside her refused to go on. She had touched the creature's mind. She knew the anguish the Word provoked. And to torture a thinking, rational being – even one of the Seer-folk – was *this* what she had come to? Was this the price of Order?

The Old Man's struggles were weakening now. Its glam was almost exhausted. To speak the last words of the canticle, to annihilate this ancient being when it was already in her power, now seemed both needless and cruel.

Maggie closed the Good Book. The last two lines of the canticle – the final cantrip that would have bound the Old Man to her will – remained unspoken.

The creature in the chunk of rock gave a kind of mental sigh.

Thank you, Maggie. I'm in your debt.

In Adam's mind, the Whisperer gave a howl of frustration. *Don't stop! Don't stop! What is, WRONG with her? Tell her to finish it – finish it NOW!*

But Maggie's attention was focused elsewhere. In her mind the Old Man's presence was unfolding like a flower. What she had failed to take by force was offering itself willingly, page by page, like an open book – text, illuminations, maps – spread out before her in glorious profusion.

'What's this?' she said.

You wanted to know me. Here I am.

And now came a cascade of images, some strange, some troublingly familiar. Stories of the Elder Age; faces and places and sigils and glams; battles and banquets and fragments of dream; heroes and monsters and long-lost friends; old betrayals, lost loves; and beneath all that, a sorrow so deep, such a world of grief and loss that Maggie, no stranger to loss herself, could hardly bear to think of it.

The Old Man was *old*, she realized. Older than the Order; older even than the Universal City. Odin, son of Bór, had seen the World Tree grow from a sapling; had seen an empire rise and fall; had seen his children grow up and die; had watched the dance of Order and Chaos as it moved across the centuries. He had cheated Death; survived in Dream; had even escaped Damnation.

And all for what? He was alone. His people were scattered, aimless, at odds. Two of his sons were dead; the third still wandered, weakened, among the Folk. Of all his people, only his grandchildren, only the twins mattered now: Modi and Magni, children of Thor, the Oak and the Ash that would rebuild the Worlds—

Maggie opened her eyes in shock. 'No – I don't believe it!'

The Old Man's voice in her mind was dry. *Believe it or not. You saw what you saw.*

'You're lying!'

I think we both know I'm not.

For a moment Maggie was too stunned to think. The landscape of the Old Man's mind went on unfolding around her, but she was unable to take it in; dwarfed by that single, mountainous truth . . .

If she was Maddy's sister, then . . .

The Old Man was her grandfather.

With a cantrip, she banished the link that bound the Old Man's mind to hers. Relief flooded through her, relief so strong that her knees gave way and she fell to the ground. She began to shake.

'What's wrong?' Adam said.

Maggie found that she could hardly speak. A mass of emotions warred in her – emotions she could barely identify. Finally she seized on one that she could really understand; one that she'd had experience of throughout her short and troubled life.

Anger.

'Why didn't you *tell* me?' she said, and her voice was enough to make Adam flinch. The air crackled with fugitive glam, raising the fine hairs on his arms.

Deep down in his mind, his passenger whispered words of caution: *Don't mess this up, boy.*

But Adam needed no warning. He'd seen Maggie angry before, and knew that she could be dangerous. 'What did it tell you, Maggie?' he said. 'Did it teach you the New Script?'

She shook her head. She knew that her rage was not against Adam himself, but still she did not trust herself. She took a deep breath, felt dizzy and clung to the bed-post for support.

'That thing,' she said. 'The Old Man – did you know he was my grandfather?'

Adam *did* know, and had dreaded the time when Maggie might find out the truth. A lie would be disastrous – she would see it in his colours at once – and so he simply nodded and said: 'I did. Oh, Maggie. I'm sorry.'

Maggie felt her rage recede, leaving her very close to tears. 'Why didn't you tell me?' she said.

'I wanted to protect you.' Adam knelt beside her. 'I thought you might never have to find out . . .' He put his arms around her. For a moment she stiffened; then she put her head into the curve of his shoulder and sobbed.

'Don't cry, Maggie,' Adam said. 'You're not the first to be taken in. My master, your sister, even me—'

'My sister?'

Adam kissed her hair. 'She's been a pawn in his game all along. He used her to get to my master, then used her again to get to you. Now he wants to claim you as well. That's why we have to deal with him fast. And with the other Seer-folk.'

Maggie nodded. It all made sense. The Old Man had misdirected her; pretended to cooperate, discovered her weakness, then dealt her this blow. Was *this* how he had claimed Maddy Smith? By playing with her loyalties?

She turned her gaze towards Adam. 'He told me they were on their way.'

'Who?' said Adam.

'The Seer-folk.'

For a moment Adam said nothing. In his mind, his passenger had suddenly grown very still and very alert. He braced himself for the creature's rage, but when the Whisperer finally spoke, its voice was calm and silky.

The Seer-folk are coming? it said. *All right. Let them come.*

You don't seem very concerned, Adam said.

I'm not, replied the Whisperer. *The road to World's End isn't easy, especially not for the likes of them. Even if they manage somehow to settle their personal differences, they'll still have the Folk to deal with. Lawmen, posses, border patrols – all those things will slow them down; test their resources; drain their glam. And if we need to intervene – well, we have our dreamer.*

'Maggie,' it said in Adam's voice. *'All this has exhausted you. For the moment you should get some rest. Tomorrow we can try again.'*

Maggie looked at him gratefully. 'Next time I'll do it right,' she said. 'I promise I won't let you down.'

And now, once more, the Whisperer spoke silently to Adam, occasionally pausing in its instructions to check that the boy had understood. Adam listened carefully, and if he was surprised at some of the things his master required, he wisely avoided comment.

A boy from the Northlands, he told himself, should never have been caught up in this battle for Worlds, and he had long since given up any desire for power. The time was approaching when he would be free, the Voice in his head assured him. All he needed to do was obey, and very soon Adam would be able to do whatever he wanted – go home, if he chose; or stay in World's End and collect his final reward.

Just do exactly as I say, and I will give you everything that you have ever wished for. All you ever dreamed . . .

No more dreams, Adam thought. *If I had a wish, that's what it would be.*

Inside his head, the Whisperer laughed. *Granted,* it said. *Now do as I say.*

Adam Scattergood obeyed.

5

THAT NIGHT, IN SPITE OF HER FATIGUE, Maggie hardly slept. The richness of their surroundings, the softness of the four-post bed, the memory of the Old Man's voice like a dark caress in her mind – all conspired to keep her awake until at last she could bear it no longer. She crept out of bed, leaving Adam asleep on the sky-blue sofa, and went over to the window, where a moon for wolves to howl at was rising over the city, gilding the roof-tops and casting panels of light and shade across the floor of the penthouse.

The Old Man was on a plinth by the bed, silent under a dust-sheet. Was it sleeping? Was it dead? A part of Maggie hoped it was. But the greater part wanted nothing more than the chance to question their prisoner; to ask him about her family – and most of all, her sister – without alerting Adam, or the dark presence inside him of which she was always conscious.

Maggie tiptoed to the plinth and gently pulled aside the sheet.

'Are you there?' she whispered.

Something flickered inside the rock. *Maggie. You seem troubled,* it said.

'I need to understand something.'

The Old Man's colours brightened again, almost like a little smile.

Let me guess. You're troubled because I showed you where you came

248

from. You're a child of the Æsir – our last encounter proved that. As if there could be any doubt in view of that runemark you carry.

The smile was even more luminous now, casting patterns of colour and light across the darkened bedroom.

Maggie frowned. 'But how can that be? I was born here, in World's End. My parents were Susan and Donal Rede. Everybody knows that.'

Really? said the Old Man. *Did you know it, Maggie? Or were you always different? Always asking questions? Always wanting something more – a thing you couldn't even name? Always looking for a place you didn't even know was there?*

Maggie's eyes widened. 'How could you know that?'

I was in Dream for a long time. I saw a lot of things there.

'You saw my dreams?' Maggie said.

Maggie, I've been watching you since the end of the Elder Age. I know how alone you must have felt, but believe this: I never forgot you. Not for a moment. All this time I've awaited my chance to bring you home to your people.

'I don't believe you!'

I think you do. Why else would you have come to me?

There was no answer to that, of course. Maggie knew that he was right. For all her suspicion, for all her rage, there was something that drew her to the Old Man; something even stronger than the thing that drew her to Adam. It was wrong – disloyal, perhaps – but there was no denying it. The knowledge that she had a family had altered the landscape of her mind. Now a range of mountains stood where once there was nothing but wasteland. Her sister. Her father. Her grandfather. All of them waiting to welcome her home . . .

'You told me they were on their way,' Maggie said.

I told you true.

'What are they coming for?'

You, of course. The Old Man's voice was tender now as it whispered and coaxed in Maggie's mind: *Magni, child of the Thunderer, I name thee; Magni, child of Thor; I name thee child of Jarnsaxa; born of Order and Misrule; I name thee Ác, Thunder Oak; sister of Aesk,*

249

Lightning Ash; I name thee Builder, Destroyer; War-bringer and Bow-breaker; Dreamer and Awakener and Mother of the Latter Age . . .

And now, as she listened to the words, Maggie began to experience a curious sensation. From feeling scratchy and restless, she began to feel almost sleepy. Her heavy eyes began to close. Her mouth curved in a little smile. Dream, in all its seduction, began to unfold its petals—

She snapped her eyes open. 'Stop that!'

She saw what it was doing now. The Old Man was trying to charm her, to take her off-balance, subdue her will, to ease her into the world of Dream, where she might be susceptible to the same kind of possession that Adam's Magister had already tried – and failed – to inflict upon her.

Panic brought her to her feet.

It's all right, said the Old Man. *Just listen for a moment more—*

But Maggie's cry had woken Adam. 'What are you doing?' he said in alarm.

The voice in her head grew urgent. *I wasn't trying to hurt you,* it said. *You must understand. I've made mistakes; I've done bad things. But I would never hurt you. We are your family, Maggie Rede. We love you. We want you. We need you—*

'I said *stop!*'

And with that Maggie flung the rune Ác with all her strength at the prisoner. There came a howl of anguish from the creature inside the rock, and the net of runes that enclosed it flared so brightly that its pattern was imprinted on her retinas for several minutes afterwards.

Maggie shielded her eyes against the sudden blaze of runelight. Then, as abruptly, the Head went dark.

'What in the Worlds were you playing at?' Adam was standing beside her.

'I couldn't sleep.' Maggie's heart was pounding like a hammer. 'I got up to talk to the Old Man, and then he tried to trick me . . .'

She looked at the darkened Head in dismay. 'I haven't killed him, have I?' she said.

Adam shook his head. 'No. But you have put him out of action. Tell me exactly what happened,' he said.

Faltering, Maggie tried to explain. About her curiosity; the urge she'd felt to speak to the thing alone and without hindrance; then how it had drawn her in, seduced her with words and canticles . . .

'What did he tell you?' Adam said.

Maggie hung her head.

'Well? Did he mention your family?' Adam's voice was relentless. 'Did he say he needed you? Wanted you? *Loved* you, perhaps?'

Maggie nodded wordlessly.

'Of course he did,' Adam said. 'I told you he was dangerous. I warned you, Maggie, didn't I? I said he'd try to seduce you.'

'I know. I *know* that,' Maggie said. 'I just thought . . .'

'You could reason with him?' Adam said in a dry voice. 'You think he really cares for you? You think because of who you are he wouldn't sacrifice you like a shot if it happened to serve his purpose?'

And now Adam told her about Maddy Smith: about how Odin One-Eye had befriended her when she was just seven years old, and groomed her into doing his work, and sent her at great peril into World Below – without so much as a warning – to find a glam of the Elder Days that the Æsir called the Whisperer . . .

'*That's* how much *he* cared for her,' Adam finished triumphantly. 'She was seven years old. An innocent. He lured her away from her family. He corrupted her. He taught her to kill. He made her into a murderer. So don't you be getting any rosy thoughts about how she might be redeemable. *None* of them are. They're the enemy. They never wanted you before, and the only reason they want you now is because you're the Rider of Carnage.'

Maggie sighed. 'I see that now. I suppose you think I'm very naïve.'

'No, Maggie. I understand better than you think.'

She looked at him. 'You do?'

'Of course. You think *I've* never been lonely? You think *I've* never wondered what it's like to have someone to love?' He turned away, and from the corner of his eye saw Maggie watching intently. 'No one's ever wanted me,' he went on in a quiet voice. 'No parents, no people, no friends. Just my master, and now—' He stopped.

'Now what?'

'Nothing. Forget it. Go back to bed,' Adam told her curtly. To an outsider, it might have looked as if he were struggling to contain some long-repressed emotion. In fact, he was trying not to laugh. 'Why should you care what *I* feel?' he said. 'I'm nothing to you, after all.'

Maggie put her hand on his arm. 'That's not true. You're my only friend—'

'I don't want to be your *friend*,' he said, turning to her abruptly. 'I've tried, but I can't. I love you—'

She looked at him, startled. '*What* did you say?'

'I love you,' he said, and touched Maggie's face. Blue eyes looked into grey-gold. Deep inside, he was grinning.

'Adam, I—'

'Shh,' he said, and drew her gently towards him. The gesture felt so natural that Maggie barely even gave it a thought. Her head sought the part of his shoulder that seemed to fit her so perfectly, and she closed her eyes with a long sigh. His hands dropped gently to her waist. He started to guide her towards the bed.

For a moment he felt resistance. Maggie, he knew, had been raised to believe in purity above all things. Over three days he had done a great deal to break down those beliefs and to replace them with those of his passenger; but even so, he knew that this was the ultimate test of her loyalty.

'I've loved you since the day we met,' he said in a dreamy, coaxing voice. 'Ever since that day in the tunnels I've thought you were the bravest, the most beautiful girl I'd ever seen in my whole life. And I'm not afraid of dying in the battle with the Seer-folk, but I'd never forgive myself if I went without at least telling you how I feel.'

And then he kissed her on the mouth, and Maggie forgot the End of the Worlds, the Old Man and the Whisperer; she forgot the Æsir, her sister and her family; she even forgot the Good Book and all its rules on modesty. In fact, she forgot everything but the touch of Adam's hands, the faint and sleepy scent of him, and the words of love he whispered to her, more potent than any runecharm . . .

And as the two of them lay entwined on the giant four-post bed, Mimir the Wise felt a tremor of joy as he finally saw his goal within reach; and the Old Man of the Wilderlands, silent in his bed of rock, kept his counsel and slept, and dreamed, like all slaves, of being master.

6

MEANWHILE NAN AND THE Horse of Air were skimming over Hel's domain. It wasn't the first time Nan had seen Hel – Crazy Nan was used to the worlds around Dream, and had spent much of her life there. Since childhood, waking or sleeping, she had always felt more comfortable in Dream than anywhere else, which was why folk had always called her daft, and had avoided her company.

Some even believed (Nat Parson among them) that her travels through Dream had robbed her of her soul as well as her sanity, and had called for her to be Examined; but in spite of the ruin-mark on her forehead – a barely recognizable corruption of the rune *Fé*—

Nan showed no other sign of possession, and so the campaign was abandoned. After all, Nan Fey had her uses. She was an excellent midwife; she had a knack with healing herbs; and for the few like Maddy Smith, who listened to her stories, she was a source of old tales, of rhymes and half-forgotten lore.

Now Nan soared over Hel and wondered what she should do for the best. She had failed to bring back the Auld Man, which was a problem, but not an insurmountable one. Odin One-Eye had a knack for dealing with problems, and besides, wherever he was, he was better off there than floating in Dream like a cork in ale, waiting for Chaos to swallow him up.

She decided to get back to Malbry. She had already spent too long in Dream, where Time works somewhat differently than in any of the other Worlds, and there were more pressing concerns at home than brooding over the Auld Man. His birdies would tell her what to do next. But with the gods having set off for World's End, the situation on Red Horse Hill was reaching a fine old crisis point, with no one left to deal with it but Nan herself – and, of course, Epona. Just *how* an old woman and a washing basket might be able to close a rift in Dream that neither Æsir nor Vanir had managed to close in the past three years, or deal with the dreamcloud that even now was spreading fast towards Malbry, reducing everything it touched to fragments of shining cinder, Nan was as yet uncertain. But the Rider whose name was Lunacy had a lunatic's optimism, believing that there was always a way; so she promptly urged the Horse of Air back towards the waking Worlds.

Some time later she was awake and sitting in her washing basket exactly as she had been when she set off on her extraordinary journey, and if it hadn't been for the fact that it was now full night and the kitchen fire had gone out, coupled with the stiffness in her old legs and the gnawing at the pit of her stomach, she might almost have thought that no time at all had passed since she and the Horse of Air had vanished over Malbry.

And speaking of the Horse of Air . . .

Nan climbed from the basket and looked out of her window. In the garden Epona was cropping the frozen grass by the door, though now her Aspect had shifted to that of a rather elderly white mare with one milky eye and one dark one, which gleamed disreputably at Nan in the moonlight, as if the old Horse wanted nothing better than to stir up trouble in one form or another.

Nan went outside. It was snowy, but clear. Gently she patted the white mare's mane and took a lump of sugar from her apron pocket. Epona accepted the sugar lump with a greedy snort and shook her head, wanting more.

255

'There's a good old girl,' said Nan. 'Ye've done very well. You have a rest now, while I feed the cats.'

Nan's cats were mostly wild, though some of them ventured inside the house. Keeping a cat for any other purpose than catching mice was not common practice in Malbry, and many of the village folk took this little foible of Nan's as further proof of her eccentricity. Nan liked her cats, however, and always fed them at half-past five every afternoon, at which time they would assemble outside the cottage and raise a plaintive chorus.

Today Nan was long overdue. The moon had been up for hours and the chorus of mewing had grown to a wail. She hurried outside with her bucket of scraps, to be greeted by more than two dozen cats – brindled and tabby and black-and-white – winding between her feet and legs and purring loudly and expectantly. So loud was this collective purr that Nan almost missed the sound of the rift between Worlds, now grown to the sound of a waterfall during the spring melt, and when she eventually heard it, she was shocked by how much its voice had increased during her few hours' absence.

She left a pan of bread-and-milk for the cats and hurried onto the Malbry road. The village lay some miles away – so far that on a still day Nan could only just make out the ringing of the church bells – but tonight the sound of the rift in Dream was very clearly audible, which meant, Nan thought, that in her absence the dreamcloud had already crept visibly closer to the village; at this rate, in a week or less it would be at their doorsteps. If she looked very hard she could see it too, snaking against the starry sky like the Serpent with its tail in its mouth, ready to devour itself.

'Oh my Laws,' said Crazy Nan.

Crawk, came a voice behind her.

She turned, and saw a raven perching on the fencepost. She recognized one of the Auld Man's birdies – the smaller one with the white head – and reached into her apron pocket for another sugar lump. She tossed it to the raven; Mandy caught it in her beak and transferred it immediately to her claws, turning it deftly round and round like a puzzle she was trying to solve.

Nan smiled. 'Here ye are. I thought I'd see ye before long. I reckon ye already know the news regarding the Auld Man?'

Ack. The raven pecked at the sugar lump. *Ack. Ack.*

'Attack,' translated Nan.

Crawk. It finished the sugar. *Kaik.*

'I don't have any cake,' said Nan. 'Ye cleaned me out last time, ye did.'

Kaik. Kaik, said the raven.

'Ach, *wait*,' said Nan. 'Ye want me to wait.'

Iar, said the bird.

Nan frowned. The Auld Man's birdies had never been what you'd call easy to deal with. The big one, Hughie, could talk all right, but rarely said anything useful. The smaller one was better at carrying and remembering messages, but tended to find speaking difficult. Now it hopped down from its perch and pecked energetically at the frozen ground.

'Wait,' repeated Nan. 'How long?'

The raven *crawk*-ed again. Once more it pecked at the cold ground. But this time its beak left a mark in the snow – a mark that stood out in the moonlight—

'What is it? A glammy?' Nan said.

Iar. Iar. Iar.

This seemed to be all the bird had to say. After several minutes of pecking the ground, of squawking, of strutting up and down, of hopping onto the fencepost and back again, Mandy finally seemed to lose heart, and with a final accusing *Crawk!* took wing and vanished into the sky.

Nan studied the mark in the snow. It certainly *looked* like a glammy. One of the New Script, likely as not; though how she was meant to use it, gods only knew.

Still, the Auld Man would find a way. He always did, she told herself. Chances were, wherever he was, he was just where he wanted to be. And if his birdies said to wait, then wait was what she had to do.

And so the Third Rider went back inside and made herself a pot of tea, while Epona cropped the grass in the yard, and on the road from Red Horse Hill the serpent of mist inched closer still, dissolving everything in its path into the stuff of dreams.

7

A WELL-EQUIPPED PARTY, TRAVELLING LIGHT and changing horses at every stop, might possibly reach World's End in a week. But it soon became clear to all concerned that the gods and their allies in Chaos could not hope to make the trip in anything under two.

It wasn't just the distance to be covered, which was significant enough, but the number of outposts they had to pass, with all the tedious formalities that entailed – credentials checked, baggage searched, names and identities called for – formalities that would, at best, cause grave delay to the party.

Better to travel cross-country, they said, avoiding the outposts as much as possible, and keeping away from the cities. It would add some time to their journey, but would save them from having to deal too often with the Folk, who, with their deep-rooted mistrust of all things Outlandish, would not make it easy to pass unchecked.

In Aspect, or in animal guise, they could have spanned the miles easily. But gone were the days (for most of them) when such glam could be used without counting the cost. Now the gods were cautious, reserving their strength for what lay ahead, knowing that every mile they crossed in this way would leave them weaker when they arrived, to face an enemy as yet unnamed.

But Heimdall (who was in charge of supplies) was painfully

aware that time itself was now in shortest supply, and that if they hoped to reach World's End before their remaining time had elapsed, then they would have to achieve something fairly impressive as far as speed and teamwork were concerned. Which was a pity, Heimdall thought, because so far neither teamwork nor speed had proved remotely achievable.

Twenty-four hours had already passed since they had set off from Malbry. In that time they had managed to cover no more than eighteen miles, or the distance between Malbry and the Hindarfell. A cheerless, mostly sleepless night had been spent in a bothy by the roadside, and the following day had been largely taken up with Freyja complaining about her feet; Frey trying to soothe her; Idun stopping to gather herbs; the Wolf Brothers eating everything in sight and chasing every rabbit that came within a mile of the road; Odin's ravens taunting the wolves; Bragi trying to cheer people up with a variety of singing styles; Skadi quarrelling with Njörd; Jolly quarrelling with Sugar; and Thor quarrelling with everyone. Nightfall had come as quite a relief, in spite of their painful progress, and by the time they stopped for the night, Heimdall was exhausted.

They found a small inn called the Moon and Stars, in which, for a generous payment (summoned, of course, by the money-rune *Fé*), the Watchman was able, first, to bribe the landlord, who claimed he had never seen such goings-on, and secondly, to pay for half a dozen rooms – not enough for all of them, but the landlord had insisted that no animals be allowed in the building, which meant that several of their number had to be banished to the barn, including Skadi, who had of course taken umbrage at having to share with the Wolf Brothers, and Njörd, who had joined them to keep the peace.

This turned out to be a mistake, as Heimdall soon discovered; for by the end of the evening Hughie and Mandy had found their way into the pantry, where they had started an impromptu party (to which only they were invited), in the course of which they managed to make so much noise and affray that the landlord was roused, and, emboldened by righteous anger as well as the prospect of generous compensation, had stormed up to Heimdall's room to demand an explanation.

It had been decided during the course of their trip that Heimdall should represent the group. He'd always been closest to the Folk; he was well-spoken and presentable as well as being a skilled negotiator, whereas Skadi's idea of negotiation was to strike first and negotiate later, and Thor didn't even know how to spell 'negotiation'.

This was why the landlord, whose name was Mr Mountjoy, had rightly assumed that Heimdall was in charge, and why the Watchman now found him, at one o'clock in the morning, standing at his bedside in nightshirt and cap, every whisker on his face bristling with outrage.

'Sir, I must protest!' he said.

Lucky for Mr Mountjoy that Heimdall slept with one eye open. If he'd wakened Thor in that way, there might have been serious consequences. As it was, the Watchman sat up and bared his teeth at the landlord.

'Couldn't this wait till morning?' he said, with dangerous composure.

'It certainly could *not*,' said Mr Mountjoy. 'May I tell you, sir, that in twenty years of being landlord of the Moon and Stars, and furthermore being, if I may say so, more than cognizant of the ways of travellers and Outlanders and Wilderlanders such as yourselves—'

Heimdall considered a silencing charm, but knew that he should preserve his glam. He simply narrowed his eyes and said: 'Please. Just get to the point, all right?'

But Mr Mountjoy was still in full flow. 'Let it be known, sir,' he went on, 'that I have *never* seen such carryings-on as I have witnessed this evening. Birds, loose women, dwarves, savage dogs, *woofs* – I'll have you know I don't hold with *woofs*, be they tamed or otherwise – roaming loose around the place, terrifying the customers—'

'But *we are the only people here*!' said Heimdall in frustration.

'Nonetheless, the principle stands.'

'All right, all right,' said the Watchman, almost snarling. 'How much to silence your . . . *principles*?'

Mr Mountjoy scratched his head. 'Well, there's four shilling for the veal pie that I was fancying for tomorrow's lunch; twenty for the two bags of sugar; ten for a churn of best butter; ten for a bushel of apples; six for the ravages done to a pudding I had laid by for Yuletime. Oh, and the bread, of course. Call it twenty. Plus distress and disturbance . . . Call it an even hundred.'

Heimdall narrowed his eyes still more. Those thrice-damned birds were becoming more than troublesome; and to judge from the sounds he had heard from behind the barn as he tried to get to sleep, he guessed that he would soon be asked to pay for damage caused to the erstwhile occupants of a henhouse by three demon wolves and a sea-eagle.

Did they think he was *made* of money? Heimdall asked himself plaintively. Even with the rune *Fé*, cash was not something he could pluck from midair without serious consequences to his glam, and the Universal City was still a long way away. In just seven days, something big was going to happen in World's End, and if he had read the signs aright, then this was a party for which none of them could afford to be late.

For the first time in his life Heimdall began to regret the absence of Loki, whose quicksilver tongue and sharp wits would have made short work of their problem.

'You'll have your money, landlord,' he said. 'Now will you let me get some sleep?'

As it happened, he managed less than an hour before the landlord was back again. Sugar-and-Sack, still more goblin than god when faced with the prospect of strong drink, had tunnelled into the cellar, where Jolly was already waiting for him, having first imbibed a whole keg of ale.

There had ensued an altercation, liberally punctuated with flagons of ale, which had rapidly descended into a fight when Jolly took umbrage at being called Stumpy, and responded by saying that Sugar was fat.

At this point the landlord had called Frederick Law, who,

entering the scene of the crime, found both perpetrators lying, blind drunk, by a silent pool of spilled ale. He carried them off to the local roundhouse; then returned with Mr Mountjoy to ensure that Heimdall was correctly informed:

'Because statute nineteen of County Law clearly states,' said the lawman, 'that a man must take responsibility for the actions of his underlings, including damage caused by same, and if these two dwarves belong to you, as I am led to believe . . .' He paused to peer at Heimdall.

'Yes?'

'It's just that we don't see many dwarves here, sir. Exactly what kind of business brings you to these parts?'

Heimdall took a deep breath. 'It's two o'clock in the morning,' he hissed. 'Wake me at nine.' Which response merely confirmed Fred Law's suspicions that the fellow with the golden teeth and the fancy armour was some kind of Wilderlands warlord with no respect for property or the Law; and so he called out his posse and set them to watching the Moon and Stars, just in case the party decided to up sticks and leave without paying their bill.

Which was why that morning at four o'clock, when Njörd and Skadi left the barn to embark on a further spot of hunting, the first thing they saw was a posse of the Folk, armed with spears and crossbows, sheltering in the porch of the inn and watching them in astonishment.

The first thing the lawman did was go and complain to Heimdall again, which gave the Watchman no choice but to order his livestock back into the barn – now secured with a padlock – and hope that nothing else happened.

His optimism – such as it was – was short-lived. He was awoken once more (this time at dawn) by the sound of raised voices. Getting up in haste to discover the cause of the commotion, he found the entire posse gathered in the smaller of the inn's two dining rooms, where Freyja, never able to resist the temptation to perform, was holding court – in Aspect – to a dozen noisy admirers; meanwhile, in the larger dining room, Thor was eating a whole roast ox while Frey attacked a side of beef, Sif was protesting loudly in front of a plate of sausages, Bragi and Idun were singing a duet, and Ethel was calmly dunking biscuits in tea while all Hel was let loose next door.

'We may have a little problem,' she said.

'Oh gods,' said Heimdall.

The scene in the smaller dining room was already beyond disastrous. The Folk were very easy to charm. Already the goddess of desire had them all competing ridiculously for her favour: eyes and noses had been blackened and bruised; pieces of furniture had been overturned in the scuffle for her attention.

One fellow lay at her feet like a dog; another hastened to bring her a cup of wine; several had tried to write poetry, with truly awful results; and even Fred Law and Mr Mountjoy were grinning like fools while Freyja – dressed all in white, her runemark gleaming guinea-gold against her bare shoulder and her long red hair spilling down her back like some kind of fabulous bridal veil – watched through modestly lowered lashes and smiled like the blade of a golden knife.

The Watchman immediately banished the charm by casting the rune *Fé*, reversed.

Freyja, in human Aspect, leaped to her feet. '*You!*' she spat at Heirndall. 'You *always* have to spoil things!'

Heimdall gave her a quelling look. 'You forget yourself, lady,' he said.

'Don't you *lady* me, you killjoy. I was having a *good* time till you came along! Why don't you just lock me in the barn with the others? Or with Sif in the piggery—'

'Sif isn't in the piggery,' protested Heimdall, glancing uneasily at the lawman.

'Well, maybe that's because she has Thor to protect her. I'm completely *alone* in the world ...' She blotted her eyes with her handkerchief. 'I have *no one at all* to care for me—'

'Stop that,' said Heimdall quickly, seeing the glazed, adoring look return to the eyes of the possemen. He strode up to Freyja and led her to the far side of the room. 'We were trying to stay *inconspicuous!*' he hissed into the goddess's ear. 'And so far, the god of war is in gaol, as is the hammer Mjølnir. Skadi and Njörd are locked up in the barn along with what the innkeeper amusingly refers to as "our livestock". So much for our so-called *allies*. All I need now is for the Witch of Ironwood to make an appearance and ...' He paused to take another breath and, just at that moment, saw Angrboda coming down the stairs, discreetly attired in thigh-high boots and a corset of fur and dragon-scale, and gave an audible moan of despair.

'Why me? *Why me?*'

Fred Law gave him a guarded look. 'I wonder if you could spare a few moments, sir? Before you move on, I still need to know your business and your plans—'

Just saving the Worlds, Heimdall thought. *If only everything were so easy.*

In the good old days of the Elder Age, he would simply have used a cantrip or two to charm the man into doing his will. Even now, he knew that between them the gods had more than enough glam to defeat a posse of the Folk. On the other hand, could they really afford to alert every lawman this side of the Hindarfell to their presence? Could they fight the Folk all the way to World's End? And how much time (and glam) would that cost?

He managed to summon a strained smile and levelled it at the lawman. 'Of course,' he said through clenched teeth. 'I'll be more than happy to answer all your questions. But first, let me buy you all breakfast'– he grimaced at Angrboda – 'while I – ah – consult with my – *colleague* here—'

'Trouble?' said Angie in a low voice as Heimdall came towards her.

'We've come eighteen miles. *Eighteen miles!*' moaned the Watchman in desperation. 'How will we ever reach World's End? We set off thirty-six hours ago, and we're barely out of the valley!'

Angie shrugged. 'You need Loki.'

Heimdall, who had harboured just the same thought, now gave a howl of frustration. 'No!'

'I don't think you have the choice,' said Angie. 'Unless *you* can think of a plausible tale to explain all this to the lawman.'

Heimdall gave Angie a hard stare. 'Given that you and your wolf brood are somewhat to blame for *all this,* as you call it . . .'

Angie bristled indignantly. She was easy-going most of the time, but any attack on her children and she reverted back to her Ironwood Aspect: cold and dark and deadly. 'Don't bring Fenris into this,' she said in a low and dangerous voice.

'Why not?' said Heimdall. '*You* did.'

'That's because we need him,' she said. 'Fenris, and the Wolf Boys.'

'Need them for *what?*' yelled Heimdall. 'All they've done so far is eat and get us into trouble! And now you're suggesting Loki – Loki, whose middle *name* is Trouble – as the best way to solve all our problems?'

The Seeress, who had observed the scene from the doorway of the larger dining room, looked at Heimdall with sympathy. 'Maybe Angie's right,' she said. 'Maybe we *do* need Loki.'

'But we have no idea where he is . . .' Heimdall began plaintively.

'Well, funny you should say that,' she said. 'In fact, I know just where to find him.'

'Where?' said Heimdall, his eyes brightening.

'He's in a cave by the Sleepers,' she said. 'And I think that by now he'll be more than happy to cooperate.'

Heimdall took a moment to think. 'But if you knew where he was all this time—'

'I wanted him *alive,*' Ethel said. 'The way you were talking yesterday, you'd have lynched him before he could open his mouth.'

Heimdall began to protest at this, then decided against it. 'So – you really think we can trust him?' he said.

'*Trust* him? Of course not.' Ethel smiled. 'This is Loki we're talking about. He's a liar, a coward, a cheat, and very probably a traitor too. But faced with a situation like this, who would Odin have asked for?'

Heimdall snorted. 'Odin's not here.'

'All the more reason to do as I say.'

Which was why, a few minutes later, a falcon might have been seen winging its way from the Hindarfell, its signature a roaring

266

blue across the hazy winter dawn. It settled some thirty minutes later on a big rock outside a cave that Ethel had described to Heimdall.

Loki, sensing its approach, felt a surge of desperate hope. He knew what such a visit meant. Either the gods wanted him dead, or else they had a job for him. He looked into Sigyn's adoring face (she was at his feet, playing the harp), and tried to suppress a shudder. Either option, he told himself, would come as a deliverance.

8

'Don't you dare say a single *word*,' snarled the Watchman as he entered the cave. He'd had time to practise this scene in his head as he flew down from the Hindarfell, and he hadn't been looking forward to it. It always rankled to ask Loki for help – and to come to him now like a penitent, clad only in gooseflesh, was beyond humiliating. Heimdall had already promised himself that if Loki cracked a single joke – Hel's teeth, if he cracked so much as a *smile* – he'd break both his arms and worry about the consequences later.

Loki read the signs, of course, and carefully assumed a neutral expression. A small, polite gesture to Sigyn earned Heimdall a suit of clothes – yes, they were ephemeral, like all Sigyn's glamours, and thus did little to keep out the cold, but at least the Watchman's dignity was safeguarded, and it was therefore with slightly less belligerence that he addressed the Trickster thus:

'Now pay attention, Dogstar. I've come to offer you a deal.' He then went on to explain in full the situation at the Moon and Stars, all the while observing Loki for any sign of inappropriate humour.

'So basically,' Loki said, still wisely keeping a straight face, 'you're saying that you need me.'

'*Rrrr*,' said Heimdall between his teeth.

'I'm a liar and a traitor and I deserve to die, but' – Loki's scarred lips twitched irrepressibly – 'all the same – you need me.'

Heimdall started to calculate exactly how many of Loki's bones he could afford to break before he lost his value. Loki saw him working it out and resisted the further temptation to gloat. 'All right. Count me in,' he said. 'I mean, anything for the family. There's just one little thing . . .' He grinned. 'If I'm going to help you all get to World's End in time, then I'll need something in return.'

'I'm not here to bargain,' Heimdall said. 'We're giving you your freedom back, which is already more than you deserve.'

'Of course.' Loki's grin widened. 'I'm just saying that I may need some support, maybe even protection, if my plan to save the day doesn't happen to meet with the full approval of the gods.'

Heimdall frowned. 'So . . . you've got a plan?'

'I *always* have a plan.' Loki grinned even more widely. 'Listen, I'm not asking for much. But you know how things are with me and the gods. Some might be – shall we say *resistant?* – to any idea coming from me.'

'What's the plan?' Heimdall said.

'Oh no,' said the Trickster. 'That is *not* the way it works. You want my help? Take me with you. Make the others do as I say. I promise, if you do that, I'll get you all to World's End by dawn on the seventh day.'

'Impossible!' Heimdall said. 'The journey takes a fortnight.'

'Trust me, it won't. You have my word. As long as you swear to do as I say.'

Heimdall narrowed his eyes at Loki, now the picture of innocence.

'I'm asking for less than a week,' said Loki. 'After which you'll be free to take whatever retribution you deem appropriate – assuming I haven't kept my word.'

There was a long pause, during which Heimdall went over in his mind all the previous instances in which the gods had been obliged to go along – albeit most reluctantly – with one or another of Loki's plans. There had been many; but in each case, even Heimdall had to admit, the Trickster always found a way.

'You're really *that* good?' he said at last.

Loki shrugged. 'I'm Loki.'

Ten minutes later, the falcon had been joined by a companion – a small, fast-moving brown hawk with a gold ring around its foot from which a fine chain dangled. That was *Eh*, the Wedlock, with Sigyn's presence now inhabiting a small gold acorn-shaped charm at the end of the little chain. Both Loki and Heimdall had tried in vain to persuade her to sever the runecharm and stay where she was; but Sigyn was unshakeable. World's End was a dangerous place. Anything could happen there. What if Loki got into trouble? What if he was injured?

Heimdall thought this only too likely, but wisely kept the thought to himself. Sigyn was welcome to come, he said, as long as she didn't get in the way. Loki agreed, rather sullenly – but an acorn on a bracelet was better than a ball and chain, and besides, he told himself as he flew, who knew what inspiration a few days on the Roads would bring?

For the present, however, he simply tried to concentrate on the immediate problem: that of conveying seven gods, five goddesses, three wolves, a person of Chaotic origin, two ravens and a hammer through four counties in less than a week without expending too much glam or attracting undue attention. Not the easiest of tasks, he knew; but he *did* have a plan, and with Heimdall's help—

He grinned to himself, and his colours brightened as he flew. Whether the plan worked or not, it promised to be a lot of fun.

And if he failed?

He banished the thought. He'd burn that bridge when he came to it.

9

I T WAS ALMOST NOON AT the Moon and Stars, which was how
long it had taken for Heimdall and Ethel to persuade the gods that
trusting Loki was their best chance. Thor and Freyja were particularly resistant to the idea: both had good cause to remember the
last time Loki had tried something like this – an occasion that had
ended up with Freyja betrothed against her will and Thor, posing
as the bride, ready to break up the party.

Skadi too would have protested most violently, if she had been
consulted at all. But with runemarks reversed and glam running
short; with little money and fewer supplies; with Sugar and Jolly
still in gaol; with the lawman and his posse pressing for information and the Wolf Brothers locked up in the barn with Skadi
and Njörd, the remaining gods were beginning to understand the
value of a little subterfuge.

'Well, I'm not dressing up as a woman again!' declared the irate
Thunderer.

'Why not? It was fun. You looked so *cute*.'

Thor lunged at the Trickster, but Heimdall intercepted the blow.
'I told you. No one touches him,' he said, and gritted his golden
teeth. 'At least, not until the seventh day – after which you can hit
him all you like.'

The subject under discussion grinned and settled himself more
comfortably into Mr Mountjoy's favourite armchair. He had

arrived in his hawk Aspect, but planned to return with more fanfare later, and had sent Frey out in wolf form to make the necessary arrangements.

'So I'll need some paper and ink,' he said. 'And paint, canvas, glue, wood, and – oh, some little bottles of water.' Having provided these supplies, the gods left him alone for an hour, whereupon he emerged, slightly inkstained, but pleased with himself, and brandishing a number of carefully lettered pages. Ethel took one and peered at it.

'*Lucky's Pocket Pan-daemonium Circus!*' she read aloud. '*A Paragon of Excellence! Beasts and Marvels! Wonders and Freaks! Brought to you from the Wacky Wilderlands, come see*' – she raised an eyebrow – '*Mr Muscles, the Strong Man! The Amazing Wolf Boys! Queen of the Pigs!*'

Sif's eyes narrowed dangerously. 'Queen of the *what?*' she said.

Loki looked modest. 'Catchy, huh? Plus there's Helga and her Huskies, Dancing Dunhilde and her Dwarves, Biddy the Bird Charmer – *plus* we'll be selling Professor Pinkerton's All-Purpose Purgative Potion (bottles of water, to you and me), the Cure for Anything at All, from baldness to incontinence – especially when we've got Idun standing nearby with a healing charm hidden up her sleeve.' Loki shot them his brilliant smile. 'So? Am I a genius, or what?'

For a few minutes the noise was too great to make out any individual responses, and Heimdall was too fully occupied in shielding his unrepentant protégé from the rain of mindbolts and missiles that ensued to give anything else much attention.

Safe behind the rune *Yr*, the cause of all this disruption just sat and watched in a bored way, and played with the gold acorn that dangled from the chain on his wrist. It was a very delicate chain, though stronger by far than it appeared, and although it still linked Loki's hands together, it gave him freedom of movement without ever allowing him to forget that it was there.

'You're mad,' said Bragi, when the noise had died down. 'We're trying to keep a low profile, and you want us to pose as a *circus!*'

Loki shrugged. 'Best way,' he said. 'No one questions a travelling show. The freakier the better. You'll be welcomed with open arms. And as long as folk are entertained, they'll pay our way in food and supplies and wave us through the outposts. Besides, you'll get to play your guitar.'

'Really?' Bragi looked hopeful.

'Queen of the *Pigs*?' repeated Sif.

'Unless you'd rather be the Bearded Lady—'

'The bearded *what*?'

Ethel smiled. 'You know,' she said, 'it might just work.'

'Queen of the *Pigs!*' protested Sif.

'Let me hammer him,' said Thor.

'You'll do no such thing,' Ethel said. 'He's under my protection now.' She paused to allow the din to subside. 'Think about it, all of you. If he *is* a traitor, then the best thing to do is keep him with us, where he can't do any harm. And if he's not' – her expression darkened – 'well, it won't really matter to any of us unless we get to World's End in time.'

Loki gave Ethel a wary look. The Seeress had never been fond of him, not even before Balder's death, and he was mightily surprised that she should speak in his defence.

'Thanks,' he said.

She smiled at him. But it was a curious, troubling smile, which did nothing to reassure him. 'And you, of course, would be Lucky,' she said. 'Ringmaster, manager . . . general?'

Loki grinned. 'Of course. Who else?'

Ethel kept on smiling.

And so the Trickster got his way, and it was with the keenest enjoyment that he now set about allocating parts, going over details, and making sure that everyone knew precisely what he wanted of them. Few of the gods warmed to the idea. But short of charming every lawman, every outpost guard, every suspicious innkeeper between the Hindarfell and the Universal City, short of keeping to their Aspects for seven whole, impossible days without the chance to replenish their glam, they had to agree – reluctantly – that Loki's way was the fastest way.

Ethel remained as serene as before, saying little, but always alert. Loki found it unnerving. Still, he thought, the Seeress had always

273

been an enigma to him, and this new side to her was doubly so. Besides, he didn't really care; he wasn't planning to stay around for long. As for Tribulation . . .

Loki had already seen one Ragnarók, and wanted no more to do with it. War with Chaos . . . the End of the Worlds – this time around he meant to be far away when all Hel broke loose. Maybe on a ship somewhere, on his way to the Outlands. There were islands there, Loki knew, where no flake of snow had ever fallen; where tropical fruit grew all year round; and where the most strenuous thing a man did all day was pour himself another drink, or decide which of the local girls was prettiest, or choose from a laden table precisely which delicacy he wanted to taste next.

He deserved this, Loki thought. He'd already saved the Worlds once. This time around, he promised himself . . .

The Æsir could manage without him.

1O

Four whole days had already passed since Maddy and
Jorgi arrived in World's End. In that time she had come to realize
that her task was far from straightforward. The Universal City
was much larger than any town she had imagined or dreamed.
It stretched out like a patchwork quilt of squares and streets and
alleyways; of arches, cobbled courtyards, minarets, walled gardens and little fountains. There were shops and markets, traders
and thieves, street performers and animal shows and off-duty
sailors with money to burn. There were colleges and cathedrals,
which, though never as huge as Nat Parson claimed, nevertheless managed to rise twice as high as the tallest tree, scraping the
sky with their gilded glass spires. There were statues of ancient
dignitaries, long since stripped of their gilding and streaked with
soot and bird-lime. There were canals with rows of houseboats
crowded in their moorings; there were filthy slums standing
alongside gracious houses surrounded by trees. In one square was
a marble plinth on which stood a giant warlord of the Sea riding
on a serpent, both intricately carved in stone and surrounded by
little jets of water that rose and fell at intervals. Looking more
closely, Maddy was almost sure that she recognized Njörd's features in the marble, though Perth assured her that this was one
of the great kings of old – a king of the Elder Age called Knut,
whose power had been so great that he could hold back the

275

waves of the One Sea and raise its beasts at his command.

Perth was full of stories. Maddy had no way of knowing whether any of them were true, but all the same she was very aware of how much she needed his guidance in this city of perilous wonders. She had not been there above an hour before she realized that finding her sister would not be the simple task she had assumed; with the truesight, it soon became clear that the city was filled with signatures – some bright, some dim, all shuttling ceaselessly like threads in an intricate tapestry. It might take weeks to find Maggie Rede – if, indeed, she found her at all.

'Ah – why do you *need* to look for her?' Perth had been asking the same questions over the course of the past four days. 'Can't we just do business here? With your skills and mine, we could reach for the sky.'

Even in such a short time, Perth had proved himself a very apt pupil in the use of the runes, picking up the fingerings with the same effortless ease that he brought to picking pockets and palming coins. His own glam was almost as bright as Maddy's own, which led her to think that the rune he bore must be one of the New Script. She began to think of it simply as *Perth*, and hoped that maybe Ethel could help identify it more clearly, if ever she managed to bring the two of them together.

But teaching Perth the runes took time. So did keeping him out of trouble. Left to his own devices, Perth's new skills would probably have landed him in gaol within the week, and when she caught him cheating at cards by using the rune *Bjarkán* to look at his opponents' hands, she had to explain to her new friend that runes were not to be trifled with.

Glam was a dangerous gift, she said, to be used only rarely, and in secret. The days of the Order might be over, but there were still hangings in World's End.

Perth listened to the lecture with every sign of contrition, then went back to doing precisely what he had before, using *Fé* to make fool's gold or *Kaen* to cheat at knucklebones, so that much of Maddy's time was taken up in trying to keep him under control.

Might as well try to tame Wildfire, she thought, and realized, with an aching heart, how badly she missed Loki. The others too – all of them. She only hoped they would understand – assuming she survived to explain – why she had misled them, and why, when she could have gone to them for help, she had chosen to act alone.

Teaching Perth was one of the reasons why Maddy had made so little progress in the Universal City. The second reason was simpler. For the first time in her life Maddy Smith was afraid. Oh, not of the dangers of the big city, or of what she might encounter on her quest; but of what she might have to do when she finally tracked down her sister.

Raised by a man who resented her for her mother's death in childbirth; the younger, plainer sister of Mae, the prettiest girl in the village, Maddy had spent her childhood dreaming of finding her true family, the tribe that would accept her for what she was. She had found it in the Æsir. She'd discovered a father (of sorts) in Thor, a grandfather in Odin. But ever since Loki had told her the truth, Maddy had longed for her unknown twin with a silent, desperate yearning. The thought that she might have a sibling out there, born into the wrong family, dreaming the same dreams and waiting for Maddy to find her, had sustained her throughout the past three years. Even after the attack on Red Horse Hill Maddy had never lost that hope. So instead of alerting the Æsir to the danger that threatened them all, she had let the Trickster take the blame and fled alone to World's End.

Now Maddy's greatest fear was that her instinct had been wrong, that Maggie *was* the enemy, and that by her actions she herself might bring about the End of the Worlds. She wished that Odin's ravens would come and tell her what to do next. Or that Odin himself would speak to her again through Dream – but the only birds she had seen so far had been the drab-looking pigeons that infested the city, and her only dreams had been troubled, broken things that made no sense when she awoke.

And so she stayed with the only friend she had managed to find in World's End. Perth knew the place like the back of his hand; plus, his work in the city markets meant that Maddy would have the opportunity to watch lots of folk go by. Some day soon, she told herself, one of them would be her sister.

BOOK FIVE

The Pan-daemonium
Circus

Never give a sucker an even break.

Old Inlandic proverb

1

MEANWHILE, ON THE RIDINGS ROAD, a spectacle the like of which had not been seen since the Elder Age was making its way to World's End just in time for Ragnarók. Travelling briskly day and night, changing horses at every stop – six hundred miles in seven days would be no small feat for those horses, even with runes of endurance sewn into their harness – and with two performances daily, Lucky's Pocket Pan-daemonium Circus, now in its third day of existence, made its way down from the Hindarfell, through the North Ridings towards World's End, performing in villages along the way – to wonder and applause from the Folk.

A circus – even a pocket-sized one – tends to attract attention, and when it boasts such enticements as (for instance) a Wolf Boy, a Queen of the Pigs, Helga and her Huskies and the Most Beautiful Woman in the World, going unnoticed generally ceases to be an option. Loki had understood this from the start, but he knew that sometimes to hide in plain sight was easier than trying to pass unseen.

Loki was enjoying it immensely, of course. He was a natural showman. His words kept the audience mesmerized, and with clever lighting and a handful of cantrips he had them in the palm of his hand. He would have been happier still if Sigyn had not been with him, but in spite of his efforts to free himself, she had remained by his side, linked to him by the fine gold chain; either in her own Aspect, or in the shape of the small golden acorn that she had assumed during her flight from Malbry.

However, not even this could detract from Loki's enjoyment. Add to the main attractions Jolly and Sugar, in colourful costumes, driving in a little car drawn by a pair of turkeys; the Wolf Brothers and Angie, in their animal Aspects; the Strongest Man in the World (that was Thor); Heimdall, in his hawk guise, in a double-act with Njörd's sea-eagle, and (or so the Trickster claimed) Lucky's Pocket Pan-daemonium Circus seemed guaranteed for success.

The gods and their associates had rather more mixed feelings. Freyja, in her current role as the Most Beautiful Woman in the World, was naturally more than satisfied. Lounging inside a gold-and-white tent, she held court to a string of admirers who, with the help of a surreptitious charm or two, were more than willing to donate supplies, money, gifts or whatever it was that Freyja (or more often Loki) desired. Bragi, now billed as the Human Nightingale, was delighted to spend his days singing and making music to a crowd of adoring womenfolk. Even Skadi, in her role as Helga, with her Huskies, was willing to tolerate the foolishness to a certain extent, although she was sure that, even with horses at every post and the continued support of the Folk, Loki would fail to get them to World's End on time, and she was rather enjoying the prospect of seeing the Trickster bite the dust – as he would, at dawn on the seventh day, if by then they had not reached the gates of the Universal City.

Sif, however, was less pleased. Petula, Queen of the Pigs, had proved almost as popular as Freyja herself, especially with the children, who always brought along baskets of food, for Loki had assured the awe-stricken crowds that the Queen of the Pigs consumed no fewer than fourteen loaves of bread *per day*, as well as six bushels of apples, a side of beef, a leg of lamb, a smoked trout, a raised chicken pie, a seed cake, a plum cake, five dozen jam tarts (Loki was partial to jam tarts), a quart of milk *and* a dozen bottles of finest ale – and this, of course, was winter-time, which, so Loki told them, was a time of fasting for the Queen of the Pigs;

otherwise she would be so heavy that even a team of oxen would find it impossible to carry her.

This convenient story ensured that Lucky's Pocket Pandaemonium Circus was always well-provisioned; although, of course, it also meant that Sif had spent the past three days in a state of perpetual fury, during which time Thor had wisely kept out of her way – that is, when he was not already engaged in lifting hay-trucks, wrestling bulls, juggling anvils and performing all the other feats expected from the World's Strongest Man.

Their journey had been going so well. The roads had been mostly clear of snow. Since passing the Hindarfell, they had managed to cover a hundred and ninety miles – excellent going for northern roads – and by evening of their third day were nearing the border into the Lowlands.

This border was marked by the river Vimur, and the only crossing place within fifty miles was through a town called Rhydian. This was a trading centre of some importance, an industrial market town filled with journeymen, farmers, weavers, stonemasons, tanners, bargemen moving their cargo downriver towards World's End; and spanning the river at its narrowest part was the marvellous Rhydian Bridge, known throughout Inland as one of the wonders of the Age.

No one remembered how old it was. Some claimed it was the work of Jonathan Gift, the genius who had designed the cathedral of St Sepulchre. Almost four hundred feet in length, suspended from four great stone pylons by sixteen cables of twisted steel, the bridge had spanned the Vimur since before anyone could remember, almost untouched by the passage of time. Legend had it that there were ancient runes embedded in the bridge's foundations that kept the stones from crumbling, the sleek steel cables from weakening. Be that as it might, the skills required to design and build such a marvel had long since been lost in the mists of time, with the result that over the centuries Rhydian had become the greatest town outside World's End, a centre of trade and industry second only to the Universal City itself.

By midafternoon, through a rising mist, they could already see the Rhydian Bridge, marooned against the darkening sky. They could even smell the smoke from the town and the tanneries on the banks of the river, a rank, unpleasant, chemical smell; but to Loki – reclining on a pile of furs in the back of his wagon, drinking from a bottle of wine and eating one of Sif's jam tarts – that was the smell of money.

Just the place for a circus, he thought. Folk with money and goods to trade were always on the lookout for entertainment. This was no Uplands village, trading in loaves of bread and bales of hay. Here there would be horses, gold, furs, fine wines, perhaps even slaves. The people, though perhaps not as sophisticated as those of World's End, would have the kind of expensive tastes that come with northern money. With luck, and the right kind of patronage, the circus could ride on the takings for at least a hundred miles or so before having to stock up again, which would put them well within crow's flight of their destination.

In any case, the travellers had no choice but to cross the Vimur by the Rhydian Bridge. The detour to the next crossing place would mean most of an extra day's journey, all of it on minor roads, and Loki couldn't afford to lose even half a day of his intricately planned itinerary. This was already the third day of their trip to World's End. By dawn on the seventh he had pledged to lead them through the city gates – which meant that they had to move fast if they wanted to make it on time.

He wasn't expecting trouble. Over three days the gods had proved more than capable of dealing with the few setbacks they had encountered: a couple of bands of outlaws, rapidly dispatched by Thor; an officious border patrol or two, who had proved no match for Freyja's charm; roads obstructed by mudslides or snow – in short, nothing unusual, and things had been going so perfectly that the Trickster had allowed himself to become just a little complacent.

Now, with Rhydian in sight and, beyond it, the broad, easy Lowlands roads, he had allowed his guard to slip . . .

That had been his one mistake.

At first it had looked so promising. First impressions count, and with this in mind, the Trickster had taken great care with the three wagons that made up his retinue, each one drawn by a pair of horses and emblazoned with these words, in gold, against a scarlet background:

LUCKY'S POCKET PAN-DAEMONIUM CIRCUS!
A PARAGON OF EXCELLENCE!
BEASTS AND MARVELS!
NEW AGE CURES!
MYSTERIES OF THE ELDER DAYS!
COME ONE, COME ALL!

This somewhat boastful display had worked very well in other towns, and the Trickster was pleased with the effect. The performers themselves flanked the wagons – Thor, stripped to the waist to show his muscles, Sif riding alongside, in Sow Aspect, in bonnet and frock. Next came Idun and Bragi – Idun throwing flower petals at the crowd (as well as her healing skills, she seemed to have the ability to produce flowers and fruit of any kind, effortlessly, in or out of season); Bragi playing his guitar.

At the rear came Angrboda with Fenris and the Wolf Boys, all three in Aspect, collared and chained, trotting obediently at her heels, while some way ahead of the convoy, Jolly and Sugar – renamed Grumpy and Stumpy by Loki, much to their indignation – rode in their turkey-drawn cart, throwing leaflets and handfuls of candies into the crowds that lined the street . . .

At least, until they reached Rhydian.

But in Rhydian there *were* no crowds. No one came out to see the show. No children ran behind the horses; no one laughed at the dwarves in their cart. Loki, who usually led the procession, was at first intrigued, then troubled, then hurt.

What in the Worlds was *wrong* with these Folk? It wasn't an excess of Orderly zeal that kept the punters away from the show; there were no Laws in Rhydian against a travelling circus. It *couldn't* be lack of interest; unless these Folk were a different race to all the others Loki had met, there ought to be plenty of takers for beasts and marvels and miracle cures.

Finally, when they'd been in Rhydian over an hour and no one but a few dogs, a road-sweeper and an old woman in a black *bergha* had turned out to see the show, Loki asked the question.

'What *is* it with this place?' he said, addressing the crone, who was sitting on the kerbside drinking a bottle of Ridings beer. 'Is there nobody here who appreciates the arts?'

The old lady shrugged and grinned at him, exposing a set of fine wooden teeth. 'A course there is, lad,' she told him. 'But ye'll have to wait till sundown. *That's* when the town comes alive, see? That's when folk come out to play.'

'Oh,' said Loki.

The crone grinned again. 'But don't ye be counting your chickens yet. We've got a circus of our own. Right up by the Meridian Bridge.' (She used the oldsters' term for the bridge, which made her one of the few left alive who remembered Rhydian's true name.) 'Damn fine show it give too. Every day at sundown. I bet they could teach *ye* a thing or two.'

'You think?' said Loki.

'Aye,' said the crone. 'I think ye'll go a long way afore ye find better than Captain Chaos's Carnival. But don't you take my word on it. See for yourselves. Be at the bridge at sundown. It's going to be a Hel of a show . . .'

And at that the old woman flashed him a grin that showed every one of her wooden teeth, and went back to drinking her Ridings beer.

2

SINCE HER LAST DISASTROUS ENCOUNTER with the Old Man in the rock, Maggie had tried twice more to question him. Both times she had failed to awaken so much as a spark from the prisoner. Maggie blamed herself for this. The battle of minds between them and the force of the blow she had struck him had left the stone Head lifeless and dark, with no clue as to when – or *if* – its occupant might reawaken.

Even so, a part of her was secretly relieved. Her last conversation with Odin had left her angry and confused, racked with self-doubt and uncertainty, ready to question even those truths that she had always lived by.

Her attempts to locate the Firefolk had been equally frustrating. At the Whisperer's request, she had tried several times to find them through Dream; but either they had shielded themselves, or the turbulence from the rift between Worlds had temporarily obscured them from sight.

To her relief, the Whisperer had shown a surprising patience. The Old Man would speak eventually – it was only a matter of time. The Seer-folk were no immediate threat; sooner or later they would be found. Meanwhile Maggie stayed in the penthouse, playing chequers with Adam, or talking, or practising her runes, and the time slipped by almost peaceably, so that she sometimes let whole hours pass without even a thought of the war, or the End of the Worlds, or the Æsir, or the Old Man, or even the Good Book.

Every day Adam would spend an hour or two outside in the city, watching their surroundings, buying supplies, and checking on the Red Horse. Maggie always stayed indoors – it wasn't safe, Adam said, for her to show her face outside. When he returned, it was always with some little gift – flowers, or fruit, or pastries, or a necklace of brightly coloured beads – which Maggie accepted in grateful surprise. It had been so long since anyone had given her a present. She wanted to give him something in return, but failing the new runes, or some kind of map indicating the position of the Seer-folk, Maggie had nothing to offer him.

Now, on her third day of idleness, she was feeling increasingly restless. The day was bright and welcoming: spring was on its way at last, and suddenly Maggie was desperate to stroll along Examiners' Walk; to smell the scent of the linden trees or maybe buy a pastry or two . . .

She glanced at the window longingly. Adam had said he'd be back by noon, but the cathedral clock had chimed two and Maggie was getting hungry.

Surely, she thought, there could be no harm in opening the window a crack. She pushed it an inch or two ajar, and the scent of the city flooded in – a complex aroma of spices and ale, of perfumes and wood-smoke and ocean salt, of garbage and flowers and roasting meat – and with it came the familiar sounds of voices and hooves on the cobbled streets; of hawkers selling their wares; of dogs and shrieking gulls and the wind across the rooftops; the multitude of city sounds that Maggie had missed so terribly.

With one hand, she cast *Bjarkán*. If there was danger anywhere, the truesight would reveal it. But nothing unusual showed itself, and so Maggie opened the window a little wider and stepped out onto the balcony. It felt good to be outside. She looked over the balcony and took a deep breath of the city air. The chophouses and coffee shops were all open for business, and the smell of cooking rose from the streets, making Maggie's mouth water.

There was a vendor just below her and his cry – '*Sweet pastries!*

Fat Boys! Marchpane for your lady!' – made her mouth water all the more.

She could be there and back again in the blink of an eye, she told herself. Gone just long enough to buy a couple of the fried, sugared dough balls that World's Enders called Fat Boys. It would mean leaving the Old Man for no more than five minutes. Surely that would do no harm.

She flicked *Bjarkán* at the Old Man. It showed no sign of wakefulness.

Below her, in the crowded street, the vendor of pastries shouted his wares.

'Marchpane! Fat Boys!'

Maggie turned towards the door. *Five minutes. That's all. What harm can five minutes do?* And with one last glance at the Old Man, she left the room, locking the door, and ran down the steps into the street.

3

THE BIRDS WERE WAITING AS SHE came in, a sugared Fat Boy in each hand. Two ravens, one perched on the window-ledge, one, with a white feather on its head, actually *inside* the room, preening its feathers and watching Maggie with eyes of a curious wedding-ring gold.

Maggie put down the Fat Boys on the bedside table. *'Out! Out!'* she said to the birds, waving her arms threateningly.

The ravens seemed quite unperturbed. The larger one cocked its head and scratched at its wing in a languid way. The smaller bird – the one with the white feather – looked at the Fat Boys by the bed and made a hopeful crowing sound.

Kaik! Kaik!

'Not a chance,' said Maggie. 'Now will you both get *out* of here?'

The larger bird hopped onto the bed.

The smaller gave its raucous cry: *Crawk. Kaik.*

'Get out,' she said again.

'Now that's hardly bein' hospitable,' said a voice at Maggie's side and, turning, she saw that the raven had turned into a rag-gedy man, dark-eyed and dressed in black, with a great deal of silver jewellery, sitting cross-legged on the coverlet and watching her with a gleaming smile.

Maggie's eyes opened wide. 'Who are you? What do you want?'

'Well, I wouldn'ae refuse a quick bite . . .' He helped himself to a Fat Boy. 'I'm Hughie, and this is Mandy, and we've come a long way tae talk wi' ye.'

The raven finished his Fat Boy with a speed that was almost uncanny, and tossed the other to his companion, who while he was speaking had assumed the Aspect of a young girl with a streak of silver in her hair and a dragon-claw ring in her left ear.

Kaik, said Mandy affably, eating the Fat Boy with lightning speed.

Maggie eyed her suspiciously. *Could* these two creatures be Seer-folk? Anything was possible. And there was something about the pair that reminded her of the Red Horse: that hint of Chaos hidden behind an Aspect that seemed almost ordinary – especially in World's End of course, where even the most Outlandish of gear barely raised an eyebrow. Each one had a tattoo on their arm – a tattoo or a runemark, Maggie wasn't sure which.

She summoned the rune *Bjarkán* and glanced at the pair through the truesight. Like Sleipnir, their Aspects were different when viewed through the circle of finger and thumb: no longer human, nor even birdlike, but some kind of nightmarish hybrid of both, the black design on their arms now shining with almost unbearable light—

Maggie quickly summoned *Tyr*, the warrior rune, behind her back. 'What are you? Demons?'

Hughie grinned. 'Messengers, hen. Just messengers.'

'What do you want?'

'To make a deal. To come to some arrangement.'

'What kind of arrangement do you mean?' The rune *Tyr* was still poised to strike.

Hughie gave her a comical look. 'Hen, if we wanted trouble,' he said, 'we could have started some by now.'

Maggie's eyes flicked towards the plinth, where the Old Man stood silent under his sheet. Nothing seemed to have been disturbed. She allowed herself to relax a little.

'So what *do* you want?'

'We want tae help. Hugin and Munin, at your service. Travellers through Nine Worlds. Erstwhile messengers to the Auld Man himself, now in need o' gainful employment.'

'What kind of gainful employment?' she said.

'Anythin' ye like, hen. We can travel through Death, through Dream. We see things. We know things. Lots o' things.'

Maggie eyed him suspiciously. 'And you think I'm going to trust you? You just told me you worked for the Old Man.'

'Ach,' said Hughie, 'not any more. *You're* the Rider of Carnage, hen. That means we belong to *you* now.'

Maggie's eyes widened. 'To *me*?' she said.

Mandy *crawk*-ed.

'You mean – like servants or something?'

Hughie scratched his armpit. 'Servants, spies, sentinels; carriers, shield-bearers, outriders, batmen, purveyors of shiny things and generally jacks of all trade. Aye. That's the basic idea. So. What do ye say, eh?'

Mandy *craw*-ed and sniffed hopefully at the bedside table for Fat Boy crumbs. Maggie found herself wanting to laugh. The creatures might well be dangerous, with their mysterious runes and their ability to change into birds, but most of all they reminded her of wild, chaotic children – strangely endearing, full of fun, fizzing with restless energy.

She cast *Bjarkán* a last time. Once more she saw the creatures in Aspect; once more she scanned their signatures. She saw a tendency to theft, a great deal of mischief, some vanity and a constant craving for sweet things and shiny objects – but there was no thread of malice there among those frenzied colours. Whatever else they intended, the ravens meant her no harm.

'How can you help me?' she said at last. 'Can you give me the new runes?'

Hughie shook his head.

'Then can you wake the Old Man?'

He shrugged. 'Sorry, hen.'

'Then what exactly *can* you do?'

'We can give ye the Seer-folk.'

And at that Hughie reached into his pocket and brought out a crumpled ball of pink paper, which he thrust at Maggie. For a moment his gold, inhuman eyes fixed on Maggie's grey ones. He dropped the ball of paper into her open hand.

Crawk, said Mandy. *Crawk. Crawk.*

Maggie unfolded the crumpled sheet. She saw a cheaply printed single page advertising some kind of show:

LUCKY'S POCKET PAN-DAEMONIUM CIRCUS!
BEASTS AND MARVELS!
WONDERS AND FREAKS!

She frowned at the page in confusion. A circus? What in the Worlds could it mean? How could a travelling circus be connected with the Seer-folk? Then her eyes widened, and she understood.

'Is *that* how they're doing it? Is that how they're going unnoticed? How close have they come? How long till they get to World's End?'

Hughie scratched his head and *crawk*-ed. 'They've come as far as Rhydian. That's a fair good speed, hen. A course, they have Loki to thank for that. He's a one that's never short of a plan – *if* his life depends on it.'

Maggie's eyes were still on the paper. 'Will they make it here in time?'

'Aye, no doubt, at this pace,' he said. 'Though perhaps there's a way tae slow them down – or stop them altogether.'

'How?'

He seemed to hesitate. 'Well, this may be a long shot . . .' he said. 'But there's something sleeping in Rhydian. Something that, if it were to awake, might just provide the solution to your problem and ours.'

'You mean, asleep like the Red Horse?' said Maggie.

'Not exactly. More like a trap, or a tripwire. I think ye'll find that it's more than enough tae deal with the likes o' the Seer-folk. But . . .' Hughie paused. 'I were ye, I wouldn't say anything tae your friend, or to his little passenger. In fact, I wouldn'ae mention us at all. Best not to let them know how ye happened to call us.'

'Call you? I did not!' she said.

'Oh, but ye did,' he told her. 'We've heard ye calling these past three days. And then ye opened the window, and gave us an offering of cake.'

'It wasn't like that,' Maggie said.

Hughie grinned. 'Nevertheless . . .'

Maggie thought hard, still looking at the crumpled piece of paper. If Hughie was right, and the Seer-folk had come as far as the Northlands border, then something needed to be done. By rights, she ought to tell Adam all this, but she didn't trust his passenger. The Whisperer had already tried to make her kill her sister. What would happen if she told it about the Seer-folk?

Frowning, she turned to Hughie again. 'You said this thing would slow them down. Like a kind of trap, you said.'

Hughie nodded. 'Aye, hen.'

'Is my sister with them?'

'No.'

'Then tell me what to do,' she said.

He smiled. 'Just dream a little dream.'

When Maggie awoke, the birds were gone and Adam was sitting beside her.

'I must have fallen asleep,' she said, with a glance at the open window. 'I'm sorry. I know I shouldn't have–'

'*Did the Old Man speak?*' he said, and she saw the Whisperer in his eyes.

Maggie shook her head. 'Not a word.'

'And nothing else happened?' The Whisperer's voice was suspicious, and dry as a handful of cemetery dust.

Once more Maggie shook her head, and any feeling of guilt she might have had at deceiving Adam slipped away. The Whisperer was too dangerous for her to confide in Adam now. Who knew what kind of punishment his master might inflict on him, and all because Maggie Rede couldn't keep her mouth shut? Besides, what had she *really* done? Opened the window an inch or two? Bought a couple of Fat Boys? Had a nap? Dreamed a dream?

She lifted her eyes to Adam's and gave him her sweetest, most open smile. 'I had the most wonderful dream,' she said. 'Now, how about a kiss?'

And as she pulled him towards her and laced her hands together at the nape of his neck, Maggie felt a surge of something inside too powerful for her to express. She had no words for it; but she knew that she would rather die than see Adam suffer because of her. If everything went to plan, she thought, the Seer-folk would soon be subdued, the Old Man would give her the new runes, and Adam would be free at last.

And as for Odin's ravens—

Maggie reached down into her pocket and felt the crumpled pink paper there. As soon as she could, she told herself, she would throw it into the fire. No trace remained of the two birds – no speck of sugar, no signature, not even a scatter of Fat Boy crumbs to indicate that they had been, there. Perhaps she had only dreamed them, and all this was just a delirium brought on by a surfeit of Fat Boys.

In any case, Maggie thought, all that was over now.

Adam didn't need to know.

4

THE SUN WAS SETTING THROUGH the mist as Loki and the other gods made their way to the Rhydian Bridge, the mass of its four stone pylons looming dark against the sky. The mist was getting thick now, rolling off the river in waves. The streets were ghostly with it; the air heavily charged with the scent of smoke.

'Gods alive, it *stinks*!' said Jolly.

For once, Sugar agreed with him. It wasn't just the smoke, he thought, or even the reek of the tanneries. It was something worse than either of those; something like the stench of death.

The townsfolk seemed not to notice. They watched with no hostility, but no apparent interest, while the circus approached the Rhydian Bridge. As the sky darkened, so Rhydian lit; first with lamps by the side of the street, suspended from metal lampposts; then with lanterns in windows; with torches, fires and braziers, and strings of multicoloured glass globes, each containing a tealight, that were stretched from building to building, giving the town a carnival look.

Loki felt his spirits lift again. A carnival meant money to spend, wine to be drunk, fat purses to be plundered. What if there *was* another circus in town? Rhydian was big enough. And besides, the Trickster couldn't see any carnival hoping to compete with Lucky's Pocket Pan-daemonium Circus.

What had the old woman said to him? That the town came alive at sundown? Well, it was sundown, and sure enough, all along the riverside, Rhydian was coming to life. Chop-houses and taverns were beginning to open their doors. From one came a scent of mulled wine; from others, fresh bread, grilled fish, fruit pies with cinnamon. The gods found their mouths watering; the meagre supplies from their last stop mostly consisted of dried food and hay for the horses, and the prospect of a home-cooked meal was suddenly very attractive. Loki began to feel quite cheerful; and even the thought of competing with Rhydian's home-grown carnival felt as if it might turn out to be not a chore, but a pleasure.

The mist had thickened even more as the gods made their way to the foot of the bridge. Now they could begin to grasp the colossal solid *scale* of the thing: those pylons reaching into the mist; those cables holding the structure in place like a cat's cradle of metal and stone. The far side of the bridge was in fog; only the lights on the pylons remained visible, like fireballs in the darkness.

'Gods, that's impressive,' said Thor (who had always appreciated a nice piece of engineering work).

'I can't see the other side at all,' said Heimdall, squinting through *Bjarkán*. 'This fog must be unusually thick.'

But Loki had other things on his mind. 'So— where's this other circus?' he said. 'And how come we can't hear it?'

'I do hear something,' Bragi said, summoning a cantrip. 'It sounds like someone playing a flute.'

Idun nodded. 'I hear it too. It's coming from down there . . .' And she pointed to some iron steps that seemed to lead *underneath* the bridge.

Loki took a step forward. There was definitely something down there. Now that he knew, he could hear it too. A sound of many voices, muffled by the weight of the fog; and music, distant music, and the scent of something delicious . . .

He squinted into the luminous mist. 'That must be the carnival,' he said. 'What say we go and check it out?'

The others seemed inclined to agree. 'It's under there,' said Freyja, pointing between the bridge's feet. 'Look, I can see the lights.'

The gods and their allies in Chaos left their wagons to take a look. Sure enough, between the pylons was gathered a crowd of people. Visibility was poor, and the crowd looked more like ghosts, but there were men, women and children down there; and pastry vendors, beer stalls, piemen, pedlars selling trinkets. The smell of food was suddenly overwhelming.

'This looks very promising,' said Loki with his crooked smile. 'We'll go down, set up the show, get ourselves a bite to eat and be off before midnight. I'm starving.'

Fenris and the Wolf Boys growled their approval of the plan.

Jolly and Sugar, who had livened up at the smell of beer, now looked almost cheerful.

Angie said, 'They have animals.'

Sure enough, a rumbling sound, like penned beasts, came from below.

'And a stage,' said Freyja, looking down the steps in her turn. 'And something written there in lights . . .'

Once more Loki squinted into the mist, and found himself wondering why he hadn't seen it before. A large square panel, surrounded by glass globe-lights, which proclaimed:

CAPTAIN CHAOS'S CARNIVAL OF CATACLYSM AND
CATASTROPHE! ALL YOUR WILDEST DREAMS
BROUGHT TO LIFE!
SEE THE MIGHTY OLIPHANT! THE MAGIC MIRROR!
THE MAN OF STEEL! THE BEST IN NINE WORLDS,
OR YOUR MONEY BACK!!!

Loki found himself caught between amusement and indignation. Clearly this Captain Chaos had no small opinion of himself.

'We can make a killing here,' he told the others. 'Wait and see. There must be a thousand people down there – that's a thousand purses ripe for the picking. A thousand satisfied customers just waiting to show their appreciation in gold.'

Only Ethel looked doubtful. 'I don't think it's a good idea,' she said. 'Can't we just cross the bridge and move on?'

'What?' said Loki. 'And miss out on the biggest prize in the whole of the North Ridings? Not to mention a decent meal . . .'

Heimdall nodded. 'Let's go,' he said. 'It's just a pity we can't take the wagons.'

Ethel shook her head. 'I'll stay. You don't need me for the show, anyway. And I don't like the look of those steps.'

Loki shrugged. 'Well, please yourself. But I still think you're missing out.'

And so gods and demons (and wolves and birds) made their way down the spiral steps that led underneath the Meridian Bridge. It was a long way down, and the steps were older and even more rickety than they had first appeared. Clearly the ironwork under the bridge was not as well-maintained as it was above, and the infrastructure made disquieting little ticking sounds as the party descended.

But when they arrived underneath, they found a scene of such merriment that all of them forgot their doubts. Loki had guessed at a thousand Folk – now he reckoned twice that number, all crowded onto the space that ran under the stone pylons – a broad stone walkway overlooking the water and lit by many lanterns that were suspended under the bridge.

The effect, especially in fog, was like that of an enormous hall with food stands and entertainers of all kinds – fire-eaters, jugglers, musicians – and merchants barking their wares at the tops of their voices while the crowd moved placidly from one entertainment to another, *ooh*-ing and *aah*-ing and tossing coins.

And there was the stage, surrounded by lights. An opulent red curtain was drawn, and a man in a spangled coat and tall hat was announcing some kind of performance. Freyja was already there, watching from the front row, her face as rapt as a child's.

Captain Chaos's Carnival, thought the Trickster, and grinned to himself; pausing only to snag a Fat Boy from a passing vendor's tray, he pushed forward through the cheering crowd to check out the opposition.

The first thing he did was cast *Bjarkán*. He wasn't expecting trouble, but information never hurt. What tricks did the circus have in store? Were there trapdoors? Illusions? What was hidden behind that curtain?

But in the glare of the stage lights, *Bjarkán* had nothing to reveal. The tiniest scrawl of a signature, something that might be a broken rune – but beyond that, try as he might, Loki couldn't make out the details. Still, he thought, it was nothing much. Just a couple of cantrips. Nothing that might challenge *him*. He settled down to enjoy the show.

Captain Chaos revealed himself to be a man of average height, with red hair under his tall hat and an impudent, lopsided grin, to which Loki immediately took exception. His manner was equally impudent, though he had an engaging style and a slick turn of phrase and a comic air that set the audience roaring.

'And now, for your delight and delectation,' he said. (What a cliché, thought Loki.) 'All the way from the depths of Dream' – a drum rolled, a guitar struck a chord – 'the delirious, delicious, utterly irresistible Diva of Desire, the Deaconess of Delight, the one and only *Dulcinea, the most Beautiful Woman in the Nine Worlds!*'

Freyja stiffened. 'How *dare* he!'

Loki put a hand on her arm. 'Shh,' he said. 'I want to see.'

'How dare he!' she said in a louder voice, slapping away the Trickster's hand. On her brow the rune *Fé* shone out in indignation. 'Most Beautiful Woman in the Worlds! That's— How *dare* he! That's *me!*'

Briefly Loki considered shutting her up with a cantrip. But the goddess of desire in a rage was not someone to be trifled with, and if Loki felt that it might be unwise for Freyja to intervene at that point, he wisely kept his thoughts to himself. Some forces are unstoppable – a jealous woman is one of them. And so he finished his Fat Boy instead, and settled down to watch as Freyja leaped in full Aspect onto the stage and into the lights.

Captain Chaos seemed unmoved by the interruption. In fact, his grin broadened a little. 'Have we had the pleasure?' he said, extending a welcoming hand.

Freyja, blinded by the lights and finding a thousand pairs of eyes suddenly fixed upon her, glared.

'Ladies and *gentlemen,*' he said. 'It appears we have a challenge. For tonight, for one night only, Dulcinea will share the stage with— er . . . ?'

Loki, seeing Freyja ready to make a fool of herself, sprang up onto the stage beside her. 'Let *me* introduce you,' he said. 'This is the Lady Gylfa, from Greenland. Gylfa the Golden, Gylfa the Great, the glorious Goddess of Gorgeousness . . .'

Captain Chaos showed his teeth. 'Very well. Name your stake. We'll match it. Winner takes all,' he said.

'Stake?' said Freyja, bewildered.

'Make a wager, lady. Best in Nine Worlds, or your money back. Isn't that the rule, folks?'

The audience roared its approval. Coins began to shower down onto the boards of the little stage.

For a moment Freyja hesitated. Then she summoned the money-rune, *Fé,* and flung down a handful of silver coins.

Captain Chaos raised an eyebrow, and Loki saw that under the dazzling lights, Freyja's coins had reverted back into the dream-stuff from which they had come, leaving only a handful of dust that glittered on the wooden boards.

He hastily put a hand into his pocket and brought out a handful of real coins. Captain Chaos grinned at him as they clinked onto the growing pile.

Once more the audience howled. Loki took a deep bow.

Captain Chaos followed suit. 'All right. Now, folks. *Let the show begin!*'

And from behind the red curtain stepped a woman of such beauty, such grace, that even the gods, who were used to such things, could not help but stop and stare. A gleaming rune adorned her brow—

— it was the reverse of the rune *Fé,* a rune of fire and destruction – and though afterwards no one who'd seen her could quite agree on the precise colour of her hair, or the fabric of her dress, Thor stared so hard that Sif slapped his face; and Fenny and the Wolf Boys almost drooled with longing; and Bragi's jaw dropped; and Idun glared; and Loki thanked his lucky stars that Sigyn was safe in her acorn-cup.

And then Dulcinea started to dance to the languid sound of a violin, and every note was a first kiss, and every step was a broken heart, and the audience began to sway and moan in a kind of voiceless ecstasy . . .

For a moment Freyja stood her ground. In Aspect, she was daz-zling. Her hair was a winter sunset, her mouth a slashed pome-granate. It seemed impossible that any woman could rival her.

But Dulcinea was like silk; like cream; like roses; like starlight. Next to her, Freyja's hair looked brassy and vulgar; her lips too full; her face too hard; her waist too pinched; her eyes angry slits; her fists clenched into ugly knots.

'Do we have a winner?' said Captain Chaos with a grin.

The audience began to chant: '*Dul-ci-ne-a! Dulcinea!*'

'Are you sure?' said Captain Chaos.

The colour dropped from Freyja's face.

'Are you *sure* that's who you want?'

'*Dul-ci-ne-a! DUL-CI-NE-A!*'

Still she faced them. The chanting grew louder. Someone called out 'Get the doxy off the stage! Let's have Dulcinea!'

And at that, with a shriek of outrage, the goddess of desire fled, crackling with runelight and wrath, to laughter and mocking ap-plause from the crowd.

Thoughtful, Loki watched her go. It wasn't that he had any sympathy for Freyja's humiliation. In fact, he quite enjoyed it. Still, there was something about all this that made him a little uneasy. Perhaps it was those dazzling lights that prevented him from using *Bjarkán* . . . He almost considered packing up and leaving. After all, they still had supplies. The horses could last another night, with runes of endurance to speed them on. After that there had to be plenty of villages down the road that would be happy to see their show.

But the thought of letting a rival win was too much for Loki to accept. Captain Chaos's Carnival *couldn't* be as good as it claimed. *The best in Nine Worlds, or your money back?*

That sounded like a challenge. A *bet*.

And if there was anything he couldn't turn down . . .

And so, without further resistance, the Trickster snagged himself another couple of Fat Boys and prepared to face the enemy.

5

PERTH LIVED IN A SMALL, narrow houseboat down by the docks, in a neighbourhood known as the Water Rats, a place where fishermen traded their wares. It was lucky for Maddy that he did, for she had soon learned that Jormungand, even in his Horse Aspect, needed more than just hay to sustain him.

On his very first day in World's End the Horse of the Sea had munched his way casually through half a dozen lobsters, a bucket of shrimp, a barrel of salt herring and a whole fresh cod before Maddy could stop him, and was now under orders to stay under the boardwalk, preferably in one of his smaller Aspects, and to feed only by night, well away from curious eyes.

Perth's suggestion that a fish-eating horse would help draw the punters in was dismissed by Maddy, whose earlier assessment of him had only been reinforced when she saw him in action. Perth could sell *anything* – from pieces of rock to sacks of potatoes – and if they were stolen property, then so much the better. He also had no scruples about picking the pockets of his customers as they left, and Maddy, trying to ensure that neither of them attracted the wrong sort of attention, found the task harder and harder.

By the time she'd been in World's End five days, Maddy was feeling desperate. According to the Seeress, the End of the Worlds was in four days' time, and still there was no sign of either the Old

Man, or Maggie, or even Odin's ravens, who might have been able to guide her in the right direction. Jorgi was worse than useless; lolling under the boardwalk by day, hunting for seals and lobsters by night, he showed no sign of clairvoyance, nor any inclination to help, and Maddy's frustration grew and grew until she could barely eat, barely sleep, in case she missed some vital clue to the problems that eluded her.

At night she paced. She gnawed her fists. She wrote out Ethel's prophecy and studied it interminably. She even took out her casting runes and tried to read her fortune, but the runestones kept stubbornly landing face-down, so that finally she put them away, half wondering whether all this – Perth, Maggie, her flight to World's End, Jormungand, all the events of the past three years – had simply been a terrible dream, from which she could expect to awake at any moment to discover that Odin was *not* dead, that Maggie was *not* her sister and that the Apocalypse predicted by the Seeress was merely a chapter in an as yet unwritten Faërie tale, to be told around a campfire to grandchildren as yet unborn.

Sadly, it was no dream; and Maddy was almost ready to give up hope and rejoin her friends when something happened to change her mind.

It was fish-market day at the Water Rats. There were four of these markets every week – one for fish, one for fabrics, one for flowers, one for fruit and vegetables. Perth was helping out at a stall selling pickled herring (and lifting the occasional purse, just to keep in practice). Jorgi was under the boardwalk as usual, snapping up anything that happened to crawl his way. And Maddy, her face half wrapped in a shawl (to try to stifle the smell of the fish), was sitting watching the people go by and feeling almost sleepy with the noise and buzz of the market-day crowd.

Suddenly she became aware of a plump little woman watching her. The woman, wearing a black *bergha*, had been walking past with some haddock in a basket. Now she stopped in her tracks and stared at Maddy with such furious persistence that Maddy was jolted from her reverie.

'So, madam!' the woman said. '*This* is where you ended up! Hanging around the Water Rats. I should have *known* it! Ha!' And she gave a contemptuous little sniff and forked the sign against the evil eye.

'I'm sorry – do I know you?' said Maddy.

'*Know* me?' said the woman. 'I should think you do, ye saucy thing. Think I don't know *ye*, Maggie Rede?'

Maddy's fatigue dropped away at once. '*What* did you call me?'

'I called ye by your *name*, Maggie Rede,' said the plump little woman vehemently. 'Ye may hide your head 'neath a shawl now, but I know what you're hiding.'

Maddy pulled away her shawl, deliberately showing her face. Her long wavy hair spilled out around her shoulders.

The little woman's eyes widened. 'What? Your *hair* . . .' she faltered. 'It was— How could—?' Then she stopped, rubbed her eyes and, with an effort, said: 'Beg pardon. My mistake.'

'Did you think I was someone else?' said Maddy, trying to conceal her excitement. Clearly this woman knew Maggie Rede. Maybe she even knew where she was.

She summoned a casual runecharm. Silver-tongued, alluring *Logr* took shape between her fingers. 'I'm sorry, Mrs . . . er?'

'Blackmore,' said the woman, still looking bewildered. 'Mrs Blackmore, so please ye, miss, and – beg pardon, but you're the *spit* of her—'

'This Maggie Rede. Who *is* she? And what exactly did she do?'

And under the soothing charm of *Logr*, Mrs Blackmore told her tale: how she had taken the wretched girl in, given her a decent home, fed her, clothed her and tried to bring her up properly; only to be repaid by Lawlessness, ingratitude and deceit. She finished by telling Maddy how the girl had come home one morning, having stayed out all night long, hair cut off like a savage's, and that terrible ruinmark at the back of her neck – and with a young man in tow, no less; a young man with eyes like a demon's.

But there Mrs Blackmore's knowledge ran dry. She could neither say who the young man had been, nor where the pair had run to; and finally Maddy let her go, feeling at the same time cheered that at last she had news of her sister, but disheartened that such a promising lead had turned out to be a dead end, a light briefly glimpsed, then lost in the dark.

6

WAITING BY THE RHYDIAN BRIDGE, Ethel was feeling uneasy. There was no apparent reason for this. *Bjarkán* had revealed no surprises. The bridge, though ancient, was just a bridge. The space underneath the pylons was just a convenient gathering place.

So what if the Folk of Rhydian were a little distant? What if the steps under the bridge were old and somewhat poorly maintained? The Seeress had stronger nerves than this, and was slightly annoyed that her weaker self – the woman who had once been Ethelberta Parson – seemed to have developed an unacceptable case of the jitters.

She had been waiting for half an hour when Odin's Mind and Spirit flew down to join her by the side of the bridge. Over the past few days Hughie and Mandy had been occasional visitors to Lucky's Pocket Pan-daemonium Circus, but the Trickster had long ceased expecting them to make any kind of valuable contribution. Sometimes they could be lured with fruit, or biscuits, or lumps of sugar; but for the most part they did as they pleased, vanishing for the whole day, then returning as if nothing had happened, cawing in their harsh voices – *Kaik. Kaik. Kaik.*

Ethel liked the ravens. They were all she had left of her husband. The Seeress part of her recalled when they had been seldom away from his side, as much a part of Allfather as his blue cloak or his broad-brimmed hat. Ragnarók had changed that, of course, as it had changed so many things. But while Hugin and Munin still travelled the skies, she felt that there could still be hope.

She reached into her pocket and brought out a handful of raisins. Scattered them onto the floor.

Ack-ack!

'There you are, my tattered ones.' She used one of Odin's names for them, and felt a surge of nostalgia. The ravens pecked at the offering, then pecked at each other viciously.

When the food was gone, they shifted back into their human Aspects and perched – Hughie on the left, Mandy on the right – on the two large ironwork pineapples that adorned the bridge's railings.

Ethel watched in mingled amusement and irritation. 'Where have you two been?' she said.

Hughie shrugged. 'Ach, here and there. World's End. Dream. The usual.'

'Any news of him?'

'Maybe. We'll know more in a little while.'

'And the Rider of Carnage?' Ethel tried to keep the impatience out of her voice.

'We're workin' on it. Give us time.' Hughie gave a massive yawn. 'It's no so easy, hen, ye know. It's no like the auld days. Things have changed.'

'I know,' said the Seeress. 'But time is short. And we have the small matter of a prophecy to fulfil.'

'Well, have ye *considered*,' Hughie said, 'that the prophecy may well be fulfilled whether or not we do anything. I mean, it depends if ye take the view that everything is predetermined, therefore it disn'ae matter *what* we do, or do ye subscribe to the theory that all actions are governed by cosmic free will?'

He paused, having noticed a raisin that he and Mandy had overlooked. Shifting to his raven form, he hopped down from his perch and pecked it up. Then he shifted Aspect again, and came to stand by Ethel's side.

'I miss him,' she said.

'I know ye do.'

'The prophecy doesn't make it clear. Are we doing the right thing?'

Hughie put his hand on her arm. His silver rings gleamed in the lamplight. 'Only time will tell, hen. Only time will tell.' Suddenly Mandy, who still looked strangely birdlike in spite of her human Aspect, *crawk*-ed.

'What's that, Mand?'

Ack-ack-ack. Crawk.

Hughie, who seemed to understand Mandy's language no matter what, listened, head cocked to one side. He frowned in concentration.

Mandy spoke again. *Crawk.* Her voice was harsh and urgent. *Crawk. Ack-ack. Crawk. Ack-ack.*

Hughie looked back at Ethel. 'Mandy says it's time,' he said.

Ethel nodded reluctantly. 'It seems like such a risk,' she said. 'And we could still lose everything . . .'

He shrugged. 'When ye're playing for everything, ye have tae risk losing everything.'

She smiled. 'You even sound like him now. Is he certain of this? Is he safe, at least?'

Hughie shrugged. 'Be sure of this: wherever he is, the Auld Man's where he wants to be.'

And with that, he resumed his raven guise, and both of Odin's birds were gone in a flurry of wings into the mist that poured from under the Rhydian Bridge.

7

CAPTAIN CHAOS'S CARNIVAL OF CONFUSION had proved to have several more tricks hidden behind its red curtain. While Freyja alternately fanned herself and indulged in mild hysterics, the artistes of Lucky's Pocket Pan-daemonium Circus, shamed at the failure of one their own, now tried to redress the balance.

Never had they encountered such a demanding audience; never had they experienced such humiliating defeat. Æsir and Vanir both shared in Freyja's mortification, and even the demons were keen to prove that their side was the strongest; with the result that Captain Chaos – his grin now broader than ever – was almost overwhelmed with folk ready to rise to the challenge.

The best in the Nine Worlds, or your money back! That had been the wager; and the scatter of coins on the little stage had now become a carpet – a sliding, chinking carpet of wealth that made the Trickster's eyes shine.

The trouble with glamorous money, of course, was that it attracted attention. It cost them glam to summon and, in a few hours, reverted back to the stuff from which it had been made: dust, sand, ashes, stones. To use it meant risking exposure – maybe even arrest – which was why the gods had had to resort to *working* their way along, the Roads.

If they won this wager, then they could pay their way to World's End without ever having to work another stroke – which was why, even now, Loki hadn't given up on the chance to win his money back.

After Freyja, the gods had discussed who should take the next turn.

'I will,' said Sif with a grunt, assuming her Battle-Sow Aspect. Freyja's lackluster performance had filled her with the utmost contempt; and although she deeply resented the role, she also knew that, as Queen of the Pigs, she had no equal in the Nine Worlds in majesty, muscle and appetite.

The bet was duly made. The fee, which had doubled since Freyja, was paid, and Petula, Queen of the Pigs, took the stage to cries of encouragement from the crowd. Loki introduced her with his usual panache, and never before had Petula been so regal, so hairy, so pink or so stout; never had she eaten so many jam tarts at one sitting, or shown such exquisite pointe-work from her gleaming trotters.

Captain Chaos watched in silence. Then, as the audience howled for more, he introduced his second act: Olivia the Oliphant, the Oligarch of Oliphants, her trunk like that of the World Tree, her appetite unquenchable. The stage was too flimsy to bear her; instead, she heaved her way through the crowd like a landed whale, pausing only to devour thirty-nine trays of Fat Boys, a dozen barrels of ale, a whole spit of roasted chickens *and* a small child from the audience – retrieved at the very last moment from between Olivia's toothless jaws, to riotous applause from the crowd.

The decision was (almost) unanimous. Captain Chaos acknowledged the merit of the challenger, but the winner was clearly Olivia, and Loki was left to pay the bill for all that she and Sif had consumed (a sum that amounted to rather more than even he cared to wager).

Next came Bragi, the Human Nightingale, paired with Linni, the Human Lark. Bragi played his guitar and sang so sweetly that the audience wept; but when his rival took to the stage (Linni was a beautiful woman with the runemark *Sól*, reversed, on her breast), some of the more susceptible audience members actually *died*, and even Skadi shed a tear (a thing Loki had believed impossible).

'It wasn't my fault,' wailed Bragi. 'I told you before. The *strings* are worn—'

'Oh, shut up,' snapped Heimdall, striding up to take the stage. 'My name is Hawk-Eyed Heimdall, and I'll wager I can outshoot *anyone* you care to name.'

But the Captain's champion was Eagle-Eyed Sam, and in spite of being almost perfectly matched, Heimdall failed – and lost the bet.

One by one, the gods tried their luck, and one by one, they were outclassed.

Njörd, the Man of the Sea, who bet that he could outswim any man alive, lost a race against Freddy Finn, the Human Fish.

The Wolf Boys and Fenris lost against an act called the Mighty Cerberus.

Even Angrboda failed to out-charm Sassy, the Snake Charmer.

Enough was enough, Loki thought.

No, he wasn't backing out. He'd lost too much to stop playing now. He'd wagered their horses, their wagons, their food; and his only hope was to win them all back before his people had to move on.

But what was he to play for? He'd already lost everything. Nothing remained – not a coin, not a rag, not even the shirt on Loki's back.

Still, this next encounter, he thought, was one that they were certain to win. Beauty, Loki told himself, was surely just a matter of taste. And animal acts were always notoriously unpredictable. But in a simple test of strength – no tricks, no blarney, just sheer *brawn* . . .

What could go wrong? Thor was quite simply the strongest man in the Nine Worlds. Even with a reversed rune, he could certainly knock the stuffing out of any of Captain Chaos's crew. It was therefore with a jaunty (if somewhat premature) sense of victory that Loki now sauntered onto the stage and, without even bothering to build up the crowd with his eloquence, announced the mighty Thunderer.

Captain Chaos seemed impressed. He too announced his

champion. The Man of Steel faced the Thunderer in front of the scarlet curtain.

The test was a familiar one. Maddy would have recognized it from Fair Days all over the North. A bell at the top of a painted pole attached to a simple counterweight. On one side, a pulley and chain, allowing the weight to move smoothly up and down the pole. On the other, a rubber pressure-pad. The test was to hit the pad hard enough to send the weight rattling up the chain fast enough to strike the bell. A wooden mallet was provided for the purpose.

Loki took one look at the mallet and laughed. 'The Man of Thunder would splinter this to smithereens with a single blow,' he said to Captain Chaos. 'Lucky for you that he brings his own tools,.' And he indicated Jolly – in his Aspect as Mjølnir – tucked neatly under Thor's arm.

This was what made the bet safe, he thought. Thor, with his hammer, Mjølnir, had no equal in the Nine Worlds. And although it was now clear to the Trickster that Captain Chaos was not what he seemed, he felt certain that, in this case, their champion was unbeatable.

For a moment Captain Chaos seemed just a little hesitant. He narrowed his eyes at Jolly, and muttered a little cantrip. Then his grin returned and he said: 'I don't see why not, friend. As long as my man can do the same. As it happens, he too prefers to work with his own instrument.'

Loki, who knew for a certain fact that nothing was stronger than Mjølnir, waved a hand in approval. The Man of Steel was big, of course – perhaps just a shade taller than Thor – but size wasn't everything. To start with, he was left-handed, while Thor favoured his right hand, which gave him a slight advantage. Plus, of course, Thor had the strength of a hundred men, and Mjølnir. There was no way that he could lose – which was good, because this time the gods had nothing left to stake.

They flipped a coin to see who went first. Thor won.

He pushed up his sleeves. Lifted Jolly. Struck the pad. The weight rattled halfway up the pole, then fell back into place with a crash.

Captain Chaos shrugged. 'First time. We'll make it the best of three, shall we?'

The second time, Thor hit the pad with every ounce of his considerable strength. The weight rattled busily up the pole, almost – but not quite – touching the bell.

A long sigh came from the crowd.

'Better,' said Captain Chaos. 'We'll give you another try. It's fair. You're maybe not used to our machine.'

Thor gritted his teeth. Tightened his belt. Flexed his muscles. Cracked his knuckles. Rubbed dust into his sweating palms to make sure Mjølnir's shaft didn't slip. Raised his mighty hammer high and brought it down with awesome strength.

The counterweight rattled up the chain – fast, then losing momentum. Only five more links to go – four – three – two – one . . .

All the gods held their breath.

Ting!

The weight just kissed the bell.

A dropped pin would have made more sound.

But Thor had beaten the machine.

The crowd applauded. Thor made a bow. Loki wiped the sweat from his eyes. And then it was time for the Man of Steel to take his turn at the challenge.

Loki watched with a little smile. Gods knew who this Man of Steel was, but it went without saying that he was no match for Thor. The hammer he had brought onstage was slightly larger than Jolly, but Loki was feeling on top of the Worlds, and he simply applauded the Man of Steel as he took his turn with the machine.

The gods and their allies in Chaos had crowded round the Trickster.

'This had better work, you,' said Heimdall, between his golden teeth. Loki noticed that Heimdall was looking rather pale, and grinned.

'Relax. You worry too much,' he said. 'There's no way he'll beat the Thunderer.'

'He'd better not,' growled Skadi. 'Because if he loses, we *all* lose. You especially, Dogstar.'

Loki made a dismissive noise, noticing that Skadi too was looking a trifle out of sorts.

'You worry too much, all of you. Your faith in me is awesome. Now just lie back. Enjoy the show. This is going to be lots of *fun*.'

The Man of Steel raised the hammer high.

The crowd held its breath . . .

The hammer crashed down. The chain rattled up the pole so fast that even the Watchman's eye couldn't follow it. The bell gave a resounding *clang* – and then, as if that wasn't enough, shot right off the top of the pole towards the underside of the bridge.

There came a distant metallic sound as the bell struck one of the bridge's struts, then, a few moments later, a splash as it fell into the river. The crowd applauded like crazy; gold coins showered onto the stage and Loki went pale to the roots of his hair.

Skadi gnashed her teeth.

'*Oops . . .*'

'Tough call,' said Captain Chaos.

For a moment Loki considered flight. In Wildfire Aspect, he could probably make it to the top of the bridge before the gods caught up with him. But Ethel was there, with the wagons; and if she didn't stop him, there was Njörd, in his sea-eagle Aspect, and Heimdall, in his bird guise; not to mention the wolves and Skadi, all of whom would be more than happy to take their frustration out on his hide.

Heimdall gave Loki a derisive glance. 'Well, that was *lots* of fun,' he said. 'Just the look on your face right now nearly makes up for the fact that you've lost all our travelling gear on a *bet*!'

But Loki wasn't listening. He suddenly felt incredibly weak. He must have overstretched his glam, because his legs wouldn't hold him. He sat down on the edge of the stage, feeling worse than ever. His head hurt; his vision swam; his signature looked so faint that even Thor, who had left the stage with the intention of breaking every bone in Loki's body, thought better of it and sat down too.

Come to think of it, thought the Thunderer, he wasn't feeling too perky himself. It wasn't often that he missed a chance to use his fists on the Trickster; but really, the little guy didn't look good. Thor hoped it was nothing catching.

'Loki, you look terrible,' said Idun, who alone of all the gods (except for Sigyn, who didn't count) still had faith in the Trickster. 'Shall I get you some apple?'

But Captain Chaos had jumped from the stage, looking more vibrant than ever. His eyes were like stars, his teeth were like quartz and his sparkly coat was dazzling. Never before had Loki seen someone who looked so completely *alive* – and in spite of the encroaching mist, his signature was a rainbow arc broader than a highway.

'Time to pay up, folks,' he said. 'It was a good fight, but a deal's a deal.'

Loki tried to stand up, and failed. 'What did you do to me?' he said.

'Nothing,' said Captain Chaos.

'You're lying,' said the Trickster. 'There's something behind that curtain. A glam – I thought I saw it before, but I couldn't make out what it was. You tricked us, somehow. Gods – *dammit*, my *head*!' A spike of pain jabbed his temple; once more his vision swam sickly.

'If I were you,' said Captain Chaos, 'I'd quit while I was still moving.' He turned to the gods. 'Time to pay up.'

'What with?' said Thor. 'You've cleaned us out.'

'Not quite,' said Captain Chaos.

'What do you mean?' said Loki, who already knew the answer.

Captain Chaos smiled at him. 'I think you know that, Trickster,' he said. 'I own you now, body and soul. Pay up and your friends can be on their way. I won't try to keep them. But if you try to renege on our deal, I'll keep you all. You know I can.'

And now at last, through the haze in his mind, Loki realized the truth. He turned to his companions, but knew that it was useless. Everyone who had taken the stage was in the same position as he: listless, drained of their glam, signature down to a low flame. No chance of shifting Aspects now, or trying to make a run for it; even just walking away at this point might prove too much in their weakened state.

Only Idun was untouched – Idun, who had not joined the game – and Loki now grabbed onto her arm like a drowning man to a flung rope.

'Please,' he whispered. 'Help me stand . . .'

It was the first time that Idun could remember the Trickster *ever* asking for help. He must be really sick, she thought; and her gentle heart swelled with compassion as she hauled him to his feet. Loki swayed, but stayed upright, and turned to face the Captain, whose arm now bore the runemark *Kaen*, unreversed and unbroken.

'It's a mirror, isn't it? No wonder Thor couldn't beat it. He was fighting his own reflection – in Aspect, with Mjølnir. And Freyja – that was *her* own Aspect she saw, another version of herself. That's why we can never match you. That's why you were able to steal our glam—'

'*Steal?*' said Captain Chaos. 'You gave it of your own accord. We had a bet, remember?' His grin broadened. 'Whatever you did, you did to *yourselves*. Haven't you ever seen a bird knock out its brains against its own reflection in a window pane?'

'What is it?' said Loki. Now that he'd stopped struggling, his strength was slowly returning. Not enough to use glam, but at least enough to see straight. 'What is it? Or should I say what are *you*?'

Once more Captain Chaos grinned. 'Well, today I'm *you*,' he said. 'Or at least a *version* of you. Tomorrow, who knows what I'll be? I have to say, I haven't enjoyed a game as much since the End of the Worlds. A travelling circus? That's genius. I take it that *was* your idea?'

'I asked what you were,' said Loki. 'Come on. You know I'm helpless. You've taken everything I had. At least give me this. What *are* you?'

Captain Chaos looked at him. 'My name was Svalinn,' he said at last, 'Remember Svalinn, the Sun Shield? I rode the skies with *Sól*, the sun. I reflected her light all over the Worlds. Now I'm stuck in Northlands, Nowhere, in the foundations of a bridge. Yes, *that's* where they put me,' the Captain said, when Loki showed his

318

surprise. 'They found me, after Ragnarók, when I'd fallen from the sky. They saw my runes and knew I had glam. And so they built me into this bridge, and–'

'And you've been here ever since. Like a spider in its web. And all these people under the bridge' – Loki indicated the crowd at his back – 'they're not quite *regular* folk, are they? They're all the folk you've collected over the last five hundred years. All of them just reflections, shadows through a dark glass–' His scarred lips twisted. 'Well, congratulations,' he said. 'You got me good. What happens now?'

The Captain gave his evil grin. *My grin*, Loki amended somewhat bitterly to himself. *Everything about him – the tricks, the talk, the treachery – was taken straight from me. And now . . .*

'Now, of course, you can't let me go. That's it, isn't it?'

It all looked horribly clear to him. The way in which they'd been drawn in: the trail of breadcrumbs they'd followed there; the fog that had concealed the trap; the glee with which the ancient being had assumed Loki's features, his manner, his style.

For a moment uncertainty crossed the Trickster's features. How *had* they fallen into the trap? He understood how the Sun Shield might have stolen glam from the Seer-folk as soon as they entered its domain, but how had it known they were coming? Who had alerted it to their approach? And how had it managed to hide itself?

The Captain's fire-green eyes shone. 'I knew you'd figure it out,' he said. 'The thing is, I don't *want* to let you go. Those others, maybe, but not you. You're the best fun I've had in five hundred years. And I don't want to have to go back to reflecting ordinary market-day crowds, or barges on the river. Besides, a deal's a deal,' he said. 'You played, you lost. I own you.'

Loki shot a desperate glance at the faces surrounding him. All were impassive, save Idun's, which was dewy with distress.

'You can't be serious,' he said. 'Besides, if you can keep the memory of what the Shield reflects, then why do you need the original?'

'Because it doesn't *last*,' said the Captain. 'I operate on borrowed glam. When it runs out, the image fades. I can't live on shadows for ever.'

Once more Loki glanced at his friends. He could see where this was heading. The audience had long since dispersed and returned to their entertainments – to the jugglers and fire-eaters and pastry vendors that crowded the riverside; now only Captain Chaos remained, facing the gods with a mocking smile. It would be too much, Loki thought, to assume that the gods would fight for him.

What had the Captain compared it to? *A bird knocking out its brains against its own reflection?*

'Ah, come on,' he said softly.

Freyja gave a contemptuous shrug. 'You brought this on yourself,' she said. 'Don't expect support from us.'

Sif bared her tusks. 'If you think we're all going to risk our lives to pay for your gambling habit—'

Idun's forget-me-not eyes were wet. 'What are you going to do to him?' she said to Captain Chaos.

The Captain grinned. 'Don't worry,' he said. 'I'm not going to hurt Loki. I mean, I *am* Loki in so many ways. Together, we could be fabulous.'

Loki thought about that for a moment, and realized that it was almost true.

'You'd be safe with me,' the Captain said. 'No one could touch you any more. Æsir, Vanir – not even Lord Surt could get to you. The End of the Worlds could come and go, but you'd be safe as houses.'

'Really?' said Loki, sitting down.

'Sure,' said Captain Chaos. 'I survived Ragnarók, didn't I? I can withstand the heat of the Sun. And if you get me out of here, then both of us can be free again. Except that you'd be invincible. Which I don't suppose you'd mind.'

Loki grinned. 'No, I don't think I would.' At last he was starting to understand what Captain Chaos wanted of him. After all, it wasn't the first time he'd encountered an artefact of the Elder Age that had gone rogue. He knew how dangerous that could be – how dangerous, and how useful. The idea of owning the Sun Shield

320

– of *possessing*, rather than being possessed – was suddenly very attractive. If he could remove it from the bridge and bind it into his service, then all his worries would be in the past.

Of course, that might not be easy. The Captain's thoughts mirrored his own. It was more than likely that, while he was contemplating deceit, his image was doing the same thing. Still . . .

I can beat him, Loki thought. *Maybe not in glam, but in guile . . .*

Idun was still looking concerned. She gave Captain Chaos a doubtful look. 'I don't think you should trust him,' she said. 'I think he's trying to trick you.'

Loki smiled. 'Not so fast. Let's explore what's on offer.'

Behind her, the gods were recovering enough to take an interest. Heimdall was looking suspicious again; Skadi's long white teeth were bared.

'Typical Trickster,' Freyja said. 'The rat, deserting the sinking ship.'

'You'd better not run out on us,' said Angie in a low voice.

'Why wouldn't he?' grunted Sif. 'It's what the weasel always does.'

Loki glanced over his shoulder. 'You'd have to get rid of them first,' he said. 'I don't want you sharing power with *them*.'

Captain Chaos raised an eyebrow. 'You're sure your friends would leave you behind?'

Loki raised his voice a little, just so the gods could hear him. 'They're no friends of mine,' he said. 'You heard what they said a moment ago. You can't believe what they've put me through. Threats, torture, snakes, *marriage* – you name it, they've done it. Twice, in some cases. Get them out of here, let them go, and *then* we can talk business.'

'Are you sure?' the Captain said. 'The deal is, I own you. If I let your friends stay, then maybe one day they'll pay back your debt. Otherwise you're mine for good.'

'Fine by me,' said Loki. 'Come on – what are the others to you? I want them gone, shadows and all. They cramp my style. Send them away—' He broke off, lowered his eyes and said: 'I mean – send them away, *Master*.'

For a moment the Captain seemed uncertain. His eyes flicked from Loki to the gods, then back to Loki once again. Then he nodded. 'Fair enough. But remember, I know you, Trickster. If you're thinking of pulling a fast one . . .'

'Why would I?' Loki said. 'Think of what you're offering. I'd be crazy to turn it down. Besides, you heard what they think of me. They think I'm a weasel, a turncoat. A rat leaving a sinking ship.' Once more the Trickster lowered his eyes, not so much out of submission as out of the need to hide a grin. 'Perhaps they're right to think so,' he said. 'I've never shown loyalty to anyone. Never done anything except for myself. Perhaps I deserve to be cast aside. No one's ever loved me. I only hope' – he gave a sniff – 'that they can sometimes think of me with something like affection. Perhaps when I'm gone, they'll remember what fun they had with Loki around, and say to themselves: *He wasn't so bad – a little wild, perhaps, but —*'

Jolly gave an explosive snort.

Idun burst into noisy tears.

The Captain looked at them thoughtfully, then addressed the Trickster. 'I guess you're right,' he said at last. 'Folks, you heard. You're free to go.'

For a moment the gods were bewildered, unsure what to do. Idun wept steadily. Freyja looked abashed. Sugar blew his nose hard and tried to pretend it was an allergy. Thor frowned at Loki. The dreadful suspicion that the Trickster might actually have done something noble began very slowly to enter his mind.

He growled: 'I can't let you do this.'

Loki gave an inward curse and waved his arms at the Thunderer. 'Go on! Get lost!' he cried. 'Forget I was ever here, all right?' He turned to Idun. 'Get them out. Give them some apple – whatever it takes – and get the Hel out of Rhydian.'

'But – what about you?' said Idun, wide-eyed.

'Forget me. I know what I'm doing.'

Now, as Idun and the weakened gods fled from the stage and its glamours, Loki looked up at his double and summoned his most ingenuous smile.

'So. Tell me where it is,' he said.

The Captain's eyes narrowed. 'The Sun Shield?'

'Well, if I'm going to free us both, I'll need to know where you keep it.'

The Captain gave a crooked smile. 'All right,' he said. 'But there's one little thing . . .' And he pushed back his shirt-cuff to reveal a golden acorn on a chain around his right wrist – the mirror-image of the one Loki had been wearing for the past five days. 'What's this?'

Loki winced. He'd been hoping to keep that secret – at least for a little longer.

'It's . . . a lucky charm,' he said.

'Take it off,' said the Captain.

'Why?'

'Just take it off,' he said. 'There's something about it that bothers me.

Privately the Trickster agreed; but something told him that in this case his ball-and-chain might be useful. 'It has . . . *sentimental* value,' he said. 'I'd rather not remove it.'

'Really, said Captain Chaos. 'You don't seem the type.' And, summoning the rune *Kaen* – now glowing, unreversed, on his arm – he levelled it at the Trickster. A ball of lurid violet light took shape around his clenched fist, hissing like a handful of snakes. 'I know it's a kind of glam,' he said. 'I can feel it on me. So don't try anything stupid – right?' He thrust the fistful of purple fire almost into Loki's face. 'A mirror has a thousand eyes. *I* won't suffer if you're blind.'

Loki's mouth went very dry. 'All right, all right, it's a glam,' he said. 'The gods put it on me five days ago. It's some kind of bindrune, that's all I know. I've tried to get it off, but I can't. They had me chained to the wagon.'

The Captain raised an eyebrow. 'So you're a prisoner too?' he said. 'Why didn't you tell me that before?'

'Oh, come on,' said Loki. 'Being led around like a dog on a chain – it was hardly my proudest moment. Forgive me for not wanting everyone in the Nine Worlds to have a good laugh at my expense.'

Close enough to the truth, he thought, for his captor to be deceived. Or so he hoped – that fireball could do a lot of damage. For a moment the Captain scrutinized him through *Bjarkán*. Then he seemed to relax again.

'All right, I believe you,' he said. 'Perhaps we can deal with that later. For now, we have a job to do.' And, still holding the fireball, he began to explain his plan to Loki, while above them, on the Rhydian Bridge, Lucky's Pocket Pan-daemonium Circus set off again at a rattling pace, and Odin's Mind and Spirit watched from underneath the Rhydian Bridge, black wings furled against the dark, beady eyes unblinking.

8

ETHEL HAD NOT BEEN AT ALL pleased to discover that Loki had been left behind. 'You *left* him there? How *could* you?' she said, when Heimdall explained the state of affairs.

Heimdall looked sullen. 'We had no choice. Besides, that's what he wanted.'

Ethel tutted. 'Since when did *that* matter? We need him!'

But Ethel was in a minority. Most of the others were inclined to consider their loss a blessing. Sif was openly gleeful, while Freyja, dabbing her eyes with a very small lace handkerchief, tried to pretend (unsuccessfully) that she wasn't utterly overjoyed at having abandoned the Trickster.

Thor looked guilty at having run; Bragi sang a mournful song; Fenny said, 'That's harsh, dude'; and Skadi was contemptuous, telling the Æsir she'd known all along that Dogstar would make a run for it and heaping scorn on Idun, who still seemed absurdly hopeful that Loki would soon catch up with them, maybe on the other side . . .

'In any case,' Heimdall said, 'why do we need him any more? I know you're fond of him, Ethel, but face it, he's a liability. We don't need him to reach World's End—'

'That isn't the point,' said Ethel. Her features, usually serene, now looked drawn and anxious. 'I won't go on without him. I'll wait alone, if I have to.'

'What if he doesn't turn up?'

'He will.'

'Is that a prophecy?' Heimdall said.

Ethel gave him a sharp look. 'What do you mean?'

Heimdall shrugged. 'You seem to know more than I do, that's all.'

'Prophecies are dangerous things,' said Ethel, looking weary. 'They start out meaning one thing, and end up meaning the opposite. Loki was meant to be here. At least, that's what I thought—'

By now they were halfway across the bridge, leaving Rhydian behind. The moon was high, the stars were bright, and the opposite bank of the river was clear, while at their back, on the Rhydian side, the pale mist hung like a floating wall, silent and oppressive. Everyone felt their spirits lift as they left the city of ghosts behind, and even Heimdall shivered at the thought that, but for Loki, they might all have remained there, drowned in shadow, weakened and lost, pale reflections of themselves . . .

Heimdall swore under his breath. He hated the thought of being in any way beholden to the Trickster. And yet, according to his personal code, he was. Even if, as Skadi maintained, Loki *had* acted out of sheer self-interest, the fact remained: he had saved them all.

The gods had reached the final pair of pylons when they felt a tremor from under the bridge. It was a brief but violent jolt that rocked the entire structure, jostling the wagons and making the horses prance nervously.

'What in Hel was that?' said Frey.

Behind them, the mist was eerily still. Not a sound, not a light, not a sign of life. There might as well be no town at all; the bridge went on for ever.

There came a second, more violent jolt. This time the horses bolted, eyes wild, hooves striking sparks against the road. One of the wagons lost a wheel; the horses dragged it anyway, metal screaming on metal, scrawling a signature of fire across the last few yards of the bridge.

'What do you *think?*' Heimdall said as they finally left the bridge.

It was shaking visibly now, the tremors coming more regularly. A distant clanging sound could be heard somewhere behind the wall of mist, and as they watched from the river bank, the gods saw the massive structure sag as if under terrible pressure. 'It's Loki, of course, damn him to Hel. Who else do we know who wreaks havoc everywhere he goes?'

Ethel smiled. 'Told you,' she said.

And so, hissing with frustration, the Watchman took to his bird form and soared into the moonlit sky, while Hugin and Munin, finding their perch suddenly unstable, shot out from under the Rhydian Bridge like Wildfire out of Netherworld.

9

WHILE ALL THIS WAS GOING ON, Wildfire himself was thinking hard. In spite of what he'd told Captain Chaos, he had no intention of pledging allegiance to yet another renegade artefact.

But the Sun Shield was a powerful glam, which – if he could control it – would give him the kind of freedom he had only ever dreamed of: independence from Asgard; physical security; protection from his enemies, be they from Order or Chaos. It was a tempting prospect, and Loki was always willing to speculate to accumulate.

But Captain Chaos had proved more dangerous than even the Trickster anticipated, and now, hanging upside-down three hundred feet above the Vimur River, from a rusty girder under a bridge that was ready to collapse at any instant, Loki was beginning to realize that his plan was riskier than he'd thought.

The Sun Shield was positioned between the first two pylons of the Rhydian Bridge, at an angle to the ground. It was convex, which meant that it reflected a good part of the city itself, as well as the bank and the river, and although the years had tarnished it, the runes upon it were clear enough: *Bjarkán; Sól; Thuris; Fé; Raedo; Úr; Kaen; Ár* – powerful runes of protection and light to guard the solar chariot.

At Ragnarók, the sun had gone out, thanks to the two Devourers – Skól and Haiti, now Skull and Big H – and their insatiable appetites. But the Shield was indestructible; and, like Mjølnir, had found its way out of Netherworld, through Dream and into the Middle Worlds.

At least, so Loki theorized; the Captain was far too busy to talk, and Loki thought it more prudent to keep his reflections to himself. Now, after a long and awkward climb, he was hanging upside-down in front of the solar mirror, while his image, watching from the ground, guided him through what was rapidly becoming a very tricky operation.

A large fishing net was spread out between the pylons, ready to catch the Shield as it fell. The plan was for Loki to pull it free, using his glam if he had to, drop it into the waiting net, then assume hawk guise and fly down from the bridge to rejoin his companion.

'If you could give me a *hand* . . .' he said. 'What are you, afraid of heights?'

Loki was *not* afraid of heights – at least, not in normal circumstances. But climbing under a metal bridge that was nearly five hundred years old, then hanging upside-down in front of a mirror-glam with a runecharm of *Tyr* in one hand, then chipping away at the metalwork that held the ancient artefact in place, with rust and soot falling into his eyes and the bridge losing stability with every second that went by, Loki was starting to feel that perhaps he *was* nervous, after all.

'Get on with it,' Captain Chaos said. 'And remember: no tricks.'

'No tricks.' Loki was uncomfortably aware of how vulnerable he was in his current position. With *Kaen* levelled at him from the ground, he was hardly likely to try anything tricky – or so he hoped the Captain would think . . . at least until it was too late. Clever of the Captain, he thought, to keep the upper hand like this; using Loki to free the Shield meant that he himself could watch from a position of safety, and that as soon as Loki dropped the Shield, he could retrieve it and use it as fast as his borrowed glam would allow him.

But Loki had a different plan. He had no intention of dropping the Shield. His double was cautious, and smart enough to anticipate some kind of trickery – but Loki too was cautious and smart,

329

and he had a suspicion that, once the Captain had the Shield, he would have more than enough glam to dispense with Loki permanently.

It was, after all, what *he* would have done, if their situations had been reversed, and Loki was conscious of a twinge – no, not of remorse, but of pique at being so very predictable.

For if the Trickster was vulnerable, Captain Chaos was far from secure. As long as Loki's image appeared in the Shield's polished surface, his double had the upper hand; but if he could slip *behind* the Shield and use it before the Captain did, then Captain Chaos would be no more, and Loki would be free . . .

These were the dangerous ideas that were passing through the Trickster's mind as he chipped away at the Sun Shield. It was rather large for a shield – about four feet across, perfectly round and inscribed with runes on its edge. The rest of it was smooth as glass, though time had given its surface a kind of smoky patina. If the mirror were removed, would the city come back to life? Would the thousands of captured souls that were caught in reflection under the bridge be freed, or would they just disappear? And what about the bridge itself? Would it still stand when the Sun Shield was gone? And – perhaps more importantly – would Loki have time to use it?

'This bridge is falling apart,' he said. 'I don't think it can take much more.'

Certainly the bridge seemed to know that the Shield was under attack. Girders moaned, rivets popped, centuries of powdery rust began to fall from the metal. It fell into Loki's clothes and hair; it filled his mouth with the taste of blood.

'Hurry,' said Captain Chaos.

Loki gave a deep sigh. He was starting to feel most uneasy. The Sun Shield was more than an artefact; he'd already seen proof of that. Captain Chaos too had proved to be far more than just a reflection. What would happen when the Sun Shield was free? Would Captain Chaos then finally have a life of his own? And what would happen to Loki himself when he was no longer needed?

Suddenly, through the falling rust, he thought he saw something

330

under the bridge. A dark shape – a bird, perhaps – was sitting on one of the girders. In no position to cast *Bjarkán*, Loki nevertheless recognized one of Odin's birds – those annoying ravens that Ethel seemed to have adopted.

He hoped they weren't trying to help him. The last thing he wanted at this stage was anyone's interference. He reached around the Sun Shield for something to hold onto. The acorn that hung from his left wrist was now concealed in the palm of his hand. He slipped it behind the Sun Shield and started to whisper a cantrip . . .

The raven gave a sharp *crawk* and hopped a little closer, bringing down a scatter of rust over the inverted Trickster. Loki saw that it had a white head, which identified it as Mandy.

Crop it into the – crawk! It said.

'What?'

Crop it. Into the creek. Gekkaway. Ack-ack! Mandy's voice was urgent and harsh; even allowing for the vocal limitations of her host body, the message was unmistakable. *Throw the Sun Shield into the river. Get away as fast as you can.*

Loki dared not raise his voice in case Captain Chaos heard him. Instead, he spoke in a whisper, barely moving his scarred lips. 'Please! Just leave me alone!' he said.

Mandy pecked at the girder. *Crawk!* Another pinch of powdery rust fell into the Trickster's eyes.

'Ouch!' He brushed the debris from his eyes, transferring *Tyr* to his right hand. The Sun Shield was almost free now; it shifted slightly beneath his grasp, and he felt the bridge shift accordingly.

'Hurry up!' said Captain Chaos.

'Got it, I think,' said the Trickster. He glanced back at the raven, and saw that it had been joined by its companion. Two pairs of gold-ringed eyes fixed on him in the darkness.

'Listen, I don't need your help,' Loki said in the same careful whisper. He knew that Captain Chaos's hearing would be at least as keen as his own, and he'd already seen how suspicious his mirror-image was of him. Once more he hissed at the ravens: 'Get lost! I can take care of this!'

Hughie assumed his human form, cross-legged on the girder. Hidden among the shadows, he was almost invisible from the ground, his silver jewellery hidden beneath the cloak of feathers that covered him.

'We know what ye're thinking,' he said.

'No you don't,' hissed Loki. 'Please. Do you want to get me killed?'

'You're planning tae steal the Sun Shield and keep it for yourself,' Hughie said.

Loki's scarred lips tightened. 'So what?'

'So – that's verra dangerous. And what about your promise, eh? What about the End of the Worlds?'

'The Worlds can end without me,' said Loki, looking down at the drop. 'I've seen the show before – and believe me, I'm in no hurry to go there again.'

'But you're *needed*,' Hughie said. 'You're a part o' the prophecy. Just throw the Shield into the river, and get away as fast as ye can. Do anything else and ye'll come to grief.'

'Who says?' muttered the Trickster.

Hughie *crawk*-ed in frustration. 'Will ye *never* do as ye're told? The survival of the Gødfolk depends on what ye do next!'

Loki shrugged (not easy to do when you're hanging upside-down from a bridge). Three hundred feet to the net, he guessed. It might take him three or four seconds to fall. Three or four seconds, exposed, in midair, to flip the Shield round and use it before Captain Chaos could intervene. Three or four seconds of terrible risk; and even if he *didn't* try to take control of the Sun Shield, what would prevent the Captain from shooting Loki out of the sky the moment the artefact was his?

He hissed: 'Because the Gødfolk care so much about *my* survival . . .'

'What are you whispering about up there?' Captain Chaos's voice was sharp.

'I've got it,' called Loki. 'It's coming free . . .'

Sure enough, the Sun Shield was coming away from its moorings at last. With a crackle of runelight, the solar disc pulled away from the pylon, and at once the bridge began to sag like a cart with a broken axle.

'Throw me the Shield,' the Captain said.

'Throw it into the river,' said Hughie. 'That'll distract him, and as ye do, ye can make your getaway. Otherwise he'll bring ye down—'

But the Trickster had another plan. Ignoring Hughie and Mandy, he whispered a little cantrip. Behind the Shield, the acorn charm resumed its Aspect as Sigyn. Cramped, confused and disoriented, she opened her mouth to scream—

'Shh, Sigyn, please . . .' he said.

Behind the Sun Shield, Sigyn's eyes widened in stupefaction. 'What are we doing here?' she said. 'Where are the others? What have you *done?*'

'Me? Nothing,' Loki hissed. 'Only saved everybody's life, and risked my skin into the bargain. Now do as I say, and everything's going to be all ri—'

A purple fireball struck the bridge barely three feet above Loki's head. Iron girders splayed like straws from the disintegrating structure.

'That was a warning shot, Trickster,' called Captain Chaos from the ground. 'I want that Shield, and I want it now!'

'Hang on a minute!' said Loki. Above him, cracks were appearing in the bridge. Chunks of stone were dropping through into the river below them.

'Sigyn, *now*! Turn the Shield—'

Ack-ack! Said the ravens, taking wing as their perch fell away.

'Turn the wha-*aaahh*!' screamed Sigyn as the girder from which Loki was hanging started to tear away in its turn. Three seconds more, and they would be falling towards the Vimur.

The second mindbolt was not a warning. It struck an inch from Loki's head, firing off the Sun Shield and into the air above Rhydian. A smattering of violet sparks, each one as lethal as a crossbow bolt, skidded across the damaged bridge and fell into the water.

Loki had time to grab the Shield before he and Sigyn began to fall. Linked fast by the Wedlock, they twisted and turned in mid-air; Loki trying to flip the Shield, Sigyn hanging on for dear life, runelight flaring from her hands. Masonry and twisted metal filled the air around them; Hugin and Munin flapped and *crawk*-ed, trying to distract the Captain; while Loki's double, on the bank, raged and screamed in fury.

His third mindbolt hit Loki smack between the shoulders, and if Sigyn hadn't been shielding them both – not with the Sun Shield, but with *Yr* – it might have been much worse for him. As it was, he fell, howling, in flames, right *through* the net and into the river.

The water was fast and very cold. For a moment the Trickster lost consciousness. Dragged under by the Sun Shield and by the weight of the Wedlock, he felt the river's terrible force crushing him and pulling him down; he opened his mouth and water rushed in, filling his lungs, consuming him-

In different circumstances it would have been an easy trick for him to have taken some different Aspect – a fish, perhaps, or a river-snake – and to swim to the bank in safety. But the mindbolt had stunned him half senseless, his glam was almost depleted; besides which there was the gold chain still fastened around his left wrist, and Sigyn, now a dead weight, dragging him deeper under the water.

The Sun Shield! Even now, the thought was foremost in the Trickster's mind. It must have fallen through the net; the undertow had taken it. He opened his eyes, but the dark was so complete that he might as well have been blind. He was moving fast too, dragged down by the undertow, breathing water, seeing stars, crashing with tremendous force against a pile of driftwood—

More stars.

Stars? Ouch!

A hand in his hair, dragging him out. More hands on his body. He felt himself being carried, then dumped onto his back on the river bank. Someone's mouth clamped over his own; air in his lungs like cold fire. His hair was singed; his shirt was charred rags; his back was burning as if he'd been branded.

Now he could hear voices; voices that seemed to come from afar; voices that he recognized . . .

'Loki, sweetheart, *talk* to me . . .'

'Is he alive?'

'He is, worse luck. Quick, let me hit him before he comes round.'

Hastily Loki opened his eyes. In the starlight, a circle of faces, blurry at first, came into view: Heimdall, Freyja, Ethel, Thor. Idun, whose voice he had first recognized, was holding a sliver of apple. As always, she looked sweet and kind; kneeling beside her, the Seeress too was watching him with a look of concern.

Then she slapped his face, hard.

'*Ouch!*' he said. 'I'm conscious.'

Ethel said, 'Just checking, dear.'

Loki sat up. 'The Sun Shield . . .'

Ethel gave him one of her looks. 'Sigyn's fine,' she said loudly. 'Just a little shaken, that's all. I'll tell her you were asking, though. You owe her your life, I hope you know that. She was the one who dragged you to the bank. She was the one who—'

'*What about the* Sun *Shield?*' Loki repeated urgently.

'Fishbait. No time to recover it. It could be halfway to Hel by now.' Ethel lowered her voice again. 'The ravens told me everything.'

'Oh,' said Loki. 'I can explain.'

'Don't bother explaining,' Ethel said, and went back to wait by the wagons.

They set off again within the hour; and the Trickster, who had fully expected Ethel to tell everybody about his failed defection, was inclined to think that she had let him off easily. Perhaps she thought he'd been punished enough – after all, he'd lost the Shield – although, looking at her impassive face as she rode alongside him down the road, Loki could see no softness there, or any sign of affection.

He noticed that she now spoke to him only out of necessity; the rest of the time she spent reading a book, or whispering to her ravens, and more than once he found himself wondering uneasily how she could seem to hate him so much, while at the same time protecting him.

Still, who really knows what an oracle thinks? The Trickster thought as they trotted along, and soon his mind was on other things as Lucky's Pocket Pan-daemonium Circus left the ruined bridge behind and began the final leg of its journey along the highway to World's End.

BOOK SIX

Brimstone and Bridey Cake

Trust me. They don't call it 'wedlock' for nothing.

Lokabrenna, 5:19

1

SEVEN DAYS HAD NOW PASSED since Maddy arrived in World's End with high hopes of finding the Old Man, solving the prophecy and contacting her sister.

None of those things had happened so far. Her search had proven fruitless. Since meeting with Mrs Blackmore, there had been no further mention of Maggie Rede, and the Old Man was as much of a mystery as it had been a week ago. Jormungand was useless, preferring to spend his time by the docks than helping Maddy in her quest. Even Odin's ravens had failed to put in an appearance.

Now, with only two days to go before the End of the Worlds, she was beginning to wonder once again whether she shouldn't simply go home when, on the Friday market day – Maddy's eighth day in the city – she saw something that changed her mind. Or rather, she saw *someone,* and the sight of him made her hackles rise just the same as they always had.

Impossible, she told herself. *What would he be doing here?*

And yet the young man reminded her so strongly of someone she'd known before. The way he moved; the set of his jaw; the way his dark-blond hair fell diagonally across his forehead . . .

It *couldn't* be. And yet it was.

He'd grown into a handsome young man – though his blue eyes were still as mean as they'd always been when he was a boy, and his walk was just as arrogant as he strode between the market stalls.

Adam? Adam Scattergood?

Adam, who had made her life so miserable when she was a child? Adam, who had done his best to bring about her downfall? Adam, who had wet his pants at her first demonstration of power?

Maddy ducked behind a tent-stall selling kitchen hardware. Perth gave her a quizzical look, but she gestured to him to hold his tongue. Through a gap in the side of the tent she watched as the young man wandered past.

For a moment her heart almost stopped as he paused at a nearby fabric stall, and fingered a roll of pale-yellow silk. 'How much for this?'

The vendor, an Outlander woman in a blue veil, murmured a price.

Adam shrugged. 'I'll take it,' he said, and threw down a handful of coins. From her place at the side of the tent, Maddy caught the gleam of gold.

So Adam was wealthy, was he, now? His clothes were of fine quality, he carried a fine blade at his side, and it was clear from his manner that he considered himself above bargaining with traders. She wondered how he had come to World's End, and what could be his business there.

The Outlander woman was folding the silk. 'Well? What are you waiting for?' Adam said. 'Wrap it up, and quickly. I don't want your dirty hands all over it.'

Maddy thought the woman's face turned a shade darker beneath her veil. 'Special occasion, sir?' she lisped.

Adam looked at her and smiled. It was not an entirely pleasant smile, but his blue eyes gleamed with amusement. 'Actually, it is,' he said. 'You see, I'm getting married.'

2

'MARRIED?' MADDY ALMOST SAID IT ALOUD. Seeing Adam here at all was already enough of a shock to her, but to hear that he was getting married – Adam, who as a boy of twelve had liked to throw firecrackers at stray cats and stones at beggars – even at gods – was too absurd to contemplate. Who would want to marry *him*? And what was he doing here, anyway?

Perth was watching her curiously, a gleam of interest in his eyes. 'Old flame?' he suggested, as soon as Adam had moved away.

'Not even close,' Maddy said, still following Adam with her gaze. She hesitated, frowned to herself, then came to a rapid decision. 'We're going after him,' she said. 'I want to know what he's up to.'

'But what about our business?' said Perth.

'Later,' said Maddy. 'Follow him first. And try to be inconspicuous.'

'You really think it's important?' said Perth.

Maddy nodded. 'It might be. Anyway,' she added, 'he's rich. You can rob him if you want to.'

Perth shrugged. 'Fair enough.' Robbery wasn't really his game, but he was always open to suggestions.

It was easy to follow Adam through the crowds and tents and market stalls. Less easy by far were the open streets, the alleys and

341

the walkways. The Universal City was vast, and had been built on a grand scale: the main streets were broad and spacious, with long, bare expanses of pavement, and only a row of linden trees providing any cover. Maddy had grabbed from a passing stall a pink *bergha*, which she now wore around her head in the manner of some World's Enders; it went poorly with her tunic and boots, which marked her as a Northerner, but at least it hid her face, she thought, and she tried to keep well behind Perth – swathed as he was in his blue robes – as they made their way, through St Sepulchre's Square with its marble fountain and its great cathedral, and straight on down Examiners' Walk into the heart of the city.

This was the largest (and most expensive) shopping street in the whole of World's End, and Maddy began to feel very conspicuous as she and Perth followed Adam past the rows of shops with coloured awnings – jewellers, drapers, milliners, coffee houses and makers of clocks, sellers of crystal and porcelain. So far Maddy's time had been spent around the docks and the Water Rats as well as the city's milling slums, and this new face of World's End came as quite a surprise to her.

Here the pavements were twelve feet across and inlaid with decorations of brass. Here there were carriages drawn by teams of horses, landaulets for dowagers and racy high-perch vehicles for the young and fashionable set. Here were ladies in bonnets made from the feathers of exotic birds; there were swaggering young men in furs and wealthy Outlanders with their strings of wives, veiled from head to foot in black, dark eyes modestly lowered.

There were servants of all races here, some running errands, some alone, some carrying parcels in their master's wake. Maddy noticed that many of these carried the mark of a brand on their arm – not quite a rune, but a symbol like two opposing arrowheads—

'What does that sign mean?' she asked.

Perth shrugged. 'Slave brand,' he said. 'People – criminals mostly, or folk who can't or won't pay their debts, or prisoners taken in battle by Outlanders and shipped here. Before the collapse of the Order, criminals just went to gaol, or were flogged, or Cleansed, or put in the stocks. But nowadays there's a slave market every three weeks in St Sepulchre's Square, and that's where most of the scallies end up. Some are sent to work building roads, or digging for stone in quarries, or working on farms as labourers. Some, if they're lucky, or if they can read, end up as house slaves to the rich and repulsive.'

Maddy gave Perth a curious glance. He'd been looking especially furtive ever since they had entered this quarter of the city, and now, halfway down Examiners' Walk, he was visibly uncomfortable. She had wondered why he dressed as he did, in the long robes of an Outlander, when he was clearly a native World's Ender (and with the accent to prove it). And now she remembered the shape of the runemark that Perth had sworn was a tattoo—

— and saw how easily it might have been changed – with iron and soot, or a tattooist's ink – from the mark of a prisoner to a new badge of freedom.

'Perth, were you a *slave?*' she exclaimed, almost forgetting in her surprise that they were meant to be shadowing Adam.

Perth winced and pulled his scarf further over his nose and mouth. 'That's right. Go on, tell everyone. I was a slave on the galleys. Have you any idea what they'll do to me if ever I get caught again?'

'I'm sorry,' said Maddy. 'I didn't know . . .'

'Your friend is getting away from us,' said Perth, with a nod towards Adam.

'Oh,' said Maddy, and quickened her pace.

The market crowd parted to let them pass.

3

Nine days had passed since Maggie had first met Adam
Goodwin in the catacombs under the old University. Since then,
a great deal had happened. In nine days Maggie's life had been
completely overturned. She'd learned that the End of the Worlds
was nigh; had spoken with demons and with gods; had ridden
through Dream on a Horse of Fire and battled with the Æsir.
The last of these had ended in a battle of wills with the Old Man,
during which the General's glam had been so thoroughly wiped
out that barely a spark of consciousness lingered inside the piece
of rock. In spite of all her efforts since then, the Old Man remained
unresponsive, and the runes of the New Script stayed where they
were, locked inside that stubborn stone Head.

But something else had happened to Maggie over those nine
days; something so unexpected, so new that it cast all her other
adventures into the shade. Maggie Rede had fallen in love – headlong, purblind, thunderous love – and Adam had asked her to
marry him, that Sunday morning at eight o'clock in the cathedral
of St Sepulchre.

The Whisperer, surprisingly, had taken the announcement with
very little protest.

'I see you're both determined,' it had said, in Adam's voice. 'I just
hope it doesn't end in tears.'

'Why should it?' said Maggie. 'You sound like my mother.'

'Oh, let Me see. The End of the Worlds?'

'I don't see what *that* has to do with it.'

'Well, one might argue,' the Whisperer said, 'that with war on the horizon, with Chaos overrunning the Middle Worlds, with demons breaking out of Hel, with the Riders of Lunacy and Treachery already on their way, and with the runes of the New Script still locked up in there ...' It used Adam's hand to gesture at the Old Man, still silent under his dust-sheet. 'With all of those things going on, some folk might just expect you to have certain priorities other than choosing fabrics.'

'Adam and I are in love. Why wait?'

'Why indeed?' said the Whisperer.

The old, suspicious Maggie might have wondered why Adam's passenger had taken the news so readily. She might even have asked herself how her forthcoming role as the Rider of Carnage was supposed to fit in with her role as a bride; but the wild exhilaration of love had clouded her suspicions.

Besides, there was more to her change of heart than just the excitement of falling in love. Maggie, who nine days ago had been more than ready to face the foe; Maggie, who had dreamed of being a part of Tribulation, now found herself dreading the idea of war. Some of her misgivings had come from the Old Man's revelations. Some of them had come from her meeting with Hugin and Munin. But mostly it was the fact that, for the first time since the Bliss had taken her family, Maggie Rede had *something to lose* – and the thought of losing Adam now was just too cruel to contemplate.

This was the reason why Maggie had tried to ensnare the gods in Rhydian. This was the reason she hadn't revealed the presence of Odin's ravens. If the Firefolk could be stopped from ever reaching World's End, then war would never happen, she thought; and the prophecy would stay unfulfilled.

And so, far from dreaming of war, the reluctant Rider of Carnage filled her days with dreams of love and, as long as the Old Man slept, was almost able to believe that battle was *not* inevitable.

As for the Whisperer, it was content. Its plan was working perfectly. The girl was in its power now. The General was defenceless. And when it had the New Script, and all the pieces were in place, *then* it would deal with the Æsir – though not before Odin had understood the extent of his defeat and humiliation; not before he realized just how much he had gambled and lost.

As far as the Whisperer was concerned, waiting enhanced the pleasure. Two days remained till the End of the Worlds; two days for the General to find his voice. No doubt he still had a trick up his sleeve; no doubt he would try to talk to the girl. The Whisperer expected it; that too was part of the plan. Maggie Rede was no longer to be seduced by the Old Man's promises. Maggie was a woman in love. And that made her very vulnerable – as well as very dangerous.

Now, on the Friday afternoon, as the Whisperer made his plans and Adam shopped for bridal silk, the subject of all this speculation was sitting by the penthouse window, as she had for the past week, looking down into the streets and feeling very bored.

A week of the same old scenery, the same instructions not to go out; a week of nothing but waiting around while Adam made arrangements and she still kept watch over the Old Man – who had not said a word since his attempt to charm her, and who seemed unlikely to try again, at least until the End of the Worlds.

Not that *that* looked likely. According to the Good Book, Tribulation was heralded by all manner of signs and portents: falling stars; rains of frogs; showers of brimstone; tidal waves and thunderstorms. Right now, Maggie thought, everything looked so ordinary. It *had* rained once or twice, but very ordinary rain, grey with the soot of the city, and without a trace of brimstone or even the smallest of amphibians. Sleipnir, munching oats in his stall, behaved just like a regular horse. There was no sign of the Æsir; no sign of the Riders of the Last Days. Even her dreams had been ordinary, dealing mostly with Adam.

But now Maggie suddenly found that she was feeling restless. Even the thrill of a wedding to plan – such a romantic wedding too, just like in the old days of chivalry – was not enough to compensate for the loss of her freedom. She wanted fresh air; she wanted her books; but most of all she wanted the waiting to be *over* – for Adam to be free at last, and all this a memory.

346

'Why do I have to stay inside? Why can't I go out with you?' she had asked Adam earlier.

He gave a narrow smile. 'Always asking questions,' he said. 'I have a wedding to arrange.'

Maggie sighed. 'I suppose so. But—'

'Don't you trust me?'

'Of course I do!'

And yet her mind refused to let go. She was filled with unanswered questions. Cathedral weddings didn't come cheap. How could Adam afford one? How had he managed to arrange such a thing at less than a week's notice? His account of a last-minute cancellation had more or less convinced her; his refusal to discuss arrangements – or to even let her out of the penthouse to go shopping – she took as proof of his concern; even so, Maggie could not help feeling slightly left out of the proceedings.

'But couldn't I come with you today?'

Adam's smile was a little forced. 'I've already told you, it isn't safe. And besides, someone has to stay and keep an eye on the Old Man.'

'Oh. *That.*'

Adam frowned. 'Remember, Maggie, it's dangerous. Don't let it draw you in again. Don't talk to it in my absence. Just watch it, and tell me if it speaks.'

She nodded.

'Good. Now wait for me. I'll try to be as quick as I can.'

And so Maggie had waited, and tried not to feel anxious or impatient. The truth was, the wedding itself was a matter of indifference to her. Maggie would much rather have been married simply, without fanfare, than sit through a lavish ceremony when so many things remained to be done. But Adam (a romantic) refused to hear of anything but a cathedral wedding. If Maggie was going to take his name, she deserved a proper ceremony. A crown; a veil of primrose silk; flowers; brideys to throw to the crowd – in short, everything a young girl dreamed of, and Maggie, who cared nothing for these things, was nevertheless moved by Adam's devotion to her, and had tried very hard to do as he said. But solitude brought reflection of the kind that Maggie hated most, and now, as she sat by the window, trying to imagine herself as a bride, the doubts that always disappeared as soon as Adam was in the room returned like a swarm of summer flies.

There was so much she didn't yet know about the man she loved. Who *was* Adam, anyway? How had he known where to find her? What did he do for a living, and how could he hope to support them? Where was he from? Who were his folk? What allegiance did he owe to the thing he called the Whisperer?

She turned away from the window. *I'm just being foolish,* she told herself. *Every bride in World's End suffers from pre-wedding jitters.*

And yet . . .

She looked at the plinth, where the Old Man's head still stood, shrouded in mystic darkness. Odin had tried to tell her something just before she had silenced him. Since then, Maggie had come to regret the violence of her reaction. Now she cast *Bjarkán* at the Head, hoping for a sign of life.

Are you awake? she whispered.

Nothing. Just the darkness.

Please, said Maggie. *I need to talk.*

And wasn't that a gleam of response, deep in the heart of the stone? Maggie's own heart beat faster. *Please. I won't hurt you. Just talk to me—*

A sound from behind her made her flinch. She turned to see a raven sitting on the balcony rail. Another was perched on the window-ledge, the single white feather on its head standing up like a warrior's crest. As Maggie approached the window, it pecked the glass impatiently.

'You again!' Maggie said, opening the window.

At once Hughie flew inside and assumed his human Aspect, looking very pleased with himself. Mandy joined him in raven form, perching on his shoulder. He was wearing a shiny pendant that Maggie hadn't seen before; a round disc, inscribed with runes, which caught the light like a mirror.

'Ye said ye wouldn'ae talk to him,' he said, with a glance at the Old Man.

Maggie shrugged. 'I wasn't,' she said. 'I don't care if he never wakes up.'

Mandy *crawk*-ed.

'No chance o' *that*. Ye'll have tae wake him soon enough. Ye'll need the new runes, for a start, before ye face the enemy.'

Mandy *crawk*-ed again. *Ack!*

'Still, there's time for that,' Hughie said. 'Good thing we're here to help ye, eh? The End o' the Worlds is nigh, hen, and we have lots to talk about. The Firefolk are on their way. The Rider of Lunacy joins them. There's war and carnage in the air, and everything's going to be *shiny!*'

Maggie shook her head. 'No thanks.'

'No *thanks?*' Hughie said. He cocked his head, looking more like a raven than ever. 'The End o' the Worlds is coming, and you're telling us no *thanks?*'

'That's right,' Maggie said. 'No thanks. I've had enough. I've fought the Seer-folk in Dream; I've stolen the Red Horse of Carnage; I've got the Old Man trapped inside a piece of rock by the side of the bed. And *this*' – she gestured towards the Good Book, propped up against the bedpost – 'all the time I believed that this Book held the answer to everything. But it doesn't, does it? I used to believe in the Nameless; in the fight for perfect Order. But now there's no Order any more; only two sides that have been at war since before the Worlds began. So what am I *doing* in all this? Who *says* I have to go to war?'

'But hen—' protested Hughie.

'I am *not* your hen!' Maggie said. 'Now listen to me, both of you. I'm getting married the day after tomorrow. Married. In the cathedral. Married to the man I love. And *nothing* – not the End of the Worlds, not the Seer-folk, not Chaos itself – is going to get in the way of that. Have I made myself quite clear?'

Hughie and Mandy exchanged looks.

Hughie shrugged.

Mandy *crawk*-ed.

'I'll take that as a yes, shall I?'

'Well, here's the thing,' Hughie said. 'On Sunday morning

349

– that's the day after tomorrow, hen, in case ye'd forgotten – there's going to be war. The Seeress predicted it. Which makes *this* the place for ravens and crows, not wedding veils and bridey cakes. And the sooner you face up tae that—'

Crawk, said Mandy lugubriously.

'Everyone keeps saying that,' Maggie said impatiently. 'War, war, the End of the Worlds – that's all anyone can talk about.'

Hughie cocked his head to one side. 'You're the Rider o' Carnage, lass. D'ye think ye can change the future? Reconcile Order and Chaos? Cancel the War of the Nine Worlds? Rewrite the Book of Apocalypse? Shiny, if ye could, but no verra *realistic.*'

Maggie made a face. 'I don't see why there has to be war.'

'Aye, that's what the God o' War says. Funny, that. But we see more. We see into all the Worlds, past and present, quick and dead, and we know *all* the prophecies. The hand that rocks the Cradle rules the Nine Worlds, so they say. It's writ on the very Foundation Stone of the cathedral. And unless the Seeress got it wrong, that hand belongs to *you,* hen, and you're going tae need all the help ye can get. Which is why we're here.'

'Well, thanks. But unless you want to be flower girls—'

'Gods, aren't ye the stubborn one? We can open Worlds, lass. We could open the gates of Hel, or of Netherworld, if ye wanted it so.'

'I don't want to open gates. Or rock cradles, for that matter.'

'What does it matter *what* ye want?' Now Hughie was getting annoyed. 'I tell ye, it's all written down. You're the one, like it or nay. *The key to the gate is a child of hate, a child of both and of neither.* That's you, or I'm a pigeon. What more do ye need, eh? Have ye any idea what will happen if the Rider o' Carnage disn'ae ride?'

Now Mandy, who had been watching the street, gave a cry of warning. *Crawk!*

'What is it, Mand?' said Hughie.

Crawk, repeated Mandy. She looked as if she were trying to speak; raucous words came out of her mouth in a language neither human nor bird.

'Someone's coming,' Hughie said. 'I'm guessing it's your young man. Now listen. This is important.' He turned once more to Mandy. 'Come on, ye can do it, hen,' he said, with an encouraging smile. 'She disn'ae speak much,' he explained, 'but when she does, folk do well tae listen.'

Mandy beat her dusty wings in mounting agitation.

Crawk! Ack-ack!

'Come on, Mand.'

And now the raven began to speak. The words were harshly accented, but nevertheless understandable, and Maggie found herself listening to the words of a nursery rhyme she'd known as a child:

'See the Cradle (crawk!)-*ing*
High above the town.
Down come the Firefolk
To bring the baby down.
All the way to Hel's gate
Firefolk are bound.
Pucker-lips, a-pucker-lips,
All (crawk!) *down.'*

And, then, as if human speech had proved too much of an effort, the white-headed raven hopped down from its perch and made for the balcony window.

Hughie followed. 'Ye heard what she said?'

'Yes, but—' Maggie protested.

'No time!' Hughie said, stepping out onto the balcony. 'The Firefolk are on their way. The End o' the Worlds is coming. Soon ye'll have tae make a choice. Ye know how tae find us.'

Maggie opened her mouth to say that no, she didn't know how to find them, and besides, she had no intention of trying, but Hughie had already reverted to bird Aspect, and before she could even find the words, both he and Mandy had taken wing, and were nothing but specks in the city sky.

4

ADAM HAD SPOTTED THE PAIR on his tail as soon as they'd left the market. He could have shaken them there and then; all he had to do was to step into a hire carriage, or walk into one of those elegant shops, or call for help and pretend he'd been robbed. But the presence of the Whisperer that always lurked in Adam's mind warned him now to be cautious, and to allow the two that shadowed him to follow his steps through the city.

Take care, boy, the Whisperer said. *Don't let them see you're aware of them.*

'Why?' said Adam. 'Who are they?'

In his mind the Whisperer made a sound of impatience. *Who do you think, idiot? Now get us home, and quickly! We have no more time to waste!*

So with Maddy and Perth in hot pursuit, Adam fled through the streets of World's End. He arrived to find Maggie waiting for him by the open window, wearing an innocent expression. Perhaps a little too innocent, but Adam did not notice it; he was too preoccupied with his own concerns.

'Did the Old Man speak?' he said.

Maggie sighed. 'The Old Man – is that all you care about?'

'No, but . . .' Adam faltered.

'I've been waiting here all day. You never ask how I spend my time. You disappear for hours, and then all you can think of is

352

that thing . . .' She gestured fiercely towards the plinth, where the stone Head stood impassively. She suddenly felt angry – not with Adam, but with the Head; the Old Man who refused to speak, whose stubbornness now stood in the way of Adam's chance at freedom.

In Adam's mind the Whisperer tried to curb its impatience. *For gods' sakes, boy, give her a kiss! The last thing I need right now is for her to be uncooperative.*

Adam gave Maggie his sweetest smile. 'I bought you a present. I chose it for you.' He dropped his parcel of silk beside her. 'Go on. Open it,' he said.

Maggie felt her anger recede. Now she only felt guilty. Once more she wondered whether she should tell Adam about the ravens. But the Whisperer might be angry, she thought; it might even punish Adam.

She took the parcel and opened it. She looked at the roll of primrose silk, soft as sunshine, sewn with pearls. *This is my wedding veil,* she thought, and her eyes were filled with sudden tears.

'I love it!' she said. 'And I love *you!*'

This time it was easier to forget the events of the afternoon. Prophecies and nursery rhymes – even rumours of a war – were easy to forget about when faced with such a gift as this.

'It's gorgeous,' she said, unfolding it and wrapping it round her shoulders. 'It must have cost you the Nine Worlds—'

'You're sure the Old Man didn't speak?'

'Not a word. Why do you ask?'

'I think we may have a problem. Someone may be spying on us. I'm almost sure I was followed here.'

'Spies?' said Maggie doubtfully, thinking of the ravens.

Adam looked at her earnestly. 'You think I *wanted* to keep you here while I went out in the city alone? We can't afford for you to be seen. And the Æsir will do whatever they can to stop us being together.'

Maggie's eyes widened. 'Why would they do that?'

Adam shrugged. 'A boy from the North marry one of the Seer-folk? Their pride would never allow it,' he said. 'If they find out,

353

they'll kill me, just as they killed your parents and friends and everyone else you've cared about—'

'Kill *you*?' Maggie's heart froze, and then began to stutter. Of all the fears she might have had regarding her long-lost family, it had never really occurred to her that the Æsir might want to hurt Adam. And for what? Their monstrous pride, which refused to accept that a child of the Fire could learn to love a child of the Folk?

'What do you mean?' she said.

Adam sighed. 'I mean they want to claim you. Everything they've done so far has been done for just that purpose. They cut you off from everything. They killed your foster-family. They made sure you were all alone before they tried to contact you. The only thing they didn't predict was that you and I might fall in love. But when they do find out – and they *will* – we'll have to be ready to fight them. And if their spies have followed me here . . .'

Once more Maggie thought of the ravens. *Could* they be spies? Of course they could. But they had offered themselves to *her*, to Maggie, the Rider of Carnage. They had shown her how to trap the Firefolk in Rhydian. But according to Hughie, the gods had escaped. And if they found out about Adam . . .

'What do you want me to do?' she said.

She knew the answer to that, of course. The ravens had predicted it. She could no longer wait, she knew, for the Old Man to find his voice again. The runes of the New Script were in that Head, waiting to reveal themselves.

Adam looked at her tenderly. 'You know it's time, don't you?' he said.

Maggie gave a long sigh. This was what she'd been dreading. Ever since she had spoken with the prisoner inside the Head; ever since he'd told her of the relationship between them, she had known that some day soon she would have to break him. She would have to make the choice between torturing the Old Man and risking the life of the man she loved. It was not a fair choice to ask her to make. She hated the thought of making it. But the Æsir had threatened Adam. To threaten Adam was to cross a line.

354

If that meant war, then let it be war. The Seer-folk had declared it.

She turned to Adam once again, her eyes like little points of steel. 'Will the new runes keep you safe?'

Adam nodded.

Maggie smiled. 'Then you'll have them, I promise,' she said. 'This time he'll tell me *everything.*'

5

THE GOOD BOOK WAS STILL LYING where Maggie had left it by the bed. A double turn of the golden key, and the Closed Chapters lay revealed. On its plinth, the Old Man stood in stony silence; but the spark of awareness that Maggie had seen earlier through the rune *Bjarkán* remained like the gleam of a half-open eye.

Odin was awake, she knew, watching every move she made.

She opened the Book of Invocations, followed the script with her finger, chose the relevant canticle and read the ritual words aloud:

'I name thee Odin, son of Bór.
I name thee Grim, Ganglàri . . .'

The words felt almost familiar now, like those of a well-practised song. This time she did not stumble or mispronounce the secret names. On her neck, the runemark *Ác* began to flare a silvery white.

Maggie? What are you doing?

The voice of the Old Man was deceptively gentle in her mind. Maggie ignored it. Instead she focused on the words, making the runes flare like molten steel, spinning them into a cradle of light.

Maggie. You don't have to do this.

Maggie ignored the coaxing voice and steeled herself for a counterattack. The Old Man was sure to try something soon, once he knew her intention.

'I name thee Ialk and Herteit.

I name thee Vakr and VarmaTyr.

I name thee Father of ravens.

I name thee one-eyed Wanderer . . .'

Now Maggie's head began to ache. Her vision doubled; trebled; swam. The light at the heart of the piece of rock started to flare like molten glass.

Please, it hurts, said the Old Man.

I'm sorry, said Maggie silently. *I have no choice. It has to be done. I name thee Father of Misrule—*

Maggie! Please!

The cradle of runes was now so bright that Maggie could barely look at it. The headache grew worse – a cap of pain tightening against her skull.

'Stop it!' Maggie cried aloud, and now, with all her glam, she *tugged* on the cradle of runelight like a choke-chain on a dangerous dog. *'A named thing is a tamed thing—'*

The voice in her head gave a howl of pain. *Mercy!*

But that was a sentiment Maggie could no longer afford. She looked up from the Good Book and focused all her glam on the Head.

'Thus are you named, and bound to my will.'

At last the struggle was over.

And now she turned to the Old Man in his net of runelight. 'I'm sorry I had to do that,' she said. 'But time's running out. You know what I want. The runes of the New Script . . .'

The prisoner gave a mental sigh. *You could just have asked me,* he told her. *Instead of subjecting me to all of this unpleasantness.*

'Yeah. Like you'd have told *me*—'

Of course I would, said the General. *The New Script is your birthright. Like your name – your true name – it is a thing of remarkable power. Be sure not to give it away unwisely.*

'What do you mean, give it away?'

Oh, you'll find out soon enough. I don't have to be an oracle to know what the Whisperer will ask of you next.

'What's that?' Maggie said.

He'll order you to kill me, of course.

Maggie protested. 'I wouldn't do that—'

Oh, but you will, said the Old Man. *You'll do it because you won't have the choice. I can even show you the runes you'll use to send me into eternity.*

'The runes,' she said.

Yes, Maggie. The runes.

And now, at last, they came. The runes. The new runes of the Younger Script, all in their colours, like pennants in the wind.

Aesk and *Ác, Eh* and *Ea, Ethel* and *Perth, Daeg, Wyn* and *Iar.* Their colours fluttered past so quickly that Maggie barely caught their names. But that didn't matter; she understood. She already knew how to use them. And she knew she could summon them at any time and bend them to her purpose.

'Nine runes. Is that all?'

No, there's one more, said the Old Man. *One last, most important rune – the one that will change the shape of the Worlds—*

'What is it? Show me!' she said.

Patience, Maggie, patience. The tenth rune is already in your possession. Although you're not aware of it yet—

'How? Where?' Maggie said.

Don't be so impatient, girl, said the Old Man in his dry voice. *If you're going to kill me, at least let me have my say first. A man may plant a sapling for any number of reasons. Perhaps the man is fond of trees. Perhaps he needs the shelter. Or perhaps he knows that some day soon he will need the firewood. Plant your seeds with care, then. From every Acorn, an Oak may grow.*

'What's all *that* supposed to mean?' Maggie said when the Old Man fell still.

You work it out, said the Old Man. *I speak as I must, and cannot be silent.*

'But who was the man you were talking about?'

I speak as I must, and cannot be silent.

'Is it someone I know?' she said.

I speak as I—

'I *do* wish you'd stop saying that!' Maggie looked at her hands. 'Please. Tell me what you've got to say.'

For a moment the Old Man paused, and the light inside the stone Head flared in satisfaction. *Maggie,* he said quietly, *I have been searching for you since the end of the Age. It has taken me longer than I thought, but believe this. I never forgot you. Not for a moment. All this time I've been trying to find a chance to bring you home to your people.*

'My people?' said Maggie, looking up. 'The Seer-folk killed my people.'

No, said the Old Man in her mind. *The Nameless killed your people. The being you call Magister, and which Adam calls the Whisperer, killed them all with a single Word—*

'That was the Bliss,' Maggie said.

There was no Bliss, said the Old Man. *Just an army of ten thousand souls, sent out to destroy the Æsir. Your sister saved the Worlds that day. But now the Whisperer has you – the Rider whose name is Carnage – and now it means to wipe out the gods and reclaim Asgard for itself—*

'You're lying!'

I can't. I'm an oracle.

For a long time Maggie sat silently, watching through the rune *Bjarkán*. Through it, the Old Man blazed with light, but she could detect no thread of deceit, nor even a flicker of a lie.

The Nameless had killed her parents.

The Whisperer was the enemy.

For a moment Maggie felt as if her whole life had been blown apart. The Order; the Good Book; Tribulation; all the immutable truths that she had been brought up to believe – suddenly it seemed that none of those things had been exactly what she'd thought. It was as if someone had told her that the Nine Worlds were *not* lodged in the branches of the World Tree, as she had always believed, but were somehow floating around in the sky, suspended by nothing but magic. It was appalling; it made no sense; and yet, she understood, it was true.

The Whisperer had caused the Bliss. The thing that inhabited Adam was a dangerous, vengeful entity sworn to destroy the

359

Firefolk. The sister she had never known had brought about the End of the Worlds, and saved the gods in the process – and now the Old Man – her grandfather – wanted *her* to do the same: to ride with them into battle and to help reclaim their lost kingdom . . .

'So— what about Adam?' she said at last.

What about him? said the Old Man.

'The Whisperer said you'd kill him. That the Æsir would never stand to see me marry a son of the Folk. Is that true? You want him dead?'

The Old Man glowed in his net of fire. *Why should I want him dead?* he said. *Maggie, I'm an oracle. This wedding isn't going to take place. However much you may want it to—*

Maggie started to interrupt, but the Old Man continued.

So Adam isn't our problem, he said. *His passenger, on the other hand, is very much our enemy. Remove one from the other, and Adam no longer concerns us.*

Maggie struggled to understand what the Old Man was telling her. The Æsir didn't want Adam dead. And yet the wedding wouldn't take place. How could that be? she asked herself. How could that be, if Adam was safe?

Eagerly she seized upon the thought that was foremost in her mind. 'Will you swear not to hurt him, then? As soon as the Whisperer sets him free?'

Of course I will.

'On your true name?'

On my true name, I swear it.

Maggie gave a sigh of relief. She knew enough to understand that the oath was binding.

Of course, if you kill me, all bets are off, the Old Man went on casually. *In fact, it's more than likely that the others will come after you both. Your sister, in particular. You're very like her, by the way. Such a shame you were raised apart . . .*

And now a series of images flicked through her mind like a fortune-teller's pack of cards; of faces and places she almost knew.

A little girl with long, wild hair sitting in the crotch of a tree; the same little girl, now older, flinging a rune at a boy with mean eyes

360

and a damp patch on his trousers. A girl on a hillside; a man with a pack sitting beside her, smoking a pipe. The same girl, older, underground, looking down into a fiery pit where a ball of molten glass bobbed up and down like a fisherman's lure. The same girl once again, on a plain that seemed to reach out for ever.

And now, somewhere in the city below, a man in a cloak and that girl again, watching through the rune *Bjarkán*.

'Is she *here?*' Maggie said. 'Is my sister here, in World's End? Did she follow Adam here? And what about the Seer-folk? Where are they now? How far away? How did they get out of Rhydian? And can they get to St Sepulchre's in time to stop the wedding?'

The Old Man sighed. *I speak as I must, and – Yadda yadda yadda. I guess you know the drill by now.*

'But what about the wedding?'

Odin sighed again. *Please, Maggie. Try to concentrate. There's more to this than wedding cake. Worlds may rise or fall on this, and even the best-laid plans may turn on as small a thing as a lover's kiss.*

And with that, the Old Man fell silent again, and Maggie Rede opened her eyes.

'What did it tell you?' Adam said. Of course, he had heard only one half of Maggie's conversation. 'Did it give you the New Script? What did it tell you about me?'

Maggie shook her head, still dazed.

'Well?' said Adam impatiently.

Maggie looked into Adam's eyes and saw the Whisperer burning there.

'First, we had a deal,' she said. 'You were going to let Adam go.'

'And so I shall,' said the Whisperer. *'Did you think I would break My word? But you have a part to play in this. After that, the boy can go free.'*

'What do you mean? What part?' she said.

The Whisperer gave a theatrical sigh. *'Always with the questions,'* it said. *'Very well. Let Me explain. In Dream, I am discorporate. But My consciousness in the Middle Worlds requires a physical presence. Until now, My young friend has served this purpose. But until I can move to a suitable host, I fear I must impose upon his goodwill for just a little longer.'*

Maggie thought about that for a while. 'A suitable host?' she repeated.

The Whisperer shrugged Adam's shoulders. *'Of course,'* it said. *'You don't think I like being trapped in this pathetic body? I need something more permanent.'*

It pointed at the stone Head. Its glam was completely dark again now, and only through *Bjarkán* could she see the net of runes that bound it. That anything could live in there was already hard enough to accept; that Adam's Magister might choose to do so was almost inconceivable.

'You'd go into *that?*' Maggie said.

'No, Maggie, not that. But something with glam.' Adam's eyes gleamed. *'Something nice, with runes, perhaps. . .'*

'Like what?' Maggie said.

'Just leave that to Me. Suffice it to say that by Sunday night, both you and I will have what we want.'

'But— what about the Old Man?'

Once more the Whisperer shrugged. *'Now that you have the new runes, we don't need it any more. When you're ready, just say the word and send it to Hel, where it belongs.'*

'You mean – kill him?' Maggie said.

'Well, of course,' said the Whisperer. *'This is Odin, General of the Æsir. Our greatest, most dangerous enemy. What did you think we were going to do? Send him to bed with a glass of milk?'*

Now Maggie saw the trap she was in, and she cursed the Old Man inwardly. Had he known this would happen? Of course. Could he have even planned it this way? That too seemed likely. This was Odin, son of Bór. His deviousness was legendary. Odin, whose plans were impenetrable; who, even at his weakest – disembodied, a prisoner – knew how to prey on his victim's mind.

She had to buy time, Maggie told herself. She had to find a way out of this. To kill the Old Man was unthinkable – at least until she had found a way of protecting Adam from the vengeance of the

Æsir. But to disobey the Whisperer – that, too, was unthinkable. Adam was still in its power; it could tear his mind apart —

'What is it, Maggie?'

The Whisperer's voice roused her from her unpleasant thoughts.

'The Old Man told me you'd say this. He said that as soon as you had the runes, you'd order me to kill him.'

'Did *he* now?' said the Whisperer silkily. '*And . . . did he tell you anything else?*'

Maggie gave a little shrug. She hoped it looked petulant, rather than guilty. She knew she would have to take great care *what* she told the Whisperer. Too little, and who knew what harm it might do to Adam before she subdued it. Too much, and she would relinquish control.

Yes, she would have to be careful, she thought.

'*Well, girl, what are you waiting for?*' said the Whisperer impatiently. '*You're getting married on Sunday. So give Me what I want – the runes – and I will give you Adam. Do we have a deal?*'

Stubbornly Maggie shook her head. 'Not until you set Adam free.'

For a moment, there was silence. Maggie could feel the Whisperer struggling to contain its rage. In a moment the thing would erupt, and Adam would be the one to suffer.

But when it finally spoke again, its voice was calm, its colours subdued.

'*Maggie, why don't you trust Me?*' it said. '*A week ago you were on My side. You believed in Me and the Order. A week ago you couldn't wait to spill a little demon blood. What did it tell you to change your mind?*'

'He *hasn't* changed my mind!' she said.

'*Then what did it* say?' said the Whisperer.

Maggie looked into Adam's eyes. She hated to hide the truth from him, but this was for his own good. If his passenger were to suspect that she was having second thoughts—

'He made a prophecy,' she said. 'Said I'd have to make a choice between my Folk and my family. And I've made my choice. If the Seer-folk come here on Sunday, I'll fight. But I won't let Adam be sacrificed. I want your word you'll keep him safe. We'll be married

363

in the cathedral at eight, and then – only *then* – I'll give you the runes and send the Old Man on his way.'

For a long time Adam was silent. '*Sunday*,' he said.

She nodded. 'At eight.'

'*And then you'll give Me the New Script?*'

'I swear it. On my true name.'

For a moment Maggie sensed the almost frightening intensity of the Whisperer's satisfaction. '*Very well*,' it said at last. '*If that's the way you want it. Fine.*' And as Maggie watched, its presence withdrew, leaving only Adam there, looking pale, but self-possessed.

She gave him a smile that Adam found almost chilling in its tenderness.

'I did it,' she said. 'You're going to be safe. And no one will stop our wedding.'

Then she turned towards the bed and picked up the piece of yellow silk. She draped it over her cropped hair; the late sun caught its folds and she was transfigured, beautiful, a goddess in Aspect, eyes like the sun . . .

Of course, Adam thought to himself, love and the right kind of lighting can make a beauty of even the plainest girl. Even so, he felt a stab of unease. She looked so like her sister had, that terrible day on the shores of Hel. Beautiful and dangerous, like something from an unnatural dream. *One more day*, he told himself. Just one more day and he would be free.

The thought was such a pleasant one that Adam felt a surge of something almost like affection, as you might feel for a stray dog that unexpectedly turns out to be quite a useful ratter.

'Maggie,' he said, 'you're going to be the most beautiful bride in World's End!'

And then he kissed her, and once again Maggie forgot everything else but Adam's face – Adam's lips, Adam's voice, Adam's eyes – while in the street below, her twin looked for her through the rune *Bjarkán*, and the Old Man slumbered, satisfied, nursing his dreams of Asgard.

6

Nan was not afraid of dreams. Dream was the lifespring of everything. Dream links Order and Chaos, she knew; Dream links Death to the Middle World. A dreamer may speak to the dead, walk with gods, build wonderful castles in the air.

And nothing dreamed is ever lost, and nothing lost forever.

Seven days had passed since Nan Fey had become the Rider of Lunacy. During that time she had followed the instructions relayed to her by the Auld Man's birds, waiting, with some apprehension, for the moment when she would be called upon to act – though what exactly she was expected to do was still something of a mystery. So far, all she had had to do was feed her cats and Epona, look after her cottage and wait as the dreamcloud from Red Horse Hill crept closer to the village.

In fact, it was no longer creeping at all. By Friday morning the cloud had become a wing spread over the valley, casting its shadow from Fettlefields right up to the shores of the Strond. Nan's house was far enough away to give her a few more days' security; but Malbry was right in its path. Already, groups of refugees had moved away as the cloud advanced – some as far as Little Bear Wood – but most of Malbry's villagers had never left the valley, and the thought of leaving it now, even in the face of such danger, was too much for them to contemplate.

Nan waited for as long as she could. But on the Friday evening, with the dreamcloud blotting out the sky and drowning even the sound of the Strond with its muted, hateful roar, she decided there was no time to lose. With or without the Auld Man's orders, she had to do *something* to help. Alone, out of Aspect, she doubted whether she would be of any use to the villagers. But perhaps if she rode Epona—

She put on her stoutest boots, her shawl and the hat she wore on festival days. Then she went out into the yard to take a look at the Horse of Air.

In her present Aspect she seemed (to Nan, who had never actually ridden a horse) much more daunting than she had when they had flown together through Dream. She bore no saddle or bridle, either; and Nan surveyed her doubtfully and wondered if she would carry her. A fall at her age could mean death; and this seemed only too likely to Nan, whose brittle old bones feared the slightest shock, and ached when it was raining.

Still, she told herself bracingly, a person who had flown through Dream in a washing basket should have nothing to fear from an old mare, and she caught hold of the Horse's mane and, standing on an old tree-stump, whispered in Epona's ear:

'Now then, old girl. We're going to ride, nice and gentle, to Malbry.'

Epona tossed her head and whinnied.

'Good girl,' said Crazy Nan. And with an effort she put her old leg over the white horse's back and hoisted herself into place, keeping hold good and tight, with her hands both clenched in the Horse's mane.

'There's my good girl,' repeated Nan as, without any further prelude, the Horse of Air began to walk, then to trot, and finally to canter down the Malbry road, while Nan held on for dear life, and the sound of the rift in Dream increased gradually from a distant roar to that of a summer thunderstorm.

Above her, two ravens circled, but the thunderous sound of the rift in Dream swallowed their cries, like everything else.

'Good girl,' Nan Fey said again, and, kicking up her heels, she rode the White Horse of the Last Days straight towards the dreamcloud, while in World's End, the Auld Man slept, and a Rider whose name was Treachery prowled the streets of the Universal City, still oblivious to the fact that the *actual* traitor was somebody else . . .

7

Even on the horse of air, Crazy Nan took ten minutes to get into Malbry. In those ten minutes the dreamcloud had crept three and a half inches closer to the gate of the Parsonage; had further eroded a grain barn belonging to Tyas Miller; had finished off a henhouse, including all its occupants; and discorporated a shaggy brown dog that had been sleeping by the door of the church, where most of the remaining citizens of Malbry and its surrounding hamlets now waited, wakeful and terrified, mothers clasping their children, in expectation of the approaching catastrophe.

Nan Fey had waited long for this. Ninety-odd years spent waiting for a time when she would be *needed* at last, when her appearance would be welcomed with sighs of relief, and not with cries of laughter and scorn. She was not of a vengeful nature, but Malbry had not treated Nan well, and now that its fate hung in her hands, she planned to enjoy her moment.

She circumvented the dreamcloud, which now towered forty feet over her, left Epona on the far side of the church, and entered by a side door. The scene that met her was pitiful. The church was lit with candles. More than two hundred villagers sat huddled against the far wall. Some were children; some were old. Some were farmers, trying hard to look tough. Some wept. Some prayed. Nan saw Mae Smith – now Mae Dean, of course – who had been on a visit to Malbry when the dreamcloud had cut off the road; and her new husband, Zebediah Dean, a rather self-important young man expected to be the new Bishop. Matt Law and his possemen were there – Tyas Miller, Dan Fletcher, Patrick Dunne, Jack Shepherd, Ben Briggs – but even they looked wide-eyed and lost, faces pale, hands outstretched, some still clasping possessions saved from their fallen houses. A shiver of sound went through the church as soon as Nan Fey opened the door; someone started a canticle, but immediately fell silent.

Instead all eyes turned towards Nan; and she found that in spite of those ninety years of being the butt of everyone's joke, she felt precious little merriment at seeing the tables thus reversed. Another kind of woman might have been tempted to crow a little, but Crazy Nan Fey had a good heart, and, seeing the villagers' misery, she raised her voice and called out to them as loudly as she could:

'Listen to me, everyone! I think I know how to help us!'

A silence greeted Nan's words. Perhaps it was a measure of their collective despair and wretchedness that no one laughed or scorned her words, but looked at her with doubt and fear (and maybe a little hope too).

'What can anyone do to help?' That was Damson Ploughman from one of the little smallholdings between Malbry and the Castle Hill Road. 'My farm's gone into the devil-mist – aye, and all my horses too, and when my son went after them—'

'Aye!' That was Mags, the ploughman's wife, a lady who some folk called lively (and others, just shrill). 'The End of the Worlds is upon us, d'ye ken! And it's *your* folk that brung it here!'

'*My* folk?' said Nan Fey.

'Aye, yourn. The Seer-folk!'

At this, a number of voices were raised in agreement. Mae Dean's cries were more strident than most (folk in Malbry had not forgotten that it had been *her* sister who had started all this). Zeb Dean listened approvingly; he'd married Mae (still a beauty) against his great-uncle Torval's advice, and he was glad to see that she, at least, had no divided sympathies.

'There, there,' he said, fondly taking his bride's hand. 'No need to fret, my darling. I still have some influence here, and you can be sure that when this comes to my great-uncle's attention, the matter will be dealt with.'

Nan listened to the angry cries and shook her old head in reproach. 'I thought you'd a learned better'n that by now,' she said, raising her own voice over the din. 'Can't ye see it's the Seer-folk that have aided ye these three years?'

'Aye!' came a mocking voice from the crowd. 'Who rid us of the Order and brought us Chaos in its place? Who brought demons from under the Hill, and now this dream-mist to drown us? We should be on our knees right now, thanking the gods for their mercy!'

That was Dan Fletcher, one of Matt's posse, known in the valley as a cynic and a freethinker; known to Nan Fey since he was a boy.

'I remember you, Dan Fletcher,' said Nan. 'I can remember when you were nobbut a lad, asking me about your dreams. You were allus dreaming in those days, even when your ma thrashed you for it.'

'Aye,' said Dan, 'and look where it got us! That mist came from off the river Dream, and don't you dare deny it.'

Nan smiled at him approvingly. Dan had always been clever, she thought, and it was good that he was here. 'I *don't* deny it, Danny,' she said, and a shiver went through the assembled folk. 'This is the start of the End of the Worlds, and it starts, as it should, at the centre. The Seer-folk have left to march on World's End, the three Horsemen are on the ride, the river Dream has broken its banks . . .' She narrowed her eyes at the refugees. '*Pucker-lips, a-pucker-lips.* Ye surely all know what *that* means.'

The villagers exchanged silent looks.

'Aye. It means nothing can save us,' said Dan. Beneath the swagger, his tone was bleak. 'We can run, we can hide, we can try to fight – it'll all come to nothing in the end. Nothing but mist and cinders.'

'Wrong,' said Nan. 'Listen to this. *The Cradle fell an age ago, But Fire and Folk shall raise her . . .*'

And now Nan quoted the prophecy the Auld Man had given

her, trying to fill her creaky old voice with the same quiet air of authority. It didn't quite work – because halfway through, Mags Ploughman piped up in her strident voice, interrupting the Oracle's words:

'What are ye listenin' to her for!' she cried. 'She's allus been mad, y'kennet, and now she's in league with the Seer-folk! I say we chuck *her* into the devil-mist, see what happens then, eh!'

'Aye,' came the voice of Mae Dean, forgetting her new refined ways and slipping into dialect. 'We'll have none of yer imaginings here, ye mad crone!'

There were cries of *'Aye!'* and *'Chuck her in!'* and now came a dozen eager hands clutching hold of Nan Fey, and a surge of people, goaded by fear, thrusting her towards the door.

But Dan Fletcher stood in their way. 'She may be as mad as ye say,' he said, 'but anyroad, you'll do her no harm.'

For a moment it seemed as if they would: fists were raised; blows threatened; someone kicked Dan in the ankle, and made him stagger.

But now Matt Law stood beside him; and Tyas Miller and Ben Briggs. Violence seemed inevitable. Someone knocked down a statue. Someone else picked up a spade. Nan pulled away from the lynch-mob and flung open the church door into the dark, where Epona, the Horse of Air, stood like a phantom in the mist.

Two tattered figures flanked her – Hugin and Munin, in true Aspect. Against the wall of mist they looked like shadows from Hel itself. The angry mob gasped and cowered.

'Demons!' said Zebediah Dean.

Nan looked at Hughie. 'Ye took your time, ye two,' she said.

'And ye were told to wait, Nan Fey.'

Nan shrugged.

Mandy *crawk*-ed. Even in this Aspect, it seemed, she still had problems with language.

Hughie reached around his neck, where a coin-sized pendant – some kind of talisman – gleamed, reflecting the candlelight. He pulled the object over his head and handed it to Nan Fey.

'What's this?' said Nan.

'A token frae the Auld Man,' said Hughie. 'Use it as ye see fit.'

And with that, he and his sibling changed into bird form, took wing and disappeared into the mist.

Nan looked at the object doubtfully. It was round, inscribed with runes, and in its mirrored surface she could see herself, upside-down, but altered, *illuminated . . .*

Behind her, the crowd of villagers had begun to recover and regroup. Soon, she knew, their fear would once more give way to the threat of violence.

But now Nan faced them in her new Aspect – the Rider whose name was Lunacy – and suddenly she *knew* what to do, and she laughed like a child at the ease of it.

'This is madness,' said Zeb Dean. 'Are we to listen to fancies and tales from a mad old crone and a couple of birds?'

Nan smiled. 'Mad?' she said. 'Aye, mebbe I *am* mad. But Madness is one of the islands of Dream, and I ken those waters *very* well.'

She lifted the pendant that Hughie had given her. From it, the light of the candles now seemed to shine out as bright as the sun. It looked a little larger too; no longer a coin, but a dinner plate.

And at that moment the broken rune *Fé* began to glow on Nan Fey's wrinkled forehead. It glowed a clear and luminous white, and as it glowed, it seemed to *shift,* so that any villager who dared raise his eyes to the old woman's face saw the ruinmark glowing there, as it changed from a dull, defective rune to a shiny bright glam of the New Script—

Mae gave a cry and shrank back. She knew a ruinmark when she saw one – and she'd seen the one on her sister's hand glow in just such a fearsome way.

'Laws save us all!' said Zeb Dean. 'This should have been reported!'

But Dan Fletcher was watching Nan, a gleam of appreciation in his eyes. 'What's this, Nan?' he said quietly. 'What mischief have you been up to now?'

Nan grinned. 'No mischief, I swear. I've sailed through the sky in a washbasket, I've floated on the islands of Dream, I've ridden a Horse of Air through the clouds and now I've come to help my Folk—'

'*Help* us?' wailed Mae. 'Ye've damned us all with your dreaming!'

Nan wondered (and not for the first time) how any sister of Maddy Smith's could have turned out to be so brainless.

'Listen to me!' she commanded. 'There never was aught to fear from dreams. That was just a story set about by the Order, who rightly feared their power.'

The villagers looked doubtful at this, most of them having believed since childhood that dreaming was terribly dangerous. Some (like Mae) had *never* dreamed; others had done so in secret. One of these was Dan Fletcher, of course, and now he looked at the Horse of Air, which was standing placidly nearby. Like most of the villagers, he knew every horse in the valley, just as he knew their owners, and this one was unfamiliar to him – besides looking strangely *insubstantial*, like the pale reflection of a horse on a piece of floodwater.

'Next you'll be saying it came here through Dream.'

Nan gave him her mischievous smile. 'Don't you underestimate Dream,' she said. 'Dream is a river that flows both ways, from Order to Chaos and back again. Dream is the wellspring of creation; even Death is no match for it. *Nothing dreamed is ever lost, and nothing lost for ever* – that's the Auld Man telling us that what's destroyed can be rebuilt – aye, even castles in the clouds!'

'Castles in the clouds,' said Dan. 'I'd settle for a bed and a meal.'

'Would ye?' said Nan, still smiling at him. 'I recall you wanting more.'

Dan looked rueful. 'What good are dreams now?'

'I'll show you,' said Nan, mounting Epona with an agility of which, only hours before, she would never have imagined herself capable. The mirror-glam from Odin's birds was now almost the size of the collection plate that Nat Parson had passed around the church after every service. Nan had no idea what it was for, but it was a glammy, for sure, she thought; and holding it in both her hands, with both heels kicking the Horse's flanks, Crazy Nan Fey urged Epona straight towards the dreamcloud.

'Don't!' cried Dan, taking a step.

But Nan just laughed. *'It flows both ways!'* And at that she entered the dreamcloud at a gallop, her long white hair streaming out behind her, and vanished into the devil-mist without so much as a backward glance.

'Now what?' said Matt Law.

'Now we wait – and pray,' said Dan.

The dreamcloud was at the entrance now, fingering the doorstep. The Folk had retreated to the church in the hope that it might provide sanctuary; but a candlestick left on the doorstep and a copy of the Good Book had both dissolved into twin piles of ash, and now the doorstep, worn to a shine by centuries of worshipful feet, was starting to turn milky and fade . . .

And then a figure stepped out of the mist.

'Demons from Chaos!' Mae screamed; but Ben Briggs reached out his hand and, bracing himself to lose it, grabbed hold of the ghostly figure and yanked it through the doorway.

For a moment there was silence as everyone stared at the apparition.

Then Damson Ploughman gave a cry.

'Gods! Thank gods!' exclaimed his wife.

It was Sam, their vanished son, and for several minutes after that the Folk were all too busy vying to touch the new arrival – pulling his hair and checking his teeth and crowing in delight and surprise at the smallest thing he did – to heed the protests of Zebediah Dean, who maintained that young Sam was a demon in disguise, and that all of them would be double-damned, and that when his uncle heard of this, there would be serious consequences—

'Ah, shut yer pie-hole, Zeb,' said Mags. 'Does he *look* like a demon to you?'

'Well, he's ugly enough, for sure, said Damson, whose eyes were still brimming.

374

Sam grinned. Everyone laughed – except, of course, for Zeb Dean and Mae.

'All you have to do is dream,' said Dan Fletcher in wonderment. 'That's what she meant. That's what this *is!'*

Sam nodded. 'I think so. I remember going into the mist – then nothing else until Nan Fey—'

'But how did she *do* it, Sam?' said Mags.

'I think— I think she *dreamed* it, Ma!'

Dan turned on the villagers. 'Well, what are we waiting for?' he said. 'If Nan can do it, so can we!'

'Us? Dream?' said Mae Dean.

'Why not?' said Matt Law, never the most imaginative of men, but dogged when he came to the point. 'What more have we to lose now?'

There was a stir among the villagers, but still no one dared approach the mist.

'What? None of you even want to *try*?' Dan Fletcher closed his eyes and plunged into the dreamcloud, to return with a shaggy dog at his heels, a brown shaggy dog, its coat still damp, its long tail wagging furiously.

'Charlie! Oh, Charlie, you rascal,' said Dan, grabbing hold of the unruly hound. 'I thought ye dead and done for, boy!' Now, turning to the villagers, he said: 'See? We can do it. We all can. All we have to do is dream, and nothing ever need be lost for ever . . .'

After that there was a rush towards the edge of the dreamcloud. Imagining had never been something that came easily, but that night the harvest exceeded any that had ever been known.

Dogs, cats, horses, birds – all as real as young Sam Ploughman – began to emerge from out of the devil-mist, *popping* into existence again like a row of bubbles containing little magical pockets of being, released back into the Middle World with just the same ease as they'd left it.

For a time, excitement made all of them a little mad. Even the cynics among them were soon joining in the free-for-all, trying to recall lost ones, prized possessions, fragments of their disrupted lives. Mags Ploughman reached into the mist and brought out her mother's music box, which she'd thought gone with the rest of her things; Joe Grocer recovered his money-counter; children rescued favourite toys. The people of Malbry soon found out that all they really had to do was concentrate on what had been lost, to remember it in every detail, to call it back from out of the mist, and sure enough it would come to them, like flotsam on the water . . .

Matt Law's posse was dispatched to make sure the church remained secure; and before long it was noticed that the mist had receded an inch or so, leaving, instead of the grass and stones that had surrounded the little church, a narrow band of sediment that gleamed in rainbow colours. No one really noticed it. Folk were too busy reknitting their lives, inch by inch, stone by stone. And when Nan Fey and the Horse of Air emerged at last from the dreamcloud, it was to a most unusual sight: a church half filled with exotic paraphernalia, in which part of a cottage (it belonged to Ben Briggs) had begun to appear, like a growth on a tree; where a group of unsupervised children had managed to summon some kittens and a red ball; and where through the roof (which had fallen in), a giant oak was now growing, in the branches of which a flock of birds were singing as if to raise the dead.

Nan Fey gave a little smile and patted the Horse of Air at her side. Soon there would be greater things than birds and lost dogs to summon. The mirror-glammy had shown her as much; it was not for nothing, she knew, that *thoughts* were known as *reflections*. Too long had thinking and dreaming been considered the work of idle hands. If the Sky Citadel were to be built, then dreams and reflections would build it. And even if the battle were lost, she knew that the Auld Man would be proud. Nan Fey had achieved what no one else could, come Hel, flood or Tribulation.

For the first time in five hundred years, the people of Malbry were dreaming.

BOOK SEVEN

The Rider of Carnage

If wishes were horses, beggars would ride.

Old folk saying

1

MUCH AS SHE WOULD HAVE LIKED to believe that this was no more than a bad dream, Maddy was *not* dreaming. Three hours had now passed since she and Perth had followed Adam to the penthouse near Examiners' Walk. There, the surprise of her old enemy's impending marriage had turned out to be nothing compared to Maddy's dismay on learning the bride's identity.

Adam Scattergood and Maggie Rede? Adam and Maggie engaged to be *wed*? Maddy realized at once that this must be part of some devious plan, although how Adam Scattergood was involved remained a mystery to her.

Did Maggie know who Adam was? How had they met? Were they in love? Could Adam really have feelings for the twin of his oldest enemy? And how in the Worlds could Maddy's twin be in love with Adam Scattergood? Adam, whose heart was as mean and sour as a late-November apple, doomed never to ripen, but to fall as soon as the first frosts came?

Now she watched through the rune *Bjarkán*, hiding in the shadows, hoping to catch a glimpse of her sister, or some clue as to what she was doing there. But there was nothing unusual to be seen except for the Red Horse in the stables. There had been no violence here – no sign of a struggle, no outbursts of glam – and although she could make out Maggie's trail, a brighter skein in the tapestry of signatures that lined the road, there was nothing there to indicate that her sister had lost her mind, or to explain what a child of Thor could see in Adam Scattergood.

It had taken all Perth's powers of persuasion to prevent Maddy from going up to the apartment there and then and simply breaking down the door.

'What do you think will happen,' he said, 'if you just go charging in?'

Maddy looked at him. 'Yes, but—'

'Listen. This needs careful thought. You don't want her calling the Law on us, or starting trouble, do you?'

Reluctantly Maddy agreed that maybe that wasn't the best plan. 'So what do we do?'

Perth shrugged. 'She knows you. If she sees you here, she'll suspect something. But if I can get in and investigate—'

'*You?*' said Maddy.

'Why not? There isn't a penthouse in World's End that I can't get into, *and* out again. Trust me. I can do it.'

Maddy smiled. '*Trust* you? Perth, if you're trying to pretend that this is about anything other than wanting to steal the silverware, or whatever other valuables might be lying around the place . . .'

Perth tried for a hurt look. 'So shoot me,' he said. 'But you know I can. And if a couple of candlesticks – or a purse, or a silver snuffbox – happen to *accidentally* find their way into my possession – well, where's the harm in *that*, eh?' He gave a broad and shameless grin, and not for the first time Maddy was struck by his resemblance to Loki. The similarity was not so much in his colouring or any of his features, but in the way he moved; in his eyes; in his changing expressions. Loki's older brother, perhaps; not quite as disruptive, but still with that quicksilver spark in him, that tiny hint of wildfire.

It occurred to her that maybe this was how One-Eye must have been in his prime, and a surge of nostalgia came over her. *Had* her old friend somehow survived? Did her sister know if he had? And what was his connection with the Old Man of the Wilderlands?

'All right,' she said, addressing Perth. 'You go. But be careful. I don't want you getting hurt. Look, don't touch, and then come back and tell me what you see. Understood?'

Perth grinned. 'Understood.'

'And no candlesticks, or snuffboxes, or anything like that. All right?'

Perth shrugged. 'Spoilsport.'

And so it was that, at sunset, a nondescript figure in drab brown climbed quickly up onto a stable roof from a back alley off Examiners' Walk, then up a drainpipe, through a gulley, over a series of ridges, their tiles half eaten up with moss, and finally onto a sloping roof overlooking the penthouse. Without his coloured Outlander's robes, Perth might have been a roofer, a chimney-sweep, or even a slave; in any case, he was well concealed, wholly invisible from the street, wedged comfortably behind a stack of chimneys.

He cast *Bjarkán* at the penthouse, and looked at the scene through his fingers. For a moment he saw only light: the curtains were pulled so that only a narrow slice of the room was visible to the naked eye, and even with the truesight, all he could see were the traces of a signature that crisscrossed the room, as if someone were pacing repeatedly behind the half-drawn curtains.

That would be Maddy's sister, he thought. Only a Fiery left such a trail. He narrowed the focus of *Bjarkán* and moved a little closer. Even from this vantage point he could see little but her signature and her movements, which both revealed agitation, and her shadow at the window, moving quickly to and fro.

Then came a sound of wings, and a bird landed on the chimney-stack just above his head. A raven of peculiar size, which looked at Perth intently.

'Shoo,' said Perth.

Crawk. Crawk.

Now another bird joined the first; a second raven, this one with a white feather on its head. It gave a harsh cry – *Ack-ack-ack!* – and pecked the larger bird on the wing.

Perth forked a runeshape. The larger bird hopped from its perch. But instead of flying away, it dropped right onto the rooftop next to him and, in a second, had taken on the Aspect of a young man in black, with disreputable hair and a broad grin.

'That's no verra polite,' he said, sitting down cross-legged on the roof.

Perth considered casting *Hagall*, then decided against it. Even if the bird-man could be deterred by such methods, the use of such a powerful glam would alert the girl in the penthouse.

'Who are you, and what do you want?'

'Call me Hughie,' said the bird. 'And that's my sister Mandy. Aides to the Rider of Carnage, and all we *want* is to see that Rider all set for the End o' the Worlds – unless ye've got such a thing as a sugar lump tae spare, or mebbe even a piece of cake—'

Kaik! Kaik! said the smaller bird, pecking at the chimney-pot.

Perth gave it a suspicious look. 'The Rider of Carnage?'

Hughie grinned. To Perth, that grin looked about as real as a purse full of glammy gold, but this was his chance to find out more about his new friend Maddy and her mysterious sister. Perth didn't know much about prophecies or tales of the Elder Age, but he knew the Song of Three Horses from the Book of Apocalypse, and it hadn't taken him long to understand that the Black Horse that Maddy called Jorgi, with its peculiar appetites and tendency to change Aspects, was no horse at all, but some creature from Dream masquerading as a horse. And here was Hughie talking about a Rider whose name was Carnage . . .

'Who *is* the Rider of Carnage?' he said. 'Is it that girl in the penthouse?'

Hughie gave his gleaming grin. 'Aye. She may be, if she rides—'

'And what has that to do with me?'

'I think it may have everything.'

Perth took a moment, thinking hard. Did Maddy know about all this? From his point of view, his new friend had been most annoyingly secretive. Since arriving in World's End she had told him almost nothing of her family, her origins, the source of her mysterious glam. Who was the girl that she had come to find? What was the Old Man of the Wilderlands? How did a girl from the Northlands come to know so much about runes? What did

382

Perth really know about Maddy? That she was new to the city; that she had a glam and knew how to use it; that she had powerful enemies.

Could she be one of the Riders? Could Jorgi be the Black Horse? It seemed to Perth that maybe he was. And the more he thought about it, the more likely it seemed that some kind of gain could be had from all this: treasure from World Below, perhaps, or knowledge for which the right person might pay.

'Tell me,' Hughie said at last. 'Have ye ever heard of a thing called the Auld Man o' the Wilderlands?'

Perth nodded. It was a phrase that he'd heard Maddy use a number of times, but he still had no idea what it was. A person? An object? A little of both?

'What is it?'

'A treasure,' Hughie said. 'A treasure out of World Below, more precious than gold and rubies.'

'Is that so?' Perth said. 'And do you know where it is?'

'Aye. It's right there, in that penthouse.'

'Really?' said Perth.

Mandy *crawk*-ed.

'And what do you want from me?' he said.

'We want ye to steal it,' Hughie replied.

'*Steal* it? But you said you were—'

'Aides to the Rider o' Carnage. Which means we serve the interests of the Rider. Even when the Rider herself disn'ae know where her interests lie.'

'And you're telling me the Rider needs—'

'A thief,' finished Hughie. 'A *verra* good thief.' His grin widened more than ever. 'One who could climb to the balcony in the middle of the night. One who could get in without a sound, and take the Auld Man from where it's hid. One who could undo the ties of glam that bind it without alerting anyone. And finally, one who could carry it back to safety, where no one could find it, and start collecting the rewards—'

'*What* rewards?' said Perth.

Hughie made a vague gesture. The silver rings on his arms

made a pleasant little clinking sound. Perth, who knew how to estimate the value of a silver ring without even measuring it, felt a pleasant shiver run from his fingertips to his money-belt.

'Anything ye like,' said Hughie. 'Gold, glam, your heart's desire . . .'

'My heart's *very* demanding.'

'And the Auld Man's *verra* obliging,' said Hughie. 'As long as ye're verra discreet.'

Once more Perth gave the matter some thought. Should he tell Maddy about this? Certainly she would want to know. But what did he *really* owe her? Clearly she too was after this prize that gave a man his heart's desire – why else would she have sent him here without even telling him what it *was*?

He considered Maddy Smith. He liked the girl. He really did. But friendship, in his experience, was rarely a sound investment, whereas money in the hand . . . well, *that* was something he understood. And much as Perth regretted having to deceive a friend, the thought of obtaining his heart's desire was enough to lull his conscience. It wasn't as if anyone was going to get hurt, after all.

He summoned the rune *Bjarkán* again and looked through the penthouse window. Through the curtains he saw the four-post bed, a velvet coverlet, a plinth, the filaments of runelight that marked the occupant's movements, and a ball of something blue that glowed . . .

'Is that it?'

Hughie nodded. 'Aye.'

And now he could almost *hear* it too: a faint, small voice at the back of his mind that whispered his name – *Perth, Perth* . . .

'It talks!' he said.

'It does more than that. But first ye have to set it free.'

'Set it free?' Perth said. 'Why? Is it a prisoner?'

'Aye, friend,' said Hughie. 'A slave.'

For a moment Perth considered the job. It didn't look too difficult. The obvious entry-point was the balcony; the greatest risk, the fifteen feet of open space between the target and the bed. The best time was during the small hours: the girl would be asleep, and he would make his escape across the roof. It all seemed quite straightforward; an easy little burglary. Of course, the climb wasn't easy, and he would have to be *very* quiet—

'Well?' said Hughie. 'Do ye have a plan?'

Perth smiled. 'I always do.'

2

THAT NIGHT, UP IN THE PENTHOUSE, Maggie was forming plans of her own. She waited till Adam had fallen asleep, then she quietly slipped out of bed. The Old Man was dark on his shadowy plinth; she guessed that he too was sleeping.

Good, thought Maggie. *Let him sleep.* This time her quarry was elsewhere. And thanks to Odin's ravens she knew just where to find them. On the road to World's End, somewhere south of Rhydian, Lucky's Pocket Pan-daemonium Circus was preparing its final performance.

She cast the rune *Bjarkán* – Dream – and let her consciousness slip away. This time she knew just what she was looking for; and her mind drifted easily into Dream, skimming its waters delicately, like a sea-bird hunting for fish.

It was so much easier now than before; Maggie almost surprised herself. The Rider of Carnage needs no Horse to dip into Dream. All she needed was to know exactly how far the Seer-folk had come; the rest of her needs could be summoned into being just as easily as the snake-thing that had almost killed Loki on Red Horse Hill.

Ah. There.

There it was. The Pocket Pan-daemonium Circus, travelling down the World's End road. Maggie moved in eagerly, taking in every detail.

So, she thought. *This is my family*. She almost smiled at the thought of it – the Queen of the Pigs, the Strong Man, the Wolf Boys, the Human Nightingale – as a child may smile at a character from a familiar story, well loved, well remembered . . .. until she remembered *why* she was here.

A voice in her head spoke dryly. *And why's that, Maggie?* It said. *Think you can stop them? Is that it?*

Maggie opened her eyes. 'Who's there?'

The Old Man, on his plinth in the dark, flickered with something like irony.

'What are you saying?' Maggie hissed. 'That no one can stop the Seer-folk?'

Oh, they can be stopped, said the Old Man. *But that won't stop Tribulation. The Rider of Carnage will ride, it says. It doesn't say: 'After the wedding the Rider of Carnage will hold a champagne reception, followed by country dancing and bridey cake.'*

'*What?*' said Maggie, wholly confused.

It doesn't matter, the Old Man said. *What I mean is, we all have our part to play in this. Adam included, more's the pity – though if you ask me, I don't understand what you see in him anyway. A child of the Folk. That* child of the Folk. *That little, conniving, weaselling boy—*

'Stop it!' she said. 'Stop saying those things! I *love* him!'

The Old Man's voice in her mind took on a terrible patience.

Maggie, you don't *love him. You don't even know him. To start with, his name isn't Goodwin. It's Scattergood. Did he tell you that? Did he tell you that for the past three years he has sought to destroy your family? That he'd stop at nothing to see us laid low? That he doesn't love you – and never did – and that this wedding was all his master's idea?*

Maggie was scornful. 'How could my wedding be part of this?'

Not your wedding, the Old Man said. *But the wedding gift . . .*

And now, in her mind, Maggie saw another series of flickering images, like pictures in a scrapbook. Herself – a little older perhaps – her hair once more covered with a *bergha*. But not one of the white scarves worn by the maidens of World's End. It was black – a widow's scarf – and on her knee she was holding a child – a boy with the mark of the Firefolk.

For a moment Maggie could hardly breathe. 'You *can't* know that,' she said. 'Nobody could know that. I *thought*, maybe, yes – but it's too soon to be sure—'

The Old Man's glow intensified. *Don't be foolish. You knew from the start. From the very moment you lay with him. You felt it. You knew because I knew. The child you bear – the fruit of the Oak – will determine the fate of the Æsir. His runemark – the gift – is the ultimate rune. The tenth rune of the New Script.*

And now the Old Man recited the prophecy of the Seeress:

The Cradle fell an age ago, but Fire and Folk shall raise her
In just twelve days, at End of Worlds; a gift within the sepulchre.
But the key to the gate is a child of hate, a child of both and
   neither.
And nothing dreamed is ever lost, and nothing lost for ever.

'Is *that* what this is all about?' said Maggie, forgetting to lower her voice. 'Are you suggesting that Adam *knew* this was going to happen? Perhaps you think he planned it this way, just to get hold of that ruinmark?'

The Old Man sighed. *I don't think. Remember, I'm an oracle. But whether your son will live to be a gift to the gods, or to their enemies – well, Maggie, that's up to you.*

For a long time Maggie stood silently next to the darkened stone Head. The runemark *Ác* at the nape of her neck flared like a patch of fever.

For a moment what the Old Man had said had almost made a kind of sense – the way that Adam had sought her out; the way his master had used her, first to recover the Red Horse and then to seek out the Old Man. And when she rebelled, it had played her, exploiting her newfound sympathies, threatening her new friend while Adam himself played on her loneliness, flattered and cajoled her, letting her think that he loved her . . .

But of course, the Old Man *would* say that.

Would he? But he can't lie . . .

He wouldn't *have* to lie, she thought. All he had to do was bend the truth to his purpose. This was Odin, after all – Odin the master manipulator. By predicting that the wedding would not take place, by playing on her fears and desires, by carefully feeding her scraps of the truth, taken out of context and from his own unique point of view, he'd hoped to erode her sympathies, to fill her with hope and doubt and mistrust, and to finally swing her allegiance back towards the Æsir.

It all made perfect sense, she thought. The Old Man wanted her loyalty. He wanted her child – his great-grandson – to be a child of the Æsir. And his pride – his legendary pride – would not allow a child of the Folk to play any part in his dynasty. So Adam's name wasn't Goodwin? So what? A man can change his name, she thought, for any number of reasons. That didn't make him a liar, or mean that he didn't love her. He'd sworn to destroy the Æsir? So had Maggie herself, once. That didn't make him dishonest, or throw any doubt upon their love. Quite the opposite, she thought. If, after all that, he could still love the child of his enemies, then didn't that make Adam *better* than they were? Didn't it make him more honourable?

And so she dismissed her dark thoughts, like a bad dream that seems real for a time, then fades away into nothingness. Love is not a candle that can be snuffed at the first breath of doubt, and Maggie was young and optimistic enough to believe that, if there *had* been deception, then it had come from the Whisperer, and not from her betrothed.

Separate Adam from his malignant passenger and everything could be started afresh. Adam, Maggie and their child: a perfect, unbroken circle of three. A family to replace what was lost; and now that she was going to be a mother, surely the wedding *must* go ahead—

Suddenly she heard a sound outside, on the balcony. Someone was trying – quietly – expertly – to open the bedroom windows.

Maggie summoned the rune *Hagall*, sharpened it to a point in her hand. She didn't know who the intruder was, but he had come at a bad time. Maggie was a mother now. It didn't matter that her child was barely a quickening. It didn't matter that her son was the key to the fate of the Nine Worlds. Some fierce and primitive instinct had been awakened inside her.

She stepped into the shadows and waited.

3

It was long after midnight when the lights in the penthouse finally dimmed. Someone was finding it hard to sleep, and Perth didn't want to make his move before he was sure of being unobserved. It was cold up on the rooftop; even the leather tunic he wore was not enough to keep out the chill. Perth shivered; his fingers ached – he stuck them under his armpits.

So far the plan was straightforward enough. As soon as he was sure that Maggie and her young man were asleep, he would climb to the penthouse. Using a rope and crampon, he would swing himself onto the balcony; open the window in silence; creep over to the plinth; slip the Old Man into a satchel slung across his back; and make his escape the way he had come.

But as far as Perth was concerned, stealing the Old Man without getting caught was just the initial stage of it. The second, rather more dangerous part was getting away from Maddy; over the rooftops seemed the best bet, although Perth wasn't sure how long he would have before she got impatient and realized the deception.

Finally the lights went out. He waited an hour longer. Then he climbed onto the balcony, opened the window (it was locked, but Perth had brought his tools) and stepped soundlessly into the room. His eyes took a moment to adjust to the darkness. Outside, the moon was full. A slow and regular breathing came from the vast canopied bed. He took a step towards the plinth, where he had seen the ball of blue light—

And stopped, frozen. A figure in white was standing beside the bed. A girl – cropped hair and big, dark eyes, holding a sliver of fire in her palm.

His first thought was astonishment at how like Maddy the girl was. He'd known they were twins, of course, but even so, he was unprepared. But for the hair, which was cut very short, she was Maddy to the life: the same stubborn mouth, the same vivid face, the same look of fierce concentration . . .

She spun the fiery thing at Perth. Perth dropped; hit the floor. The weapon – some kind of mindbolt, he thought – went over his head and struck the wall. There was a crash and a flare of light; Perth sprang towards the plinth, forking *Yr* to protect himself. His hand was actually touching the thing that Maddy called the Old Man – and then something hit him in the back with dizzying, spectacular force, and he went down, seeing stars, onto the floor of the penthouse.

The Old Man fell with him, and narrowly missed crushing his skull as he hit the floor. As it was, it glanced off his shoulder and rolled to a halt beside him.

Perth swore and lashed out in pain; on his arm the runemark *Perth* lit an ominous rose-red. He saw the girl standing over him, one hand extended, holding the glam, the other clasped over her belly.

'Put it down,' said the girl.

Perth's eyes flicked to the rune in her hand. It was *Hagall*, the Destroyer. No time to cast a protective glam; if she hit him, he was toast. Of course, that was true of the girl too: if she fired a mindbolt now she wouldn't have time to protect herself. His glam might knock her down – but hers would probably pulverize him.

The thing was: did *she* know that?

He got up very slowly, still holding the rune in the palm of his hand. *Perth* and *Hagall* faced each other head to head, like hammers.

'Drop the glammy,' said the girl.

'Why don't *you* drop the glammy?' said Perth.

'Because this is *Hagall*, the Destroyer,' she said. 'If I decide to hit you with this, you're going to have more than a headache.'

'Well, this is *Perth*,' retorted Perth, with rather more confidence than he felt. '*Perth*, the – *er* – the All Powerful. And if *I* hit you with *that*, then . . .'

Maggie looked sceptical. 'Well?' she said.

'Well, it won't be pretty,' said Perth, edging towards the window.

Maggie's eyes flickered. The hand at her belly moved protectively downwards.

'You look a lot like your sister,' said Perth.

'Yes, I've been told that before,' Maggie said. 'Is she the one who sent you here?'

Perth nodded.

'To kill me?'

'No.'

She glanced at him through the rune *Bjarkán*. For a long time she said nothing. *Bjarkán* lit her face with a clear blue light; in her hand the rune *Hagall* shone with its lethal silvery glow. Finally she banished the runes and levelled her granite-gold gaze at Perth.

'Go back to my sister,' she said, 'and tell her I'm not going to war. Tell her that when Tribulation comes, they're going to be short of a Rider.'

'You're letting me *go*?' Perth said.

Maggie nodded.

'Just like that?'

She gave a rueful little smile. 'Would you rather I knocked you about a bit first?'

'Er, not particularly,' said Perth.

'Then just deliver the message,' she said. 'And if I ever see you again, I'll kill you. Do you understand?'

It must be some kind of a trap, Perth thought. The girl must have known he was bluffing. With his shoulder still numb from the blow he'd received, he guessed there was one slam left in his glam, after which he was hers for the taking. And yet she had chosen to let him go . . .

'Why?' he said.

Maggie seemed about to reply. Then came a sound from the four-post bed. Maggie flinched. Perth summoned his glam. Adam had finally woken up.

'What's going on?' he said.

Perth turned to run.

'Maggie, stop him! He's getting away!'

Perth's foot struck against the Old Man's head. Quickly he bent to scoop it up—

And at that, Adam grabbed the first thing that came to hand – which happened, ironically, to be a silver candlestick – and threw it as hard as he could at the intruder. It hit Perth on the side of the head. A glancing blow, but painful. He staggered; instinctively he discharged his mindbolt against the wall.

Runelight exploded onto the scene; through a haze of pain Perth recognized the fair young man from the marketplace. He flung another mindbolt – instinct taking over from fear – and a spray of red sparks like firecrackers scattered across the bedroom.

Adam shielded his face with his arm; Maggie cast *Yr* to protect them both; and, throwing the Old Man into the satchel that was slung around his shoulder, Perth closed his eyes and ran full-tilt at the little balcony.

He didn't use the rope, but simply *hurled* himself into the night, arms wheeling, legs pumping; two hundred feet to the cobbles below and nothing but moonlight to cling to.

But Perth did not fall; a dozen feet down he caught hold of a loose piece of guttering, and, in spite of the pain in his shoulders and back, managed to haul himself up into a lead-lined gulley; from there onto a ridged roof, then down a slope, round a chimney-stack, and across the rooftops like a cat, the Old Man in the satchel bouncing against his hip as he ran, until at last he could run no more, and slid down a drainpipe into the back of an alley that ran alongside a drainage canal.

Here he stopped to catch his breath. That had been too close, he thought. If he'd known how the girl could throw her glam, he might have thought twice before breaking in. As it was, he'd been lucky, he told himself. He'd escaped with nothing but bruises; had managed to steal the Old Man *and* get clear of Maddy all at the same time.

He was feeling rather pleased with himself, and had almost decided to celebrate in one of the local taverns, when a voice at his back said: 'Stop in the name of the Law!' and a hand fell on his shoulder.

Perth froze. His glam was all gone; he had no strength to run or fight. He turned: two lawmen, with weighted sticks, were standing in the alley mouth. The third, with a hand on Perth's shoulder, eyed the satchel suspiciously. Had they seen him on the roof? If so, he was in trouble. If not – and this seemed more likely – then maybe he could brazen it out. He tried for a smile.

'Officers. How can I help?'

The lawman closest to him growled, 'What's in the bag?'

'What? This?' said Perth. He opened the satchel that hid the Old Man, taking care not to move too fast. Some lawmen had been known to be overzealous with their nightsticks, and Perth had no intention of giving them the least excuse to use them. The Old Man in the satchel looked just like a lump of rock – a piece of volcanic glass, perhaps, or a block of cinder.

The lawmen inspected it closely, with identical looks of suspicion.

At last: 'What is it?' one of them said.

Perth looked hurt. 'It's a sculpture. Can't you see? It's a stone head. I mean, it isn't finished, but surely you can see the craftsmanship. The nobility of the features. The loftiness of the brow. The craggy wisdom of the nose—'

'And these?' The lawman indicated the tools that Perth had brought with him: the glass-cutting knife; the jemmy; the small hammer for breaking and entering.

'Those are the tools of my trade,' said Perth. 'Can't you see I'm an *artist*?' And such was his air of injury that even the Law was taken in, as the three officers looked solemnly at the stone Head and acknowledged that, yes, it *did* have a certain something, and that Perth was free to go.

And then, just as they were about to leave, one of the lawmen – an older man, with cold blue eyes under his hat – dropped his gaze and stiffened. Perth had rolled up his coat sleeves when he'd broken into the penthouse. Now, in a sliver of moonlight, the runemark showed against his skin as clearly as a splash of ink.

'What's this?' said the lawman.

'That's an Outlands tattoo,' said Perth.

'It looks like a brand,' said the lawman. 'A slave brand that's been tampered with.'

Perth could see his position weakening rapidly. The lawmen, already suspicious, had now discovered his runemark In a moment one of them would suggest that he accompany them to the round-house . . .

He turned to run. It seemed the best plan. He might even have made it too, without the Old Man and the satchel. But the lawman's hand caught the satchel strap, and in the second it took to release it, the other two lawmen had moved in close. Before Perth could summon his glam, or even think of a plausible lie, one of those weighted sticks had caught him on the side of the head, and within seconds his hands were cuffed, and he – and the contents of the satchel – were on their way to the roundhouse.

Ten minutes later, stripped of his tools and of anything else that might help him escape, Perth was sitting in a cell underneath the roundhouse at St Sepulchre's Gate. His head ached, his hands were cuffed, and through the trapdoor that led to the cell – a dark and windowless hole in the ground – the arresting officer read him his rights as set down in the Book of the Law.

Of course, as he pointed out, if Perth really *was* a runaway – a fact that would surely emerge under Examination – then he had no rights anyway, and, unless he was claimed by his master, would end up in the mines, or on the galleys, or, more likely, the gallows, which was undoubtedly where such as he belonged.

Perth said nothing. He'd learned that in these circumstances silence was always the best reply. So far he had refused to give the lawmen anything – not even his name – which might just buy him a day's respite, he hoped, before the giant machine of the Law returned in force to crush him. By then he hoped to have thought of a plan. It wasn't the first time he'd been in a cell, and he fully understood the need to play it soft, and carefully.

'Lost your tongue, eh, scally?' said the lawman nastily. 'You'll be lucky if that's *all* you lose once the Courts have done with you.'

Still Perth said nothing.

'Sure you don't want to give us your name? We'll get it out of you anyway, so you might as well save us the trouble.'

Perth pretended to go to sleep.

'All right then,' said the lawman. 'But if you want to eat, or drink, or sleep under a blanket – and I'm warning you, it gets chilly down there – you're going to have to give us your name.'

Once more Perth said nothing.

Annoyed by his prisoner's lack of response, the lawman concluded this little speech by tossing a heavy object through the trapdoor. It almost hit Perth – it was meant to – but he saw it coming and dodged, and the thing hit the floor with a dull thud.

In the dark it was hard to determine what the object actually *was*; but just as the lawman shut the trap, he paused to deliver his parting shot and, in doing so, solved the mystery:

'Oh, and by the way,' he said, 'here's your precious sculpture.'

4

PERTH SAT DOWN ON THE FLOOR of the cell and reviewed the situation. All in all, it didn't look good. The cell was six feet square, baked earth, windowless, dark, and smelled as if something had died there. Most likely the previous occupant, Perth told himself sourly; and so far the chances of its current tenant's continued survival didn't look at all promising.

He cast the rune *Bjarkán* and took a look at the décor. For a moment or two *Bjarkán* revealed little that Perth's nose hadn't already told him, but now he saw the Old Man, the mysterious object that had landed him in this fix in the first place, gleaming with runelight and bindrunes, its blue heart glowing like a ball of thread woven with strands of starlight.

He reached out with his bound hands. The Head felt warm, as if touched by the sun. It brightened at the contact, a rose-coloured glow appearing where his fingers pressed the rock. He pulled his hands away; the glow dimmed. He touched the rock; the glow returned.

Perth. Perth.

That voice. That whispering voice. He thought he might have imagined it. What in the Worlds had he stolen?

Once more he peered at the Old Man through the circle of finger and thumb. It looked like no gemstone he'd ever seen, though the ravens had called it a treasure. But they had also called it a

398

slave, and now Perth understood what they meant: there was a consciousness trapped within the rock, something that whispered in his mind—

PERTH! WE DON'T HAVE TIME FOR THIS!

He pulled back his hands as if they'd been burned. The voice in his mind was louder – *much* louder – as soon as he put his hands on the rock; when he took his hands away, the voice went back to a comforting drone.

Perth. Listen to me, Perth.

Cautiously he extended his hands. Touched the rock with his fingertips. Once more the trapped blue heart pulsed in its web of runelight.

Thank the gods for that, said the voice with a trace of irritation. *In case you hadn't noticed, neither of us has much time. Now I want you to listen—*

'Hang on,' said Perth. 'And what do *I* get?'

There came a chuckle from the rock. *You get the chance to listen to me. What did you want? Three wishes?*

'Well . . .'

We're talking about Ragnarók. The war between Order and Chaos. The chance to make better Worlds—

'Fine,' said Perth. 'But what's in it for me?'

Gods, you sound like my brother. The Old Man sighed. *Very well,* he said. *Do as I say and I'll give you whatever your heart most desires. All right? Is that enough to tempt your grasping little soul?*

Perth shrugged. 'It'll do. But I'm warning you: my soul may be little, but my *price—*'

Understood, said the Old Man. *Unlimited wealth. Ultimate power. Runes to charm any woman – or man. Adventure. Excitement. Freedom—*

'Freedom?' said Perth.

The Old Man glowed. *Of course,* he said. *Come closer, Perth, and listen . . .*

5

MEANWHILE, BACK IN THE PENTHOUSE, Maggie Rede seemed strangely unmoved, both by the theft of the Old Man and by the rage of the Whisperer.

She had not attempted to follow Perth as he fled across the rooftops, nor had she seemed at all concerned as Adam's dark passenger vented its fury, hurling objects across the room, tearing at the drapes, breaking ornaments and generally behaving like a drunken bard following a particularly unsuccessful performance.

Why did she let him get AWAY? it howled.

Adam asked the question.

Maggie shrugged. 'We'll get him back. I had other things on my mind.'

'Other THINGS?' snarled the Whisperer. *'What kind of things? Your wedding dress? Canapes for the party, perhaps? You practically hand over the Old Man to some sneak-thief from the rooftops, and you have the nerve, the almighty GALL—'*

Maggie's only response was to give Adam a long and measuring look.

'Is your name really Goodwin?' she said.

Adam stared at her. 'Of course. Why do you ask?'

She smiled at him. 'Because,' she said, 'when our son is born I want him to have his father's name. A name that he can be proud of. Be that Goodwin . . . or Scattergood.'

Adam's mouth opened, but nothing came out. In his mind, the Whisperer had suddenly fallen very still.

Be careful, boy. She knows . . .

But how?

'That's why I let him go,' she said. 'I couldn't risk him hurting our child. You see that, don't you?' Her voice was soft. 'You understand why I couldn't fight?'

Adam nodded silently. In fact, he was even more confused. How had Maggie even known she was carrying a child? Was he supposed to congratulate her? Why was the Whisperer in his mind capering like a lunatic?

'You spoke to the Old Man,' he said. 'That's how you knew, isn't it?'

Maggie nodded.

'What else did it say?'

For a long time Maggie said nothing. Instead, she looked at Adam's face, trying to understand what had changed.

A week ago, that face had seemed as noble as it was handsome. The face of a hero from one of her books, honest, brave and true. But now, somehow, the mask had slipped; and she could see behind his features to the mean-eyed boy who had pissed his pants when Maddy had hit him on Red Horse Hill. She could see his confusion now, his weakness and his terrible fear.

That was the Old Man's gift to her, and she knew, with a painful twist of the heart, that she would never be able to see Adam in quite the same light again.

But Love is the greatest of glamours, making folk see what they most want to see, rewriting the past, gilding the future, making the ugly beautiful. To a lover, any vice becomes a hidden virtue; any betrayal a challenge. Adam was only human, she thought. And yes, perhaps he *had* lied to her. But now that they were a family, surely things would be different. And what was a storybook hero compared to the father of her child?

'Don't lie to me any more,' she said. 'You can't build a marriage on a lie. And now that you're going to be a father, you have to be responsible.'

'B-but . . . how? I mean, what did he tell you?'

She shrugged. 'That doesn't matter now. It only matters that it's true. And that you love me . . .' She looked at him with such intensity that Adam felt his knees go weak. 'You *do* love me, don't you?' she said.

'Yes,' said Adam. 'Yes. Yes.' And he nodded so emphatically that his teeth almost rattled in his head.

'All right. Good,' said Maggie, and smiled. 'That's really all that matters. We have a wedding to think about, and one more day to prepare for it—'

'But what about the Old Man?' said Adam in a trembling voice. 'We can't let him fall into enemy hands. What about the New Script? What about the Seer-folk? And what about me, Maggie? What about *me?*'

Maggie smiled. 'Don't worry,' she said. 'Let me handle all that. And as for *you*' – here Adam knew that she was addressing the Whisperer – 'all I want of you is your word that you won't try to interfere. This wedding is going ahead as planned. I don't care what the Old Man says. I won't have my son telling folk that his parents were married over the broom. Is that understood?'

Adam's head nodded vigorously.

'Good,' said Maggie. 'That's settled then. Now – Adam. You deal with the wedding. We still have things to organize, and I don't want anything going wrong at the last minute. Everything's going to be perfect. Nothing's going to spoil my day.'

'B-but . . .' stammered Adam. 'What about you?'

Maggie gave him a tender look. He really was just a boy, she thought. A frightened and uncertain boy, as new to all this as she was. Perhaps he *had* deceived her. Perhaps he'd lied to her – at first. But now that they were a family, everything was bound to change.

The old, suspicious Maggie would have cast the rune *Bjarkán* at this point, if only to *know* that his love was true. But the Maggie who had let the Old Man go rather than risk her unborn child had no need for that kind of proof. Love is built on trust, she knew; to question trust was to murder love.

And so she took his love on trust, and found herself loving him even more.

'Don't you fret about me,' she said. 'Of course, I'll be working too. But I don't want you getting hurt. This business of mine might be dangerous.'

Adam's eyes widened. 'What will you do?'

'What I should have done from the start.' Maggie turned to him and smiled. 'I'm going to deal with the Seer-folk.'

Adam and his passenger watched as Maggie went onto the balcony. The moonlight shone on her cropped hair, giving her a silver crown. The runemark at the nape of her neck glowed with an eerie intensity.

For a moment she stood there in silence, barefoot, in her nightdress. Then she murmured a cantrip and held out her arms to the night.

For a long time nothing happened. Then came a sound of beating wings.

Two ravens – one with a white head – alighted on the balcony rail. They looked at Maggie and *crawk*-ed – *Almost as if they were talking to her*, Adam thought uneasily.

In his mind the Whisperer hissed and writhed like a nest of snakes. *They* are *talking to her*, it said. *Hel's teeth, how did she summon them? How did she even* know *about them?*

Adam could sense how badly his passenger longed to eavesdrop, and how afraid it was to do so. He tried to hear what Maggie was saying, but caught only the raucous cries of the two ravens, and a few broken phrases in Maggie's voice of something like a nursery rhyme:

'See the Cradle rocking
High above the town.
Down come the Firefolk
To bring the baby down.
All the way to Hel's gate
Firefolk are bound . . .'

It made no sense to Adam at all, and Adam found he didn't care. One more day, and he would be free. The rest was none of his business.

He'd always known Maggie was dangerous. He'd sensed that almost from the start. But this was a different Maggie Rede to the one he'd found in the catacombs; the lonely, suspicious little girl who'd wanted nothing more than to follow him. That girl was gone, and for the first time in over three years Adam Scattergood felt afraid of someone who wasn't the Whisperer.

Something had changed her. What had she said? *You're going to be a father?* How could she know that, anyway? How could anyone possibly know?

Whatever the reason, Adam thought, there was something new in Maggie's eyes; a dark and murderous knowledge that had not been there the day before. It frightened him, and not for the first time he offered up a silent prayer to whatever gods might be listening:

Please, don't let her find me out . . .

Because whatever she might have been once, Maggie Rede had undergone a kind of transformation. It was like watching a milkweed pod that had ripened slowly throughout the year suddenly burst and release its seeds into the hungry summer wind.

What had the Old Man said to her?

What was his dark passenger's plan?

And what were those birds, those ravens, whose language she seemed to understand?

Adam didn't want to know the answer to either of these questions. He'd had enough of oracles – and of talking birds, and glamours, and dreams – to last him a dozen lifetimes. But one thing he was certain of: he couldn't afford to anger her. She was no longer the Maggie he'd known; the one who had been such easy prey.

Somehow, in barely an hour, she had become the Rider whose name was Carnage.

6

THE LAST TIME MAGGIE HAD RIDDEN the Red Horse through Dream, the Whisperer had guided her steps. This time things were different. This time Maggie herself was in charge. Dreams no longer frightened her. Maggie had learned that Dream was just another World to explore – a World in which she was powerful enough to challenge even the gods themselves.

While Maddy was waiting for Perth outside in the alley behind the penthouse, Maggie was already making plans. By the time she was ready to leave, the moon had dipped below the city rooftops, and the first fine strands of a pale predawn had begun to cling to the horizon.

Maggie pinned her *bergha* in place and went down to the stables, where the Red Horse of the Last Days was placidly eating a bag of oats.

He looked up and snorted at her approach.

Above the stables, in Aspect, Hugin and Munin were circling.

Ironically it had been the birds that had given Maggie the idea. An idea for a plan that both the Whisperer and the Old Man himself might have dismissed as impossible – a plan that would solve all her problems, contradictory as that seemed; so that in just one move, the war would be stopped, bloodshed prevented, Adam freed, and their child born into a world at peace.

Rhydian had been a mistake. Somehow, the Seer-folk had

escaped. But this time, Maggie told herself, there would be no confusion. This time not even the Trickster would see the trap as it closed upon him – or at any rate, not until long after it was too late. This time there would be no escape; no confusion; no mercy.

Beside her, Adam's passenger was showing signs of restlessness.

'*I demand you tell Me what's going on!*' it complained, in Adam's voice.

Maggie gave Adam a tender smile. 'Trust me. I know what I'm doing,' she said. 'Take care. I'll be back as soon as I can.'

'*I'm going with you —*' the Whisperer said.

'No, not this time,' Maggie replied, and then, with a cantrip of Ós, she was off, ignoring the Whisperer's protests as it tried in vain to enter her mind.

She turned her attention once more to the birds that circled and crowed overhead. They'd said that they belonged to her. But would they really obey her commands?

Crawk.

As she rose, in Aspect, to join the course of the river Dream, she found that she could hear them dimly in the back of her mind.

Of course we'll do what ye say, hen.

You're the Rider o' Carnage.

'Then take me to the Seer-folk!' Maggie said, and she and Sleipnir rose above the city streets like St Sepulchre's Fire, and vanished into the early mist that was rising from the World's End road.

They caught up with the Seer-folk some thirty miles from the city. Their colours, filtered by the mist, flared up into the rosy sky. For a long time Maggie did nothing but watch as Lucky's Pocket Pandaemonium Circus drew closer along the World's End road, the three little red-painted caravans moving along at a steady pace, three wolves bringing up the rear, a sharp-eyed hawk observing the road.

That was their Watchman, she already knew. The first thing she would have to do was to hide herself from his piercing gaze. That mist would do it, she told herself; if only it were thicker . . .

She murmured a cantrip of *Isa*.

A chill seemed to descend from the clouds. The thin bright gilding on the horizon faded to a tarnished grey. The hawk seemed to sense a change in the air and flew down onto one of the wagons, where it resumed the Aspect of Heimdall, huddled under a wolf-skin cloak.

Now Maggie cast the rune *Bjarkán* and looked through its lens at the enemy. They were already so close, she thought. Closer even than she'd feared. How had they managed to get there in time? How much did they already know?

'This had better work,' she said, 'or they'll be in the city by nightfall.'

Hughie *crawk*-ed. *It's the only way.*

Once more Maggie looked down at the Seer-folk through the rune *Bjarkán*. They looked so harmless, so helpless now, with their little caravans. From one of the wagons she could hear the lilting sound of Bragi's guitar, a scatter of bright little notes in the grey, and a sudden sadness came over her, a fleeting desire to join the group in spite of the discord she sensed within—

No, she had *not* had a change of heart. She still rejected her ancestry with every drop of her demon blood, but something inside her mourned the choice she had to make – the family she had made with Adam, or the family she had never even met.

No one chooses their family, Maggie Rede told herself. Hers was wicked through and through; a nest of thieves and murderers. She'd read all about them in her books; she knew their crimes, their betrayals.

And there they were at last, she thought. Completely at her mercy. It would be easy to ride them down, to cut them all to pieces – and yet she could not do it.

She was, after all, a mother now. A mother should not be a murderer. And how could she explain to her son that she'd killed their people as they slept?

And yet, when they reached the city gates . . .

Pucker-lips, a-pucker-lips, all fall down. Maggie knew what that meant. It meant the Apocalypse, the End of the Worlds, the second

Tribulation; all the things she'd once desired, and which now she rejected with all her heart. The Rider whose name was Carnage wanted nothing more than to see her child born into a world at peace, and to live with her husband, quietly, away from the noise of the Universal City.

It seemed at first glance impossible. The Rider of Carnage was fated to ride as soon as the Firefolk entered the gates. But if she joined forces with the gods, the Whisperer would kill Adam. And if she stood against them, then she would be forced to destroy the Old Man, at which point the Æsir would take their revenge, with Adam once more as their target.

She had not forgotten the vision that the Old Man had shown her: the picture of herself, with her child, wearing a widow's black *bergha*. Whichever choice Maggie made would put Adam in the line of fire . . .

Unless the gods never reached those gates . . .

And now at last, thanks to those birds and their rhyme, Maggie had a plan so simple that she wondered why she'd never thought of it before. She barely had to do anything. Just a series of glamours, and Adam and their child would be safe.

Maggie whispered a cantrip of *Raedo – Reid kveda rossom vaesta –* and fingered the rune with her left hand.

See the Cradle rocking
High above the town . . .

Beneath her, a ghostly filament unfurled across the landscape.

Down come the Firefolk
To bring the baby down.

Once more Maggie whispered a cantrip – this time a version of *Bjarkán* – and made the sign with her fingers. The mist began to thicken. Slowly at first, then creeping out of fissures in the stony ground; from rivers and streamlets and cracks in the road, until it became a white cloud that lay softly over the land like snow, making ghosts of everything, so that even the three red caravans looked grey and mournful and lost.

Good.

All the way to Hel's gate
Firefolk are bound . . .

And now, with a click of her fingers, Maggie reversed the Journeyman rune, and began to draw the silver skeins of mist through the circle of finger and thumb. As she did so, she began to sing another cantrip of *Raedo:*

Rad byth on recyde, rinca gehwylcum . . .

Below her, the white cloud thickened and churned. Marsh-lights flickered at its heart. The ravens shuttled busily through the mist, tracing a scrawl of runelight, while Sleipnir, in his fiery Aspect, spanned the sky like St Sepulchre's Fire, his long legs reaching from horizon to horizon.

The result was like a cat's cradle, of light in every imaginable colour, from which a column of mist was spun like pale wool on a spindle.

All the way to Hel's gate
Firefolk are bound . . .

And on the road to World's End, the Firefolk vanished into the cloud, and Sleipnir's eight legs spun spidery webs, and Odin's Mind and Spirit swooped with ever-increasing frenzy, and sun and moon and stars went out, as Maggie Rede went riding.

7

MADDY HAD WAITED TILL FIRST LIGHT for Perth to come down from the penthouse roof. Even then, it was a measure of her belief in her new friend that it took her till after breakfast to understand that he wouldn't be back.

She had found herself a place to wait at the window of a coffee shop. There, she had breakfast – bacon and eggs and a pot of strong World's End coffee – and kept watch over the penthouse. But as the sun rose over St Sepulchre's Gate and the city returned to life, Maddy began to realize that something must have gone terribly wrong. Perth should have been back hours ago; and, watching now through the rune *Bjarkán,* Maddy could see his signature slashed across the building's façade, along with some splashes of runelight that told an eloquent story.

Climbing up the fire escape that ran around the back of the building, Maddy took a closer look. There had been a struggle, she saw. Perth had fought with her sister. Perth's rose-red signature was clear, and Maggie's was unmistakable. But what was that third signature-trail, and why did it seem so familiar?

Could it be the Old Man?

And was the Old Man the Whisperer?

Until now she had been certain it was. And yet those colours were somehow wrong. The Whisperer's trail had been harsh and bright, like lightning in a bottle. But this was something different – different and unmistakable – those splashes of runelight, kingfisher-blue, and that trace in the air of *Raedo*, reversed . . .

One-Eye?

Odin?

Could it be? Maddy could barely believe it. And yet her old friend's signature was scrawled across the rooftops. *Raedo*, reversed, in his colours. Which meant that the being he had called the Old Man, the thing he had ordered her to find, was none other than his own self, embodied, like the Whisperer, in that piece of volcanic rock.

Maddy's head was spinning now. She sat down on the fire escape. Why had Odin not told her the truth? Why had he misled her? Where was Perth, and why had he run? Was he hurt? Was he lying low? Or had he simply turned his coat, and delivered One-Eye into enemy hands?

Maddy sat for a long time, trying to make sense of it all. She had none of Perth's climbing skills. Impossible to follow his path across those perilous rooftops. But the Old Man's signature, she hoped, should be possible to find, especially now the trail was fresh; and so she returned to Examiners' Walk to search for traces of her friend.

It was no simple task, she found. The Universal City was always thick with signatures, and even a trail like Odin's or Perth's could easily be lost in the crowd. Hours passed: not a trace of the pair. Maddy grew tired, disheartened and cold. She had walked around in circles for hours without picking up so much as a broken cantrip. Noon struck in Cathedral Square. Still no sign of her vanished friends. According to Ethel's prophecy, she had less than twenty-four hours to go before Ragnarók and the End of the Worlds, by which time she needed to find Perth, retrieve the Old Man, ride the Black Horse of Treachery *and* find out why her sister was marrying Adam Scattergood . . .

Face it, she thought. *It's impossible. I've failed them. I've failed everyone.*

At lunch time she bought flatbread and sour herrings from one of the stalls in St Sepulchre's Square, and sat down by the fountain to eat them. As she did so, her eye was drawn by something pinned to a noticeboard nearby.

This board was a public display space usually taken up by wedding announcements, market times, lost dogs, property auctions, Court rulings and Cleansings. Normally Maddy would not have paid very much attention to these, but this time a sign at the top of the board caught her eye. The sign read:

SLAVE AUCTION THIS SUNDAY AT 8.00
UNIVERSITY MAIN QUAD

Below was a list detailing some of the auction's highlights, including: a matched set of four nineteen-year-old Outlands dancers; a cook specializing in Ridings food; two bodyguards with knowledge of edged weapons and hand-to-hand combat; any number of house slaves, body slaves and ordinary labourers; seven common criminals . . . and, right at the bottom, a short addition, just six words, hand written below the print:

Unidentified runaway. Suitable for galley work.

Maddy felt her throat contract. There must be dozens of runaways in the Universal City. Why should she be so certain that those six words referred to her friend? And yet she was sure of it. Perth was her man.

What had happened? Had he been caught climbing on the rooftops? Had he meant to come back after all? And what about the Old Man? Had it been found by the lawmen, or had Perth managed to hide it?

'So, yell have seen the notice, then,' said a familiar voice at her back.

Maddy turned. It was Hughie, in human Aspect, lounging on the rim of the fountain, while Mandy, in raven form, was perching on the head of one of the stone serpents that adorned it.

'*You!*' said Maddy.

Kaik, said the bird.

Maddy glanced around the square. It was busy, as always on Saturdays, but no one seemed to notice them. Ragged, disreputable folk were in abundance in the city, and anyone looking at Hughie would just assume he was an Outlander trader; dark, exotic, dangerous.

'What are you doing here?' she said, lowering her voice to a hiss.

Hughie flashed his perfect teeth. 'You might seem more pleased tae see us,' he said.

'Really?' said Maddy. 'And why's that? You send me here on a wild-goose chase; you don't give me *any* of the facts; you leave me on my own for a week without so much as a single word; and then you turn up as if nothing had happened—'

'Oh, but it has,' Hughie said. 'We've seen plenty of action. Haven't we, Mand?'

Mandy *crawk*-ed mournfully, though whether this was in agreement or in protest at the absence of cake, Maddy could not be certain.

'All right. What's your news?' Maddy said. 'Be quick. I have to find my friend.'

'Ye do?' said Hughie. 'Well, we can help ye there. Your friend's in the city roundhouse. More germane tae the point, hen—'

'Yes, he took the Old Man.' Maddy glared at Hughie. 'Who just *happens* to be Odin. Which no one saw fit to tell *me* . . .'

Hughie shrugged. 'Orders, hen. He didn'ae *want* us tae tell ye.'

'Why not? Doesn't he trust me?'

'Ach, ye know the General.' Hughie gave his salesman's smile. 'He disn'ae trust *hisself* half the time.'

Maddy took a deep breath. When – if ever – she saw him again, she'd have a few words with the General – on the subject of trust, and other things. For the moment . . .

'What about my friends?'

'Riding fast towards World's End. Thirty easy miles to go – ye'll see them in the morning.'

Maddy gave a sigh of relief. 'Thank gods for that. I was starting to think I'd have to fight all of Chaos without them.' She grinned, feeling suddenly giddy, and threw her arms around Hughie's neck. 'Thank you. *Thank* you for coming back! I was so worried I'd done the wrong thing. But now things are coming together at last. Odin's giving orders again. The others managed to make it in time. Now all we need is to rescue Perth.'

'Perth?' said Hughie.

'Yes, of course. You saw the notice, didn't you? They'll send him to the galleys. And if he knows where the General is—'

'Wait a minute,' Hughie said.

But Maddy's mind was racing ahead, already making rescue plans. Alone, she knew she had no chance. The roundhouse was nothing like the tiny lock-up in Malbry village. The Order had always prided itself on its prison's security. She could not attack it on her own. But with the World Serpent on her side, and with Odin's Mind and Spirit—

'Wait. *Wait!*' Hughie said, putting his hand on Maddy's arm. On top of the fountain, Mandy flapped her wings and *crawk*-ed.

'I don't have time to wait!' Maddy said. 'Perth's my friend. You think I'd just abandon him?'

'And your sister? Will ye abandon *her*?'

Maddy paused. 'My sister?

'Aye,' said Hughie. 'I thought ye'd seen it. There – up *there* . . .' And he pointed towards the parchment sheet that covered half the notice board. Maddy looked up and saw a long list, written in heavily gilded script:

WEDDINGS

THIS SUNDAY:

8.00: Maggie Rede, to Adam Goodwin
8.15: Priscilla Page, to Franklin Bard
8.30: Jennet Price, to Owen Marchant

And so on, at fifteen-minute intervals, until five o'clock, which was when the evening service began. Weddings were lucrative business in the Universal City, and that fifteen-minute cathedral ceremony could cost as much as five hundred crowns – the price of a coach-and-four, or the rent of a penthouse suite for a month.

She shook her head impatiently. 'I know about that already,' she said. 'What matters now is saving Perth.'

Hughie frowned. 'No. Your friend can look after himself. What matters now is your sister and this wedding that she's planned. That ceremony must *not* take place. No matter what ye have tae do.'

'Who says?'

'The Auld Man. Who do ye think?'

By now Maddy had forgotten all about keeping her voice down. 'To *Hel* with the Old Man!' she cried. 'I'm sick of following orders! Sick of being kept in the dark! Sick of prophecies! Sick of dreams! Sick of fish-eating horses and cake-eating birds! So you'd better tell me what's going on, because otherwise I shall *wring your neck!*'

Hughie waited patiently until Maddy had run out of breath.

'Feeling better, hen?' he said.

Maddy found that, actually, she was.

'Then listen to me. Listen to *him*. This is what he wants you to do.'

And Hughie explained the General's plan, while Maddy listened in silence, her face growing paler and paler.

Suddenly the Saturday crowds seemed to her like an army of distant ghosts; the bright dome of the cathedral like a tarnished shield in the sun. Nothing felt real to her any more. Her head felt like a Fair Day balloon; her heart was a drumbeat that filled the Worlds.

'And this is what he wants?' she said, when Hughie at last fell silent.

'Aye,' said Hughie.

'I don't understand.'

'He disn'ae *need* ye to understand. He simply needs ye to do as he says. Will ye, Maddy? Do as he says? Will ye trust him, Maggie?'

'I'll try.'

Hughie gave a sigh of relief. 'Shiny.'

Maddy almost laughed. If asked for suitable words to describe the current dreadful state of affairs, *shiny* would not have made the list.

She looked at Hughie hopefully. 'But he must have another plan? Since when did the General not have a plan?'

Hughie shrugged. 'This *is* the plan. Beyond that, there's nothing. If this wedding goes ahead, then we lose everything: Asgard; your sister; the future of the Firefolk. And there's no one else to stop it but you, and only one way to do it.'

'Are you sure there's no other way?'

'The General was verra clear. If ye want to save the Worlds, *you have to kill Adam Goodwin.*'

8

As crazy nan had already found, in Dream, time has no meaning. Seconds can stretch into minutes, to hours; hours can pass in the blink of an eye. Maggie, on Sleipnir, had no idea how much time remained to her; but as she skimmed the islets of Dream for traces of her quarry, she could feel the weight of Worlds gathering like thunderclouds; a surge of something about to break that filled the air around her with barbed little notes of static.

So far it had gone better than Maggie had expected. But dealing with the Firefolk had been the easy part of the plan. Now came the second throw of the dice: her move against the Whisperer.

Maggie had known from the start that this would be the hardest task of all. The Whisperer was already alert to every suspicious movement; and Maggie knew that if she failed, Adam would be its target. She needed the Old Man; and for that, she needed to track down the man who had stolen it from the penthouse. Her brief encounter with Perth had left her filled with curiosity. He looked like an everyday scally; a rooftop sneak-thief of the kind that World's End had in abundance. But his glam was one of the new runes, *and* he knew her sister.

Whoever he was, Maggie thought, he was proving hard to find. She'd searched through Dream for what seemed like hours without so much as a sign of the thief, or of what he'd stolen. Was he shielding the Old Man? Did he know she was hunting him?

Now, as she searched in vain for Perth, Maggie began to feel very tired. The effort of her ride through Dream had taken its toll on her weakened glam. Her ravens had vanished long ago; even the Red Horse was starting to show signs of fatigue.

She clenched her fists in frustration. Where was he? Didn't he sleep? Had *no one* seen his face that day?

And then she found it – a wisp of dream, no bigger than a speck of down. A lawman off the night shift, reviewing his list of arrests for the day. The man was no dreamer, but he had sensed a strangeness in one of his prisoners. The memory had lodged in his mind; had become this broken fragment of dream.

Maggie grasped it eagerly. There was Perth, locked in a cell below the city roundhouse. She frowned. *That* was annoying. There was no sign in the lawman's dream of either her sister or the Old Man, but Maggie was sure that by the time she and Sleipnir had finished with him, Perth would be more than willing to cooperate.

And so she spurred the Red Horse out of Dream into World Below, where the labyrinth that for three years had been her playground and hideaway was about to become the scene of one of the Middle World's greatest escapes.

9

IT WAS LATE AFTERNOON IN World's End. Almost twelve hours had already passed since Maggie had disappeared into Dream – a deeply troubling length of time for Adam and his passenger.

Where is she? WHERE IS SHE?

The Whisperer's voice, angry at first, had dropped to a kind of plaintive drone. Adam ignored it. He didn't care. In fact, if he'd heard that Maggie Rede had met with a fatal accident, he wouldn't have cared at all – but for the fact that she'd promised him freedom from his passenger.

He had watched from his balcony as the sun rose high over the Universal City, and listened to the distant sounds of tradesmen, carts on the cobblestones, birds singing, delivery boys – all the familiar sounds of a life that now seemed very far away.

He found it hard to imagine ever going back to that life – harder still to remember that he had once been part of it. For the first time in many months he found himself thinking of Malbry. He'd been so eager to escape; to experience life in the city. Now he remembered Red Horse Hill, and Little Bear Wood, and the river bank where he and the other boys had played throughout the long sweet summers of his childhood. He thought of his mother and the Seven Sleepers Inn and his own little room under the eaves, and his toy soldiers lined up on the windowsill, and the plum tree that grew by his window.

All of it seemed so distant now – he'd had dreams that felt more real – and he was aware of a pain in his chest, a dull, low throbbing, like a bruise. Adam was not much given to thinking about his feelings. If he had been, he might have recognized that dull pain as homesickness. The Whisperer *did* recognize it, and its contempt was scathing. But over three years Adam had learned to tune out the sneering Voice in his head.

And so he just sat by the window and waited for Maggie to come out of Dream, unaware of the tears on his face, or the fact that his fists were so painfully clenched that his fingernails had scored the skin. In fact, he was so lost to the world that, when Maggie finally came home, it took him a moment to understand that she was not part of some waking dream, but the person he had promised to wed the following day at St Sepulchre's.

She looked terrible, he thought. Her clothes were scorched, she was missing a shoe, her *bergha* had been torn off. A cut above her eyebrow had bled into her cropped hair; there was a bruise on the side of her face; her knuckles were shredded and bleeding.

'What in Hel happened?' Adam said.

Maggie gave him a tired smile. 'Rough ride. I need to rest. Is there anything to eat?'

Adam looked around the room. 'I . . . could get something from one of the chophouses. But—'

'Good,' said Maggie. 'I'm starving. But I've done it. I've dealt with everything.'

In Adam's mind, the Whisperer was seething and buzzing with outrage. *Am I to be her servant now? Am I to be at her beck and call? I DEMAND that she tells Me what happened! Tell her I will not be kept in the dark!*

Adam relayed the message as tactfully as he could. 'My master was wondering . . .'

'I know,' she said. 'Tell him I did it. I fixed the Old Man. That's all it needs to know.'

'But *how*? Where is it?' Adam wailed.

She shook her head. 'I blasted it. Sent it to Hel, like the Magister said.'

'WHAT?' said the Whisperer. *'You did what?'*

Maggie could see Adam's passenger watching her through Adam's eyes. It felt as though she were looking into a pit of snakes and spiders.

Speaking low in Adam's voice, it said: *'But I wanted to see it done.'*

'I know you did,' Maggie said. 'If I could have brought him back—'

'To have him in front of Me, helpless, fully aware of what he had lost, knowing that I and I alone was the one who caused his downfall. THAT was what I wanted, girl. THAT was what you and I agreed.'

Maggie could see the Whisperer's rage building with every syllable. She knew she would have to be careful now: the creature was horribly alert, and would strike at the first sign of weakness. She faced it unflinchingly, even though her heart was ready to burst with fear, and addressed it in a voice that was calm almost to the point of indifference.

'That would have been a bonus,' she said. 'But we have bigger fish to fry. We can't afford the luxury of gloating over our enemies.'

Adam's eyes widened in disbelief. *'Are you presuming to lecture ME?'*

'Not at all,' Maggie said, still holding the Whisperer's furious gaze. 'But you know the Old Man was dangerous. You saw how he tried to turn me. I couldn't afford to let him live.'

She indicated her ragged self. 'Look at me, I'm exhausted,' she said. 'A battle of wills would have finished me. And so I did what had to be done. I kept my promise. And you'll do the same.'

For a long time the Whisperer glared at her from Adam's eyes. Coolly, Maggie held its gaze, knowing that everything hung on this: her future with Adam; her child; her life. In twenty-four hours, she told herself, when she looked into those eyes, there would only be Adam looking back. The passenger would be gone for good, and there would be no more lies, no more fear . . .

'And now I need to eat. To sleep. I need to have a hot bath. Tomorrow's my big day and I don't want to see or hear from you till then. Do you understand me?'

For a moment longer the Whisperer paused. Maggie could feel its anger, but there was something else as well: something like amusement; almost like satisfaction.

'*You're growing up at last,*' it said. '*Odin would have been proud of you.*'

Then it withdrew, and Adam was back, his blue eyes wide and fearful.

'You really did it? You killed that thing?'

'I don't want to talk any more,' Maggie said. 'Please, Adam. Leave me alone.'

At the back of his mind, his passenger's Voice whispered a silent warning. *No more questions. Do as she says. We can't have her risking the baby.*

Adam shrugged. 'All right,' he said. 'I'll go and get you something to eat.'

Maggie turned to hide her relief, and started to run the bath. Hot water splashed into the tub from a tap in the shape of a silver swan.

'Then get me a dozen Fat Boys,' she said. 'And some roast lamb, and some fried rice – and bean soup – oh, and chestnuts. Pork dumplings, if they have them. Flatbread with olives and anchovies. Bacon rolls. Spiced chicken. Fish pie. Sausages. Fruit cake. And jam tarts. I've got such a *craving* for jam tarts . . .'

One day more, she told herself as Adam followed her instructions. After that she would be free. A wife; a mother; a child of the Folk. The Rider of Carnage would be no more, and all the events of the past nine days – her sister, the Red Horse, the Old Man – could be folded back into the Book of Words where they belonged, and just as quickly forgotten. As long as she could be strong enough. As long as this worked . . .

Please, make it work!

And as Adam scoured Examiners' Walk for all the items on Maggie's list, the reluctant Rider of Carnage stepped into the claw-footed bathtub and washed away the dust of Dream in a million rose-scented bubbles. After which, when Adam returned, she managed, in spite of her fatigue, to do more than justice to

422

a meal that would have put the Queen of the Pigs to shame, then finally collapsed into bed, and slept without dreams until morning.

10

THE SUN HAD SET ON CATHEDRAL SQUARE, but Maddy had never felt less like sleeping in her life. Long after Odin's birds had gone, she had remained by the fountain, watching the Saturday market-folk go by in a kind of dream-haze. As the shadows lengthened, the crowds began at last to disperse; but even as the people left, the square was alive with their signatures: vendors, hawkers, jugglers, thieves; sightseers, dancers, entertainers of all kinds. The day's last wedding procession went by – the bride in white, with her long saffron veil, laughing and throwing flowers.

Maddy watched her go inside, hand in hand with her betrothed. Their signatures rose in the darkening air, entwined like columns of starlight.

That could be my sister, she thought.

She found that she was trembling. Tears were running down her face. She must have been crying for some time, she thought, because her skin was raw with it. Maddy Smith, who never cried, who never flinched at anything.

Pull yourself together, she thought. *This is no time to fall apart.* What was it Crazy Nan used to say? *Desperate times call for desperate plans . . .*

But what kind of desperation was this? Since when did one of the General's plans involve her killing an innocent?

Well, perhaps not an innocent, Maddy thought with a wry smile.

But Adam was no threat to the gods. He was just an innkeeper's boy. To kill him would be murder – and if Maggie really loved him, then it would break her sister's heart.

Could she do that to Maggie, even if the Worlds depended on it? And if she could, then how could her twin *ever* forgive the Æsir?

Maddy took a deep breath. Odin had asked her to trust him. But how could she trust him when clearly he didn't trust *her*? If only he'd given a *reason*, she thought, instead of issuing orders in that typically imperious way.

If the wedding goes ahead, then everything we've fought for is lost.

But how *could* the wedding go ahead? The gods were only a few miles away. By morning they'd be in the city and the second Ragnarók would begin. The End of the Worlds was not going to wait for one little girl to get married. Especially if that little girl was also the Rider of Carnage . . .

Maddy frowned. What would happen, she wondered, if the Rider of Carnage *didn't* ride? Could *this* be what Odin feared? This war was just a means to an end – its purpose: to regain Asgard. Could this be his way of making sure that Maggie was ready to fulfil her part of the prophecy? And if so, what about Maddy herself? Was she too just playing a role? Or could it be that both of them were nothing more than pieces – counters on a chequer board, set up by a master player whose only thought was to *win the game?*

Odin would never do that, she thought. *That would be too cruel.*

And yet, as her heart protested, the rational part of her knew that he could. Maddy knew Odin far too well to be blinded by her feelings for him. He *could* be cruel, manipulative; he could even be treacherous. Hard as it was to admit it, Odin had a long history of betrayal, violence and deceit. And now that he was back in the Worlds – albeit inside a stone Head – she guessed that he might be willing to do almost anything to regain his stronghold, his Aspect.

Maddy looked up and was startled to see that night had fallen on the square. A few bright stars pierced the sky; to Maddy they looked bleak and cold. She was hungry again, and tired, and stiff; stretching her limbs, she realized that she had been sitting there thinking for hours. And yet she felt better; lighter, somehow. As if she had come to a difficult truth. Her face took on an implacable look, which, if Adam had seen it, he would have recognized instantly.

Now was the time, she told herself, to decide who she *really* wanted to be. The Rider of Treachery? Maggie's twin? Odin's grandchild? Perth's friend? The future of the Æsir? The defender of the Folk? Or something else entirely – something she'd chosen for *herself*?

Maddy stood up and started to walk. She knew just where she was going. Finally she'd had enough of messengers and mind games. Whatever her role in this circus, she would be no one's instrument. If she had to choose between betraying her sister and betraying her tribe, then she was done with minions.

The ravens could go to Hel, she thought.

Maddy needed to talk to the Head.

BOOK EIGHT
Bif-rost

When the 'bow breaks, the Cradle will fall . . .
Northlands nursery rhyme

1

OVER FOUR HUNDRED YEARS HAD passed since the creation of the Universal City. The man who designed it was long gone; and the skills that had gone into its construction had been forgotten for centuries. But nothing is ever lost, they say, and if Maggie Rede had paid more attention to the contents of those dry old histories, instead of studying tales of adventure, she might have remembered the name of a certain architect, once a Professor of Mathematics at the University of Immutable Truths, who, at the end of the Winter War, had almost single-handedly redesigned and rebuilt World's End, beginning with a single stone from the fallen Citadel, and, topping it with spires and domes, had renamed it the Universal City.

This man's name was Jonathan Gift, and according to legend, after his death he had been entombed in the city cathedral, whose giant crystal roof-dome had been his most ambitious undertaking. But by the time the Order emerged, the name of Jonathan Gift had been forgotten, and only his legacy had remained. His sepulchre – the Foundation Stone – had become a place of reverence throughout World's End and the Southlands.

Carved with runes and canticles that no one now remembered, the Foundation Stone of World's End – or the Kissing Stone, as it soon became known – had acquired a mythical status. Folk came here to be married, or blessed, to kiss the Stone for good luck;

and there were reports of miracles, tales of unexpected cures – of voices and visions of Worlds Beyond.

These tales had become so widespread that at last the Order had declared Gift a saint – Saint Sepulchre, of the Holy Fire – and in the Good Book told the tale of how he, with the help of the Nameless, had rebuilt the city in seven days, on nothing but fasting and canticles.

Odin could have told them more. But right now Odin had problems of his own – his death being only one of them. Loki too knew the truth, although right now he had more pressing concerns than filling in the gaps in World's End history. On the sixth day of their journey, with the spires of the city almost within sight, Lucky's Pocket Pan-daemonium Circus had come to a frustrating halt.

That morning had brought a ground-mist that rolled over them as they approached. At first it had caused them no concern; the road was broad and well-travelled, and though they could barely see the verge, they all knew where they were heading.

But the mist was cold and persistent; it robbed them of their energy. Hughie and Mandy, in raven form, who until then had been in the air, settled on top of the wagon, feathers plumped against the cold. Angie joined them, in bird Aspect, bright colours muted in the fog. The demon wolves slunk closer and whined; even Jolly lost some of his natural aggression and stumped along behind his master, muttering darkly to himself.

'More fog,' grumbled Heimdall, moodily casting the rune *Sól*. 'I thought we'd left that in Rhydian.'

Loki shot him a dirty look. 'Like I needed reminding of that.'

Heimdall didn't see the look, hidden as it was in the mist. In fact, beyond *Sól's* influence, there was nothing to be seen, even through the rune *Bjarkán*, but a maze of jumbled signatures, and the mist that dampened everything.

'All right,' said the Trickster. 'Let's see what this looks like from the air.'

And so Odin's ravens were duly dispatched to survey the terrain from above. Hours later, they had not returned, and the mist showed no sign of lifting.

The gods travelled slowly. Hours passed. The mist, if anything, thickened.

Finally night began to fall.

'Are we nearly there yet?' said Jolly, whose stomach had been telling him that dinner time was long overdue.

'Yes, for the ninth time,' said Loki.

Ethel gave him a sidelong glance. 'Something wrong?' she asked him.

Loki shrugged. 'No, not at all. What could possibly be wrong?'

In fact, he was feeling uncomfortable. The absence of stars made it hard to be sure, but Loki was almost certain that they should have reached the city by now. That morning they had seen it – its spires, its docks; even the ocean, for gods' sakes – rising at them from out of the mist like one of the skerries of Dream – and now . . .

Nothing. Just endless road.

Something was wrong, he told himself; and as they continued through the fog (which showed no sign of lifting) he started to feel a growing unease somewhere between his shoulder blades. He blamed it on his frayed nerves, on the night, on fatigue, and then hunger; but when the Watchman called a halt some three or four hours later, Loki was finally forced to admit that on the only road to World's End, the gods had somehow lost their way.

Everyone blamed him, of course.

'This is ridiculous,' Freyja said. 'We've been going in circles for hours and *hours*!'

'Not in circles,' Loki said. 'There's only one road. We're on it.'

'Then why aren't we bloody *there* yet?' said Jolly, who wanted his dinner.

Loki shrugged. 'Don't look at me. I wasn't driving. Maybe Shorty went to sleep.'

Sugar shot him a dirty look. 'I did *not* go to sleep,' he said. 'And do *not* call me Shorty.'

'Well, I say we just make camp here,' suggested Njörd sensibly. 'In the morning the fog will be gone, and we'll be able to find our path again.'

'In the *morning*?' Loki said.

Heimdall bared his golden teeth.

'We can't be more than a few miles away,' said Frey. 'So why not keep going?' Loki said.

'Why don't we take a vote?' said Njörd. 'See what everyone else thinks?'

Loki looked down at the sandy ground and considered his situation. He already had a good idea of what everyone else would say. For six days he'd played his role to full and shameless advantage, forcing them all to dance to his tune, on the understanding that if he failed to get them to World's End within the time agreed, then Heimdall's reluctant protection would cease. To wait until dawn would be to admit a defeat of which the consequences, he guessed, might not be pleasant.

But now another possibility suggested itself in the Trickster's mind. He knelt down to inspect the terrain; scratched out a sample of the soil. The road ahead was sandy, speckled with mica and pieces of quartz. No vegetation grew nearby; nor was there anything to suggest how they could have strayed off the road to World's End.

Hiding his growing anxiety, Loki stood and addressed the smirking Watchman. 'Our little agreement stands till dawn. That means officially, I'm still in charge.'

Heimdall raised an eyebrow. 'And . . .?'

'And if you remove my authority,' said Loki with his crooked smile, 'then regrettably, all bets would be off, including any – ahem! – *penalties* for failure to deliver.'

Angie grinned. 'I said he was smart.'

Loki shrugged. 'It's only fair.'

'Does that mean I can't hammer him?' said Thor.

Heimdall scowled. 'Not yet,' he said.

'When can I hammer him, please?' said Thor.

'At dawn on the seventh day, of course,' said Angie, her grin broadening.

'Which means that you still do as I say,' Loki said, 'unless you declare our agreement void. So *I* say, keep on walking.'

432

For a moment Heimdall glowered at him. *Did* Loki have a plan, he thought, or was this just a play for time? He quickly fingered the rune *Bjarkán,* and was rewarded with a split-second glimpse of Loki's unguarded colours – a flash of unease; a flare of deceit; a silver plume of bravado – before Loki managed to shield himself, using a form of the rune *Yr,* though not before Heimdall had concluded that Loki was bluffing, after all.

There was no plan. The Trickster was lost – just as lost as the rest of them. Sometime during the night, he guessed, Loki would probably try to escape – in bird form, or in his Wildfire Aspect – and Heimdall would be waiting for him. The prospect was so enjoyable that he actually smiled, showing his golden teeth to full advantage as he said: 'All right. You win.'

'I *win*?' said Loki, slightly nonplussed.

'Yes. We're in your hands. At least, until tomorrow.'

Loki was looking uneasy now. 'You're sure? I mean, we could all use some sleep . . .'

'No, I wouldn't dream of it,' said Heimdall in his sweetest voice. 'I mean, you've led us all this far – it's only fair that we allow you to finish what you started. Unless you want to admit you're lost—'

'I know exactly where we are.'

'Terrific. There's no problem, then.'

Loki smiled between clenched teeth. His mind was racing furiously. He'd managed to gain a little time, though to what advantage he did not know. On the plus side, he had until dawn. On the other hand, if he was right, then that might be a long time coming.

Alone – except for Sigyn, of course – Loki considered his options. Any attempt at escape, he assumed, would result in swift retribution. Still, if his suspicions were correct, then they might have strayed so far from their path that escape was no longer on the cards. For Loki had recognized that road – its sandy soil, its fugitive gleam, the chill that covered everything.

'Why me?' howled the Trickster, burying his face in his hands. 'Why do these things always happen to *me?'*

'There, there,' Sigyn said, putting a gentle hand on his head, and it was a measure of Loki's distress that in that moment of anguish, even the sympathy of the most annoying woman in the Nine Worlds was not altogether unwelcome. Because if he was right, he told himself, then he *did* know where they were heading. Somehow, on the way to World's End, their path had been diverted. It led to a place where dawn never broke, a road on which they might travel for years without ever reaching *anywhere*.

This wasn't the road to World's End at all.

This was the road to Hel.

2

AFTER LEAVING ST SEPULCHRE'S SQUARE, Maddy made for
the Water Rats. There she found Jormungand under the pier, looking even more sluggish than usual. The Serpent Aspect he seemed
to prefer was rather less conspicuous there, plus he was able to
indulge his taste for shellfish without attracting undue attention.

Maddy assumed from his bearing that he had been out hunting
seals all day, which explained his bloated appearance and apparent disinclination to do anything but gape and loll (and vent an
occasional fishy belch).

There was no point, Maddy knew, in trying to appeal to his
sense of shame. Jorgi had no work ethic to speak of, and if he
didn't want to move, there wasn't much she could do to force him.
However, she could try.

'Jorgi, I need your help,' she began.

Jorgi gave a monumental belch that shook the entire boardwalk.

Maddy squared her shoulders. 'Seriously, Jorgi,' she said. 'I
really, *really* need your help.'

Jorgi's display of indifference was almost overwhelming.

'Come on,' said Maddy bracingly. 'You're the Black Horse of
Treachery, for gods' sakes. You're one of the harbingers of the Last
Days. You can't just hide under the pier and eat yourself silly all
the time . . .'

Jorgi gave a loathsome shrug.

'*Please,*' said Maddy. 'We have to find the General. For that, we have to rescue Perth. And Perth is in the roundhouse. Which means I need your help to get in. Because obviously I'm not just going to march in there and demand his release, am I? Whereas if you take me through Dream – Jorgi, are you listening?'

Jorgi opened one eye.

'That's better. I promise you that when we're done, you can have all the fish you want. But now we have to look for Perth. Got that?'

Jorgi resumed his Black Horse Aspect, looking even more disreputable than ever. He smelled quite strongly of fish too, although compared to his Serpent Aspect he was positively fragrant. His long black mane was greasy – probably with seal blubber, Maddy thought – but he seemed docile enough as they set off at a slow trot towards the city roundhouse.

This was situated some ten blocks away from St Sepulchre's Square, in a complex known as the Armouries. The Order had used it as a training centre for young prentices, away from the distractions of the University. Now it was a prison, a barracks, a weapons store and a place of execution.

It was also the site of a passageway that led from under the Armouries to the Magisterial Quad, which ran alongside the University Library. Even in the Order's day, very few people had known about this; now only one person knew – the person responsible for the scene that faced Maddy and Jorgi as they approached.

Maddy saw the runelight even before she saw the fire. Her sister's signature in the sky was like a giant's handwriting – huge, unformed, unmistakable. It lit the sky above the Armouries like a second sunset – astonishing splashes of runelight that lingered over the rooftops, staining the buildings ochre and red, blotting out the stars.

There had been a battle here, Maddy knew; and recently. In the distance, a smell of smoke and the dark-red glow of a building on fire. She urged Jorgi on through the narrow streets until she reached the heart of the Armouries – the city roundhouse on Capital Square, where she stopped to take in a scene of purest carnage.

The roundhouse was gone. Two walls still stood, but the

436

building itself had been torn apart. Maddy had heard of earth-quakes – usually in the far North – that had had the same effect as this: deep fissures in the earth, buildings reduced to piles of stone. Timbers scattered like jackstraws; fire; the air still thick with dust. Whatever had happened, she told herself, must have been only hours ago: the fires were under control now, the scene still ringed with lawmen.

One saw her coming. 'Keep clear,' he said. 'Some of these build-ings may collapse.'

'What happened?' said Maddy.

The lawman shrugged. 'We don't know. Maybe an earthquake.'

He did not mention runelight, or glam, which Maddy found un-usual; most of these lawmen had served the Order at one time or another, and should be more than familiar with the signs of magic. Maddy took this to mean that the man was deliberately avoiding telling her the truth – and why should he? She was nobody. Just a girl from the Northlands.

Still, she had to know about Perth. Had he been in the round-house when the attack had taken place? And if so, how could he have survived? Gods, the place was rubble. All she could hope was that he had been in transit to some other location at the time, or at least that his end had been quick.

'Did anyone escape?' she asked. 'Did any of the prisoners—?'

But the lawman seemed not to be listening. Jorgi had caught his attention. The smell, perhaps; or the fishy eyes; or the unappealing way he moved. Maddy suddenly realized that this was no place to be noticed. There might still be folk here who recognized glam-ours at work; an inner core of lawmen who still remembered the Order.

'That's a very unusual horse.' The lawman's voice was cool and bland.

'Yes. He belongs to a relative.'

'What is it, some kind of Outlands breed?'

Maddy nodded. 'I think so.' She started to bring the Horse round – but the lawman's hand shot out suddenly and grabbed hold of Jorgi's bridle.

'I think you'd better come with me, miss,' he said, and that was when Maddy knew that she wasn't just going to slip away: there was a look on the lawman's face that told her all she needed to know.

'Is there a problem?' she said, fingering *Isa* behind her back.

'We've had reports of a fugitive, miss. A young lady fitting your description, and riding a most unusual horse.. We have reason to believe that this young lady may have been responsible for – er – *damage* to city property.'

'Really?' said Maddy. 'How terrible.'

She glanced up to see three more lawmen making their way towards her. Another moment and she would be surrounded. She knew she ought to be gone. But Maddy was torn between the instinct to flee and the need to know more:

'What did she do?'

'You really don't know?' said the lawman. He was a man of middle years, tall and broad-shouldered in his uniform. His greying hair was neatly tied back. His eyes were a cold and piercing blue.

He looks like an Examiner.

Of course, that wasn't possible, Maddy told herself at once. The Examiners were all gone. But the Order did have guards, she thought; a network of spies and enforcers. Who knew how many were still left? Who knew what secrets they possessed?

'It was a red horse,' the lawman said (though Maddy no longer really believed that this man *was* a lawman). 'A red horse, and now a black—'

His hand fastened around Maddy's wrist. His eyes locked with hers. '*I know you,*' he said. 'There's something about you. Something uncanny. Just like that fellow I brought in today. The one who wouldn't give me his name.'

Maddy suddenly realized that he was trying to charm her. Not with the Word, of course, but with the sheer force of his personality. Behind her, the three other lawmen were barely a dozen feet away. In a moment they would be on her.

She summoned *Isa*, the Icy One, and flung it at the lawman. At

438

once, the man was frozen in place. His comrades held back, startled, and in the moment it took them to react, Maddy had grabbed Jorgi's bridle, and, kicking her heels into his sides, she cried: 'Jorgi! Get us *out of here!*'

There followed a moment's confusion. Shadows blurred; runelight flashed; the air was suddenly filled with dust. Darkness fell – a darkness so dense that Maddy could almost touch it. It felt powdery, like soot; it even smelled like stale smoke.

Jorgi had once more changed Aspect to that of the World Serpent. Maddy could feel his mane in her hands; it was like holding onto a fringe of dead squid.

Then he stopped, and Maddy slid from the Serpent's back onto cold stone.

'Where is this? Dream?'

She was still blind. Casting *Sól*, she found herself in a brick-lined passageway, feathered with cobwebs, soft with dust.

'Haven't we been here before?'

Maddy's voice echoed against the stone, and she began to understand. This wasn't Dream. They were underground. Jorgi must have taken them underneath the city, just as he had the day they arrived. This was one of the passageways that led to the University, unused since the end of the Order, cocooned in the dust of centuries.

'Well done, Jorgi!'

She realized that they were *under* the Armouries. A section of the passageway had partially collapsed ahead of them, spilling stone and bricks and rubble into the vault below. And now, looking through the rune *Bjarkán*, Maddy saw something that made her cry out. A signature, a recent one – faint but recognizable – running alongside the pile of rocks and leading into the darkness.

Perth?

And wasn't there something else too: a silvery trace of the rune *Ác* that cut through the shadows like a blade, and with it, a scrawl of kingfisher-blue that could only belong to the General?

So *that* was how Maggie had done it, she thought. First through

439

Dream, on Sleipnir, and then through the underground labyrinth to strike where least expected.

'Jorgi, I could *kiss* you! If only you didn't *smell* so bad.'

Jorgi belched and expanded his Aspect to fill the whole of the passageway. Now he looked like a giant slug – slimy and very pleased with himself.

'Can you take me where it leads?' Maddy indicated the trail.

Jorgi shrugged again and began to move through the passageway. Maddy held on as hard as she could; pressing herself into Jorgi's side as he oozed past various obstacles. Their progress was slow and slimy, but the World Serpent was agile and surprisingly good at squeezing through small spaces. Before long they had left the Armouries, and were working their way down a tunnel that was largely free of signatures – except for that triple trail that led into the darkness.

Now Maddy followed the trail on foot. Perth's glam was very faint. The traces that overlaid it were dazzling in comparison, the spackle of runelight against the walls like the sign of some violent eruption. There must have been a fight, she thought. But who had been the victor?

She found Perth a hundred yards further down, in a place where the roof had partly collapsed, curled up, almost hidden beneath a pile of rubble and dust; for a moment Maddy was sure he was dead.

She gave a cry and started to clear the debris; under it, her friend lay still. His glam was so low she could barely see it, even through the rune *Bjarkán*. Barely conscious; smothered in dust; torn and bruised and bleeding. And yet he was breathing; he was alive.

Perth coughed. 'Water. Please.'

Quickly Maddy found a place where water had seeped through the ceiling. It looked clean; she collected some between her cupped hands and made him drink. It seemed to revive him; he coughed again and sat up with an effort.

'What is it that the slave dreams?'

Maddy frowned at him, puzzled. 'What?'

'It's an old riddle we used to tell, when I was in the galleys. *What is it that the slave dreams? The slave dreams of being master.* I thought of it just a moment ago, for the first time in years and years.' He put a hand to his head. 'It hurts. I must have hit it on something.'

'No kidding,' Maddy said. 'What happened? You look terrible.'

'There was an altercation.' Perth looked up at Maddy and grinned. 'One minute I was in my cell, trying to get some much-needed rest, then *boom!* I tell you, if I'd known it was going to be so much trouble, I wouldn't have stolen that Head for the Worlds.'

Maddy was trembling with relief. 'I should have told you the truth,' she said. 'You could have been killed. If you had—'

Perth shrugged. 'If wishes were horses, beggars would ride.'

Maddy felt her heart clench. 'I had a friend who used to say that.'

'Really? What happened?'

She shook her head. 'Never mind. It's over now. And if my sister has the Head . . .'

Perth looked surprised. 'But she hasn't,' he said.

Maddy stared at him. 'What?'

He grinned. 'I told you. There was an altercation. And I have to say that I'm disappointed by your assumption that, in a fight between me and a little girl, the little girl would always win . . .'

Maddy's head was spinning. 'Please, Perth. For gods' sakes, stop *talking!*'

Perth assumed an injured look.

'You don't mean you've still *got* it?' she said.

Once more Perth grinned. Reaching behind him into the pile of rubble, he pulled out a piece of volcanic rock that Maddy remembered only too well. She'd last seen it on the plains of Hel, when Sugar had thrown it into Dream . . .

For a moment her heart was too full to speak. She reached out to take the stone Head. Was it really the General? Could he tell her what to do to avert the coming Apocalypse?

With trembling hands, she took it. Then, summoning the rune *Bjarkán*, she looked into its stony heart.

'Odin? One-Eye? Are you there?'

No reply. Not a trace of glam.

'It's Maddy. Odin, are you there?'

Still there came no answering gleam.

She tried again, with all her glam, but *Bjarkán* revealed no sign of life. No cantrips would awaken it; Maddy grew hoarse from trying.

At last, when she had tried every rune, every cantrip she had learned, Maddy finally understood. The Head was simply an empty husk. Not even the faintest glimmer remained. The rock was a rock, and nothing more.

Whatever had been inside was gone.

3

THERE'S AN OLD NORTHLANDS SAYING that goes like this: *When lies don't help, try telling the truth.* Loki knew it well, of course, but much preferred his own version, which was: *When lies don't help, tell better lies.*

Loki was an excellent liar. Having realized where they were heading, he had decided to play for time, and, assuming an air of insouciance, had assured the anxious gods that everything was going to plan.

'What plan?' Skadi said. 'Your plan to get us nowhere?'

Loki waved a cheery hand. 'We're going to leave the wagons behind. They're only holding us up,' he said. 'Those who can take bird Aspect will; as for the rest, you can leave them to me.'

The Æsir looked doubtful at this. Vanir and Chaos folk could change Aspect at will; but they, with their broken runemarks, were quite unable to do so.

'You're playing for time,' Skadi said. 'This is a trick to split us up so you can make your getaway.'

Loki shook his head. 'Please. Just how far do you think I'd get?'

'All right. What's the plan?' she said.

Loki shrugged. 'Just wait and see.'

The gods spent the next few hours trying to work out how Loki could fly Ethel, Thor *and* the Queen of the Pigs across an

443

indeterminate stretch of countryside – not to mention their weapons, of course, and the clothes that the Vanir would certainly need when resuming their human Aspects.

No one believed he could do it. In fact, Thor was looking forward to the moment when Loki at last admitted defeat, and he could finally hammer him.

'You're going to change their Aspects,' said Idun, who, with Bragi, liked a good tale, and had joined in the guessing game with enthusiasm (she was in fact the only one who still believed Loki's promise). 'You'll turn us all into acorns and carry us into the city.'

Loki shook his head. 'No.'

Idun looked at him, wide-eyed. 'All right. You're going to ask the Tunnel Folk to build a magnificent flying machine . . .'

Loki sighed. 'Wrong,' he said.

Bragi made a suggestion. 'You're going to summon Jormungand, your monstrous son, to take us into the city through Dream . . .'

'Nope, said Loki. 'Wrong again.'

In fact, this would have been an excellent solution, but for two simple drawbacks. One, Loki had no idea how to summon Jormungand. Two, the World Serpent was far more likely to crunch him up like a fish-biscuit than to help him in any way.

No, Loki's solution was simpler. He was planning to run away.

The only obstacle to this was attached to his wrist by the Wedlock; and Loki knew that if he fled, Sigyn would certainly raise the alarm, after which he didn't rate his chances of survival.

He'd tried everything he could – everything but the truth, of course. Nothing had worked. Sigyn was impervious to flattery; to argument; to charm or tears or declarations of love. She was reasonable, but adamant; and Loki was keenly reminded of the woman who, five hundred years before, had collected the droplets of poison dripping from the fangs of the snake that Skadi had hung above his face, while sweetly but firmly refusing his pleas to release him from his manacles.

Finally the lies had run out. They'd marched the whole day and most of the night, and still there was nothing to be seen – not the dawn, nor the sea, nor Odin's birds, nor the battlements of the Universal City. The road ahead was endless, the landscape around them was swimming in fog, and even Thor was getting tired, which made him all the keener to hammer the cause of his annoyance.

Only Sigyn still seemed to believe that Loki really had a plan; which Loki found so annoying that finally he turned her back into an acorn and called a halt.

'Er, listen, folks,' he told the gods. 'I haven't *quite* been straight with you. The *good* news is that I know where we are. The bad news is . . .'

'*Do* tell,' said Thor.

Loki told them the bad news.

After that, he sat and waited for the noise to die down. After five minutes or so, it did, and once again he tried to explain how this time it *really* wasn't his fault.

'I know how it looks,' he admitted.

'It *looks* like a trap,' said Heimdall, narrowing his steel-blue eyes. 'It *looks* as though you led us here on a fool's errand, talked about plans, and basically wasted as much time as you could to keep us away from things at World's End.'

'Well, I didn't,' said Loki.

'Please. Let me hammer him,' said Thor.

'I'm telling the *truth*,' Loki insisted.

'Let me hammer him anyway.'

For a moment Loki stood up, trying to hold back the angry gods. 'Please!' he yelled. 'Just *listen* to me! I think I know what's happening here!'

Little by little the noise died down again, barring some muttered invective.

Then Loki took a deep breath and summoned all his eloquence.

'I know that most of you hate me,' he said, 'and none of you really trust me. But please, just *think* for a minute.' He spread his hands appealingly. 'How could I have done all this? Opened the Worlds, taken us through, created this fog to confuse everyone . . .' He shrugged. 'I've never had the kind of glam it would take to play a trick like that, and even if I had, I'd be burned out by now. So before you play jump-rope with my spine—'

'You could have had help,' said Heimdall.

'Yes, because I have *so* many friends,' Loki told him bitterly. 'Tell me, does anyone remember what happened last time I was here? I called in a favour from Hel, who swore that she'd kill me if I ever showed my face here again, so trust me when I tell you that I'm not exactly *thrilled* to be back.'

'He has a point,' said Angie, who until then had been silent. 'You told us you knew what was happening,' she said, addressing the Trickster.

'Yes, but you're not going to like it.'

Ethel raised an eyebrow. 'At this stage,' she said quietly, 'I don't think you have much to lose. Why don't you tell us?'

Loki gave his crooked smile. 'I have to admit, you got me,' he said. 'You got me good and proper. The Wedlock . . .' He glanced at his wrist, where *Eh* still gleamed, with Sigyn, in her acorn form, dangling from the end of the chain. 'I assumed all that was Skadi's idea, to keep me out of mischief. But it wasn't, was it, Seeress?'

Smiling, Ethel shook her head.

'Of course, I should have known something was wrong. Since when did *you* care what happened to me? Since when did you try to protect me? You've always hated my guts. And perhaps – just perhaps – I deserved it. So why would you, of all people, help *me?* At first I thought it was because you needed me to get to World's End. But that wasn't the reason. You needed me for something else. Something no one else knew about.'

Ethel's eyes shone. 'Well done. I wondered if you'd work it out.'

'Well, Trickery *is* my middle name. And I knew Angie couldn't be working alone. That runemark of hers could only have come from someone with access to the New Script. Someone who can cross between Worlds. Someone who can speak with the dead. Someone who's an *oracle* . . .'

Ethel smiled. 'Go on,' she said.

'It was a good performance, though.' Loki's grin was cold and hard. 'You had me completely fooled. I thought there was nothing left in the Worlds that had the power to surprise me. But you – you, with your tea and cake and *shall-I-be-Mother?* – gods! What an *act*! If only I'd known . . .'

'Known what?' said Thor.

'Haven't you worked it out yet? The Oracle predicted this. She knew we were coming here all along. Perhaps she even brought it about. She knew, because she'd made a deal. *That* was why she needed me.'

Loki was looking beyond them now, to a point ahead on the road. *'I see a Rainbow riding high; of cheating Death the legacy.* Cheating Death. I should have known.'

He raised his voice and called through the mist. 'A life for a life, Hel, isn't that right? Isn't that the currency of choice? Wasn't that *always* your bargain?'

For a moment no one answered him. Then the mist began to roll away, leaving the road ahead of them bare, and the landscape around them familiar.

They had all seen Hel's kingdom before, and yet the barren scale of it, the sickening wasteland all around and the sky like a lid on a cauldron filled their hearts with fear and dismay. Nothing relieved its emptiness; no desert of the Middle Worlds could mirror its bleak magnificence.

And now there was someone standing ahead of them, a woman with a face like the moon, that changed as she moved it left and right, and a smile like a mouthful of broken bones as she turned her dead eye on the Trickster.

It had been years since Hel the Half-Born had felt anything remotely like enjoyment. And yet, she thought, this might qualify. To see Loki like this, at her mercy, betrayed by one of his own kin. Her dead eye lingered on him. It saw so much more than her living one. Fear, hatred, anguish, despair – these were the colours that Hel loved most, and they were present now in abundance.

But when he spoke, the Trickster's tone was as light and mocking as ever. 'So tell me – who is it?' Loki said. 'Who am I redeeming today? Golden Boy Balder? Too obvious. Besides, he's too much of a goody-two-shoes to get involved with something like this. No, it has to be someone else. Now let me guess – who *could* it be? Who could be worth such a sacrifice?'

Ethel shrugged. 'You got me,' she said. 'Believe me, it's nothing personal. You all heard the prophecy. The future of Asgard depends on this. If I could have thought of another way to bring my husband back from the dead—'

'So, you made a deal with Hel. My life for the General's. Was this your idea, or his?'

Ethel smiled. 'A bit of both.'

'Well. You got a bargain.'

Loki looked around at the circle of gods. From their expressions it was clear that most of them agreed with him. Only Idun seemed distressed; her blue eyes went from Ethel to Loki, then back to Ethel again, as if she expected one of them to pull off a mask and shout, *Surprise!*

'This isn't happening,' she said at last. 'Ethel would never betray one of us. Not even to save the General. Not even if it was Loki . . .'

'Idun, sweetheart,' Loki said, 'we're *gods*, not saints. Everyone lies. Everyone cheats. Everyone scores off everyone else. Well, maybe not *you*. What I don't understand is this: how did we get here, Seeress? You can't have brought us to Hel on your own. You must have had help from someone.'

Ethel just smiled.

Loki thought hard. 'The ravens!' he said. 'Odin's messengers. *They* can travel from World to World – through Death, Dream and Damnation. They must have acted as go-betweens. My darling daughter did the rest. And Angie – I thought you *liked* me.'

The Temptress shrugged. 'Oh, sweetheart, I do. But I wanted my hall in Asgard. I wanted to be on the winning team. And I wanted *this* . . .' She showed him the runemark on her arm, gleaming in its violet light.

'So protecting me was just a ruse to ensure I survived to cement your deal.' Loki appealed to the party of gods. 'You're really going along with this? You're going to watch them sacrifice me? Sif, we've had our differences, but . . .'

The goddess of grace and plenty smiled. 'You bet I'm going to watch,' she said. 'I only wish we had popcorn.'

'Thor,' said Loki. 'We're old friends . . .'

Thor shrugged. 'What choice do we have? It's either you or the General.'

'Heimdall . . . Bragi . . . Tyr . . . Frey . . .'

The Watchman showed his golden teeth. 'We'll tell everyone you died bravely.'

'I'll write you an epic poem,' said Bragi.

'Nothing personal,' said Frey. 'Consider this a debt repaid.'

'Idun . . . Njörd . . . Freyja. *Please* . . .'

One by one the gods turned away. Sugar gave him a rueful look. Jolly spread his hands and grinned. Idun wiped away a tear. Bragi played a sad little tune. Angrboda blew him a kiss.

Fenris said: 'Tough call, dude.'

'Well, thanks a bunch,' said the Trickster. 'It's nice to know who your friends are. And to think I risked my *life* for you!' His green eyes narrowed suddenly. 'That's why Maddy isn't here. You guessed she wouldn't play along. So you sent the ravens to lure her away with some half-baked story about her twin.' He gave a bitter little laugh. 'I wondered why you were helping me, Seeress, offering me your protection. I thought you'd decided to give me a break. Maybe even forgiven me. Turns out you needed a sacrifice . . .'

Ethel shrugged. '*Forgiven* you? You caused the death of my only son. You think I'm going to let you off?'

'That was a *misunderstanding* —'

'A life for a life,' Ethel said. 'It's time to keep our bargain.'

Hel took a lurching step forward. Even through her living eye she could see that Loki was afraid. A shiver of pleasure ran through her, and she paused to savour the moment a while. Pleasures were so very few, here in the Kingdom of the Dead. And if the End of Everything was as close as it was rumoured to be, then she meant to enjoy every pleasure she could before the darkness claimed them all.

She raised the binding rope of runes that was her most powerful weapon. Woven from the rune *Naudr*, it gleamed with a livid malevolence.

'I made you a promise, Loki,' she said. 'I made it right here, three years ago. And Hel *always* keeps her promises – as I'm sure you already know . . .'

And with that she flicked out the rune *Naudr*, which wrapped itself tightly around. Loki's neck. Tugged at it. Loki fell to his knees. Once more Hel closed her living eye and concentrated on Loki's signature. Through the rune *Bjarkán* it shone, a skein of violet against the dark. Now Hel extended her withered hand and grasped the violet filament between her skeletal fingers. It brightened as Loki struggled in vain to pull himself free from the stranglehold of *Naudr*. It was impossible, he knew. Death conquers all – even Wildfire.

He looked up at the circle of gods. *Naudr*, the Binder, bit into his throat. He tried to speak – to plead his case – but the binding rope had cut off his voice.

'A life for a life,' Hel intoned, bringing the violet skein to her mouth. 'Odin, son of Bór, arise!'

There was a moment of anticipation. Then another. In the deserts of Hel, the bone-white wind blew drifts of dust across the dunes.

'Odin, son of Bór,' said Hel, 'Father of Thor, General of Asgard, Allfather of the Middle Worlds – I summon you to life! *Arise!*'

Once again, nothing happened. The wind keened over the bitter ground. The dead, sensing something momentous, distressed the chilly air in droves. But no one arose. The dead stayed dead. Odin was not among them.

Ethel turned to Hel, 'Oh. This is rather embarrassing.'

'What?' said Hel, looking confused.

'Well, clearly my husband isn't here.'

'Impossible,' said Hel. 'He died. You *saw* him die, all of you.' She tugged at the rope around Loki's neck. 'You promised me. We had a deal—'

'But you can't keep your side of it. Why would I give you Loki?'

'So— take somebody else,' said Hel, beginning to look agitated.

450

'I'll give you your son Balder, if you like. Or anyone. But Loki's *mine!'*

For a moment Ethel looked down at the Trickster, on his knees. *Naudr* had robbed him of his voice, but his eyes still pleaded eloquently. She shook her head. 'I don't think so,' she said. 'Our deal was for Odin. No one else.'

The living side of Hel's face took on a look of disbelief. 'No,' she said. 'He belongs to me. This time I don't care if the Nine Worlds end . . .'

And, like a seamstress trimming loose thread, she nipped at Loki's lifeline with teeth that were white on one side of her mouth, worn black stumps on the other.

The Trickster uttered a blasphemous prayer as he felt her sever his life.

Goodbye, cruel Worlds!

He closed his eyes—

And opened them to find himself looking up at Hel's living profile, her features now distorted with anger and bewilderment. Between her fingers, his signature shone as bright and unbroken as ever.

'What went wrong?' Heimdall said. 'I thought you were supposed to *cut* his life, not floss your teeth with it.'

'Does this mean Loki *doesn't* die?' said Sif, looking disgusted.

Ethel smiled. 'Apparently so. As we have already seen, Death's guardian cannot break her word without suffering serious consequences.'

Once more, and with growing impatience, Hel tried to break the violet thread. Nothing happened. The signature glowed. She tore at the thread with her fingernails . . .

'Do you mind? That tickles.' Loki had loosened the binding rope, and was now sitting cross-legged on the sandy ground, looking more confident than he felt. He still had no idea why Hel had failed to take his life, but his keen sense of the ridiculous had temporarily suspended his fear.

He looked up at the circle of gods now staring at him in surprise. Only Ethel seemed unmoved, her face serene as always.

'Of cheating Death the legacy,' quoted Loki, with a smile. 'Of course. I see now. *Cheating Death.* You pushed her to this, Seeress. You cheated Death. You pushed Hel into breaking her word, using me as bait. Did you plan this from the start? Did you know this would happen?'

Ethel shrugged. 'Hel's always had a bit of a moral blind spot where you were concerned. I wonder why.'

Now Hel's living features were dark with rage. Even her dead side looked angry. It occurred to her that the only time she ever felt rage was when the Trickster was around. How could he have cheated Death? What could be protecting him?

She focused her blind eye on Loki.

There! How could she have missed it? Almost invisible around his wrist, something glittered. A golden chain. Hel had been too preoccupied with gloating over her enemy to notice the chain, or the little charm that dangled from it – a gleaming golden acorn. Now her all-seeing dead eye registered its significance, and she ground her teeth together in wrath as she saw the Wedlock.

She glared at Ethel. 'What's this?' she said.

Ethel gave her gentle smile. 'Security, of course,' she said. 'In case you tried to renege on our deal.'

A cantrip, and the acorn charm turned back into Loki's ex-wife.

'Sweetheart, what have they *done* to you?' she wailed, on seeing the Trickster. She rounded in fury on the gods, a fierce, diminutive figure with a flushed round face and blue eyes flashing like angry stars. 'You cowards!' she shrieked. 'How *could* you? After everything he's done for you, how could you treat the poor angel this way?'

The gods – even Heimdall – looked taken aback.

Ethel said: 'Well done, my dear.'

The poor angel grinned and looked up at his wife. 'I never thought I'd say this,' he said, 'but Sigyn, it's *great* to see you.'

Hel's mouth twisted as she focused once more on Loki. 'I may not be able to kill him,' she said, 'but I *can* make sure he never leaves. And if the rest of you ever want to find your way back, then I suggest you give him to me.'

Sigyn drew herself up to full height. It wasn't very impressive, but she stood fast between Hel and Loki, her face set in determination.

'Are you out of your mind?' said Hel.

Stubbornly Sigyn shook her head.

'I'm warning you. Get out of my way—'

'Not on your life,' said Sigyn.

And now the Guardian of the Dead looked up and saw a light in the sky; a light that shone with the force of a sun. And for the second time in five hundred and three years her ancient heart leaped in surprise as something bore down on the plains of Hel; something that looked – though it *couldn't* be – exactly like an old washing basket, gleaming with unearthly fire . . .

4

MAGGIE AWOKE THAT MORNING FEELING tired and unrefreshed. That was to be expected, of course. It was, after all, her wedding day. She could expect to be feeling jittery, especially in her condition. It was also the morning of Ragnarók, and the dawn sky was apocalyptic in rose-gold and marshmallow-pink, though Maggie was naive enough to take this as a good sign.

Maddy knew just what it meant, having been raised in the rustic North. *Red sky at night, shepherd's delight. Red sky in the morning, shepherd's warning.* There might not be many shepherds in the Universal City, but on the day of the End of the Worlds, she thought, *everybody* might do well to take heed of that old wives' saying.

It had been dark when she and Perth had returned with Jorgi to the Water Rats, and by then neither of them felt much like talking. Perth was exhausted, his glam burned out, his body covered in bruises. Maddy was equally drained, her hope of avoiding the inevitable dashed by the loss of the Old Man. Only Jorgi seemed cheerful – probably at the prospect of another night's hunting for seals – and, on arrival, promptly assumed his Serpent form and slid back into the water. Maddy did not try to stop him. The Rider of Treachery needed no horse for what she had to do the next day; although her heart sank at betraying her twin, the General had given her no choice but to murder Adam Scattergood.

That night she had tried to sleep, but sleep had never been more elusive. Guilt, grief and worry kept her awake, and by three in the morning she was so wide awake that she abandoned all hope of rest and got up to prepare for treachery.

Perth, on the other hand, was deeply asleep, and did not stir when she entered his room – not even when Maddy cast the rune *Sól* and, in its glow, looked at her friend. She would have welcomed his company in the task that lay ahead, but he looked so innocent as he slept, his head at a childish angle, that she was reluctant to wake him.

And so she went alone to Examiners' Walk, as the first light of the Last Day began, to colour the eastern sky, and, shivering, waited in the alleyway for Maggie to make her appearance.

Maggie too had been awake since well before first light. Even though she had never been vain, there was pleasure to be had in bathing and pampering; in the choosing of scent; in the painting of palms with ochre in the traditional designs; and finally, in the pinning of the white *bergha* around the head, upon which the wedding veil would lie beneath its garland of roses.

It was almost a quarter to eight.

'Aren't you ready *yet?*' said Adam, pacing the floor of the penthouse.

Maggie turned and looked at him. Handsome in his white silk, his fair hair cut in the latest World's End fashion, he looked just like an angel. A little pale, perhaps, she thought – though that was understandable. All young men were nervous on their wedding morning.

'Nearly,' she said. 'How do I look?'

She slipped on her veil – the one she had made from the yellow silk that Adam had brought – and, placing the rose garland on her head, looked at her reflection.

Adam smiled. It was not an especially friendly smile, but Maggie, still watching her mirror-self, failed to notice its lack of warmth. She was thinking of the ceremony soon to be held at St Sepulchre's, when she and Adam would stand before the Kissing Stone and declare their love in the ritual words of the Good Book:

455

My hand to your hand,
My soul to your soul,
My name to your name,
For ever, one.

Adam too was thinking of the words of the wedding ceremony. He had no idea why his passenger should find them so important, but in his mind the Whisperer was almost swooning with excitement. It would soon be over now. His passenger would be gone. And so Adam smiled at his bride-to-be, and said in a voice that trembled with anticipation:

'Darling, you look ready.'

In the street below, Maddy didn't feel ready at all. The day was going to be perfect, she thought: the red sky had veered to angelic blue; the sun was shining; there were no clouds. In just a few minutes, she told herself, the bells of St Sepulchre would ring, and Maggie Rede would say her vows of marriage to Adam Scattergood.

A wedding, even a modest one, always attracts attention, and Adam, it seemed, had spared no expense. A piper, a drummer, a flower-decked carriage, to be drawn – by none other than the Red Horse of the Last Days – to the cathedral of St Sepulchre, where the couple would be wed in front of the Kissing Stone, according to a tradition dating back over five hundred years.

A little crowd had already gathered around the wedding carriage, dancing to the piper's tune; most were children, hands held out and clamouring for brideys – the little heart-shaped biscuits traditionally thrown to the revellers.

Maddy's heart sank lower still. This wasn't going to be easy. The idea of murdering a young man at his own wedding was bad enough; to do it in a crowd of children, any one of whom might be hit, was almost unthinkable. But those were the General's orders, clear and unambiguous, and whatever chance she might have had to question his plan had been lost.

She wished that he were with her now. She didn't want to do

456

this alone. Everything about it felt wrong, but with so little time till the crucial event, Maddy could think of no other way of preventing her sister's wedding.

It was already ten minutes to the hour. The bride was more than fashionably late. For a moment Maddy dared to hope that Maggie might have changed her mind, that somehow she might have realized the terrible mistake she'd made . . .

And then came a mighty cheer from the crowd, and the bride and groom made their appearance.

Maddy stared at them from her hiding place in the alleyway. Maggie wore a yellow veil and carried a basket of brideys; Adam was resplendent in white. The little crowd cheered as they emerged, the children clamouring for brideys, and the piper began to play a sprightly traditional tune called *The Kissing Dance*, which Maddy recognized at once from weddings in her own village.

She moved a little closer, out from the mouth of the alleyway. Drawn in by the trail of children, mesmerized by the vivid faces, the rosy flush on her sister's cheek, the way she laughed and traded jokes with the folk who now lined Examiners' Walk – some crowding the carriage, others simply waving at her – Maddy joined the little gathering, and she needed no truesight to tell her that this was no performance. Her sister's happiness was real; she practically glowed with excitement.

Could Adam have changed? Maddy thought. Could it be that the mean little boy had turned into someone her sister could love? Could it be that he loved *her*?

No. The thought was unbearable. The only way she could do this was if Adam were a genuine threat; but the more she tried to picture it, the more she seemed to remember that distant day on Red Horse Hill, when she had flung the mindbolt and Adam had wet his pants in fear . . .

In a moment the procession would leave. It would have to be done soon. Done soon and done right; there would be no second chance. She moved a little closer. The wedding carriage was now no more than twenty feet away from her, and, approaching, Maddy lowered her head, as if to pick up one of the brideys that had fallen to the cobbles, and started to summon the rune *Hagall*.

But – a quirk of Fate, perhaps – the gesture that should have concealed her attracted Maggie's attention. The girl froze just as she was flinging a handful of brideys into the crowd, and as Maddy glanced up instinctively, she found herself looking into a pair of grey eyes as gold-flecked and curious as her own . . .

For less than a second her own eyes went wide.

Startled, Maggie caught her breath.

Something passed between them – a force much greater than *Aesk* or *Ác* – that flashed across their twin consciousness. Adam, seeing Maddy there, flinched and instinctively threw up his arm. *Same old Adam,* Maddy thought, and started to raise the mindbolt . . .

But Maggie was reaching out her hand, a shy little smile on her lips. 'Oh, Maddy, I knew you'd—' she began.

Looking back later, Maddy knew that this had been her moment. This – this second of readiness, this ultimate test of her loyalty.

And she failed it, the rune *Hagall* discharging harmlessly into the ground just as Maggie saw what was happening.

'Maggie, wait . . .' Maddy said.

But Maggie was already out of reach. Her eyes, so hopeful a moment before, now blazed with betrayal and horror. She raised a fist that was suddenly bristling with runelight.

'I thought you were different,' she said. 'I thought you were on *my* side. Turns out you were one of them, just like that *thing* said you were . . .'

And, hurling a fistful of cantrips, she urged the Red Horse of Carnage on, and drove him at a brisk trot down Examiners' Walk, scattering the little crowd (the children still calling for brideys), the runes snapping like firecrackers all across the cobbled street, the drummer and piper running behind, the garland slipping from her head to tumble into the gutter.

The Folk all reacted in different ways.

Someone shouted: 'Fireworks!' Others went on dancing. Others gaped into the sky, aware that they'd seen *something* strange, but unable to put it into words. Some heard the voices of people long

458

dead; some laughed, a little wildly; some wept – but then, doesn't everyone cry at weddings?

Maggie looked back once, wild-eyed, deathly under her veil. Then both she and Adam were gone.

5

MADDY WATCHED AS THE WEDDING CARRIAGE clattered away down the road. Her mind was a blur of misery. What now? She'd ruined everything. She'd failed the General and the gods. But to ask her to murder a human being, even Adam Scattergood . . .

Had Odin *really* believed she could? He was certainly capable of ruthlessness, deceit, coldness, even cruelty. But he'd always had a soft spot for the Folk, and Maddy wondered if even Death could have changed him so much from the man she knew.

Odin, I'm sorry. I let you down.

But it was too late for regrets, she knew. So many chances already lost. So many missed opportunities. And with so little time, even guilt was a luxury that would have to wait. It was too late to save Odin now. Too late to do what he'd ordered her to; but perhaps not too late to intervene.

She'd been unable to kill Adam Scattergood, but might there not be another way to divert the path of Chaos?

If only I knew where to start, she thought.

But maybe she *did*, she realized. Why had she not seen it before? It had been staring her in the face ever since she came to World's End. There all along in the prophecy, like a finger pointing up at the sky:

The Cradle fell an age ago, but Fire and Folk shall raise her
In just twelve days, at End of Worlds; a gift within the

'*Sepulchre!*' Maddy's eyes opened wide. 'The cathedral of Saint Sepulchre! That's where I'm supposed to be!'

'Aye,' said a voice at Maddy's back. 'So why are ye still standing here, hen?'

Maddy turned in surprise to see Odin's Mind and Spirit standing by the side of the road. Both were more or less in human form, though Mandy still had her raven's wings, folded like a feather cloak over her skinny, bejewelled arms, and both were looking twitchy and tense, with ruffled feathers and shifty eyes.

Alongside them was Jorgi in Black Horse Aspect, looking especially greasy and drab in the morning sunlight. Maddy noticed that even the revellers gave the Black Horse a wide berth. Some forked signs against bad luck; some averted their gaze as they passed. And behind the Horse of Treachery stood a figure in a blue robe, his face half concealed under a hat.

'Perth! What are you doing here?'

'I might ask the same of ye,' Hughie said. 'I take it ye didn'ae heed the Auld Man's instructions.'

Maddy shook her head. 'No. I couldn't do what he asked me.'

Hughie gave a derisive *crawk*. 'Aye. I should have known that. Ye've too kind a heart to kill anyone. Still – we may have a chance yet. As long as we stop that sister of yours.'

'Stop her from what?' Maddy said.

Mandy *craw*-ed impatiently. *Crawk. Ack. No time*, she said.

Hughie turned to Maddy again. 'There's no time for explanations now. Ye'll have tae trust me. Will ye, lass?'

Maddy nodded. 'I'll have to,' she said. 'But – if you're Odin's Spirit and Mind, then how come you're still here at all? I mean – he died. Didn't he? I found the Head. There was nothing there.'

Hughie shrugged. 'He's been dead before.'

'You mean . . .'

'Ach, he'll have a plan. The General *always* has a plan.'

Maddy looked at him helplessly. 'I don't see how—'

Crawk. Crawk. No time!

'All right.' She looked at Jormungand. 'I don't suppose you'd let me ride? We have to get there as fast as we can, and I don't think being inconspicuous is going to help at this stage . . .'

Jorgi gave a fishy belch. He seemed to understand, though. In a moment the Horse was gone, to be replaced by the World Serpent in his original Aspect: big and black and fearsome; his mane bristling with runelight; his eyes like portholes of black glass.

'You're going to ride *that?*' Perth said. 'It smells *awful.*' He put out a hand. Then he took hold of Jorgi's mane and made as if to pull himself up.

'No, not you,' Maddy said. 'I mean, it could be dangerous . . .'

'We've both seen how well you manage without me,' Perth told her with a grin. 'Besides, it's a wedding, isn't it? Purses to cut? Pockets to pick? You really think I'm the type to miss out on a little bit of free enterprise?'

Maddy shook her head. 'No. I've lost too many friends. I don't want to lose another . . .'

Perth grinned at her again. 'I can look after myself,' he said. 'Now, will you get a grip, girl? We have a wedding to go to!'

6

'WHAT IN HEL IS THAT?' said Thor as the object hurtled towards them. Seen through the lens of the rune *Bjarkán*, it looked like a flying creature – a Horse of Air, or maybe a sky-dragon – though to the naked eye its Aspect was simply that of an old woman sitting in a washing basket, a scruffy shawl over her shoulders, her hair streaming out behind. The sky in her wake wheeled and yawned like a child's kaleidoscope, as colours that had never before been seen in Hel's kingdom bloomed across its horizon.

'Hey! You!' yelled Crazy Nan. 'I made it! I made it! With help from the Folk!'

Hel observed Nan through her dead eye. She was feeling exceptionally weary. Contact with Loki often had this effect on her, and now Hel wanted nothing more than to sleep through the next five hundred years.

She gave a deep sigh – not that she *needed* to breathe, of course – and the whole of Hel sighed around her, rocks and stones shifting suddenly, the sandy desert of Death's domain shrugging in tired frustration.

She turned the eye on Loki. 'Why do these things only ever happen when you're around?' she demanded.

'Just dumb luck, I guess,' said the Trickster as Crazy Nan landed her washing basket and got out – rather shakily. On the plain of Hel, her Aspect was no longer that of a frail old crone, but of a

463

woman in her prime, white hair to her waist, her eyes a wicked, snapping blue.

The broken rune that had once been hers now shone out a brilliant silver. Ethel recognized it at once. It was *Iar*, the Beaver, fourth rune of the New Script, rune of earth and water and air. *Iar*, the Master Builder—

She smiled. 'It's good to see you, Nan. Any news yet from the Old Man?'

Nan grinned. 'You know what he's like.' Her gaze fell upon the Trickster. 'So, you're not dead?' she said cheerily.

'No thanks to any of you,' Loki said. 'Look, I hate to be a grouch, but could someone *please* tell me what's going on?'

'Don't like being left out of the loop, eh?' Nan's eyes shone with mischief. 'Well, it's all in the prophecy. If you'd just made the effort to work it all out, instead of trying to avoid responsibility . . .'

Loki's eyes widened. 'You're blaming *me*? I'm not the guilty party here. Over the past couple of weeks I've been chained, accused, bullied, hit, threatened, tied up, married, sold out, used as a bargaining chip with Hel and now—'

'Oh, leave it out,' snapped the Guardian of the Dead. 'So on *one* occasion in five hundred years you turn out to be innocent.' She turned to the little party of gods. 'And I suppose that gives *you* the right to enter my kingdom and do all *this?*' With her dead hand, she gestured at the sky, where the colours that had accompanied Crazy Nan's arrival now filled the horizon with unearthly light 'I mean, what *is* that, anyway?'

'Excellent question,' said Heimdall.

In the wake of Nan's arrival, no one had really looked at the sky. Now they did, their faces upturned, their eyes alight with wonder.

The river Dream has many tributaries, both in and out of the Middle Worlds. Even Malbry's river Strond was linked to that oldest of rivers. But Dream also crosses the Firmament, where it runs into the river of stars that the Folk call the Milky Way. And when the Sky Citadel was built, back in the days of the Elder Age, Dream had linked the earth and sky in the form of Bif-rost, the legendary Rainbow Bridge that had fallen to earth when Asgard fell, back in the days of Ragnarók. Now scarcely anyone remembered it, except the gods, the Faërie, and the old wives, who passed on the tale in skipping songs and nursery rhymes:

When the 'bow breaks, the Cradle will fall . . .

None of them had ever expected to see the likes of Bif-rost again. And yet there it stood before them now – a rainbow bright enough to climb – rising out of the sudden mist, while beyond it, the sky flickered and gasped with colours that shifted from ice-blue to fire-green, to amber and to marshmallow-pink, like a giant lantern-show in which, if the gods had narrowed their eyes and watched closely through the rune *Bjarkán,* they might just have been able to see the surprising variety of shapes and shadows that seemed to make up the edifice, swimming in and out of sight like the distant skerries of Dream.

There were fields of flowers and groves of trees; there were kittens and puppies and balls of string; there were rocking horses, forbidden fruit, antique furniture, pieces of eight; there were dreams of waking up suddenly surrounded by ladies' underwear; there were dragons and goblins and pirate ships. There was roast beef and chocolate cake. There were angels and goblins and two-headed dogs and roads that led nowhere and castles in the sky.

In fact, *all* the dreams of five hundred years were floating above the plains of Hel, and even the gods found it hard to believe as they stared at the gleaming edifice.

And at the end of the rainbow was a disc of gold that reflected a thousand prisms of light back at them like a glowing sun.

'That *can't* be what it looks like,' said Thor. 'It has to be northlights, or something.'

Fenny, Skull and Big H turned their yellow eyes to the sky.

'*Dude,*' said Fenris dreamily. 'No *way* is that northlights. Far out . . .'

'The Folk call this Saint Sepulchre's Fire,' said Ethel in her quiet voice. 'I suppose even they still remember. *Nothing dreamed is ever lost, and nothing lost for ever.* Nan knew that from the start, of course. Nan Fey, the Master Builder.'

The gods all turned to stare at Nan, who gave a little curtsey. 'It's not quite finished,' she said modestly, 'but – well, you get the picture.'

Loki was staring at the sky with an expression, not of awe, but of growing realization. 'I may be missing something here,' he said in a tone of exaggerated sarcasm, 'but it seems to me that the Seeress has been keeping quite a few secrets that the rest of us might have found useful to know. And – forgive me if I seem naive' – he indicated the golden disc – 'but isn't that the Sun Shield?'

Ethel shrugged. 'Of course it is. You don't really think I'd have let it go? My ravens rescued it from the river and delivered it to somebody who could be trusted to use it properly, and for the good of us all.'

'You mean you knew it was there, all along? And you sent me, knowing full well what would—' The Trickster choked. For a moment something almost as rare as the sight that they had just witnessed occurred: Loki was totally lost for words.

Finally he turned to Nan. 'And you . . . *you* made this? All by yourself?' he said, indicating the Rainbow Bridge.

'Well, it wasn't just me,' said Nan. 'I had help from the Folk, of course, and the Shield – and my old Horse Epona.'

The gods followed Crazy Nan's gaze.

'But that's just an old basket . . .' Freyja said.

Ethel smiled. 'Don't you know the nursery rhyme? The one about the old lady who flies to the Land of Roast Beef in a basket?'

Loki, who *did* know it, pulled a face. 'Oh, well. Why didn't you say? If I'd known that Ragnarók was going to be fought with old wives' tales—'

'Old wives know more than you think,' said Ethel, with a sideways glance at Sigyn, still linked to the Trickster by the wrist. '*Ex*-wives too, if it comes to that. In fact, I think yours just saved your life. Perhaps you should be grateful.'

Loki shrugged. 'Whatever,' he said. 'The question is, what brings us here? Why not push straight on to World's End? I'm assuming

466

you didn't bring me here to give me couples' counselling.'

Ethel sighed. 'You're incorrigible. But you're right. The Rainbow Bridge of the Elder Age was not just the road to Asgard. It was a highway that gave us entry into eight of the Nine Worlds, free and in full Aspect. But I knew that Hel would never allow us a foothold in her kingdom – at least, not without something to bargain with. Of course, I thought of you at once.'

'Thanks. I'm flattered,' Loki said. 'And what if you'd been wrong, eh? What if Odin *hadn't* got out? Would you have handed me over to Hel?'

'As the Fenris Wolf might say: *Tough call, Trickster, dude.*'

Loki shook his head. 'Gods. And I thought I was the devious one. So – what do we do next, huh? Or shouldn't I ask?'

'Well, you might want to run . . .'

'Run?' said Loki.

'Yes, run,' Ethel said, jumping into Nan's basket. It changed Aspect immediately, becoming the Horse of Air once more; a madman's dream of a white horse, with legs that spanned the sky and a mane flung out like a sheaf of cloud. 'If you make for the Bridge as fast as you can, then we can be at Saint Sepulchre's Gate before they manage to reach World's End—'

'*They?*' said Loki, looking round.

And then the Trickster saw what was coming, and took to his Wildfire Aspect at once. Behind him, Thor reached for his hammer and Heimdall pulled out his mindsword, then thought better of trying to fight and took to his bird form in a hurry.

The others – even Thor – followed suit, and it was a strangely assorted group of gods, wolves and mythical birds that scattered across Death's domain and fled towards the Rainbow Bridge.

The last time Hel had broken her word, the disruption had temporarily breached the gates of Netherworld, causing Dream to burst its banks and creating untold damage. This time the breach was more than a rift. A wall of darkness, like a wave, now emerged from the Ninth World to roll across the plain of Hel. From a distance it looked slow – just as, from afar, it seemed soundless; but as it approached, it became all too clear that the wave was moving

467

at monstrous speed, blotting out everything in its path – ground, sky, landscape.

Hel took one look at the wave and fled. Even the dead sensed its approach and blew away like dust in its path. Then, minutes later, came the sound – so loud that it struck like a mindbolt, making the whole of the Nine Worlds resonate with its power.

In the valley of the Strond the Folk heard it as an unearthly roar that vented from the open Hill.

In World's End Maggie heard it as a peal of bells from Cathedral Square.

Freyja heard it as the breaking of a thousand mirrors.

Frey heard it as a thresher's flail.

Thor heard it as thunder so loud that his ears began to bleed.

Tyr heard it as a clashing of swords.

Bragi heard it as a lost chord.

Odin's ravens heard it, and grinned.

The Wolf Brothers heard it, and howled in unison.

In Hel, the Trickster, in hawk guise, half fell out of the sky as it struck, and was saved only by the intervention of Njörd's sea-eagle, which seized him between its talons and rode the shock-wave to the Bridge, where Crazy Nan and the Horse of Air, with Ethel riding shotgun, had already joined the rest of the gods, way up, over the rainbow.

7

THE GREAT CATHEDRAL OF St Sepulchre was known throughout Inland as one of the few remaining wonders of the Nine Worlds.
Tribulation had swallowed most of the rest: the Sky Citadel, the
Rainbow Bridge, the University Library, the Hall of the Heroes,
the Observatory, the Planetarium, the Hundred Year Clock, the
Twelvemonth Fountain – even the fleet of merchant ships that had
once sailed as far as World Beyond.

Five hundred and three years after Ragnarók, the skills that had
gone into the making – even the conceiving – of such things had
long since been banned or forgotten. What little remained commanded an almost religious respect in the minds of the Folk of the
Universal City, a respect that the Order had been quick to identify
and put to its own purposes.

Now this last vestige of the wonders of the Elder Age had
become primarily a means of raising money – hence the invasion
of traders and the increasingly high Cathedral Tax that every
World's Ender had to pay.

Maggie was in many ways a typical World's Ender. While visitors from all over Inland queued (and paid) to see the cathedral,
she had never actually been inside, preferring to enjoy the view
from the square – a view that could be had for free. Pilgrims paid
a premium, of course; but native World's Enders knew better.
Anyone who paid to see the city's sights deserved to be fleeced, or

so Maggie had always thought – at least until Adam had changed her mind.

But Adam was a romantic, of course. Adam had wanted them to be married properly, in the cathedral. *And* by a bishop, no less – Maggie had not dared think how much such a luxury would cost. But Adam had been determined; and now, as Maggie approached the square, she could not help a shiver of awe as she looked up to see the great glass dome designed by the architect of World's End – the man who, many years after his death, had been renamed St Sepulchre.

Maggie knew his story, having read it in one of her old books from the Department of Records, but had never quite made the connection between Jonathan Gift, the mathematician, and the saint whose celebrated martyrdom (at the hands of uncanny forces which had never been fully explained) had been one of the few bedtime stories that children were allowed to hear, back in the days of the Order.

In fact, the truth was stranger than the fiction. According to records, Jonathan Gift had simply disappeared one day, following an argument with one of his chief stonemasons. The man, whose name was James Carver, had apparently disputed an order from Gift about the design on a marble frieze, and had been heard to threaten Gift on the day he disappeared. The stonemason's temper was well-known, and when later the architect was reported missing, it was assumed that Carver had killed him. Carver denied it – but then, he would. He went to the scaffold denying the crime, by which time Gift's legend was already half established, and the rumours were spreading like wildfire. By the end of the century (Gift's great architectural project had, in fact, taken thirty years, and not the mere seven days of the Order's later version), rumours and stories were all that was left, and no one remembered the man any more.

Now, as Maggie approached the square, she tried to recapture the joy she had felt earlier that morning. The encounter with Maddy had ruined all that. Even the fact that Adam would finally soon be free failed to banish her growing sense that something very wrong was afoot.

Perhaps she sensed it in Adam's face; or in the powdery feel of the air; or even in the cathedral bells – their ringing sounding strangely off-key, like chimes heard underwater.

She glanced up at the sky. Even that had changed: a greenish light now shone from the north-east. Not the dawn, but something else – northlights, perhaps? St Sepulchre's Fire? She could not tell. But she felt the change.

The Red Horse stopped at the cathedral gate, the group of revellers in his wake beginning to disperse at last. The brideys were gone. A little girl who had followed the carriage from Examiners' Walk looked at Maggie and stuck out her tongue.

Adam was already climbing down from the carriage, careful not to mark his white silk.

For a moment Maggie thought she saw a curious expression on his face, and she found herself fighting the urge to ask him if he was *really* sure that this was what he wanted. But that would be to admit to herself that there was still a doubt in her mind; and what kind of bride has doubts about her husband on their wedding day?

Adam looked up at her and smiled. 'Maggie,' he said. 'I owe you so much. How can I ever pay you back?'

He reached out a hand to help her down from the carriage. The Red Horse blew through his nostrils and stamped.

'You really mean that?' Maggie said.

Once more Adam smiled at her. 'Maggie, I'm going to be free,' he said. 'Now we belong to each other. You and me, and our baby.' And he put his arms around her and kissed her softly on the mouth.

In his head a tiny Voice, barely even a whisper, said: *Good.*

'What was that?' Maggie said.

'Just my heart,' he told her.

And with that, the two young people walked hand in hand out of the light and into the great cathedral, where the Kissing Stone of St Sepulchre – the altar that for centuries the Folk of World's End had used and revered without understanding what it *was* – was now finally ready to serve its purpose.

8

THEY WOULD HAVE MADE IT IN TIME, she thought, but for the
fishmonger's barrow. A tempting array of lobsters and prawns,
tastefully bedded on seaweed, on one of the many food stalls at the
far end of Examiners' Walk – precisely the kind of seafood snack
that Jormungand enjoyed the most. In spite of Maddy's entreaties,
he stopped, resumed his Black Horse Aspect, and languidly began
to graze.

'You can't do that now!' Maddy cried. 'You're taking us to
Cathedral Square!'

She glanced at the sky. The light had changed from sunny blue
to uneasy green. It was beautiful, but ominous; a luminous curtain
that hid the sun.

'What's that? Northlights?' Maddy said.

Above her head, Mandy *crawk*-ed: '*Quick! Quick! No time!*'

The Black Horse of the Last Days thoughtfully crunched on a
lobster.

Perth tugged at his bridle, but could not persuade him to move
an inch.

The fishmonger, a thickset young man in a dirty white cap,
eyed them disapprovingly. He didn't much care for foreigners, or
their Outlandish livestock, especially not when they helped themselves to his wares without asking. 'I 'ope you've got money,' he

observed. "Cos it don't cost you anyfink to look, but what you taste gets paid for.'

The Horse whose Rider was Treachery finished the lobsters and started on the prawns.

'I said, I 'ope you can pay fer that,' said the fishmonger in a louder voice.

'Of course we can, my good fellow,' said Perth, reaching into his pocket and bringing out a handful of gold summoned by the money-rune *Fé*.

The fishmonger eyed it suspiciously. 'What kind of money is this?' he said.

'Gold. What does it matter?' said Perth.

'Come on, come *on!*' said Maddy, almost shrieking with frustration.

The fishmonger narrowed his eyes at them, then turned his gaze back to the pieces of gold. Fish-eating horses were one thing, he thought. Even talking birds, at a pinch. But the coins that Perth had just handed him looked like nothing he'd ever seen: four great cartwheels of new-minted gold with an animal on one side and some kind of ruinmark on the reverse.

The fishmonger had no idea what they were. Nor did Maddy – such coins had been out of circulation five hundred years before she was born. Odin, had he been available for consultation, would have told them that this type of coin – it was called an Otter – had been part of the currency of World's End back in the days of the Elder Age. No one had used or seen such coins in five hundred years, and as for these in particular . . .

As the fishmonger watched in surprise, the four pieces of gold suddenly became eight. Then sixteen. Then thirty-two. Gold coins showered onto the ground. The fishmonger, no intellect, frowned at the increasing pile. The money-rune shone merrily from every single gleaming coin.

Perth shrugged apologetically. 'I guess I'm not used to this runemark,' he said, by way of explanation.

'Oy,' said the fishmonger. 'I ain't takin' dodgy gold . . .'

No one paid any attention to him. Jormungand finished the

prawns and belched, then started on the seaweed. The bells of St Sepulchre started to ring. Maddy tugged at the Horse's bridle. 'Jorgi! Please! Come *on!*' she said. 'That means the ceremony's about to start!'

But Perth was looking at the sky. 'We have a situation,' he said.

Maddy followed his gaze. 'Oh.'

The sky was changing once again. A bank of cloud was moving in fast, obliterating the northlights. A dark and swift and ominous cloud, shot through with shards of lightning. And the worst of it was that the cloud was moving, not with the wind, but *against* it.

'We have to go,' said Maddy. 'Now.'

The fishmonger clamped a hand on her arm. 'What about me fish?' he said.

'Damn the fish!' said Perth. 'Let's go!'

The fishmonger's face took on a dangerous expression. *'What did you just say?'* he said, transferring his grip from Maddy's arm to the back of Perth's neck.

Which was why, a second later, when Jormungand resumed his true Aspect, he had acquired an extra passenger. Perth had found himself unable to detach the fishmonger's hand in time and, giving up the struggle, had simply clung on for dear life as Jorgi, making up for lost time, headed for St Sepulchre's Square at twenty times the speed of Dream, arriving only minutes too late. The great cathedral doors were shut and barred with steel from the inside. The last few revellers had dispersed. Even the bells were silent.

'What now?' said Maddy.

Perth shrugged. 'I guess we missed the party.'

He dismounted from Jormungand and went over to the strawberry roan still harnessed to the wedding carriage. The Red Horse gave a whinny and tugged wildly against the harness.

'There, old friend. It's all right.' Perth's voice seemed to have a calming effect, and he was able to free the Red Horse and lead him by his bridle to where Maddy was already waiting.

Anyone else might been deceived by Sleipnir's humble Aspect; but the runelight that surrounded him was quick to reveal his nature. Even without the rune *Bjarkán* Maddy had always known

Odin's Horse, and she was amazed at how easily Perth now managed to handle him.

'Be careful,' she said. 'That's no common Horse.'

Perth shrugged. 'I'm good with horses.'

The fishmonger, who had watched all this in growing alarm and bewilderment, opened his mouth like a landed trout as the Red Horse assumed his true Aspect, his legs becoming spidery, his mane a spray of coloured lights.

'What about me fish?' he said, clinging in desperation to the only reality he knew.

'Sorry. There's no time for that,' said Perth, getting onto Sleipnir's back. 'Now I can only suggest you run. As far and as fast as you possibly can.'

'Perth . . . ?' said Maddy uncertainly.

Perth looked down at her and grinned. And perhaps it was that grin, she thought – or the wink that accompanied it, or the Horse – but at that moment he reminded her so much of the One-Eye of her childhood that she almost forgot to breathe. She said: *'You're* the Rider of Carnage?'

Perth shrugged. 'Who else?'

'But Sleipnir belongs to—'

'Grim,' said Perth, and looked beyond her at the sky.

And then there came an almighty *crash* as the sky split open and something appeared against the mass of approaching cloud. A rainbow, but so much brighter than any rainbow Maddy had ever seen, and in its band of colours she saw the signatures of the Æsir and the Vanir in their original Aspects, riding the sky as if Ragnarók had never even happened.

'Blimey,' said the fishmonger, and promptly followed Perth's advice. In seconds he had disappeared, leaving Maddy still staring at her friend, now looking very much at ease astride the Red Horse of Carnage.

'What the Hel?' said Maddy to Perth. 'And how do you even *know* that name?'

Perth sighed. 'I may be experiencing a few . . . adjustment difficulties, but I do remember my names,' he said. 'And besides, if you'd done as you were told, we wouldn't have to deal with all this.'

Maddy's eyes grew wide. 'What?'

'I guess I should have known,' he said. 'Your record's hardly unblemished when it comes to following orders.'

Maddy continued to stare at Perth. She found that in spite of everything that was happening around her, she could not take her eyes off him.

She cast the rune *Bjarkán* and saw, entwined in his rose-red signature, a skein of brilliant kingfisher-blue that she would have recognized anywhere.

Perth's grin broadened a notch. Now it looked as wide as a road. His blue eyes gleamed with wicked humour, and this time there could be no doubt: his features might belong to Perth, but that smile belonged to Odin.

'Odin? It can't be. You were dead . . .'

Perth shrugged. 'It's happened before. Why else do you think I have so many names? Aspects come, Aspects go – this time I was lucky enough to find an Aspect that suited me, *and* with a brand-new runemark, just when I happened to need it most . . .'

For a moment Maddy was torn between joy and speechless horror. Joy that Odin had survived – but at what price? Perth was her friend. If Odin possessed him against his will, then he was no better than the Whisperer. And though Maddy's affection for One-Eye ran deep, she sensed that he was capable of worse things than helping himself to another person's body if his own happened to be unavailable.

'What about Perth?' she demanded.

Sarcastically: 'I'm fine, thanks.'

'How did you even get *in* there?'

Perth – or was it Odin? – shrugged. 'How do you think I got in?' he said. 'The usual way. Dreams, of course. *The slave dreams of being master*.' He looked at Maddy. 'What?' he said. 'Did you think I'd enslaved your friend? Thanks for the vote of confidence.'

Once more he glanced at the view overhead. The rainbow was spectacular – a double arc of runelight with the Sun Shield on its brow. Beyond it, the bank of cloud still approached, stitched through with points of lightning.

'Maddy' he said, 'Perth isn't *gone*, any more than Ethel Parson or any of the others are gone. Ethel gave the Seeress her runemark and her name. No one can do that against their will. Perth and I have been linked for years in Dream – you even sensed me once. Remember the very first time we met? You thought you saw something in my signature. You thought I looked familiar . . .'

'I thought you looked like Loki,' she said.

'We're brothers,' said Perth. 'What did you expect?'

Maddy gave a long sigh. 'Please. Tell me what happened,' she said.

'What, *now?*' Perth looked at the sky. 'Is this really the time, do you think?'

'I need to know,' Maddy said. 'I need to know who you really are.'

'Always with the questions,' said Perth. 'Well, I was trapped in that damned Head. Trapped and floating around in Dream. And so I sent you to find me. We both know how *that* worked out. There was a little unpleasantness, during which I was briefly reacquainted with my old friend Mimir the Wise. Your sister Maggie tortured me. She's very like you, by the way. Nice girl, if highly strung. She made me give her the New Script. I issued my instructions to you – which you ignored, as per usual. Then I sent Hugin and Munin to find Perth and bring him to me. After which – you know the rest.'

'But what about my sister?' said Maddy. 'You said – *Perth* said —'

'Your sister found the Head just as you did,' said Perth, a trifle impatiently. 'I imagine the discovery led her to jump to the same conclusion. In any case, she never guessed that I'd simply vacated the premises for something a little more comfortable. And now for the final chapter. I'm assuming you've studied the prophecy?'

Sleipnir responded by shaking his mane and pawing the ground frantically. Jorgi, who until then had been calm, now seemed to respond to Sleipnir, blowing through his nostrils and shaking his mane of runelight. Maddy put a soothing hand on his flank, just as Hughie and Mandy, who had been following Jormungand at a distance, came in to land in Cathedral Square.

'General!' said Hughie to Perth.

Kaik, said Mandy. *Kaik. Kaik.*

Perth put a hand in his pocket and came up with a Fat Boy. He tossed it to Mandy, who caught it, then he looked down at Maddy again. 'Maddy, please. Just get on your Horse.'

Kaik.

'Do it, Maddy,' he said.

Maddy obeyed. 'What's going *on?*' she said plaintively, trying to calm the Horse of the Sea, who, sensing her agitation, was growling and shaking his slimy mane, showing his appalling teeth.

'Tribulation,' Hughie said.

'*Kaik,*' said Mandy happily.

'We don't have time to discuss it,' said Perth. 'The enemy is on the way. The rest of the gods – if they made it this far – are about to come up against Chaos itself – Dream in its purest, most deadly form – so for the moment let's just assume that I know what I'm doing, shall we?'

'And do you?' said Maddy.

'No,' said Perth.

After which no one said anything much, because that was when Maggie kissed the Stone, the Gødfolk arrived, and all Hel broke loose.

9

'WHAT IN HEL IS GOING *ON*?' yelled Loki, clinging onto the Bridge, while attempting to dislodge Njörd from his back. 'I appreciate the gesture, Njörd, but if you could just get your claws out of me . . .'

But as he spoke, the Man of the Sea had already regained his Aspect. His *true* Aspect, runemark intact, and clothed in the traditional garb – blue scale tunic and harpoon – in which the Folk had always pictured him.

'That's going to leave a mark,' Loki said, peering at his shoulder; then, looking down at himself and back across at his colleagues, he grinned. 'Oh,' he said. 'Oh *yes.*'

Dream, of course, has no physical laws. Anything is possible. In Dream the ravages of Time, even of Death, can be reversed. And Bif-rost was a thing of dreams, born of the rift from Red Horse Hill, bearing the party of demons and gods at phenomenal speed out of Hel's domain.

Now all of them were just like Njörd: runes unreversed, unblemished, young. Clad in their age-old Aspects once more – the Reaper with his gleaming sword; the Huntress with her runewhip; Thor with Mjølnir in his hand; Freyja shining like the sun. Ethel was no longer drab. Nan Fey was no longer old. Sif (who was no longer dumpy) was radiant with happiness; Bragi's guitar was back in tune; even Idun, who was not usually moved by ordinary

479

events, looked more focused than usual, flinging handfuls of flowers in the wake of the speeding rainbow.

Tyr, in his Aspect as god of war, was fully armoured in red and gold, and the hand that Fenris had bitten off, back in the days of the Elder Age, was now a mindweapon in its own right, a glamorous gauntlet of runic power that hissed and sizzled with energy.

Angrboda, whose nature as a child of Chaos permitted her to take any form she chose, was much the same as she always was; but Fenris, Skull and Big H had taken to their wolf forms. Bigger and badder than ever in Dream, there was nothing clumsy about them now; nothing remotely amusing. Their teeth were as long as a man's forearm, their fur was electric with runelight. Tyr, who, though taller than usual, still had Sugar's cautious approach, took several steps backwards on seeing them and almost fell off the Rainbow Bridge.

The best part, from Loki's perspective, was that he was no longer a prisoner. The fine gold chain that bound his wrist had vanished, though the Wedlock remained, now in the form of a simple gold ring that shone from his middle finger, and that no amount of twisting could remove.

Sigyn was standing by his side, dressed in sensible green and grey, the runemark *Eh* gleaming from her brow. In this Aspect she was beautiful, and Loki found himself vaguely surprised that he had never noticed it before.

He tried a single cantrip. His runemark gave a burst of glam, and a corresponding stream of light shot out like a flare in their wake.

'I like it!' he said, grinning again. 'If I'm going to die today, the least I can do is look *fabulous* while I'm doing it.'

Ethel gave him a quelling look. 'Save your glam,' she advised him. 'We're going to need every spark of it.'

Loki squinted at the black cloud still following them out of Hel. 'Right. I get the point,' he said. 'So – where are we going, exactly?'

'We're going to fulfil my prophecy. So far I think it's been reasonably clear—'

'*Clear*?' said Loki. 'Clear how?'

Ethel gave him a mischievous smile. 'How does it feel to be kept in the dark?'

Loki made a rude gesture.

'Be nice and she'll tell you,' Sigyn said.

'All right, all right.'

Once more Ethel smiled. '*I see a mighty Ash that stands beside a mighty Oak tree*. We already know who the Ash is, of course, and very soon we'll be meeting the Oak. Both are instrumental in the rebuilding of Asgard. *I see a Rainbow riding high; of cheating Death the legacy*. That part, as I'm sure you know, refers to recent events in Hel.'

Loki scowled. 'That much, at least, was very clear,' he said in a tone of exaggerated politeness. 'I was the bait with which you planned to lure Hel into breaking her oath, which in its turn would release Dream into the Worlds in full force – with which force I'm assuming *you* – presumably, with the General's help – propose to rebuild Asgard. Nice' – he gave her a dark look – 'if a little . . . *risky*.'

Loki silently promised himself that if he ever saw the General again, Odin would get a piece of his mind. This was twice that the General had colluded with a stratagem that involved handing Loki over to his enemies just before Ragnarók. Neither occasion had been pleasant. And if past history was anything to go by, the next twenty-four hours would probably end in the death of the gods, the End of the Worlds and a great deal of unnecessary noise. Right now the Trickster felt that what he really needed most was a dose of peace and harmony, preferably on an island somewhere, with hammocks and lots of pretty girls.

Ethel went on with the prophecy: '*But Treachery and Carnage ride with Lunacy across the sky. And when the 'bow breaks, the Cradle will fall—*'

'Which I don't like the sound of at all,' Loki said. 'So if you could maybe drop me off before all the treachery and carnage begin—'

'Too late,' said Ethel, not without sympathy. 'Tribulation has already begun. We have no choice but to stand and fight, and to hope that the General's plan works out.'

'The General's plan . . . I thought as much.'

There was a long and ominous pause as the Trickster reassessed events. He should have known, he told himself, that he wouldn't escape so easily. He hoped that when the General finally made his appearance, his current Aspect would at least turn out to be something unappealing – a pig, a disembodied Head, or perhaps a toothless old woman. That would be payback, Loki thought. That might make them about square.

Around them, the scenery blurred and spun and finally stopped moving as the Bridge across the Firmament, which spans all Worlds at the speed of Dream, settled itself into position in the sky above the cathedral, once known as the Cradle of the gods, and now the site of the End of the Worlds or, as the Folk called it, *Apocalypse*.

'Apocalypse,' said Loki at last. 'What kind of a word *is* that, anyway?'

BOOK NINE

Asgard

The End of the World always starts with a kiss.

Lokabrenna, 19:12

1

FOR A MOMENT MAGGIE WAS STUNNED by the sheer size and splendour of the cathedral. The famous glass dome, which from outside looked like a dish-cover made of tarnished brass, was as different from the inside as she could ever have imagined. The sunlight streamed in from the ceiling through a thousand – ten thousand – panes of cut glass, cleverly angled to catch the light at every conceivable time of day. Maggie had never seen diamonds, but if she had she might have been reminded of a giant multi-faceted gem that scattered light over the walls and arches and pillars and floors of the great cathedral, making it a place of light even on the dullest of days.

Today it was especially radiant, every pane shooting prisms and rainbows, so that Adam, in his white suit, was a harlequin of reds and greens, and Maggie, who was not often given to levity, laughed out loud in delight as she saw the solemn cathedral lit up like a magic-lantern show.

The place was almost empty. No guests had been invited, of course, and Adam had paid a premium for the cathedral to be closed for the fifteen minutes of the ceremony. Only the folk who worked the organ and a few cathedral staff – the Confessor in his wooden box, the Shriver with his long black gloves, and the Steward with his pouch and bell – joined the Bishop as witnesses.

The Machina Brava, an organ so large that it needed five men

485

to play it, dated back almost to Tribulation, and Maggie watched with curiosity as the great pipes – each one as tall as a tree and carved with runes from head to foot – began to shiver and resonate as the machinists plied the levers and wheels that would coax the Machina Brava to life.

The organ emitted a squealing sound, then a series of belches. It was an ancient, temperamental thing, but when it finally found its voice it was like nothing Maggie had ever heard before. It was like a forest of trees given voice; like the sea; like voices from the dead. It awed her; and it was with a new timidity that she stepped up with Adam to the Kissing Stone, where the Bishop was waiting to bless them both.

Her veil caught on the buckle of one of her shoes. She struggled to release it. She was suddenly filled with a sense of panic, an urgency to have it done; for everything to be over.

The Bishop spoke. 'We are gathered here today to unite two young folk in wedlock. Adam Goodwin and Maggie Rede – take your places before the Stone.'

Adam and Maggie exchanged a look. Maggie tried to smile. Soon it would be over, she thought. Soon she and Adam would be free to begin their new life together, as one.

Mimir the Wise had been waiting for this since long before Tribulation. His plans had been thwarted once before, but his giant ambition had never waned. Now the moment had almost come when Mimir the Wise would take his place among the ranks of the Æsir; the culmination of five hundred years of hate and thwarted ambition – his enemies vanquished, his kingdom rebuilt, himself reborn as Allfather.

And all this with a single kiss . . .

The Kissing Stone of St Sepulchre was larger than Maggie had expected. A piece of black volcanic rock, five feet thick and twelve feet high, and inscribed, like the pipes of the organ, with runes that ran up and down its surface like neat little columns of ants, too small for Maggie to decipher. On the near surface, a smoother patch marked the spot that had earned the Kissing Stone its name: for five hundred years pilgrims and penitents, brides and grooms had kissed the place in which a mark – like a stone kiss – had been cut deeply into the rock.

And now the Bishop read aloud the ancient wedding canticle. Maggie and Adam repeated the words – Adam's voice trembling a little, Maggie's clear and confident:

'*My hand to your hand,*
My soul to your soul . . .

Of course, it had never occurred to Maggie that, like everything in the Good Book, that simple little canticle might be a thing of power. To Maggie, it was just a tradition, like the brideys and the wedding dress. The Whisperer knew better, of course, and its fierce old heart rejoiced.

'*My name to your name,*
For ever, one.'

'Now you may kiss the Stone,' said the Bishop, a middle-aged, ambitious man, who, like the Shriver, the Confessor, the Steward and the five machinists, now had only seconds to live.

Maggie knelt to kiss the Stone. It felt curiously warm to her touch, as of some vestige of heat remained from the long-dead fires of its creation. There was a kind of vibration too; and a hum like that of a hive of bees, which moved up through her fingertips and set her heart a-fluttering.

She looked up at Adam and saw him transfixed. Her young heart swelled with happiness. All the doubts she'd ever had – her fears, her insecurities – vanished as she saw Adam's face illuminated with rapture.

Of course, Adam's joy had nothing to do with making his vows to Maggie. But *something* had happened, all the same; something that made him want to shout and scream and dance like a savage.

After three years of slavery the Whisperer was finally gone. *Gone for ever*, Adam thought. *No more darkness. No more dreams—*

He looked down at his new wife and almost didn't hate her. His eyes were bright, his face was flushed, he felt reborn to perfect bliss.

Maggie kissed the Stone . . .

And then—

All these things happened at once:

The glass dome of St Sepulchre split right down the middle, revealing a sky that in its turn was split into halves, one dark, one bright, with Bif-rost as the dividing line, like a shield against the night.

A sound like the slamming of every door that had ever existed in the World erupted into the cathedral.

A single titanic bolt of glam shot out from the heart of the Kissing Stone, sending a ripple of runic energy to all points of the compass at once. At the same time a beam of light emerged from the carving that looked so much like a kiss . . .

And the Bishop, his colleagues – in fact, every living being in the place, with just one single exception – instantly collapsed to the ground, nose and ears gushing blood. The Bishop was dead in a second, along with the Confessor, the machinists, the Shriver, the cathedral's substantial colony of rats – and, of course, Adam Scattergood, who had just enough time to remind himself to *never trust an oracle* before he was expelled from his body with the force of a crossbow bolt and projected towards the surging black cloud that had already swallowed half the sky, and which, with his new-found perspective, he could now identify as Dream in its most chaotic Aspect – known to the Folk as Pan-daemonium, the World of Countless Demons.

2

THERE'S A SAYING AMONG THE Inland Folk: *Sticks and stones will break my bones, but words can never slay me.* How ridiculous, Loki thought as he watched the approaching cloud. Words were far from harmless. A well-placed word can bring down a foe; a speech can take down an empire. The Trickster knew the power of words – they'd saved his life a thousand times – but he also knew that, like himself, words could be misleading. They liked to hide, to reverse themselves, to warp and turn into something else.

Take that word: *Apocalypse.* Passed down through generations of Folk; a word of power and mystery, the sense of it lost over the years until only the children knew what it meant, in skipping songs and playground games:

See the Cradle rocking
High above the town . . .
Pucker-lips, a-pucker-lips,
All fall down.

Once more Loki considered the black cloud. It wasn't really a cloud, he knew, any more than Dream was a river, but there was a kind of comfort in being able to see it as something familiar. Its shadow, now less than a mile away, had already breached the city walls. In the shadow there was a void. The shadow eclipsed everything.

He glanced over at the parapet of the Bridge, where Æsir and Vanir waited and watched. None of them were talkative. Thor's Hammer was at the ready; Frey stood by with his mindsword. Freyja was in her Carrion form, bat-winged and skull-headed. Even Sif was in armour. Skadi and Njörd stood side by side with Angie and her demon wolves. Ethel waited to give the word as soon as action was required. Sigyn was standing behind her, her rune *Eh* at the ready in the shape of a golden binding rope very like Skadi's runewhip.

All looked tense but focused, waiting in that oppressive silence that heralds the bloodiest battles.

Only Tyr seemed uncertain. Outwardly resplendent in his Aspect as god of war, he was still Sugar-and-Sack at heart, and the red and gold of his signature was tinged with the grey of anxiety. He glanced at Loki nervously. 'What are we waiting for?' he said.

Loki shrugged. 'Why ask me? *I'm* not in charge. If I were, I'd be running like Hel, instead of awaiting the inevitable.'

Sugar looked even more nervous. 'You mean – you think we can't possibly win?'

'Sure we can.' Loki grinned. 'With a couple of armies, a fortress, perhaps – and maybe a flying pig or two?'

'Oh,' said Sugar.

'Feel better now?'

'Not as such.'

Ethel smiled. 'It won't be long now.'

'And that's a *good* thing?' said Loki. 'Look, you *said* you had a plan. In fact, you mentioned the *General's* plan. So, if you *have* the General tucked away somewhere – which I very much doubt – now's the time to reveal him. Otherwise, running sounds good.'

'Too late for that,' said Ethel. 'Besides, I trust the General.'

'Well, I have issues with trust,' said Loki. 'Especially where my life is concerned.'

Sigyn, who had followed all this with the indulgent look of a nursery nurse looking after a fractious patient, now put a hand on Loki's arm. 'I'll look after you,' she said. 'There's nothing to be afraid of.'

'Well, that's terrific,' said Loki. 'Because *nothing*' – he pointed at the cloud – 'is exactly what's coming after us. And— *What in Hel is that?*'

For just at that moment there came a blinding burst of light and a massive explosion that rocked the Bridge, throwing Æsir and Vanir off-balance and vaporizing the few white clouds that marked the sky under Bif-rost. Loki flung himself onto his belly with his hands over his head. Thor gave a snarl of rage and prepared to wield Mjølnir. Sugar-and-Sack was astonished to find his new, glamorous hand working by itself, mindsword at the ready.

Ethel simply smiled, and said: 'Good.'

'Why? What's happening?' Loki said. 'Are we under attack?'

'No.' She shook her head. 'Not yet. But soon. Which is why, when we get the signal, we are going to have to work quickly.'

'Doing what?' Sugar said.

'Building,' said Ethel. 'As fast as we can, because when that shadowcloud gets here, we're going to need protection.'

At that, Loki's eyes began to gleam. A slow smile touched his scarred lips. He looked up at the shadowcloud, now only a few dozen feet away. Soon it would be on top of them, eclipsing the light from the Sun Shield, obliterating the runelight that shone from the heart of the Kissing Stone. They might be able to hold it back for five or ten minutes, maximum. But whether that would be enough . . .

'Building,' said Sugar. 'Building what?'

'Asgard,' said Loki softly, and grinned.

3

OUTSIDE THE CATHEDRAL, Maddy and Perth raced for cover as glass showered down over the streets like hail. Above them stood the Rainbow Bridge, the one remaining barrier between Order and Pan-daemonium. Looking over her shoulder now, Maddy could see the shadowcloud; a wall of darkness at her back, moving inexorably towards the cathedral.

Once, when she was ten years old, Maddy had seen an eclipse of the sun. Others had stayed in their houses, afraid, or had huddled together in the church as Nat Parson told them bastardized tales of demon wolves that ran through the sky. But One-Eye had explained it to her: the movements of the sun and moon, and the dance they performed together. How quickly it had moved, she thought. How quickly the moon's shadow had raced across the valley. And how *cold* it had been, she remembered; how cold and strange the light had been as the sun turned to blood at midday.

The shadowcloud was not as fast. And yet she could see it approaching – moving as fast as a man can walk – towards the ruined cathedral. Both she and Perth could outrun it, she knew: Perth was mounted on Sleipnir; Maddy was riding Jormungand – and getting the worst of the deal, she thought, because though Sleipnir simply *looked* freakish, Jormungand *smelled* terrible.

But Maggie was still in the building – dead or alive, she did not know – and inside, the Kissing Stone still shone, projecting a column of dazzling light towards the heart of the rainbow, where the Sun Shield caught its rays and projected them outwards like a cradle in the sky.

Perth flung up the rune *Yr* as a shield against the blinding light; Maddy did the same with *Ác*, the rune she had learned from her sister.

They came to a halt some distance away in one of the side streets off Cathedral Square, from which they were able to observe the collapse of the dome of St Sepulchre and everything that followed it. On every side, the Folk of World's End clutched at their gushing noses and fell to their knees as the aftershock of what had occurred at the Kissing Stone reverberated throughout the Universal City, bringing carnage in its wake.

Some, closest to the centre, died. Most had survived the initial attack, but were seized with panic and, seeing the sky, ran for their homes, or went insane, or fled raving in search of someone to blame. Some blamed the Faërie; others the old gods; others the wave of foreigners. Some fell to their knees and prayed, remembering tales of the Bliss. Shops were looted; people were robbed, old scores settled under cover of Chaos.

Disaster always strengthens faith, and in the city the old beliefs that had been so quickly eclipsed by greed now returned to new life. Mrs Blackmore, Maggie's old landlady, rapidly rediscovered prayer, donned a black *bergha* and fled through the streets, screaming that this was Last Days, and that everyone should repent or be Cleansed. The lawman who had arrested Perth remembered the girl on the Red Horse, and called his remaining colleagues to arms. The Outlanders and traders who had settled themselves so comfortably in the old University found themselves being attacked on all sides by native World's Enders, who, like most people in crisis, afraid and in need of a scapegoat, had decided to punish the foreigners for the coming Apocalypse.

And in the middle of it all Perth simply sat on his Horse and smiled like a gambler wagering his last coin.

It was a look that Maddy knew – she'd last seen it on Odin three years ago, on the shores of Hel – and she knew only too well what it meant.

She glanced at the ruined cathedral, shielding her eyes from the column of light. 'What happened?' she said. 'Is my sister dead?'

It seemed more than likely: the building was wrecked, its dome collapsed like a rotten egg. No movement came from the rubble; and, looking through *Bjarkán* at the scene, Maddy could see no signatures, no sign of anything left alive; just that eerie finger of light pointing into the turbulent sky . . .

And then there it was, that fugitive gleam, shining through the drifting dust. The colour of Maggie's presence, her glam, silvery-white against the destruction. Heart pounding, Maddy moved to urge Jormungand towards the source of the signature—

'Don't,' said Perth.

'Why not?'

'Just don't.' He looked more than ever like Odin now. 'You disobeyed me once before, and all the Worlds will pay the price. But forsake your duty now, and everything we've worked for is lost. Your sister's alive. Be glad of it. If you want her to stay that way, then we have a prophecy to fulfil.'

'But I thought that my *sister* was meant to be the Rider whose name was Carnage. The Seeress practically said so!'

'Never trust an oracle.' Now he had Odin's voice too; Maddy's eyes began to sting. 'Your sister's part in this is done. For good or ill, the child of hate has opened the gate to Asgard. Our job now is to protect it.'

'How do you know?' Maddy said.

'Because I was dead,' Perth replied, 'and that gives quite a unique perspective on things. Now, if you don't have any more questions—'

Maddy looked up into the sky. 'I don't understand. How could my sister have done all this? She was only here to get *married*.'

Perth shrugged. 'You think so?' he said. He gestured towards the cathedral. '*The Cradle fell an age ago, but Fire and Folk shall raise her; in just twelve days, at End of Worlds; a gift within the sepulchre.*

'*Cathedral. Cradle.* Such similar words. You think that was just a

494

coincidence? And what about the architect? Where do you *think* Jonathan Gift found the means to build this place? And who do you think instructed him?'

Maddy's eyes widened. 'The Whisperer?'

Perth nodded. 'Exactly,' he said. 'The Universal City wasn't just built *on* the ruins of Asgard. It was built *from* the ruins of Asgard. And the thing you Folk call the Kissing Stone – inscribed all over with runes of power – *that* was the First Stone of Asgard, the Foundation Stone of the Sky Citadel, linked through Bif-rost, the Rainbow Bridge, to every one of the Nine Worlds.'

He frowned at Maddy impatiently. 'For five hundred years that stone has lain here, waiting for someone to awaken it. Jonathan Gift knew what he had. He made sure the Stone was kept safe, deep in the heart of the city. For centuries the Order guarded it, not understanding what it was. But the Nameless understood. It knew, and it watched, and bided its time, waiting for someone to come along – someone with sufficient glam to speak the Word and release the power.'

Maddy stared. 'My sister,' she said. 'But why would the Nameless – the Whisperer – *want* to rebuild Asgard?'

'To own it for itself, of course,' said Perth with a twisted smile. 'In spite of all his power in World's End, Mimir was a prisoner. Bodiless and robbed of his glam, he could never hope to escape. Ending the Worlds was one way out; but far better, if he could manage it, was to steal an Aspect from one of us, and use it to get into Asgard.'

'One of *us*?'

He nodded. 'That's right. Preferably someone like you, whose rune was intact and full of power. He tried with you in Hel, and failed. But now—'

'He has my sister?' she said.

Perth put a hand on her arm. 'There's nothing you can do any more. Maggie gave herself willingly. She spoke the words on the Kissing Stone; the words inscribed for that purpose over five hundred years ago. And then she sealed the oath with a kiss . . .' He sketched the runesign in the air—

495

'Which also happens to be a rune – *Gabe* – a gift, in the language of the Elder Age. Though it's more than likely that her gift will end up being the death of us all.'

'Is that a prophecy?' Maddy said.

'No. An educated guess. So now – suppose we do our job? We have a citadel to build, and she can't be a part of it.'

Stubbornly Maddy shook her head. 'That thing has taken my sister,' she said. 'There's no way I'm going to leave her like this.'

Perth made an impatient sound. Now he looked like the One-Eye of the old days in one of his blackest, foulest moods. 'How obtuse can you be?' he snapped. 'There's nothing you can do for her. She's lost to us now. What's done is done. And both of us have a job to do. This glam is a gift to the Æsir . . .' He indicated the column of light that had been released from the Kissing Stone. 'We can use it to fight the enemy. To arm ourselves – to rebuild our fortress – or we can watch it be consumed while you waste time in sentiment . . .'

But Maddy was barely listening. 'I fought the Whisperer before. I can do it again,' she said. 'Together, we can cast it out.' Her heart was pounding. 'It's worth a try!'

Perth glared. 'Damn you,' he said. 'Are you going to betray me *again*?'

Maddy held his gaze. 'I can't abandon my sister,' she said. 'If Mimir has her—'

'He doesn't,' he said.

'But you just told me—'

'I *said* she gave herself willingly. But she was never the main prize. The Whisperer tried to control her once. It knew it couldn't possess her. It knew that she – or *you* – would expel it long before it reached Asgard.

'So what's the problem?' said Maddy, confused. 'If it *doesn't* have Maggie after all, then why does she have to be lost to us?'

But Perth never got the chance to answer Maddy's question,

because just then there came a sound and a movement from the ruined dome. For a moment she hardly recognized the approaching figure as Maggie Rede. Her yellow veil was black with dust, her face blank and blurry with tears and soot. She climbed out from the debris, eyes fixed on the stony ground, moving as slowly and carefully as if she were a hundred years old. Grief and rage marked her signature in lurid shades of green and red.

'Maddy, trust me,' Perth said. 'You *really* don't want to be part of this.'

But Maddy wasn't listening. She stepped away from the Serpent's flank and softly spoke her sister's name.

Slowly Maggie lifted her head. A pair of grey-gold eyes met hers. For a moment Oak and Ash stood face to face under Bif-rost.

Then Maggie's eyes lost their blurry look and acquired a deadly focus. A smile of peculiar sweetness came over her ravaged features.

'Run. *Now*,' Perth said, kicking his heels into Sleipnir's flanks.

But it was already too late. Maggie's eyes fixed on the General. The runemark at the back of her neck flared with sudden brilliance.

'You killed Adam, demon,' she said, and the rune *Ác*, crossed with *Úr* and *Hagall*, whickered through the dusty air. Perth's reflexes were fast – and, combined with Odin's lifelong skills, the result was impressive.

Perth, combined with *Raedo* and *Úr*, deflected the mindbolt against a wall, and Maddy had just enough time to admire the deftness with which her old friend handled the runes before he went on the offensive, fanning out a handful of runes with astonishing speed and power towards the source of the attack.

So this is what he used to be like before his runemark was reversed, thought Maddy, just as the mindbolt struck, showering Maggie with shards of glam. And with that thought came the certainty that Perth would try to kill Maggie – just as *she* would try to kill *him*, if Maddy did not intervene.

'You killed Adam,' said Maggie again, and hurled another handful of runes. The runes were unskilled but effective, each one breaking into small, sharp pieces, scattering potent little missiles across the whole area. A stray shard hit. Perth in the face, and he slumped across his saddle-bow.

Sleipnir took to the air at once, long legs straddling the sky, so that Maddy had no time to see where or how badly Perth was hit. She flung up a shield to protect herself; *Aesk* and *Yr* dispersed the glam. She knew she ought to get away – Perth was hurt, and needed help. But still she couldn't leave Maggie.

'Maggie, please. Let me explain—'

'You killed Adam,' Maggie said. Her voice was dull and expressionless. It was as if the grief of her loss had burned the heart right out of her.

'I *didn't* kill him!' Maddy said. 'I wanted to, but I couldn't. You saw—'

'*Why?*' said Maggie. 'Did you hate us so much?'

'No!' said Maddy desperately. 'I wanted to save you – to stop all this. Nobody *wanted* Adam to die . . .'

Stubbornly Maggie shook her head. 'Oh yes they did. They wanted him dead because he was a man of the Folk. Because he was in love with me. And because I'm pregnant with his child—'

His child? Oh gods. My sister's child?

Suddenly Maddy could hardly breathe. She understood now what Perth had meant when he'd said that Maggie was lost to them. Maggie Rede had never been the Whisperer's primary target. The girl was already too strong, too volatile to serve as a host. But her unborn child – a child of the Fire, with glam passed down from its mother's side – would be wide open and easy to shape. Its character, as yet unformed, would become that of the Whisperer. And Maggie, of course, would be there to protect her child from any who threatened it – which meant that the Whisperer's Aspect was safe until its powers were fully grown.

Maddy's voice grew urgent now. 'Maggie, you have to listen to me. The Whisperer has possessed your child. It means to use it – and you too – to get back into Asgard.'

But Maggie wasn't listening. A double fistful of mindrunes flew like razor-blades and peppered the wall around Maddy's shield. 'You're lying!' she said in a harsh voice. 'First Adam, and now my baby as well! I wish I'd killed you when I had the chance! I wish I'd killed *all* the Seer-folk!'

Once more Maddy tried to reason with her sister, but in her heart she knew that she'd already lost. Maggie was working on a rune that would cut through her mindshield. A combination of *Úr* and *Hagall* took shape between her fingers.

Behind her, the shadowcloud had reached the walls of the cathedral. Massive, it stood at Maggie's back, hissing with destructive energy.

'Get away from the shadow!' Maddy said. 'Maggie, whether you trust me or not, don't go near the shadowcloud!'

Maggie flung the weapon at her. It broke against the mindshield. Wild-eyed, she started again, summoning her strongest glam.

Maddy tried to work out in her mind the distance back to Jormungand. She could make it in thirty seconds, she thought, as long as the mindshield held that long. She cast a version of *Aesk,* and sent a handful of jagged little runes spinning out like sycamore keys. Their purpose was not to harm, but to confuse, to buy herself a little time. One of them sliced across Maggie's palm, making her flinch and look away, and in that second, Maddy leaped on Jorgi's back and spurred him into action. Above them, the arch of the Rainbow Bridge. Below them, a city in chaos.

And at the centre of it all, the light from the Kissing Stone still shone against the Sun Shield, pinning World's End like an insect, and Maggie Rede hurled runes at the sky and swore vengeance against the Æsir, while in her belly something so small that it barely had a heartbeat smiled and whispered to itself, and dreamed of Worlds to conquer.

4

PERTH REACHED BIF-ROST JUST IN time to witness the onset of Chaos. Not that he saw very much at first: the bolt that Maggie had thrown at him had struck him squarely in the face, and for most of his flight he had had to rely on Sleipnir to guide him home. His eyes hurt, but as he approached, he found that he was not blind, although it took him some time to understand what it was he was seeing.

The inky cloud had become a wall that towered over the Rainbow Bridge, its dark mass dwarfing the sprawl of World's End. On one side of the Bridge there was light; the other was nothing but shadow, its furious depths filled with turbulence and roiling with ephemera. It was impressive; even the General, who had witnessed Aspects of Chaos before, had never seen such a concentration over such an enormous area. Ten thousand times as potent as the dreamcloud erupting from Red Horse Hill, this was the raw stuff of all the Worlds, the wellspring of Destruction and Creation, which starts in Chaos and finds its place, sometimes after millions of years, as a natural part of the Order of things.

On the parapet of the Bridge, the gods had begun to mount their defence – Æsir on the right side, Vanir on the other; both sides working frantically to hold back the approach of the cloud. Bragi sang a song of war that scattered musical shrapnel. Njörd set up a sea wall. Tyr flexed the fingers of his new hand. Hawk-Eyed

500

Heimdall, with his glass, charted the path of the enemy. Thor, with Mjølnir in his hand, swept a deadly arc through the air. Idun stood by with her healing kit; Skadi mounted an ice-shield. In the centre stood Angie, with her wolves on either side – Skól the Devourer to her left, Haiti and Fenris to her right – the Temptress herself in her Hag Aspect: ancient, skeletal and cold.

The shadowcloud was very close now. Thirty feet away, maybe less. A mindbolt flung against it slowed its pace by a second or two; after which it began its approach again, sending out ephemeral tendrils towards the little group of gods. These tendrils could be cut, Perth knew; mindswords and rune-staves would do it but the shadowcloud was capable of generating so much more, and, including himself, the defenders of Worlds only numbered twenty-one.

Half blinded by Maggie's mindbolt, Perth reined in Sleipnir on the bright side of the Bridge. Hugin and Munin, in raven form, wheeled and *crawk*-ed around him. Perth touched his eyes with his hand. The fingers came away red, and now he could feel the clean, shallow cut that ran between his left eyebrow and cheekbone. The eye was swollen shut. It hurt; still, he knew it could have been worse. He tore off a piece of his shirt and made a pad and a bandage to keep it in place. Ethel came to help him; there was no time for celebration now, but her look told him all he needed to know.

He smiled. 'It's been a long time.'

'Longer for the rest of us.'

Meanwhile Loki, whose contribution to Bif-rost's defence had been from the safer side of the Bridge, came over to see what was going on. Anyone else might have been reasonably chastened by recent events, but the Trickster was in high spirits, his eyes gleaming maliciously, his scarred lips stretched in a broad grin.

'Welcome to the party,' he said. 'I hope you brought a bottle.'

Perth gave a reluctant smile. The Trickster could be annoying, he thought, but still, it was good to see him again. 'So how was Hel?'

'You should know.' Loki gave him a dark look. 'Nice Aspect, by the way.' He jerked his head at the wall of cloud. 'So, I'm told you have a plan?'

'Of sorts,' responded Perth.

'Of *sorts*? What the Hel does that mean?'

'Well, it hasn't exactly been tested yet.' Perth shrugged. 'But as you know, I'm at my best when I'm being creative.'

'Terrific,' said Loki. 'So – when do we start?'

There was a slightly uncomfortable pause. Then Perth said, 'Well, that's the thing.'

'The *thing*?' demanded the Trickster.

'I'm waiting for one more development,' said Perth, in a casual voice. 'We have almost everything in place – the Bridge, the building blocks of Dream, the Sun Shield, the runes from the First Stone of Asgard – all we need now is Carnage, Madness and Treachery, and we'll have ourselves a construction team.' He gave his broadest, most brilliant smile.

Loki knew that smile of old. He'd seen it too many times before – and in too many unpleasant situations – to believe that it promised anything good. 'Hang on,' he said. 'If that's the case – we already have Sleipnir and Epona. So – where's Jorgi? And Maddy, of course—'

'They'll be here any second now.'

'Really?' said Loki, peering down over the Bridge's parapet. 'Because I don't know if you'd noticed, but things aren't looking too good down there.'

Loki was right. The End of the Worlds had finally come to World's End. One half of the city remained in light; the rest was eclipsed in shadow. The gods had seen that shadow before, three years ago in Netherworld, and they knew that it was only a matter of time before Chaos released its most lethal Aspect of all: that of Surt, the Destroyer, a being that was defined more by absence than presence, but whose shadow was that of a black bird that left only nothingness in its wake.

Death and Dream were part of the Worlds; even Chaos had its place. But in that bird shadow nothing remained, not even Death; just an eternal emptiness beyond imagination or redemption.

Loki didn't *want* to imagine it. Loki's imagination was much happier roaming the islands beyond the One Sea, maybe drinking a cocktail or two and watching pretty girls walk by. But Chaos had already eclipsed more than half of the fallen cathedral, and as far as Loki could tell, they had only minutes before the end.

'I hate to rush one of your plans—' he began.

'Get to your post,' said the General.

'But—'

'Captain, *get to your post!*' said Perth, and that was when the shadowcloud began to collapse towards the Bridge like a tidal wave of darkness.

5

THE FIRST WAVE HIT THEM broadside, rocking the Bridge to its foundations. The Sun Shield trembled, the double arc shook, and a wave of ephemera broke from the cloud like a giant swarm of killer bees. The creatures stung relentlessly, defying the runes of protection; swords and hammers were useless against their poison needles.

Thor gave a roar of fury and flailed with Jolly at the ephemeral cloud; Frey was stung on the ankle and fell, numbness surging through him. Bragi picked up his guitar and picked out a series of quick little notes, sending them spinning into the swarm. The bees converged on the player now, two arms of ephemera pulling him into a deadly embrace; but Bragi's music played on – sweeter, more melodic now, so that the bees grew drowsy and flagged, dropping away from the Rainbow Bridge as if they had been hit by smoke.

Idun gave pieces of apple to everyone who had been stung. The gods prepared for another assault. Nan Fey stood by with Ethel and Perth to watch for Maddy's arrival.

Meanwhile Maddy and Jormungand were hurtling towards Bifrost. The shadowcloud hung over the Bridge, monstrous, inescapable. Distinguishable only by their signatures, which blazed like torches against the night, the gods fought on in Aspect with all the force of their recovered glam. Above their heads the Sun Shield blazed; below them, the column of runelight that rose from the ruined cathedral gathered like wool on a spindle, turning, spinning, reflecting.

It was a strangely moving sight – Æsir and Vanir fighting side by side, just as they had at Ragnarók, and fighting now alongside them were the very beings that had caused their fall: the Fenris Wolf, the World Serpent, the Temptress, the Devourers.

Would it be enough? she thought. Would their allies in Chaos be enough to turn the tide of Dream? Was the promise of a hall in Asgard really enough to buy their loyalty? And if Chaos got the upper hand, could Angie not just turn her coat again and rejoin the enemy?

But Chaos was not forgiving: Loki was proof of that. Chaos has no sentiment, no understanding, no clemency. Its imagination is boundless, its penalties extreme. Chaos offers no second chances; Angrboda knew that. She and her demon brood, like the gods, were in this to the very end.

Maddy kicked against Jorgi's flanks, urging him towards the Bridge.

The second attack was under way. This time, bees had been replaced by a wave of four-legged predators: wild dogs, ice bears, black wolves of enormous size with jaws that snapped wildly even as their heads were cut off and their bodies sent plummeting down to World's End.

With great sweeps of his hammer, Thor kept Bif-rost clear of the creatures, while Freyja and Angie, in Carrion form, flew from side to side of the Bridge to beat off the invaders with burning wings and raking claws.

The god of war, however, was suffering from a conflict of personalities. His glamorous arm seemed to have ideas of its own about how to handle a battle, while Sugar-and-Sack's first instinct had always been to run for cover at the first sign of trouble. He was also finding it difficult to adjust his style to his new height: Sugar's humble fighting skills had always been tailored to suit his size (which was more or less that of a small dog), and he found it rather daunting now to be in a position to strike for

505

the head, when before he'd been lucky to go for the knees.

Fenris, in wolf form, snarled at him. He and the other two demon wolves had positioned themselves on the Bridge, ready to take Thor's place if he fell.

'Some god of war you turned out to be,' he growled as Sugar's glamorous arm flailed wildly at an oncoming ice bear.

'Well, I'm not used to dealin' with woofs,' said Sugar, dispatching the creature (mostly by chance) with a sweep of his mindsword.

Fenris sniggered. 'Dude. *Ragnarók?*'

Sugar shot him a nervous look. 'Yeah, kennet. You bit off my arm. But I was someone else then. Now we're supposed to be allies.'

'Yeah. Right. Allies,' said Fenny. 'As if a little noob like you was ever going to fight with me.' He paused to bite the heads off three oncoming wolverines – like a dog snapping heads off marigolds.

'I am *not* a noob,' said Sugar. 'And you got *killed* at Ragnarók. All the stories say so.'

The demon wolf grinned and showed his teeth. 'Here's something the stories *didn't* say . . .'

'What's that?' said Sugar.

'You were *tasty*.'

Sugar gritted his teeth and tried to concentrate on the fight in hand. He wasn't at all comfortable with Fenris standing at his back. As far as he was concerned, one demon wolf was much like another, and the fact that they were supposed to be on the same side was hardly reassurance. He didn't trust Fenris, never had, and he edged away warily, making for the far side of the Bridge, where Loki was hurling fire-runes and holding a running commentary on the battle, to which no one but he was listening.

'And Thor gets in behind Frey and— *Wham! Boom!* That's got to hurt. And Loki *scores*! This boy's on *fire*!' And Loki did a little dance on the parapet of the Bridge, shooting runes into the air like a spray of fireworks.

'Calm down, and save your glam,' Perth advised him. 'Maddy's here.'

Loki looked down. 'About bloody time.' The second wave was

over. The creatures drew back into the cloud to regroup and take another shape. Idun came round with her apples. Skadi, who, fighting in wolf form, had sustained a number of slashes and bites, took two pieces.

With his spyglass, Heimdall was trying to see what might come next. He squinted for several seconds, then levelled his gaze at Loki. 'This one's for you,' he said with a grin.

'Let me guess,' said Loki. 'Snakes.'

Snakes it was – ten thousand of them, heaving and wriggling out of the cloud. Snakes of all colours, poisonous snakes, constrictors, serpents as big as a dozen men. They slithered onto the Rainbow Bridge with an unspeakable *papery* sound, heads raised, fangs bared.

'Hold them!' said Perth. 'Hold them *back*!'

Loki shifted to his Wildfire Aspect. The smell of burning snakes rose from the parapet of the Bridge. Perth smiled. Loki could be trouble, he thought, but he always came through in a crisis. He turned to Maddy, who had just arrived with Jormungand at the far side of the Bridge. In Aspect, she looked ready to face anything.

Nan took Jormungand's bridle.

Maddy stared at her. 'Crazy *Nan*?'

'Long story,' said Perth. 'No time for that now. Nan and I need your help.'

'Of course!' said Maddy, drawing her mindsword.

Perth shook his head. 'Not that. The others can handle the shadowcloud. What we have to do – and *fast* – is build.'

'Build?' said Maddy. 'What with?'

6

RIGHT AT THE START OF THE Elder Age, when Odin – and the
Worlds – were young, the stuff of Creation was always Dream.
Dream in its purest, sweetest form, channelled through a single
mind. But Dream, like all rivers, is a fragile ecosystem, subject
to contamination and pollution. Over the centuries Dream had
become a place of diverse influences – some healthy, some lethal –
as Faërie and Folk and demons and gods all dipped into its lavish
flow. Now it was a toxic mess, as likely to kill as to restore. And
yet it retained a crude energy that, when harnessed and refined,
might yet have the power to heal the Worlds.

Crazy Nan had already seen some of that power on Red Horse
Hill. There, the rift in Dream had been small compared with what
assailed them now; just as the imaginations of the Folk were small
compared with those of the gods. If Nan could use the rift in the
Hill and the dreams of the Folk to build Bif-rost, then surely,
with the Sun Shield's help, from the dreams of gods and from the
almost infinite resources of the shadowcloud, a new Sky Citadel
might arise.

At least, this was what Perth believed. There was only one way
of testing it.

'It's not so much a plan,' he explained, 'as a work in progress.'

Behind them, Æsir and Vanir fought to hold back a living
wall of snakes. Maddy tried to ignore them, but the sound was

inescapable – a hideous slithering, crackling sound – and there was a stench of burning and venom. Of course, she was used to Jormungand, who seemed oafishly disinterested in what was going on, except when stray ephemera ventured his way, at which point he simply opened his jaws and swallowed the intruder. It didn't surprise Maddy at all that Jorgi was a cannibal. In fact, she would have been surprised if he wasn't. Jorgi's appetites seemed to run equally to gods, ephemera and seafood.

'We'll need the Three Horses to do the work,' shouted Perth over the noise. 'Nan, we'll need you *there* . . .' He gestured to a point at the foot of the Bridge. 'Maddy, *there'* – at the far end – 'and I'll be up there with Sleipnir, pulling it together.' He pointed upwards, and Maddy thought she'd never seen him look happier. The End of the Worlds was upon them, the maw of Chaos was opening, and the General was immersed in a plan that seemed, at best, rudimentary.

Still, what choice did they have now? Looking down at World's End, Maddy saw that the cathedral was almost in shadow. She tried not to wonder what her sister might be doing. She jumped back onto Jormungand – who was just sucking the tail end of a snake into the side of his mouth – and manoeuvred him into position. Nan and Perth remounted, and suddenly Maddy could see what the General was aiming for.

Now Treachery and Carnage ride with Lunacy across the sky . . .

And now she could see the light from World's End, no longer a column, but a skein; a skein that was woven from hundreds of runes – hundreds, maybe thousands . . . maybe even *tens* of thousands of them, feeding up into the sky from the Kissing Stone of St Sepulchre. Maggie had released that glam; glam that spooled into the sky like yarn.

Perth and Nan were in place too – Nan turning the Sun Shield as if it were a spinning wheel; Sleipnir in his Aspect with his spidery legs spanning eight Worlds and spinning, spinning the skein of runelight into shapes that Maddy could almost recognize – starry, elegant, spiderweb shapes that hung against the darkening sky like the strands of a necklace.

And in the strands there were hundreds of runes; binding to-gether, making links, reflecting each other, connecting too fast for the eye to follow, knitting together the fabric of Worlds into a blaze of colours and glam.

Gods, thought Maddy. *It's beautiful . . .*

Of course, she had never seen Odin unleashed, in his primary Aspect. She'd never even considered the gods as anything but a spent force. Now she began to understand everything the Æsir had lost; everything they were fighting for. In Asgard, their As-pects would be complete, their powers restored to what they had been. Who would turn away from the chance to wield that kind of power again? To shine so brightly? To be a god?

Nan too was hard at work. Maddy didn't really see why the Horse whose Rider was Lunacy should prefer to adopt the Aspect of an old washing basket rather than something more impressive, but Crazy Nan seemed happy enough as she darted around the Sun Shield, flitting and shuttling to and fro between the strands of runelight. The web gained substance each time she passed; Maddy could hear her laughing.

'Cat's cradle!' yelled Nan. 'We're making a cat's cradle!'

Then she aimed straight for the shadowcloud—

'Nan! *No!*' Maddy cried.

But it was already too late – the Horse of Air and Crazy Nan had disappeared into shadow. Maddy stared at the cloud in dismay.

'Now, Maddy!' Perth called across the cat's cradle of runelight. 'Now, Maddy, for gods' sakes, *dream!*'

Below, the light from the Kissing Stone was finally beginning to fail. The shadowcloud had reached it at last; a wedge of darkness lay at its base. The runes that had shone so brightly now began to go out, one by one. And as they did so, the Rainbow Bridge also began to unravel and fade, its far end sinking into the cloud. At the same time the Sun Shield was darkening at the edge; once it was eclipsed, Maddy knew, the Bridge would hold no longer.

'Dream, Maddy! Dream for your life!' The General's voice was urgent.

Maddy opened her mouth to say that she had no idea what she had to do – she was only a girl from the Northlands . . .

But *dream?* That she *could* do. She had dreamed for most of her young life, while people like Nat Parson had warned her of its dangers. Now she could see those dangers for herself, coming out of the shadowcloud. The wave of snakes had given way to a more generalized assault as the cloud continued its slow collapse over the Bridge and its guardians.

Now the whole of Dream laid siege to the fragment of rainbow. There were war machines with teeth of flame, spiders as big as houses; there were columns of faceless soldiers and armies of the walking dead, mechanical skinning devices and carrion birds with human faces; there were dreams of drowning, dreams of dismemberment, dreams of being helpless and hungry and old, dreams of forgetfulness, dreams of the past; and, of course, there were dreams of the dead.

For Thor, the enemy was Old Age; for Njörd it was snow and ice; for Skadi it was drowning; for Loki it was more snakes. And behind it all, the beating of wings: *something* was approaching. A black bird shadow with feathers of flame, bringing silence in its wake.

Maddy saw only fragments as she urged the Serpent towards the cloud. There was no time to fear for her friends, or to intervene in their struggles. She saw now what Perth meant to do, and she understood that time was short. The rainbow was only a temporary bridge, a bridge that might soon be swept away. And *when the 'bow breaks, the Cradle will fall* – which meant that if, by the time it fell, the Citadel was incomplete . . .

She dug her heels into Jorgi's flanks. The cloud was only seconds away. The motherlode of Dream; the heart of everything ephemeral. But dreams had never failed her yet, Maddy Smith told herself. *And nothing dreamed is ever lost . . .*

Dream for your life, Perth had said.

She dived headlong into the cloud.

She closed her eyes as she reached it, half expecting an impact; but Jorgi was used to moving through Worlds, and the shadow parted to let them through like a whispering curtain of black lace.

7

FROM THE RUINS OF World's End, Maggie Rede was watching the sky. She was in a rubble-filled alleyway on the brighter side of the cathedral, from which she could watch events as they unfurled. The shadowcloud had bisected the square as neatly as an apple – half a cathedral, half an arch, half a marble fountain, its jets still gushing merrily from half a hundred cherubs' mouths . . .

At the meeting of light and dark, the column of glam from the Kissing Stone spooled up into the turbulent sky to make an intricate latticework, radiant as northlights.

Without a doubt, it was beautiful; and yet Maggie hated it. That was the Cradle of the gods. The reason for which Adam had died. When complete, it would become the Sky Citadel of the Æsir; the stronghold of the Firefolk.

Now Maggie could see why Folk had called it the Cradle. She'd made such cradles herself once, in the days before the Bliss. Cats' cradles, the old folk called them; and Maggie remembered her mother and brothers showing her how to hold the silk – just *so*, between her fingers – and to make those intricate patterns like a spider spinning thread . . .

Tears would have been a relief; but she touched her eyes and found them dry. No matter – that would come later. Even revenge would have to wait. For now, she had to protect her child.

She looked down at her bleeding palm, where Maddy's rune

had cut her. She pulled off what was left of her *bergha* – little more than a rag now – and wadded it tight against the cut. The runemark *Ác* at the nape of her neck itched and burned like an insect bite. Maggie flexed her fingers. Good. The damage was insignificant.

She turned her eyes to her immediate surroundings. The streets at her back were deserted; facing her was a wall of cloud. For all she knew, she might be the only person left alive; the blast of glam from the Kissing Stone had dispatched everyone inside the cathedral, and there was nothing to indicate whether or not the whole of World's End had met with the same fate.

But Maggie was used to being alone. The catacombs under the old University could serve once more as a refuge against whatever came out of the shadowcloud. There was food down there, and shelter, and books; she could seal the entrance with runes, and after the cloud had passed (as it certainly would) there would be time to plan her revenge.

Once more she glanced up at the Cradle, then turned her back on the shadowcloud. The University wasn't far; she could make it in less than five minutes. After that, the Worlds could end as far as Maggie Rede was concerned; she and her unborn child would be safe, cocooned underground and swaddled in glam.

And then Maggie began to run as the shadow fell onto the Kissing Stone, and the Sun Shield was cut to a paring of light, and the Rainbow Bridge began to give way, sending fragments of prismic light cascading down onto World's End.

8

MADDY HAD TRAVELLED THROUGH Dream before. First in Hel, five years ago; more recently with Jormungand. She thought she knew the rules – even hoped that she might have built up a tolerance. But as she entered the shadowcloud, she knew what a foolish hope that had been. Dream had no rules, no allies, no laws. Dream was Disorder incarnate.

Loki had once described Netherworld as drowning in a sea of lost dreams. That's what it felt like to Maddy now, as she and Jorgi plunged deeper into the dark heart of the shadowcloud.

Here, Maddy looked for the dreams that had given her comfort in troubled times. Dreams of far places, of oceans and islands; dreams of tables piled with food; of demons and Faërie; of warriors and kings; of animals and talking birds. Dreams of flying; dreams of ships; dreams of distant continents. But here, in the heart of the shadowcloud, the sweet dreams of her childhood seemed nothing but fragments lost in time, flashes from a distant past.

Here instead were her childhood fears: the fear of failure, of drowning, of wolves; the fear of being alone at night with the bare trees tapping against the window and the moonlight shining onto the floor. Here too was the cold sweat of nightmare; here were monsters of all kinds; and here was the truth at the heart of it all – the fear of loss, the death of a friend, the fear of the dark, the awareness of death.

Dream for your life, Perth had said.

But Maddy had no idea where to start. *What am I even looking for?* she asked herself in growing despair. *There's nothing here but darkness . . .*

And then came Crazy Nan's voice: *Nothing dreamed is ever lost* – and suddenly it came to her. It was obvious, she told herself. It didn't *have* to be like this. Nothing was lost for ever. What was broken could be rebuilt; what was impossible could be achieved. The dead could be remembered; the fallen could be raised anew. And out of the darkness . . .

Let there be light!

And suddenly, for Maddy, there was.

There was her father, Jed Smith, when Maddy was a little girl. She remembered his forge, and the light at its heart; the way she had watched as her father twisted and turned and folded the steel and hammered it into intricate shapes. There was her sister Mae, playing with her dolls on the green; and One-Eye, her old teacher and friend, known to some as Allfather.

There was Crazy Nan Fey, with her cats and her stories. And then there was Malbry; the valley; the green; the river with its little boats; the pastures high in the mountains; the sunlight on the winter snow; the smell of hay at Harvestmonth; the first ray of sunshine over the Hindarfell after three whole months of darkness.

This was where Maddy's dreams had begun: in Malbry, under Red Horse Hill. And this, she finally understood, was what Crazy Nan had meant. She took a deep breath and closed her eyes and tried to hold onto what she had found. Then she kicked her heels into Jormungand's flanks and spurred him back towards the Bridge. And as they emerged from the shadowcloud, she summoned the dream with all her glam and *flung* it at the Sun Shield at the heart of the Cradle, so that all the force of *Aesk,* the Ash, and *Iar,* the Builder, and *Perth,* the Gambler, held it suspended in runelight like a droplet on a spider's web; a fragment of World above the Worlds.

Gods! thought Maddy. *It's beautiful . . .*

Had the General planned all this? Had he foreseen this moment?

Had he intended from the start to draw out the forces of Chaos, so that when the time came, he and his friends could use the enemy's own power – the infinite power of Dream – to build the Cradle of the gods in time to ward off their attack? Had he *known* it would work this way? Or had he simply played the odds and made up the plot as he went along?

But there was no time for questions now. The Rainbow Bridge was already half gone, and the signatures that flared along its diminishing arc were fading and exhausted. Maddy tried not to look, but even at a cursory glance she could tell that the gods were in a bad way: exhausted, outnumbered, bleeding from wounds that Idun had no time to heal.

Thor, with Mjølnir, still kept clear the threshold of the Bridge; Loki, in his Wildfire Aspect, holding the parapet to his left, with Hawk-Eyed Heimdall keeping watch. Frey and Freyja held the right; Bragi played a triumphal march; Njörd and Skadi fought side by side as a pair of giant eagles, their wings scorched by ephemera.

Tyr's glamorous left arm still ripped and flailed into the shadowcloud, but his right arm was useless, his glam almost out. As Maddy plunged once more into Dream, he stumbled and fell to one knee; the Bridge rocked; the Sun Shield flickered; the Fenris Wolf came up behind him to take his place against the advancing enemy—

Now Maddy was working at desperate speed, plunging in and out of Dream like a shuttle on a weaving loom. Crazy Nan was doing the same, casting glamours at the sky. And out of the glamours, the First World slowly began to take shape. It looked like no kind of citadel Maddy Smith had ever seen; there was nothing yet to connect it all. Here she recognized a lake in the mountains by Farnley Tyas. There was the Hall of the Sleepers with its hanging ceiling of stalactites. Here was a cottage with hollyhocks around the door – Nan's old house, Maddy realized, with her cats on the doorstep. There was Malbry church – and the docks where Perth had had his lodgings. There was the cathedral of St Sepulchre with its glass dome and marble floor. Here was Jed Smith's workshop.

Here was the smell of bluebells in spring, and the sound of cur-lews in summer. Here were fields of barley, and goats high up in the summer pastures. And there – right there – was Red Horse Hill, with the rabbit-tail grass growing down one side and the Red Horse cut into the clay just as if nothing had happened at all . . .

And then everyone heard it: a beating of wings in the shadow-cloud like the beating of a giant heart.

Surt, the Destroyer, was there at last.

Maddy heard the sound and stopped, half in, half out of Dream.

Heimdall *saw* it coming, and swore.

Skadi heard it, and spread her wings.

Sigyn heard it, and took Loki's hand.

Bragi heard it, and began to play a deathsong to its pounding rhythm.

Angrboda heard it, and smiled, and said to the three demon wolves at her side: 'Now's *the time, boys. Make Ma proud.*'

Brave-Hearted Tyr heard, and looked across at the Fenris Wolf.

Ethel heard it and closed her eyes .

Loki heard it, and thought: *Here goes* . . .

The General heard it, and knew it was time.

'*Dream! All of you! DREAM!*' he roared, and his voice was almost loud enough to drown out the sound of beating wings. Everyone heard the order; and Æsir and Vanir moved to obey – even Heim-dall and Skadi, whose loyalty to Odin had suffered more than one blow over the years since Ragnarók.

Even Loki obeyed the command, shifting to his falcon Aspect and plunging headlong into Dream as the last of the glam from the Kissing Stone died and the wave of shadow finally broke, smash-ing through the Rainbow Bridge, toppling the Sun Shield into the maw of darkness.

'*Dream like you've never dreamed before!*' thundered the voice of Allfather. No time to explain it further; no more time to hold the Bridge. It had been a desperate game – and for very high stakes, he knew that. An attempt to use the power of Dream against the forces of Chaos; and in one single move to reestablish the balance of Worlds, raise Asgard, reinstate the gods *and* send the pendulum hurtling back, with Order in its place again.

But if the Destroyer broke through the cloud, then the game was over. And it was going to be *very* close – they were out of time, the Bridge was lost, and Asgard, the fortress in which they appeared in their true, most powerful Aspects, was still some distance from completion. Which meant that as soon as the Bridge was gone, they would have to face the enemy in human Aspect – runemarks reversed – and Surt would wipe them out for good with a single beat of his flame-edged wing.

'DREAM!' Odin raged for the last time, seeing the broken Bridge give way. The Vanir – Heimdall, Skadi and Njörd, Frey and Freyja, Bragi and Idun – all shifted to bird form and scattered into the dreamcloud. Shards of runelight flashed from the cloud; but in the confusion no one could see how much of Asgard remained to be built. Was it just a castle in the air, or could it be a Citadel?

Below him, Thor, with Mjølnir in hand, was trying to keep his footing on what was left of the broken Bridge. Thor was no dreamer, but he understood the urgency of the General's command. He tried to summon Asgard from the cloud of ephemera, but all he could think of was Sif, his wife, sitting in front of her looking glass, combing out her golden hair . . .

Sif was faring a little better. Interior furnishings had always been more important to her than to Thor, and she had had five years to plan the design of her hall in Asgard. Rugs, columns, tapestries, marble floors and gilded chairs, four-post beds and cages of doves all took shape with the speed of Dream as Bright-Haired Sif summoned them out of the cloud.

Loki was in a quandary. The snake-woman sent to kill him, that first day on Red Horse Hill, had prophesied that he would have no hall in the new Asgard. Now Loki's mistrust of oracles was starting to verge on the paranoid, but from the start he'd taken this to mean that either the gods would refuse him entry to the new Sky Citadel, or that he would fall in battle before it was completed. Neither option appealed to him much, and now he was faced with a difficult choice – that of dreaming Asgard in place without any guarantee that he would benefit, or cutting his losses, saving his glam and making a dash for the open sky.

Only the Wedlock stood in his way, but while Sigyn was working, he thought that, in Aspect, he might have a chance.

He narrowed his eyes and focused his glam on *Eh*. It gleamed on his middle finger, a narrow golden band of light. Slyly the Trickster fingered a rune; it was *Tyr*, and its blade was small but sharp.

He glanced at Sigyn's profile. She seemed quite unaware of his plan; her eyes were closed, her earnest face a study in concentration. What would she do if he left her? he thought. *She* couldn't shift to bird form . . .

Come on, Loki told himself. *Now is definitely not the time to find out you've got a conscience.*

He brought the rune *Tyr* in closer. The Wedlock began to glow. It burned; and still he held the rune, thinking: *Sorry, Sig. I have to go. I'm really not the marrying kind—*

Just then there came a terrific lurch from the fading Bridge. Loki was knocked off-balance and fell. *That's it*, he thought. *I'm out of here . . .*

But as he was about to shift, he felt Sigyn's hand take hold of his, and she dragged him forward into a dream of a place that was like the cave by the Sleepers, except that he wasn't a prisoner there, and two little boys played at his feet – two little boys with red hair .

The dream-Sigyn smiled at Loki. It wasn't *quite* a comforting smile – it was rather too maternal for that – but it was kind, nevertheless.

'Where are we?' said Loki.

'Home,' she said.

'Home? Where?'

'Asgard, of course,' she said with a smile. 'Remember? Your hall in Asgard?'

'I don't get a hall in Asgard,' said Loki. 'Remember? The Oracle told me.'

Sigyn laughed. 'So share mine. There's plenty of room for two.'

'Don't get me wrong,' said Loki. 'I mean, that's very generous, but actually, I don't really need—'

'Everyone needs someone,' she said. 'Everyone – even someone like you – needs a place to come home to.'

Loki's keenness to escape was suspended by curiosity. 'What?' he said. 'You'd take me in? After everything I've done? I mean, I'm hardly the faithful spouse . . .'

'Of course I would,' said Sigyn.

'You must be crazy,' Loki said.

'So I'm crazy,' said Sigyn. 'Who cares? Now dream!'

Why not? thought Loki, and closed his eyes . . .

And stepped into the shadowcloud.

Around him, the gods were doing the same. Frey dreamed of banqueting halls; Freyja of mirrors and jewellery; Heimdall of horizons and hills; and Ethel of Balder, her long-lost son, with perfect, loving clarity.

Skadi dreamed of a hall of ice; Njörd dreamed of a hall in the Sea; Idun dreamed of orchards and gardens; Bragi dreamed of music.

And Perth and Sleipnir dreamed of *walls* – walls as thick as a man was tall; battlements; ramparts; bulwarks and buttresses; drawbridges and parapets and towers.

They had only seconds now, but time works differently in Dream, and seconds was all they needed – as long as the black bird shadow held back. Surt must have sensed the urgency. The beating of wings grew louder. A wing-tip grazed the Bridge . . .

Now only Tyr and the demon wolves stood between Asgard and Chaos. Fenris, Skull and Big H were poised on the last piece of parapet, ready to strike as the black bird broke through. No dreamers, but seasoned Devourers, the three now entered into their own, jaws snapping, eyes wild, fangs bared at the shadow-cloud. Every second was valuable; every second might mean the chance to snatch a victory even as the Rainbow Bridge dissolved into air—

'NOW!' came Perth's voice from above. '*Give it everything you've got!*'

Brave-Hearted Tyr, whose powers had never run to flying even at the best of times, felt himself begin to fall. His Aspect was failing. His glamorous arm flickered and started to fade. Below him – *far* below – World's End: a chequerboard of light and shade.

Beside him, the Fenris Wolf gave him an appraising look. His grey-gold eyes were shining. 'Think you can ride on my back, noob?'

Sugar looked down. 'Where to?' he said.

Fenris jerked his head at the cloud.

'Dude,' said Skull. 'We don't stand a chance.'

'That's Surt,' said Big H. '*Surt*, man. The Destroyer . . .'

Fenris showed his teeth. 'Yeah. I say we go in there and kick his ass.'

Skull and Big H exchanged looks. Beneath them, the Bridge was nothing but air.

Sugar swallowed. 'Sounds like a plan.' He grabbed hold of Fenny's mane with both hands.

Fenny gave an approving growl. 'The noob says we have a plan. Are you with me, boys?' Then he opened his jaws and leaped, howling, at the oncoming cloud just as the tip of the Destroyer's wing came down like a blade over Bif-rost.

9

PUCKER-LIPS, A-PUCKER-LIPS, *all fall down,* said the words of the ancient rock-a-bye. And that was what started to happen, of course, as the last of the Bridge disappeared, tumbling Sun Shield and dreamers into the empty, merciless sky.

At the same time the shadowcloud gave a seismic shudder, spitting the Vanir into the air like seeds into a hurricane. Loki shifted to bird form and shot off over Asgard, carrying Sigyn between his claws as a golden acorn. The Vanir scattered, some stunned by the blast, some swept aside by the turbulence. Chaos had finally understood the danger their dreams represented, and had slammed its doors against them with all the force it could summon.

Maddy gave a moan of dismay and looked up at the Cradle. No longer ephemeral, it shone like a glacier in the sun, rising glamorous from the clouds in a thousand glassy turrets and spires. It was by far the most wonderful thing that she had ever seen or dreamed: a city in the Firmament, all ringed about with northlights. But *still* it wasn't finished, she sensed, as Jormungand moved in and out of Dream, so that if she stopped to save her friends, the whole delicate, intricate structure might dissolve just like the Rainbow Bridge, leaving nothing to cling to but vapours and clouds.

She looked up to where Perth and Sleipnir stood on the city's battlements. The General's Aspect was very dim, his glam burned down to nothing at all. Through the rune *Bjarkán* she could see that he was barely conscious. Nan too was at a halt; Dream is a devourer of glam, and the energy required to build had already taken most of hers. Maddy's own glam was down to a spark; but she had come late to the battle and, with luck, a little remained. Enough for just one more attempt – one last, desperate flight of fancy .

Time! I need more time! she thought. *A second, even a second more . . .*

She saw the black bird shadow rise. Sugar was riding Fenris. She gave a cry as the shadow fell, and Sugar glanced at her, his golden eyes alight, his hand extended towards the shadowcloud. His glamorous arm reappeared as soon as it touched the fabric of Dream, and for a second – maybe less – his Aspect was that of Brave-Hearted Tyr, his signature flaring a brilliant red, mounted on a demon wolf with fur that crackled with runelight.

Fenris opened his jaws wide. The Devourer faced the Destroyer. For a second the shadow faltered, and Maddy plunged once more into Dream . . .

She felt the tip of the black bird's wing graze her shoulder as she passed. There was no pain, but her arm went numb and her glam dipped like a dying flame. She ignored it and reached for the final time into the seething heart of Dream.

And now at last Maddy dreamed of her friends. She dreamed of the Seer-folk and Firefolk; of the Trickster with his crooked smile, the Watchman and the Thunderer, the Seeress and the General, the Healer and the Poet, the Huntress and the Man of the Sea. She dreamed of Bright-Haired Sif, of Frey and Freyja, of Crazy Nan Fey – and especially of Brave-Hearted Tyr, who had once been Sugar-and-Sack, a cowardly goblin from Red Horse Hill, and who had fearlessly given his all to earn her that last precious second of time.

Spurring Jorgi out of the cloud, she felt the bird shadow come down again, so close that it clipped her left heel. Numbness engulfed her; but Maddy sped on, trying not to think of her friends plummeting through the air to their deaths; summoning

Aesk, the Lightning Ash, with every flicker of glam she had left.

But instead of the flare of runelight there came the dry click of a breaking twig as *Aesk,* the Ash, guttered and died.

The rune had failed.

It was over.

Maddy stared at the mark on her palm. She knew its shape better than anything; she'd had it since the day she was born. A rusty runemark – a blemish, they'd said – that had given her the power of gods.

But now it had changed, and in her fatigue and confusion it took her an instant to understand why it looked so strange and unfamiliar—

It was reversed.

'No, please,' Maddy said, in sudden comprehension. 'Not now we're so *close* . . .'

And now she saw a black bird's wing emerging from the seething shadowcloud. Surt, the Destroyer, in Aspect, was entering the Middle Worlds . . .

'No!' said Maddy once again, and spurred Jormungand at the cloud. No matter that, with her rune reversed, she didn't have any hope of success. All she could think of was: *If I don't try something, at least, then Sugar will have died in vain* . . .

The thing that was not really a bird sensed her approach and halted. It had no feelings of pleasure or pain – in fact that ancient intelligence had no feelings at all of the kind that Maddy could have identified – but it did possess a cold curiosity, even a kind of humour.

Scrutinizing the girl and the snake, it concluded that they posed no threat, and began to move forward once again, summoning its vast resources to annihilate the last of those who sought to resist it.

Now Maddy lifted her right palm with its rusty, faded mark. *Aesk,* reversed, gave out barely a glow. She climbed off Jorgi's back and gave him one last whispered instruction. Then, with her left hand, she summoned *Bjarkán,* and stepped into the mouth of Chaos.

10

FROM THE BATTLEMENTS OF THE Sky Citadel the General looked on helplessly. Hugin and Munin wheeled frantically around his head; Sleipnir was tethered close by. They had come so very close, he thought. They had almost won the war. But now it was over. The Cradle would fall. Surely nothing could save them now . . .

And then he saw something far below; a gleam from out of the darkness. World's End was mostly in shadow now, its spires and turrets fallen. But still there remained that point of light, so dim that he might have imagined it – a single speck of brightness, like a mote against the dark.

Maggie Rede, thought the General. That glam could belong to no one else. His mind, always on the alert for anything that might be useful to him, began to consider the girl's potential. Above him, his Mind and Spirit, looking increasingly agitated, gave harsh cries of encouragement.

So – Maggie was alive, he thought. What of it? Well, she still had glam. But for her to use it on his behalf – that was surely too much to expect. *Unless . . .*

Perth's undamaged eye widened.

Of course!

He turned to look at Sleipnir. The Red Horse stood on the battlements, his weirdly elongated legs spanning most of the hectic sky.

Perth gave a little smile and turned to address his ravens. 'Go,' he said. 'You know what to do . . .'

And so, at the speed of Dream, the Horse whose Rider is Carnage shook his mane of runelight and plummeted down towards World's End.

11

ALL THIS HAPPENED SO MUCH faster than the time it takes to tell. But time is not always objective. A second can stretch for minutes – for *hours* – depending on the circumstances.

Dreamtime is one of these; so are moments of pain; and so, as the Thunderer now realized, is the interval between falling from a great height and the inevitable moment of impact – for it seemed to him that he had been falling for half an eternity, rather than the six seconds or so that had actually passed since Bif-rost went down.

World's End hurtled towards him now with the speed of Jormungand crashing through Dream. It made him feel slightly nauseous, and he closed his eyes – which were watering from the icy wind – and tried not to count the seconds.

One. Two. Three. Four . . .

Surely the ground couldn't be far.

Five. Six. Seven. Eight . . .

Thor opened a cautious eye. Then another. Jolly, who had shifted to his inanimate Aspect as soon as they had begun to fall, reverted to his goblin self and looked around in puzzlement.

'Oy – what's goin' on 'ere?'

Thor blinked. He was flying. Below him was Jorgi, his Aspect now that of a black sky-dragon, undulating through the air like heavily greased lightning. He had already picked up the rest of the Æsir, who clung to his spiny back and mane with varying expressions of unease; for the present the Serpent was on their side, but his motives had never been clear to them. Above, a red-and-purple bird, eccentric both in proportion and design, fluttered and tumbled along in his wake. The Serpent's flight had generated a great deal of turbulence, but this was nothing compared to the shadowcloud now descending over Asgard. It filled the sky, spanned horizons, leaving only the narrowest band of light between itself and the battlements of the Sky Citadel.

Chaos must still be uncertain, thought the Thunderer as he sped through the sky towards Asgard. As well it might: they could have won. Even now, set one foot on Asgard's completed battlements, and his Aspect, as well as those of his friends, would be instantly restored. But as yet Asgard *wasn't* complete, and all of them were out of glam. They'd lost Tyr in the shadowcloud; the Fenris Wolf had fallen. The Sun Shield was lost; the General spent. Even Nan was out of dreams. And as for Maddy . . .

He sought her now, frantically, without success. Her signature streaked the darkening sky, vanishing into the shadowcloud.

Thor's heart gave a desperate lurch as he realized what Maddy had done. She must have known that Jormungand needed time to get away, so she had sent him after the Æsir while she remained to hold back the cloud.

For a moment the Thunderer was torn between grief and a choking pride. He'd never wanted a daughter; had hardly bothered to hide his dismay when Modi, his long-lost son and heir, had turned out to be Maddy instead; and he'd felt nothing but disgust when the second son of the prophecy, Magni, had proved to be not only a traitor, but a second daughter (which was worse).

Now he felt profoundly ashamed. Maddy had made a gesture so brave and so generous that he hardly understood it himself, and now there would be no chance to explain, or to tell her that no son of his could have made him half as proud.

'I wish I could have told her . . .' he said, unaware he was speaking aloud, still less of the tears that rolled down his face and into his fiery beard.

'Told who what?' said Jolly.

Thor sighed. 'Oh, nothing,' he said.

They hurtled towards Asgard.

12

DOWN IN THE CITY, Maggie had reached the site of the old University. But the buildings that had first housed scholars and historians, then the devotees of the Order, then the traders and merchants who had rushed in after the Bliss, were now filled with refugees – terrified and cowering.

Some were native World's Enders; some were the foreigners Maggie despised. Some were wealthy; some were slaves; some were old; some, children. But in the face of the shadowcloud, everyone was equal. Equal in terror, equal in grief. Race, money, influence – none of those things mattered now. Fear had united World's End at last. Fear, and the need for a scapegoat.

The thought gave Maggie a bitter kind of pleasure. *This is what it feels like,* she thought. *Everyone in the same boat. Everyone has lost someone: a friend, a child, a relative.* A woman was sitting on the floor just under the pulpit that concealed the secret entrance to the labyrinth under the University. Quite a young woman, Maggie saw, tangled hair over her face, singing a little rock-a-bye. There was a baby in her arms, bundled into a blanket.

Instinctively Maggie fingered *Bjarkán* – but she didn't need the truesight to tell her that the baby was dead.

The woman looked up at her hopefully. 'Are you a healer, lady?' she said in a heavily accented voice. She was an Outlander, Maggie saw; her hands were tattooed with Outlandish designs. She held the bundle out to Maggie. 'Please. My baby. My baby is sick.'

'Your baby's dead,' said Maggie. 'I'm sorry. I can't help you.'

Maggie had thought she was empty inside after watching Adam die, but the wail that the Outlander woman gave changed her mind immediately. She put a hand to her own belly, where the germ of a new life was already so strong in her that she could actually *feel* it there, calling out to her, whispering; and the love she felt for that tiny life was greater than anything she'd ever felt. Greater than her love for Adam; greater than her need for revenge. She knelt down beside the Outlander woman and took one of her hands.

'I'm sorry,' she said. 'I'm so sorry.'

The Outlander woman looked up at her. 'Do *you* have a child?'

'Not yet,' Maggie said.

'Then you don't know,' said the woman, and went back to her singing and rocking. Maggie heard the words of the song:

'Rock-a-bye baby on the treetop.
When the wind blows, the Cradle will rock . . .'

She tried to feel inside herself for something to comfort the woman. Of course, Maggie had had no formal instruction in how to cast runes. But she *was* a child of the Fire, and now she reached for the fingerings that might soothe a mother's grief.

With new-found skill, she fingered *Bjarkán*, the rune of revelation and dream. Then came *Sól*, the Bright One: sunshine and renewal.

'Close your eyes,' Maggie said. 'You must be so tired. Try to sleep.'

Then she sketched *Madr*, the rune of compassion, on the woman's forehead – and crossed it with *Úr*, the Mighty Ox, to give her strength and endurance.

The runes flared briefly, then dispersed. The Outlander woman closed her eyes. Maggie knew that runes alone could not compete with the death of a child, but sleep itself was a healer of sorts, and Dream, she knew, was a haven for those for whom the waking world has become unbearable. She watched as the Outlander woman began to drift slowly into Dream, and with a last gentle touch of her hand Maggie drew the new rune *Gabe* – a gift – in the air above her.

The woman would sleep now, Maggie thought. Sleep and, if she was lucky, dream – and if she never awoke from the dream, then perhaps it would be for the best. Because something was coming – a darkness – from which Dream might be the only escape.

She opened the entrance to World Below concealed beneath the pulpit.

'What's that?' said the woman sleepily.

'That's where I'm going,' she told her. 'Come with me, and you might survive.'

It suddenly seemed very important to her to save at least someone from the disaster. She stood up and addressed the refugees. 'There's a hiding place under the city,' she said. 'I've been there before. You'll be safe with me. Anyone want to come along?'

Silence.

'Someone? *Anyone?*'

Still there was silence from the group. The Outlander woman was asleep. Others shielded their faces or made the sign against evil. Everyone had seen her cast her glam at the Outlander woman.

And now Maggie understood for the first time that the runemark that shone from the nape of her neck did more than give her powers; it marked her for ever as one of a tribe that had devastated World's End more times than the Folk could remember – a tribe that had wiped out the Order and had now brought this Chaos onto their heads.

'It's all right!' she tried to explain. She took a step towards them.

A man who looked like a country parson moved to intercept her. 'Get back to Netherworld, demon!' he cried, and pushed at her with both hands.

He took her by surprise; Maggie fell, and at that moment she felt the runes forming at her fingertips – *Hagall, Isa, Naudr, Úr* – and, with them, a searing, blinding rage, a rage that exploded out of her with uncontrolled ferocity.

'How *dare* you touch me!' Maggie said. 'How dare you put your hands on me! I ought to kill the lot of you . . .'

And for a moment she almost did; the mindbolt levelled and ready to strike at anyone who dared to move . . .

The parson saw it and held out his hands. 'Lady, mercy . . .' He dropped to his knees.

The others just stared in horror at her, looking like frightened children.

Maggie gave a stricken cry and dispersed the runes against the floor, hard enough to crack the marble.

I am a demon, she told herself. *I could have killed them – I wanted to . . .*

For a moment, she saw herself as they did. A monster, shorn, bare-headed; black with the dust of destruction; that ruinmark gleaming from her skin and her dead eyes like those of a murderer.

And am I not a murderer? If I had listened to the Old Man, wouldn't Adam still be alive?

The thought came from somewhere inside her; some deep and secret place of hurt. It dragged at her heart – her cold, dead heart – and suddenly her eyes were wet.

The eyes of the Folk were merciless. Staring now at the monster, the freak; staring in horror, in hatred, in fear; but mostly in growing hostility. They had no idea of Maggie's strength; her glam aside, she looked just like any other seventeen-year-old girl; but filthy, ragged, and now weak.

A little boy threw a stone.

It missed, but Maggie was startled. She looked up to see the refugees gathering their forces: sticks; knives; chunks of rock.

'Please. I don't want to hurt you . . .' she said.

Another stone flew. This time it hit. Maggie felt a pain in her wrist. The pain was sharper than the glam that had sliced into her palm; it came as a surprise; once more she felt a wetness on her face.

She summoned her glam again. A shield made up of *Yr*, the Protector. Several stones bounced off the shield as the little crowd grew bolder.

'Stop this,' Maggie said. 'You don't know what you're doing!'

Now a knife glanced off the shield; a man's face, distorted with rage, pressing against empty air.

The parson had found his courage again. 'Pray, pray!' he urged the crowd. 'The demons are powerless against prayer!'

Once more Maggie tried to protest. But their voices rose against her – a babble of cries in which she repeatedly heard the words: *demon, Fiery, Order, Cleansed.*

Suddenly the crowd fell still. Their gaze moved upward, a hundred eyes suddenly reflecting the sky.

The Cradle of St Sepulchre's Fire blazed down onto World's End; and now, through the broken ceiling of the derelict University, they saw an eight-legged nightmare descending on them, with a mane of runelight, a tail of fire and spidery legs that spanned the sky.

Maggie recognized Sleipnir at once; but Sleipnir in his primary Aspect was a fearsome sight indeed, and once more the group of refugees shrank away and covered their eyes. Some made the sign against evil; some prayed aloud; some wailed; some called for their mothers; some wept.

'Ach, typical Folk,' said a voice. 'Never know what's good for them.' And now, astride the Red Horse, Maggie saw Hughie and Mandy, both of them in human Aspect as Sleipnir alit on the cracked marble floor. 'Still, nae harm done, eh?'

Crawk, said Mandy. *No harm. Crawk!*

Hughie gave his brilliant smile. 'We've come tae pick you up, hen.'

'Pick me *up*?' said Maggie.

Hughie looked apologetic. 'Well, what with the End of the Worlds, the Auld Man thought ye'd be safer up *there* . . .' He nodded up at the Cradle that burned and rocked in the hectic sky. 'Besides, your sister needs your help.'

Maggie made a dry sound that might have been laughter, or a sob. 'My husband's dead,' she told him, feeling the runes once more beginning to itch against her palm. 'You think I care what happens to *her*? Or any of the Firefolk?'

535

'Ach, I'm sorry for your loss.' Hughie tugged at the silver ring that dangled from his earlobe. 'But ye can see how popular ye are now with the Folk of World's End. *We* are your true family. We love you for ever, no matter what—'

'*You?*' said Maggie.

Hughie shrugged. 'We speak for the Auld Man. We're his Mind and Spirit, ken? He says no hard feelings for the wound ye gave him when ye glammied him in the face. Perhaps he deserved it a little, he says. And scars, of course, add character.'

'That was *him?*' Maggie said, curious in spite of herself.

'Aye, or one of his Aspects. He sends his regards to his grand-child. He says he doubts ye'll meet again.'

And with that Hughie remounted Sleipnir, while Mandy reverted to raven form.

'Seems a shame for the wean,' he said, almost as an afterthought.

Maggie's hand crept to her belly. 'What?'

'Well, I can see *you* not wantin' to live, but I thought you might do it for the wean. I *meant* the baby,' he said helpfully, dazzling Maggie with his smile.

'What do you mean?' Maggie said.

He indicated the shadowcloud. 'What did you think it was, eh? Rain, to make the flowers grow? That's Chaos coming for all of us, lass, with Surt himself as vanguard. When that cloud covers Asgard, then all the Worlds will come to an end, and no one – not you, not me, not even Death herself – will survive. Surely ye've heard the prophecy:

'When the 'bow breaks, the Cradle will fall,
And down will come baby, Cradle an' all—'

'But that's just a rock-a-bye,' Maggie said.

Craw, said Mandy. *Crawk. Craw.*

Hughie shrugged. 'She says we should go. She's not the most patient, I'm afraid ...' He glanced once more at the open roof, through which the sky blazed purple-black. 'Perhaps we could fill ye in on the way. I'm afraid we dinnae have much time. But if ye'd oblige him, the Auld Man gives his solemn word that he'll give ye a hall in Asgard, and he'll not raise a hand against ye or your child – neither he, nor any of his folk – no, not until the End of the Worlds.'

Maggie narrowed her eyes at him. 'How do I know he'll keep his word?'

'Because he has to,' Hughie said. 'Now, are ye comin', or are ye not?'

13

*I*T FEELS LIKE DROWNING, Loki had said. *Drowning in a sea of lost dreams.* Now Maddy *really* knew what he'd meant: without Jorgi to keep her afloat, she was tumbled and turned this way and that like a bundle of rags brought in on the tide. Above her, the black bird shadow, poised like the sails of a deathly ship; beneath her, the multiplicity of Dream, in all its confusion and splendour.

Why am I still alive? she thought. *What can Chaos want of me?*

The answer came almost immediately – though not in words, of course. Words are the language of Order; but in Chaos the language is that of sensation alone; wordless; incorruptible. To Maddy it felt like plunging into a sink of ice-cold water; every nerve, every sense, every part of her was immersed in that knowledge, so that the spoken word seemed clumsy by comparison, while the clever fingers of Chaos now turned her over and over, unravelling her secret thoughts like a spindle laden with wool.

The presence that did this was nothing like any creature of Maddy's experience. She sensed its curiosity, its alienness, its caution. Its rage was overwhelming; and yet it was an impersonal rage, like thunderstorms and earthquakes, untainted by contact with Faërie or Folk; cool; remote; relentless.

Dreamingdreamingdreamdream . . . There were no words in the presence's voice; just a buzz of conscious static, something like a swarm of bees. *Sleepsleep perchancetodream* . . . still turning her over this way and that; unwrapping her like a parcel .

What do you want? Maddy tried to say.

Dreamdreamdreaming. Dream. The buzz of static intensified, urging her to surrender. She began to feel her mind give way; her subconscious begin to unravel. *The best way to know an enemy is to understand his dreams,* she thought; and on that realization (which came in a burst of memories: herself at four, on Red Horse Hill, asleep and dreaming of goblins) came a sudden understanding: Chaos was trying to enter her mind, not in the way the Whisperer had, by force of personality, but by a process of close inspection and slow analysis that, when complete, would give away not only Asgard's defences, but the inner workings of those who had built it.

It doesn't know, Maddy thought. *It doesn't know how helpless we are* . . .

She hid the thought as best she could inside another memory – a dream of running through the woods on all fours, like a hunting wolf. A ghost moon capered overhead; the earth was fragrant underfoot. Maddy lifted her head and howled . . .

In the distance, another howl seemed to answer Maddy's cry. It sounded familiar – not part of the dream – and her heart gave a lurch of surprise and hope.

Fenris? Fenny? Is that you?

The cry came again, so distantly that she could barely hear it at all. The static in her mind increased – *dreamdreamdreamDREAM* – until all Maddy really wanted to do was dip under the black bird's shadow and feel nothing any more . . .

Dream. Dream of Asgard. Dream . . . And now she could feel her mind coming apart, dropping her secrets like petals from a blown rose. Here was Asgard's gateway, with its double row of pillars. Here was an orchard of cherry trees, the petals scattered in the wind. Here was a tower, there a lake; and Maddy could feel them dissolving away as Chaos reclaimed what she had stolen. She tried to keep what was dearest to her hidden closest to her heart, but even so, it would not be long before it had taken everything.

They'd been close – so very close! But this was surely the end of the line. She could feel her mind letting go, like a man holding onto a high branch, losing his grip, a finger at a time. Soon there would be nothing left. Nothing but forgetfulness. Was that really so bad?

Here a smile from an old friend. There the shadow of a rose. Runes, cantrips, memories; everything dissolved like smoke, leaving nothing but darkness. *Goodbye, Sugar-and-Sack,* she thought. *Goodbye, Jed Smith. Goodbye, Mae, goodbye, Nan, goodbye, Malbry and Red Horse Hill. And Maggie, my sister, wherever you are – I wish I'd known you better . . .*

And then, from behind her, there came a sound like the beating of giant wings. *It's over,* she thought with a kind of relief. *No more fighting. No more loss. I'm sorry, Odin – Perth, my old friend – but this is as far as I can go . . .*

And now, at last, the black bird shadow descended once more. Maddy didn't even look up. Why bother to look? There was nowhere to go. She closed her eyes and tried to hold onto those last small fragments of memory:

The scent of bonfires in fall-time. A red-haired young man called Lucky. A journeyman with his travelling bag. Wild geese over the mountains. A shape – a *blemish* – on her hand that somehow meant something important . . .

And then Maddy heard a rushing sound, and opened her eyes in astonishment as someone said: *'Oh no, you don't,'* and something hard rammed into her side, knocking her out of the black bird's shadow just as it grazed the heel of her boot . . .

And now she was hurtling out of the shadowcloud at a speed that even Jormungand might have found hard to match. Instinctively she clung to the mane of the creature that had rescued her. It was Sleipnir, she remembered; the Horse's name was Sleipnir. And on his back were the ravens, Hughie, Mandy and . . .

'Maggie?'

Maggie gave her a sidelong glance in which Maddy read both anger and a grudging kind of pride. 'What in the Worlds were you doing?' Maggie said. 'What did you think you could do here alone?'

Maddy shrugged. 'I wasn't exactly overwhelmed with options.'

'Well, you were lucky. Lucky I got here in time.' She looked at Maddy again, and said: 'Do you know your rune's reversed?'

Maddy nodded. 'I know,' she said.

'Pfff,' said Maggie scornfully as, with a giant stretch of his spidery legs, Sleipnir bore them out of the cloud. Above them, the Cradle was rocking like a rowing boat in a high wind, with the gods – now in their human Aspects again – looking down from the battlements.

Crazy Nan saw Maddy and cheered. 'I knew it!' she cackled. 'You made it!'

Perth was standing next to her, with Hughie and Mandy, who had flown to join him as soon as they had left the shadowcloud, perched upon his shoulders. Behind him, Loki – now back in human Aspect, and therefore clad in nothing but skin – offered a desperate, blasphemous prayer to any deity who might care: *Please, don't let me die like this – naked and married, for gods' sakes* . . .

'Dream, Maddy, dream!' he yelled.

Perth's voice rang out in support. Soon the others were joining in, their voices rising thinly above the sound of the approaching shadow.

Maddy turned to Maggie. 'I can't. You have to help me!' Maggie nodded. 'Take my hand.'

Maddy did, and a bolt of glam passed between the sisters. It was like being hit by a thunderbolt, Maddy thought to herself as it struck; she stumbled, half blinded, as *Ac*, the Thunder Oak, lit up like summer lightning.

At the same time *Aesk*, the Lightning Ash, lit up with sudden intensity. It was reversed, but still it shone; and now the tiniest spark of glam began to take shape at her fingertips. Not enough to build a bridge, or to raise a citadel, but maybe – just maybe – enough to dream ..

'Come on, Maddy! *Dream!*' said Thor, leaning over the battlements.

'You can do it, sweetheart!' said Sif.

Maddy closed her eyes and dreamed. At her side, Maggie did the same. Their dreams were strangely similar, if only they had known it. Both dreamed of places they'd loved – Maddy of Little Bear Wood in the spring; Maggie of her catacombs. Both of them dreamed of absent friends: Maddy remembered Sugar-and-Sack; Maggie, Adam Scattergood. And both of them dreamed of Inland – its little hedges and winding roads; farms and markets; cities and towns and, most especially, the Folk . . .

Nothing dreamed is ever lost, thought Maddy, opening her eyes as, from out of the shadowcloud, came something dark and hungry and *huge* – not a black bird shadow, but—

'*Fenny!*' cried Skull and Big H, dancing on the parapet. 'Aw, man, we thought you were dead!'

Fenny was still in Devourer Aspect, fangs bared, eyes aflame. He leaped onto the parapet, then turned to the black bird shadow that now dipped out of the dreamcloud, and opened his jaws in a silent snarl.

'Do it, Maddy! Do it *now!*' he growled, and faced the Destroyer.

And so Maddy summoned her last spark of glam, reached for her last precious fragments of Dream, and *hurled* them at the Citadel with every bit of strength she had. Maggie joined her glam to Maddy's, and for a time Oak and Ash stood together beneath the Cradle.

Will it be enough? Maddy thought. *Or will it be too little, too late?*

She looked back at her sister. Maggie's gaze was fixed on a point somewhere above the Citadel, and her face was distorted with concentration. The silvery light of Ác, the Oak, streamed and flared from her body, shooting from her fingertips, her eyes, even the ends of her hair. But there was something else, Maddy saw: Ác was no longer alone. Another signature was there, almost hidden inside the light, a filament of rose-pink, like a worm in a baby's eye . . .

And then there came a sudden flare of northlights over Asgard. The whole of the Cradle blazed with a light so bright that it almost blinded her. A burst of music accompanied it: Bragi's guitar was back in tune, and he was already celebrating.

Above the Citadel, Jormungand formed an arch of victory. Crazy Nan danced a little jig.

Hugin and Munin wheeled and soared, *crawk*-ing to each other.

Heimdall reached for his spyglass to scrutinize the shadow-cloud. He thought he could already see a change – the tiniest hint of translucency. That might have been wishful thinking, of course, except that it had ceased to advance; it simply stood there, glowering, less than twelve feet from Asgard's gates.

On the parapet, one by one, the gods felt their primary Aspects return. Loki found himself fully dressed, with the rune *Kaen* (no longer reversed) shining from his signature. Odin, both his runes restored, drew himself up to his full height. Thor shot Mjølnir into the cloud; the black bird shadow faltered and stopped.

They felt its confusion – *What's this?* – its triumph faltering into dismay.

Once more Thor struck with Mjølnir. Its brightness turned the shadowcloud a dusty, bloated purple. The black bird shadow began to retreat, the flame of its wings changing colour to match.

'What's happening?' said Maggie.

Maddy shook her head. 'I think that when we finished the Cradle, we weren't just building a fortress. We were trying to re-establish Order in the Nine Worlds. We remade the First World, where the Æsir can take back their Aspects and push back the shadows of Chaos . . .'

Maggie looked at the black bird. It had almost withdrawn, but for a single wing-tip. Fenris, his Devourer Aspect fearsome to behold, made a lunge at the tip of the wing. There was a tearing, rending sound. The black bird vanished into the cloud.

'I think it lost some feathers,' she said.

Maddy grinned. 'I think it did.'

Sleipnir was moving faster now, ready to take the sisters home. Fenris, snarling, jaws agape, gave one last snap at the shadow-cloud and leaped back onto the battlements, his Aspect changing from that of a demon wolf to that of a pale young man in World's End garb, wearing an earring shaped like a skull.

'Fenny! *Dude!*' The Wolf Brothers were delirious with happiness. 'You totally *owned* that shadow-thing . . .'

'I mean, you were, like – *grrr, woawr* —'

'Fierce!'

'Yeah! *Totally* fierce . . .'

'Why are they talking like that?' Maggie said, stepping down from Sleipnir's back onto Asgard's parapet.

But Maddy had something else on her mind. She stepped up to the Fenris Wolf, who was already on his way to explore his new hall in Asgard – as imagined by the Wolf Brothers, and lavishly decorated with skulls (as far as the Wolf Brothers were concerned, skulls were the design concept of the future).

He saw her coming. 'Er, yeah . . .' he said.

Maddy knew what *that* meant. 'You're sure?' she said in a small voice, thinking that maybe he was wrong, that Sugar might somehow have survived, as Odin had on the shores of Hel. He *was* a creature of Faërie, she thought. Chaos should have been in his blood. And Fenris had survived, after all . . .

Fenny shrugged. 'I'm sure,' he said. 'He did pretty good for a noob, though.'

Maddy nodded silently. Tears were burning her eyelids. It seemed so very hard to believe that Sugar-and-Sack was gone for good. Odin's death on the shores of Hel had left her under a cloud of grief; but the death of the little goblin felt like a bruise on Maddy's soul. Perhaps because Sugar had been the final link between Asgard and Malbry; or maybe simply because of the fact that a cowardly goblin from under the Hill had shown the heart of an oliphant.

At Asgard's gates, the shadowcloud was already starting to move away. A pale glow in the eastern sky had begun to light the horizon. A brisk little wind started to blow; soon, Maddy thought, all traces of the shadowcloud would be blown away.

Maggie was looking down at World's End. Soon that too would be clear of the cloud. The survivors would start to rebuild in their turn. Maybe this time they could create a wiser, kinder, happier place. Maybe this time they'd get it right.

All around Maddy came sounds of celebration from the gods. As Order reestablished itself, all her friends hastened to explore what lay in the new Asgard. Built from memory and Dream, it was not the same as the original Sky Citadel, although of course it had Aspects of that. But it also had Aspects of World's End, including the whole of St Sepulchre's Square, the fountain and the cathedral, as well as a stretch of the Water Rats (probably dreamed up by Perth); and Aspects of Malbry, including Red Horse Hill in late summer and several of its houses, among them the Parsonage, which Ethel had dreamed slightly larger (and with that new wallpaper she'd always been meaning to hang).

There was a version of Jed Smith's forge, transformed into something a little more grand, with a series of dressing rooms for Sif and a large, vaulted banqueting hall for when Thor's friends came round. There was also a chamber for Jolly, who, retaining his goblin Aspect, had demanded a place of his own, not too far away from Thor, but well-supplied with plenty of ale and some pies, in case he got peckish.

Angie had her own hall, as promised, close to Ironwood, which the Wolf Brothers had brought (at least in part) and positioned not far from Skadi's domain – a natural habitat for wolves.

In fact, *all* the gods and their allies had imagined their ideal surroundings, which meant that the new Sky Citadel was a strange and colourful patchwork of mountains and caves, turrets and tunnels, fragments of city and rural retreats, all packed into an area which, if it had been forced to obey the strictest rules of space and scale, might have covered, at best, a few square miles.

Luckily the rules of Dream are fluid, like its substance, and given that Asgard was built from dreams, everyone had what they dreamed of most. Bragi had a concert hall, Idun a series of gardens and groves. Heimdall had a lighthouse, Skadi a labyrinth of caves. Njörd had an underwater hall, Frey a banqueting hall, Freyja a hall of mirrors. Nan had her old cottage, her cats, her spinning wheel and Epona. And Perth (as well as his hideaway at the Water Rats) had the University, now even grander than before, with a bell tower for his ravens and a personal study and library in which to retreat when the responsibilities of office became too demanding.

Only two people had no hall: Maggie, because she had come too late to contribute anything much more than glam; and Loki, who had never had a hall in Asgard in the first place, and whose energy had mostly gone into trying to break the Wedlock.

Of course, he'd failed to do that, and now he found himself standing in front of the place that Sigyn had dreamed for them. It looked like the cave by the Sleepers, but larger and more practical, with a little cabbage-patch by the door and a stream running behind it. It was simple and cheerful and modest – in fact it was everything that the Trickster most despised – and yet there was something pleasant about it, something almost relaxing.

He glanced at the Wedlock on his hand. Even in Aspect, he couldn't take it off. But maybe he could live with that.

He took a step towards the door. Sigyn was sitting inside, on a chair. Her long brown hair fell loose onto the shoulders of her white dress. Once again Loki thought how very beautiful she was. It wasn't a typical thought, and might have disturbed him in different circumstances, but today he was feeling unusual – *But after all, he told himself, it isn't often that you come back from the dead, beat Hel at her own game, give Pan-daemonium a kicking, and rebuild Asgard, all in a day . . .*

Sigyn looked up as he came in. 'Sweetheart,' she said. 'What took you so long?' She stood up and kissed him on the mouth. The sensation was really quite pleasant, he thought – after all, it had been five hundred years since anyone had wanted to do anything with his mouth except perhaps to shut it for good.

He closed his eyes. Sigyn's hands linked together in the small of his back and pressed, and for the first time in over five hundred years the Trickster surrendered to something like . . .

Love?

And then came a sound from behind them, and Loki's eyes snapped open again.

In the doorway, hand in hand, stood two little boys – aged maybe three or four, with bright red hair and eyes of identical flame-green. Loki recognized the boys he'd seen in the dream he'd shared with Sigyn; and thinking back five hundred years, he thought of his sons, and how they had died so long ago, and how he'd seen them in Hel's domain . . .

They killed us, they'd told him that day in Hel. *They killed us both because of you.*

Loki shook his head. 'No. They died. Sig, it's impossible.'

Sigyn smiled. 'They died,' she agreed. 'But Hel was open, its Guardian fled – and besides, didn't the prophecy say: *Nothing dreamed is ever lost, and nothing lost for ever?*'

A terrible thought occurred to him. 'You don't think Balder might be back?'

'Stranger things have happened.'

Not for the first time that long, hard day, Loki was at a loss for words. 'So now I'm a father again?' he said. 'Because we all know how *that* works out . . .'

Sigyn laughed. '*Sweetheart*,' she said. 'You're so *negative*. You get a chance to start again, with a wife who thinks the Worlds of you, two lovely children and your dream home – and you're being all *passive-aggressive* about it. Now come and say hello to the boys, and I'll make a start on dinner.'

Loki's mouth went suddenly dry. *Perfect*, he thought. *It sounds perfect.*

'Well, what are you waiting for?'

'Er – gotta check on Maddy,' he said; and, shifting to hawk Aspect as if all Hel were on his tail, he fled from his dream home with barely a pang of regret, having decided right at that moment that perfection was really *not* his style – and landing five minutes later by a small and somewhat familiar part of what had once been Little Bear Wood, where Maddy was sitting alone by a tree and sobbing as if her heart would break.

'What's up?' said Loki, reverting to Aspect (of course, fully clothed in Asgard).

Maddy turned her face away.

Loki sat down on the mossy ground. 'You're not going home?' he said at last.

'This is it,' Maddy said, with a listless gesture. 'Everything I could save, at least: Red Horse Hill, and Little Bear Wood, and my father's cottage, and the Seven Sleepers Inn, and that funny little crossing place on the road to Farnley Tyas . . .'

Loki shrugged. 'Each to his own. Apparently, mine is a *dream home*.' He looked at the Wedlock on his hand. 'I'm going to build myself a shed,' he told her with a sudden grin. 'Preferably somewhere a *long* way away . . .'

Maddy gave a tired smile. 'I can't believe Sugar's gone. I still half expect to see him, you know, peering out from behind a tree.'

Loki grinned. 'A cellar, more like. Especially if there's an inn nearby.'

Maddy's eyes widened. '*What* did you say?'

'I said—' began Loki. 'Hey, where are you going?'

Maddy was already on her feet. 'The cellar,' she said in a choking voice. 'That's it, Loki – the *cellar*!'

The cellar was dark and smelled of rats. Loki wasn't at all impressed.

'Well, if *I* were building a dream home, I'd try to fix it up, at least.' He glanced at the brick-lined floor, where a hole the size of a foxhole gaped, and a messy strew of rubble, earth, pieces of brick and broken kegs littered the storage area. 'Must have had a party,' he said, tapping one of the empty kegs. 'Looks like *someone* had a good time.'

But Maddy wasn't listening. Instead, she knelt at the mouth of the hole, heedless of dust and spiders, and whispered something into the dark.

'*I name you Smá-rakki*,' she whispered.

Silence. Just the empty house.

'*A named thing is a tamed thing*,' said Maddy. 'Sugar-and-Sack – oh *please*, if you're there . . .'

There came the smallest of movements from behind the pile of kegs. Maddy turned, her eyes alight.

'It's only a rat,' said Loki.

Maddy stood up, shaking her head. 'I know rats,' she whispered. 'Sugar, are you there?' And then she pushed the keg aside (finding it suspiciously light), revealing a small bewhiskered face and eyes of a curious wedding-ring gold beneath a battered helmet. Maddy saw that the runemark *Tyr* no longer shone from his signature.

'Now I know what yer going to say, miss.' The goblin held out his furry hands. 'But I swear – on my Captain's life – I dunno *what* happened to all this ale—'

'*Sugar!*' cried Maddy, sweeping him up.

'Oy!' protested the goblin.

'I thought you were dead!' Maddy said, beginning to cry all over again.

Sugar gave her a cautious look. Clearly, she was crazy. But she did have a powerful glam, and . . .

'*Captain?*' he said as Loki emerged from the shadows under the cellar steps.

Loki grinned. 'None other,' he said. 'Back from the dead, and *fabulous*— What in Hel are you crying at *now*?' That was to Maddy, who couldn't seem to control her tears, although she was half laughing too at the look of confusion on Sugar's face.

'He doesn't remember, does he?' she said, wiping her eyes with the back of her hand.

'Remember what?' said Sugar.

'Oh, nothing,' Maddy said. 'Just that you helped save the Worlds – twice. That you took on the Aspect of Brave-Hearted Tyr, that you rode against Surt on a demon wolf, that you died in battle, that you were my friend . . .'

Sugar's eyes were like saucers now. 'I did all that?'

'All that, and more.'

Sugar eyed her doubtfully. 'That ale must be stronger than I thought. You sure you haven't had some yerself, miss? 'Cos ale can have very *narsty* effects on them as isn't used to drinking it.'

Maddy smiled. 'I'll bear that in mind . . .'

'I don't mind bein' your friend, though.'

'That's all right, then,' Maddy said.

She went back out into the sunlight.

14

Now a single figure remained standing on Asgard's battlements. As the shadow slowly cleared and Æsir and Vanir explored their new territories, Maggie Rede was left alone, looking down on World's End. The Rainbow Bridge, once more rebuilt, spanned the gap between earth and sky in a dazzling band of coloured light. And as the shadowcloud dispersed, rain fell softly on World's End.

A tremendous feeling of weariness now fell like a blanket over her, and the tears she had not shed for Adam now began to run down her face. Not *really* for Adam, Maggie thought; or for the ruins of World's End, or even for her unborn child, who would never know his father . . .

A shadow fell on the parapet. Someone was standing behind her. A tall figure, blue-cloaked, his eyes half hidden beneath his hat. There was a scar across his left eye, where Maggie's glam had struck him; it looked just like the rune *Raedo*, and shone with a dim luminescence.

Odin in Allfather Aspect still looked a lot like Perth. Maddy, if she'd been there, would have known that he also looked like One-Eye; but younger, stronger, and yet more alone, remote and somehow forbidding. Hugin and Munin fluttered down onto the battlements and *crawk*-ed.

'So. You got what you wanted, then,' Maggie said, still looking down at World's End.

This is what the Firefolk see, she told herself silently. *Little fields. Little streets. An ocean like a cloak of blue. How small it all is! How very small!*

Odin gave a weary sigh. Idun's fruit might heal his wounds, but it could do nothing for his aching heart. 'Yes. I got what I wanted,' he said. 'At a price. And you?'

'A hall in Asgard. You promised me. And safety for my baby.'

'I keep my word,' said Odin. 'Even though the child you bear may live to make us both sorry.'

Maggie looked up at that. 'My sister said that my child was possessed. That the Whisperer was just using me to get back into Asgard.' She lowered her voice and went on. 'Just as it used Adam,' she said, 'to get to the runes in the Kissing Stone.'

Odin shrugged. 'She may be wrong.'

'You don't think so, do you?' she said.

'No, Maggie. I don't think so.'

Maggie considered Odin's words. Something inside her believed him – was actually convinced of the truth. And yet what she felt for the tiny life that was growing steadily inside her was so overwhelming, so *potent*, that the truth was barely relevant.

Whatever it might one day become, whatever might be wrong with it, this was her child – *Adam's* child – and she would protect it with her life. Anything that possessed it – as Adam too had been possessed – would first have Maggie to deal with, and that would be no easy task. Maggie Rede, as once was; then Maggie Goodwin; Magni, the Oak; and now, at last, Maggie Scattergood, widow and mother of World's End.

'I'm keeping my child,' said Maggie.

'Of course you are,' Odin said.

'And I'm calling him Adam, after his father.'

Odin gave a twisted smile.

'But as for that hall in Asgard' – she lifted her granite-gold eyes to his – 'I don't think I'm going to need it right now. At least, not for a while.'

Odin said nothing, but his good eye was alight with speculation.

Maggie went on: 'You promised me that the Firefolk would do no harm to me, or my son.'

Odin nodded. 'You have my word.'

'Then take me home,' Maggie said, stepping down from the parapet. 'Tell my sister I said goodbye, and tell her not to look for me. I'll find her if – *when* –the time comes.'

Odin looked at her. 'Home?' he said.

Maggie nodded. 'Where else would I go? That's where I want my son to be born. In World's End, where his father died. Besides,' – she gave a wry little smile – 'who else is there to rebuild the place? To unearth the library, raise the dome, reopen the University – after all, if I can raise Asgard from Dream, World's End should be a piece of cake.'

Odin gave a low laugh. 'You're very like your sister,' he said.

'Tell her I'll see her again some day.'

And at that Maggie stepped onto Bif-rost, and with a quick flick of the rune *Raedo* – the rune of roads still to be travelled, of riders in the wake of the storm, of journeymen and explorers and gods – she was gone, down the rainbow and into the mists of World's End.

15

'But *why*?' said Maddy once more when she arrived to find Maggie gone. 'Why would she do that? Leave this place? Leave her friends, her *family*! For gods' sakes, she's seventeen. She's pregnant. She's completely alone. And if we're right, the Whisperer—'

'If we're right, then World's End is the best place for her,' said Odin in a calm voice. 'If the Whisperer *has* taken hold of her child, then all we can do is try to keep that child from entering Asgard. Because if it ever finds its way here, and Mimir regains his Aspect, then we will have civil war on our hands, and the Order for which we fought so hard will descend once more into Chaos.'

Maddy was silent for a while. 'Oh,' she said. 'It's not over, then.'

'Maddy, it's *never* over.'

They sat for a while in silence, watching the light bloom over World's End. The shadow had completely dispersed; the rain had stopped and now the sun shone faintly through the ring of white clouds that hedged the Sky Citadel.

'How long do we have?' she said.

'Till what?'

'Till it happens again.'

He shrugged. 'Who knows how these things happen? The Worlds have ended so often before. So many gods have been and gone. Order and Chaos have their tides, just as the One Sea ebbs and flows. We may have hundreds of years before Chaos bursts its banks again. What the Hel are you grinning at *now*?'

She smiled. 'It's just that it sounds kind of funny, with you still looking so like Perth and sounding so like One-Eye.'

He shrugged again. 'Maddy, we're gods. We have to be all things to all men. I'm Odin, Allfather, son of Bór. I'm also the Rider of Carnage. To you I was One-Eye. Then I was Perth. Now I'm all those things, and more.'

Maddy sighed and closed her eyes. The sun was warm on her eyelids. It felt so safe, so familiar. She might have been on Red Horse Hill, lying on her back in the grass, chewing a stem of clover and listening to the crickets sing. Instead she was miles above the Worlds in a Cradle built from runelight and dreams.

'We've come a long way from Red Horse Hill,' she said, unaware that she'd spoken aloud.

'Not as far as you'd think,' he said. 'Remember, you brought it with you.'

Maddy smiled. 'So I did. Want to come with me? Smoke a pipe? Watch the clouds from the Horse's Eye? Dream a little dream? Waste time? Play cards? Or doesn't Allfather do those things?' she said, a little wistfully.

'Maddy, I'm sorry. I don't think he does. Allfather has work to do. But as for *Perth*—' He broke off and gave her a flash of his salesman's smile. 'Perth is never too busy to dream. Perth never turns down a game of chance. And as for wasting time with you – what better way to waste it?'

They took the long way to Red Horse Hill. By then the light was almost gone. A band of luminescence had appeared against the western sky. It shimmered, moving gently, like the sails of a giant ship, shifting from green, to pink, to blue as it sailed across the Firmament.

'Northlights,' Maddy said. 'I've always wanted to see them. You know, they're supposed to bring good luck?'

'Bring it on,' said Perth.